The Defector's Diary

Books by Ray C Doyle

The Blind Pigeon
Lara's Secret

Contact at:
www.facebook.com/AuthorRaymondStone

The Defector's Diary

Ray C Doyle

ALL RIGHTS RESERVED

This novel is entirely a work of fiction. The names, characters and incidents portrayed in it are the work of the author's imagination. Any resemblance to actual persons, living or dead, events or localities is entirely coincidental.

Ray C Doyle asserts the moral right to be identified as the author of this work.

Copyright: Ray C Doyle ©2023

Published by Hardboiled Press

Dedication

To Ant Gavin Smits

Acknowledgments

To Ant Gavin Smits and his wife, Paula, my friends and fellow artists who produced the book and designed a great cover and inspired me with excellent advice that kept me going to the finish line.

I thank Kimber Coleman, my soulmate, who was instrumental in helping me devise how my characters solved clues that played across a chess board.

To Emily Hetherington, who edited with much patience during many changes I made with a complicated plot. I applaud her and am deeply grateful.

For Anton Johnson and his wife, Jan, lifetime friends whose words of wisdom made life bearable as I worked on this book. For all my many friends I left in Cyprus, Malta, and Washington State, USA, who supported me over the last twenty-seven years, I thank you.

Finally, to my sister, Susan, who looks after me through thick and thin. Nothing would have seen the light of day without her.

Cover design by Ant Gavin Smits

Chapter One

DIANNE CAME BOUNDING up the stairs and rushed into the bathroom. I took the note and envelope waved at me and read the message scrawled across one side of the paper. Puzzled, I recognised the Czechian name.

Aurora, if anything happens to me, you must find a diary a Czechia agent stole from Jozef Novotney. She wants to cross the road and will bring the diary. Listen to her and trust her and no one else. Pete will know who should have the diary. Stay away from the British Embassy.

"It was in the post today," said Dianne breathlessly. "Adam is in some sort of trouble."

I sat, looking at her for a moment. Adam and Valerie's wedding was set for the end of September in Prague, six weeks away.

"From how Adam has written this message, I'd guess he's gone into hiding. That's why he didn't call you." I picked up the envelope off the shelf. "He's a diplomat, for Christ's sake. You bet he's in trouble."

A small card lay inside the envelope dated August 12th, 2019. I pulled the card out. The legend read: Capo & Café Cocktail Bar, and underneath a message neatly written:

Every Tuesday— 7.00 pm—Table 22.

I studied the note again. "Jozef Novotney is an EU commissioner. He's heading a committee that's going through a tough trade negotiation with the Ukrainians."

"But what has that got to do with a defector? What would Adam know about this Novotney?" Dianne rubbed her forehead and sighed.

"I've no idea," I answered. "We need to tread carefully here.

Adam's asking us to break the law. Let's think this through. The obvious thing to do is call the authorities."

Dianne reached out to touch my arm. "Surely, we can do something. I'll try to ring him before you do that."

I turned the note over. A sentence in Czech was handwritten across the page. I took little notice of it and turned my attention to the card.

"Try, by all means, but I'm sure you'll get no reply," I said and held up the card. "This is interesting. I could go along and meet whoever turns up."

"Trust you," said Dianne. "Just remember this is a friend of mine."

"Yes, of course," I agreed, "but one who appears to be in a lot of trouble. From the tone of this message, I'd say he's skipped the Embassy, and if he has, there will be an almighty panic going on in Whitehall. Whatever, I think you should calm down and we can sort things out after breakfast."

Dianne took the note from me and returned downstairs.

The mouth-watering smell of sizzling bacon and eggs wafted around me as I followed her a minute later.

Dianne sat munching toast and marmalade. "I've just been reading an article about Prague," she said without looking up.

I leaned over and kissed her cheek, enjoying a moment of capturing Gardenia over bacon and eggs. Her long, blonde hair was pinned up as usual when around the house. It was her large blue eyes and Scandinavian look that seduced me four years earlier. I was hopelessly in love with her, and we married two years later.

Our marriage was a happy one, which surprised many of our friends, mainly because we could not have been more diverse socially, something I was reminded of on occasion. My middle-class parents died while I was still at school, and with no siblings, I was brought up by an aunt. Dianne, daughter of a Swedish industrialist, grew up in British high society, got tired of the social merry-go-round, and made her way into photographic journalism, but

The Defector's Diary

kept touch with what, much to her annoyance, I called the 'Rich and Infamous Set'.

"So, what's going on in Prague?" I asked.

I picked up the teapot and poured the Darjeeling before dropping a single cube of sugar into my cup. Dianne fluttered her long, slender fingers at me from behind the newspaper.

"The Bilderberg Club is meeting there in six weeks at the same time as Adam's wedding."

She looked apprehensively at me. "That's if the wedding takes place."

"I know," I answered, trying to make light of the situation. "Just think, we might get to see Richard's best Downing Street friend, complete with SIS toadies from the dirt factory. Wouldn't that be something? The city will be teeming with spies."

It was strange, I thought, that Prague had once earned the reputation as a romantic spy centre. The word romantic far from painted an accurate picture of the modern world of politics. What dark side there was, lay carefully hidden behind plastic smiles and barbed innuendos that were well-practiced within Whitehall and the Secret Intelligence Services HQ, affectionately nicknamed 'The Dirt Factory' by me. Times changed since the Cold War.

Foreign spies, the old raincoat types, were now scarce on the ground, replaced by a more dangerous kind. The new spy terrorist was the enemy within our ranks.

Dianne gave me a cold stare and folded the newspaper, slapping it on the table. "Can we have breakfast without you making silly jokes about the PM, please? Let's talk about Adam and Valerie, yes?"

There was not much I knew about Adam Denton. Dianne met him after going to an art gallery in Paris. He held a post as a junior diplomat at the British Embassy where they met at some foreign trade reception. Their friendship continued after Dianne moved to New York a year later to start a career with the New York Herald. They remained in touch ever since, as far as I knew. After a whirlwind romance in Prague, according to Dianne, Adam proposed to Valerie after just three months.

I winked and continued eating while Dianne raised the newspaper and resumed reading. Still thinking about my first visit to Prague, I closed my eyes. The paper rustled again.

"What are you doing?"

I opened my eyes as she lowered the paper. "I was trying to visualize the Charles Bridge over the Vltava River. You know, the bridge you cross to get to the castle where the Bilderberg conference is held. I remember the first time I walked across it. It was raining hard. I was soaked after being held up by two Russian soldiers stopping people to check identity papers. Can you imagine the security involved this year for that damned conference?"

We finished breakfast before dealing with Prague again.

"You try calling Adam, and I'll contact our newsroom desk to see if anything interesting has come in overnight. You and Adam were pretty close at one time?" I added.

"We have always been good friends," she replied.

I picked up my cell phone, already regretting that I had not probed Dianne more on Adam to get a broad background, but worried Dianne might feel I was treading on the privacy of her pre-Pete ground. If Adam had gone missing for whatever reason, the Secret Intelligence Service (SIS) would be on to Dianne as soon as her name came up as a friend or a past romance, especially as she was a journalist. That was the last thing I wanted if a big story was about to break. Max, my editor, would be getting calls from the owner of the Herald, Richard Hart, and then I would be involved. It would be best to remain ignorant about the letter.

I decided to see how things played out.

The gruff voice of George O'Connor sounded loud in my ear.

"Morning, Pete. No, nothing for you."

"I haven't asked you anything yet," I replied.

"I've known you for fifteen years. Go back to bed. You're off

The Defector's Diary

for four weeks. Now leave me alone."

The phone went dead. So, there was nothing on the wire about a missing diplomat. I waited for Dianne to finish her call. She looked up and shook her head.

"I'll call the Embassy and see if he's there," she said.

"No, I've got a better idea. It occurred to me that it might be wiser for us to assume there is nothing wrong at all. It could be that Adam has a situation he cannot manage himself and is hoping we can help and get him out of what could be a right mess. As I have already said, I think we should wait until we know what is going on and then decide whether or not to go to the authorities?"

Dianne looked at me with her eyes lowered. "Adam is not the kind of man to dabble in things that don't concern him."

Maybe," I persisted, "but he's a junior diplomat, I believe. Supposing he stumbled across something or someone and saw a way to further his career. Too late, he realized he was in over his head and could not go to the Embassy to explain, as he should have right from the start."

"That's silly, Pete." Dianne folded her arms. "He is not an idiot. If anything happened like that, he would do what was expected of him. He must have been prevented from doing so, and that's why he wrote to us."

"Whatever, darling. You might be right. I've never met him. The point is, he has something important to hide—being a spy, for goodness' sake, or so he says. I would guess he's perfectly okay and going about his normal duties while keeping quiet until we contact him."

"But he warned us not to go near the Embassy and trust no one. I can't raise him anyway."

I could see Dianne getting more agitated. She had decided for us to fly to Prague the following weekend, plenty of time before the wedding. As I wondered if I should go earlier, an absurd thought crossed my mind. After years of expecting the unexpected in politics, I looked at this situation and stored a scenario in my memory that was highly probable but too fictional to voice aloud.

"Why don't you get us on an earlier flight and change our hotel booking? We can then go and find him."

Dianne smiled and left me to enjoy another coffee.

Although I never met Adam, she had told me about him, but strangely more about his family, career, the embassy receptions, and dinners they attended. There had never been mention of their social life away from jobs, and I guessed they had been more than friends, hence the concern.

I picked up the paper and turned to the article Dianne was reading. The Bilderberg Club was a secret society. The media widely knew about its annual meeting place and guessed the agenda. Heads of state, presidents, industry captains, and even royalty were invited to discuss world events, finance, and industry. They were meeting in Prague Castle, the official residence of the president of Czechia.

I looked through the rest of the news, most of which I was already aware of, but could not keep my thoughts away from Adam's letter. The card seemed more of a mystery than the message itself. I felt a tinge of excitement at the idea there might be a great story here, but as always, Max never liked me going off on my own assignments. There was no need to mention a thing to him. He knew we were heading to Prague for a wedding anyway. Dianne's concerns toned down my enthusiasm.

Despite my feelings, Adam was a close friend of hers, and treading softly until I had a clearer picture was imperative.

Dianne's head appeared as the door opened. With cell phone to ear, she whispered, "I'm just on the phone to the airline. I'm afraid it will cost another three hundred and eighty pounds."

I cringed dramatically. "That's okay. I'll pay the mortgage later. We got away with that before."

The Defector's Diary

She frowned at me and disappeared down the passage as my phone rang. It was Max.

His gritty voice invaded my ear. "Get your backside here and bring Dianne with you."

As always, Max was straight to the point. I love the man, but he still has a habit of annoying me with calls like this one.

"Well, good morning, Max. Yes, I'm fine, thanks. How are you? Sorry, but I have a few weeks off. Perhaps you would like to speak to Dianne? She's just preparing our dinner for tonight. You know, in our limited social life that revolves around a damn newspaper, we have guests coming."

"None of your bloody sarcasm, Pete. Something big has come up and I need someone with in-depth savvy in diplomacy despite your obvious cynicism about those who practice it."

"Well, that was a funny line, Max." There was a loud cough. "I'm going to a wedding, and whatever you have will have to go to someone else. Surely, another journalist can be assigned, and anyway, I have a column of my own. I'm no longer a damn run-of-the-mill correspondent. What the hell, Max?"

"It's right up your street, literally. I need you in Prague."

Any other time, I would have argued with him, but it sounded as though I was about to hear what Adam Denton may have done.

"Don't blame me if my wife slaps you. Be there as soon as. And by the way, try not smoking and shouting at the same time."

"Bollocks." The phone went dead.

I slipped my shoes on and went looking for Dianne. If I was going to get involved in Adam's plight, I needed to talk to her and agree on what we would or wouldn't tell Max, depending on the breaking news he was about to reveal.

True, there was a promise of a big story, but with it came the risk of breaking the law. Keeping Dianne out of trouble was going to be hard too. I had already decided what I wanted to do. Her reaction to my plan was immediate.

"No, Pete. You're not leaving me behind!"

"I'm not advocating that," I explained. "All I'm suggesting is that I go a week early on my own and see what's what. If I do get into a sticky patch, I can have you, if necessary, sort things with Max or the authorities on this end. No one knows about the note. If Max has something that involves Adam, we can tell him about the letter. If not, we keep it to ourselves, at least until I've found Adam, or made sure this is not a damp squib."

"I don't like the idea of you going it alone. You're not a young man anymore."

I laughed. "Well, thanks a lot."

She gave me a playful push. "What if this isn't a damp squid? How long are you going to keep this to yourself?"

"If it stinks," I replied, "I'll call Max, knowing we have a big story. He can inform the authorities and give me time before anyone knows the Herald's involved."

Dianne put her arms around me. "What about Adam?"

I wanted to ask her about Adam but thought better of it.

"I'll look for him, but you should know if he's involved in anything naughty, I'll report things as is. I'm not going to hide anything to help him."

She kissed me gently. "I wouldn't expect anything else from you. Thank you. Okay, I'll call the airline and sort things out, but I'm warning you, if you get into trouble with the authorities, I can assure you, that will be nothing compared to dealing with me."

Chapter Two

AS SHE SHOWERED, Dianne tried to relax. The Post brought Adam's warning letter that morning, causing more stress. A medical report the day before had crushed her emotionally. After two years of marital bliss, she had agreed with Pete that having a family would be fantastic, something he enthusiastically welcomed. They had seen a specialist, and both were given a medical. They waited with impatience to receive the results, and Pete's arrived days before. When hers came, she did not wait to open it with Pete as promised. She was glad she had not.

The medical found fibroid tumours and suggested a further exam. There was a possibility that a hysterectomy might be necessary. There was still hope. Emotion overwhelmed her as she looked at the unopened box in the corner of the kitchen. Pete put it there, ready to fix the baby bouncer sling and spring to a hook in the doorframe. She dismissed her feelings and instead gave the forthcoming wedding and invitation from Adam more thought.

The wedding gave her something to worry about, something that would happen, although she hoped she would steer Pete away from trouble. Pete had a habit of courting trouble every time he heard a whisper of wrongdoing from or around Whitehall. Her worry was the Bilderberg Club conference being held in Prague Castle that coincided with the wedding. Pete was already looking forward to going to Prague, his third time, according to him. He had upset Whitehall over an article he wrote about the Club a year previously.

Dianne had managed a smile, knowing how ridiculous it was

keeping Pete out of things. She pushed the letter from the clinic to the back of her mind.

Her marriage had been a success so far, although her colleagues and close friends were a little surprised, not at the age difference of fifteen years, but that Pete's social background was the exact opposite of hers. A bachelor for several years, his innocence and awkwardness over matters of the heart appealed to her. His persistence at reporting the truth without fearing backlash if his work upset Westminster, had gained her total respect. He was something of a maverick among journalists. His unending enthusiasm and dedication to 'keeping Joe public informed of the truth' enflamed her, and she fell in love with the rebel within him.

She remembered their affair had not been without many angry spats as she fought to make the marriage work without changing the maverick. It was during that period that their love for each other deepened to a point of no return. It had been hard going but successful.

Adam's letter that morning stunned her. At first, it looked as though he mailed an empty envelope, a silly joke, or a reminder of the wedding perhaps. Dianne knew it was from him. The Czech stamps gave it away.

Anger coursed through her, mixed with concern for Adam's safety. The content of the letter was alarming, demanding attention. The affectionate name 'Aurora' could not be ignored either. Her immediate thought was that Adam might be reminding her of his feelings for her that she had rejected. The affair had ended. She sighed, hoping Pete would understand. Perhaps it was Adam's final reminder before he married Valerie of a relationship that could have been a lot more.

His feelings of yesteryear were hidden innocently behind the affectionate name.

Chapter Three

WAPPING IS NOT THE MOST ATTRACTIVE location in Central London. Traffic at ten in the morning was usually slow-moving among the mass of tall, uninteresting glass architectures thrust together with historic masonry to create an ugly skyline. At St Katharine's dock, under a grey sky, the procession of frustrated drivers came to a halt at the junction leading to Wapping High Street.

Dianne sat silently beside me, annoyed, lips tightly closed. Max was not playing on her mind. It was Adam. Jealousy is not part of my makeup, but not knowing much about the man left me feeling a little frustrated, unable to find the right words of comfort. I decided killing conversation would be better than trying to cheer her up. Worse still, it began to rain, adding more gloom to the day. As we drove across the junction, I inwardly cursed Max. He was a great editor and colleague, and our mutual respect paid dividends when I needed him to keep me out of trouble. Unfortunately, his whole life revolved around the Herald. A widower, he lived near Canary Wharf in a modest townhouse and spent his spare time keeping tabs on Number Ten incumbents, as well as many influential backbenchers from both sides of the House. If anyone heard whispers first, it was Max.

Dianne agreed with me not to say a word to Max unless he brought up Adam's name. Whatever was going on in Prague was significant, or Max wouldn't have called me. I had read through the Herald a second time but saw nothing that could hint at what he wanted with us. The Bilderberg meeting was all I could think of, and that was already news.

It took another ten minutes before we parked and hurried into the Herald reception out of the rain. The elevator took us to the third floor, and an unusually worried-looking Max was waiting impatiently.

"Okay, Max, we're here. What's going on? Is our beloved paper going bust?"

Dianne gave me a nudge and pushed me forward.

"I'm warning you, Pete. No bloody cheek." Max motioned us into armchairs. "I've had Richard on the line practically all bloody night. He asked for you to manage this."

I whistled. "It must be a dirty job."

Dianne sank into an armchair and crossed her legs. I couldn't help feeling a little out of place. She was a woman who looked attractive no matter what she wore. My worn corduroy trousers and outdoor waterproof jacket that had seen better days looked drab against her smart suit neatly displaying the curves of a beautiful woman. It was, I reasoned to myself, the weekend, and this was my day off, officially. I tried to look unconcerned about my pair of scuffed and unpolished brown leather shoes.

Max pushed wavy white hair away from his eyes and pulled a cigar from a pouch on the desk, avoiding Dianne's wary stare. Seconds later, clouds of blue smoke drifted up to the ceiling. Mindful of Dianne's aversion to smoke, I stepped to the wall to turn on the extractor fans before sinking back into the armchair.

"What do you know about Jozef Novotney?" Max asked. He blew smoke from his nostrils and picked a small piece of cigar leaf from the tip of his tongue with a little finger.

So that was it. There it was a connection to the letter from Adam. I remained silent and glanced sideways at Dianne.

She feigned ignorance. "I can't remember what he does, but I'm pretty sure he's in the European Parliament in Brussels. EU trade secretary, perhaps." She shrugged and looked at me.

"No," I corrected. "Jozef Novotney is an EU commissioner for Czechia."

The Defector's Diary

Max coughed. "Not anymore, he's not. Someone bumped him off a couple of days ago in his Prague office." He paused to let the news sink in. "The rumour has it that he was corrupt. He annoyed someone, and that person or persons got rid of him. That's a load of crap, and you know it. I smell an EU cover-up for some reason, so Richard wants you there."

He raised a hand as I opened my mouth.

"In a minute. Just let me finish. Brussels is screaming about the lack of security, and the Czechia government is recalling its EU trade secretary for an urgent meeting. The bloody Americans, believe it or not, are worried about security arrangements for their attendees at this year's Bilderberg conference. And they'll have dozens of security agents there."

Brussels and the European Union were no different. There were so many so-called security agents around, that one could trip over them. As I had experienced over several years, the rise in terrorist activity meant security personnel had doubled.

Max drew deeply on his cigar. "That can only mean the bloody President or some White House gofer is going to attend. Bloody stupid secret society."

I nodded. Was there another connection? "You're probably right, Max, although I doubt Novotney's death has anything to do with the Bilderberg Club."

Max rolled the cigar between his fingers. "And don't start thinking you're getting involved in that. I know the way your mind works. We had enough trouble over your interference last time you investigated them. You were damn lucky you didn't land in jail. Leave well alone, Pete, or so help me, I'll bloody throttle you myself. This job needs your full attention, so you will not go off down another road because you have some politician in your sights. Even if he's been a naughty boy." He pointed the cigar at me. "No matter what you think, Richard wants a professional profile on Novotney. Forget any skeletons he might have been hiding. Novotney hosted the Prime Minister's visit to Czechia last year."

I closed my eyes. "That figures. Why the hell me, Max? This story is a reporter's job, not a journalist with a column. Surely the conference is worth a few lines."

"Did you hear what I just said?" Max glared at Dianne. "For Christ's sake, can you please keep him in line? Journalists have looked into that organization and found nothing harmless about them. Novotney had nothing to do with them."

I sighed, remembering the incident three years earlier when a fellow journalist I was working with interested me to look into the Bilderberg Club, which just met in Saltzberg. He was writing an article about the Club and wanted any thoughts I had about them.

What made these conferences special, the Bilderberg Club was a secret society formed in 1954. A steerage committee put together a list of subjects for discussion ranging from world finance, manufacturing, global warming, and terrorism. Attendees included captains of industry, banking, nuclear power, and European politicians who discussed all the topics, but no minutes existed. The original concept was to foster dialogue between Europe and North America. Later, my colleague moved on and Max was on leave.

I took full advantage of the situation. With a little tongue in cheek, mixed with serious undertones, I wrote an article, asking the question, 'Was there a long-term plan to change the way the world is governed?' The article was a 'what if' conversation piece. It worked. The readers loved and hated it, and all Wapping print went crazy for a week.

Richard Hart went mad on the phone to Max, demanding I resign. As a life-long supporter of the Tory Party, he was subjected to several embarrassing questions from Number 10, who suggested I may have broken terms of the Official Secrets Act. Lots of threats followed, but Max sailed through them all. Six months later, I got my column as a political correspondent. It was not a reward, far from it. Max had a more significant say in things.

"I suppose you two are still having time off for a break and a wedding, and that's fine as long as you, Pete, get me a quick opening story on the murder with statements from the police and EU officials. You can follow up with a fuller account on Wednesday." Max snapped his fingers at me. "And don't forget the Americans. Hart reckons it may have been a political robbery. If it is, then we need it out by tomorrow night."

"That means a flight out within hours, Max."

"Here." He tossed an envelope into my lap. "Four this afternoon from Heathrow." He looked through cigar smoke at Dianne. "Not you. You still have a week here before you go."

I was pleased. Despite Dianne's agreement, Max had confirmed she was staying home anyway. "Why the rush?" I asked.

"Ukraine and Russia. They hate each other. Moscow sees the EU as courting their former territories and undermining their trade deals."

"You think or you know?"

Max drew on the cigar until the tip glowed red. A lump of ash fell onto the desk. He brushed it away. "The police found Novotney's attaché case empty on the floor beside his bed. There's no telling what was in it, but he'd recently been working on a trade deal Brussels was putting the final touches to with Ukraine, so there might be a connection to Moscow."

He pointed the finger at me as I opened my mouth.

"Richard knows about the case. He got the news last night from Novotney's secretary. She's an old friend of Richard's, so talk to her, but tread lightly. She used to work for him in New York and, as I understand it, they're still close." He opened a drawer. 'Just a minute. I have her details here somewhere."

I remained quiet while he rummaged through notes in the drawer. He seemed nervous and on edge, the cigar never leaving his lips. So, Hart had asked for me because his old secretary was involved. There was history there, but Hart knew he could trust me not to dig into that part of his life.

"Here it is," Max eventually announced. He held a small sheet of paper with the secretary's details scrawled across it and scowled at me. "Whatever their relationship is, it has nothing to do with you. Focus on the attaché case, not Richard's love life. Don't annoy him. He's coming here next week, and I don't want you getting him upset over some stupid remarks or a situation you've got yourself into."

"I wouldn't dream of it, Max," I quipped. "It's bad enough tip-toeing around his love affair with the Prime Minister."

Max glared at me. "That's exactly the kind of thing I'm talking about." He took a long draw from the cigar, then drank steaming coffee from his mug while smoke escaped from his nose.

I often wondered if he enjoyed his coffee that way. Max reminded me of Frank Sinatra performing as a melancholy drinker, smoking, and singing, One for my Baby in the empty nightclub scene. I smiled inwardly. Max didn't sing, he yelled.

"This is not the time for wit, Pete. And another thing. I don't want to hear reports or have urgent calls from you or Dianne telling me that the bloody Russians are after you. If I do, I'll call bloody Putin myself and tell him where you are. Are we clear?"

I nodded and asked, "Is there a way you can get hold of a list of Bilderberg attendees?"

Max put the mug down, placed the cigar loosely between his lips, and studied me over the rim of his glasses. "If you think there's a connection here, you're way off. What the hell would Novotney's death have to do with that organization?"

I could see lots of connections and wondered if Max was not telling all.

"Could be nothing," interrupted Dianne, "but I don't believe in coincidence times three." She stood and straightened her jacket. "Novotney worked in government and lived in Prague, and most probably engaged in some way with the conference. If

The Defector's Diary

he wasn't attending himself, someone he knew in the Czechian government is on the list. As you say, Pete could be way off, but I doubt it."

Max ignored her. "Don't get involved with anything other than the Commissioner, Pete, you hear me?" he growled. "Enjoy the wedding, Dianne, but please keep an eye on him."

His eyes darted to me and back to her. "Forget the bloody conference, and don't use it as an excuse to start pulling politicians apart."

I joined Dianne at the door and crossed my heart. "Promise I'll stick to the plot. You know me, Max."

He raised one eyebrow and waved us out. "Call me tonight whatever the time."

I wanted to discuss Adam and the Bilderberg Club on the way home. Still, Dianne was unusually quiet, and matrimonial experience taught me to be wary about talking business or cracking jokes to lighten the atmosphere at such moments. It was time to keep my mouth shut.

Max would have his story, and with luck, there might be one or two politicians to 'pull apart.' Despite the warning, Max thrived on political intrigue for his editorials. Past lessons told me that within every political faux pas, whether departmental or something to do with the private life of a politician, there was always a story being hidden. Still, Adam's letter needed investigating, and that was just as important. I was sure a phone call would alleviate Dianne's worries.

"You're flying out this afternoon," Dianne announced as we turned onto Mews Lane. There was a slight tremble in her voice. "Let's get you packed now, and then you can take me to lunch at the Hilton." She leaned into me and kissed my cheek. "Thank you."

"Why? Not that it matters," I added quickly, parking the car opposite our front gate.

"For not getting all excited about the Bilderberg conference and Adam. Let's discuss him over lunch."

My phone rang. It was Max sounding unusually quiet.

"I forgot, Pete." He lowered his voice. "I should have told you, but SIS is gagging the press for now. So, keep this to yourself. There's a lot of flak flying about at the Cross. Our government appears to have lost its European trade secretary in Prague. Keep your eyes and ears open but don't get involved. SIS is all over it. You might get something I can use, but please stay with Novotney. If those bastards find out we're making inquiries, there could be serious consequences."

"Who's missing?" I asked.

"Michael Myer. Look him up. That's all I know. These are two separate incidents; one you follow and the other you do not. I thought you should know in case Myer turns up dead as well. Get onto Novotney's death, Pete, and don't forget I want a call every twenty-four." There was a pause. "Be careful. Situations like this can and do turn nasty. Just make sure you stay out of harm's way. You're going to be there longer than a week, and I'll take care of Dianne after the wedding. I want her back here and not chasing about with you."

"Thanks, Max."

"Good. Don't take any chances on Dianne's safety while she's with you."

"What about mine?"

There was a loud cough. "Yeah, what about it?"

I was on the verge of telling him all about Adam and the note we received but thought better of it. There was no need to start raising Max's temperature until I found out if all the players took part in one plot.

"Okay, I'll call you tonight." The line went dead. I was always grateful to Max for thinking about Dianne. He had a soft spot for her and knew she would insist on staying in Prague, something I did not want if things turned out the way he was painting the picture. He was rarely wrong.

The Defector's Diary

SIS was involved, and I guessed several agents from the Vauxhall Cross would be scampering about Prague. Max was right. We needed to be there and running before the rest of the journalistic hoards got wind of a missing politician, but it was best to keep a distance from SIS, already involved in this.

Dianne shook her head. "What couldn't he keep to himself?"

I told her, and we both sat, wondering if there was another connection in any way to Adam. With Novotney to worry about and a little irritated that Dianne was so concerned about Adam, someone I had never met, I had an extra unease I did not need.

On a lighter note, I asked, "I don't suppose you had your letter from the clinic yet?"

"No, so please stop asking me. I'll let you know when it arrives. Let's just get you packed and concentrate on Adam for the time being."

She seemed a little preoccupied, which was disappointing, but I put the thought of family to the back of my mind.

"Okay, you pack for me, and then I'm going to treat you to a great lunch, which you can pay for."

I could not help feeling a slight shiver of excitement as we walked up the path to our front door. Writing a column was a great privilege, but one drawback was the anchor tying me closer to Westminster and the daily political fare. True, there were many trips to Brussels, Paris, and DC, but I missed the early years, the cut and thrust of European and world politics.

With my enthusiasm in check, I smiled at Dianne.

Chapter Four

THERE WERE OVER FIFTY letters in all, neatly tied into a bundle with a red ribbon, hidden beneath several old diaries in a shoebox. The envelopes were posted with a variety of stamps from England, the USA, France, and Chechnya.

Two on top of the bundle were stamped from Portugal.

Dianne slid out the first envelope and unfolded the letter. She read, Dearest Dianne, and then closed her eyes as pictures of that last time they spent together vividly played out before her.

She recalled the late-night call two days after she moved into her New York apartment. Adam surprised her with a birthday gift. A long weekend in Portugal had been booked for her, including an airline ticket. Adam was staying on for another week in Lisbon as a temporary aide to the British Embassy. A staff illness had to be covered before he returned to London. They agreed to take it in turns to fly the Atlantic whenever work permitted and see how their relationship worked out.

Dianne opened her eyes and read the first four lines as a tear formed in the corner of her eye.

Darling, I am so sorry we quarrelled. I should have told you while you were in New York that I was being transferred to Prague. Please forgive me. I wanted the weekend to be so special.

She dabbed the eye with a tissue and remembered how she had worried about reporting to the New York Herald and putting off her start date for a few days, but things worked out, and the following weekend, she arrived in Lisbon.

Adam met her at the airport and they explored the city, enjoyed a wonderful evening meal, and later made passionate love.

The Defector's Diary

She felt sure he would ask 'the question'. The following morning over a champagne breakfast, he announced his transfer to Prague. He promised they would see each other, and things would work out. She felt betrayed and hurt. After a brief argument, she packed and left, telling him they were finished. The letter arrived a week later after many unanswered phone calls.

She never replied and spent the next year engrossed in work. It was not until she attended a Thanksgiving celebration party given by a congressman visiting London that she recalled meeting Adam again. After an initial frosty greeting, she forgave him, and they agreed to remain friends. They e-mailed each other until he only remembered her birthday and a card at Christmas.

She folded the letter and sighed. It was during that period that she met Pete after moving to the Herald in London. She didn't love him at first sight. He grew on her and eventually won her heart even though he was an awkward and sometimes infuriating man.

"Do you need any help, Dianne?" Pete's voice interrupted her train of thought.

"No, I'm fine," she answered. "I won't be too long. Why don't you book a cab for thirty minutes?"

She replaced the letter and put the box back on the wardrobe shelf, deep in thought. She felt no love for Adam, but there was something special about him. Perhaps regret at the way she walked out in a huff on him. She was unsure but was pleased that things had turned out the way they had. That was until the letter came.

Minutes later, she finished packing and placed Pete's suitcase out on the landing.

"Okay, Pete!" she called. "You can check your case now. Did you call a cab?"

He appeared at the top of the stairs. "It'll be here in half an hour. Let's leave my luggage here and collect it after lunch."

As they passed on the landing, she inwardly smiled again.

Letters were one thing Pete never sent. Text or Messenger, as long as it was electronic communication, he was fine. Yet there was a part of him that was so romantic, something about his body language, gentle touch, and smile whenever he was near. Whatever it was, it was a part of him she enjoyed.

Chapter Five

WE HAD A TABLE WITH A VIEW on the twenty-eighth floor. The Hilton's top restaurant was Dianne's favourite place for its excellent cuisine. It was not our regular daily eatery. There were special occasions such as birthdays and perhaps the odd lunch I had with some Westminster know-it-all. As luxurious and relaxed as it was, my salary laughed at the menu. On the other hand, Dianne had a private trust fund set up by her father, which sufficed when needed.

My mind was full of Max's assignment, mixed with my feelings on edge over Dianne's clear concern for Adam.

She seemed a little too concerned, and I felt guilty thinking that way. That said, there was something in Max's warning that was a little more important than my wife's history. Max never exaggerated. If he was worried, it meant he was suspicious that something might happen in connection to what was going on in Prague. Still a hunch, he just gave me a heads-up, but I knew, if necessary, he would shout.

I took my seat and looked out at Hyde Park, watching a colourful kaleidoscope of traffic and umbrellas pounded by pouring rain. The weather forecast predicted either rain or occasional showers in Prague, according to which forecast I checked. It rained the last time I was there on a quick visit to cover an EU function celebrating the Czech Republic's membership anniversary that year. I hoped it would clear by the time I arrived.

Dianne joined me at the table, shaking her head slowly, a worried look on her face. "I just called Adam, but he's still not answering."

"You know, I'm sure you're worrying over nothing. I bet I'll find the problem has been sorted out. As you say, Adam is a man who can be trusted and is level-headed. Let's think clearly about the letter and what I should or shouldn't do when I get there."

Dianne picked up the menu. "I don't want you doing anything until you find him."

"Excuse me?" I said.

She looked up. "Sorry, I didn't mean the way it sounded. I just meant that before we report the letter to an official, we try our best to get hold of Adam."

"Twenty-four hours," I replied. "Otherwise, we're putting ourselves in the clink."

After ordering lunch and a bottle of Chianti, Dianne again approached the subject of Adam and the diary.

"At any other time, you know what I would think?"

I knew only too well. Despite typically getting my way, she would fire a warning shot across my enthusiasm to unravel a mystery or embark on something that involved the risk of being fired, or ruining the Herald's reputation. This time, things were different. A friend was in trouble.

"Promise me you'll sort this out, won't you?" She hesitated. "I tried calling Adam several times now, but there's no response. I'm worried, Pete. I'm beginning to think the worst."

She gave me that helpless little girl look that worked every time. It was pointless saying no.

"Absolutely, and I promise I'll not get us into trouble…on purpose," I answered.

We looked at each other, then burst into laughter. My record for not getting into trouble wasn't good, but at least, I managed to have a few happy endings to my scrapes with authority.

"Pete…"

There followed one of those pregnant moments when one feels a little uneasy. Slender fingers tipped with red nails glided across the table and touched mine. I said nothing as our eyes met.

The Defector's Diary

"Aurora is the name of a Roman goddess—goddess of dawn. Adam used to call me that. I—"

I should have kept quiet and let her finish. "That's none of my business," I said softly. "No need to explain. I'm sure Adam loved you just as much as I do now."

"I'm not too sure about that, but I thought I should explain. It was a silly pet name, that's all." Her eyes darted away, a little embarrassed look on her face as she pulled a napkin from its holder.

The sommelier arrived, his pandering causing the soft scent of gardenias to fill the air around us. Dianne lowered her eyes. A half-smile accentuated by partly open lips set my heart thumping against my chest. I could not imagine a time when I would not be madly in love with her. She mouthed 'thank you' and placed her napkin on her lap as the sommelier uncorked the bottle.

We chatted over lunch about other matters, but despite trying to lighten the atmosphere for her sake, Adam's strange message played on my mind. I waited for coffee before pulling the note from my pocket.

The message was genuine. What disturbed me, the page had not been cut from the diary but torn out in apparent hurry. The words were scribbled, something one would not expect from a diplomat. Then again, the whole thing, I reasoned, could end up as a non-event, some misunderstanding. Dealing with the dead commissioner's story was the priority. There was a connection, the diary, but that was all it was for the time being.

"The message is quite straightforward," I said, "but there's nothing I can do until we meet the Czech who has the diary. I assume she'll be at the Da Capo Café and Cocktail Bar. I have two days before that happens, if it happens at all. I suggest I go to a meeting as per the card's message. I'll contact Novotney's secretary after I see the police. Afterward, I can follow up with any other inquiries."

"I have Adam's address," Dianne replied. "Perhaps you could

call on him as soon as you get there. He lives off Wenceslas Square."

"If it'll stop you worrying," I answered. "But if we have not heard or seen anything of Adam by the following morning, I'll have to let Max know. He can deal with the authorities while I do what I'm there for."

"The embassies are out, and I assume the SIS too?" said Dianne. "Surely, if this agent is defecting, she'll have to see someone at some embassy."

I was ahead of her. "Probably the British is out if Adam found something that made it a no-go, which also means no SIS. He would be wary of them. Adam is right. Trust no one. My problem is Max. If Novotney was up to his eyes in all this, then I have a huge story. But that's if there is a story, darling. All of this is supposition and maybe's and ifs over a note containing what? A defecting agent? Do you know how many of these rumours surface each year?"

"None of them are to do with Adam, though."

Her determination frustrated me. I changed the subject. "Another thing, you need to get that list of attendees of the conference and send it to me."

Dianne studied the torn page and pushed it in front of me. "What do you make of these entries?"

The page was quite large, suggesting an A4 diary divided into two days. The first date showed two appointments three hours apart. In the next day's space, Novotney had written, Pořadí bude zahájena první fáze v Londýněpo příštívšeobecnévolby.

The words were neatly handwritten across the page. "I have no idea how Adam would get involved in this. Concerning the sentence, I think you should translate it through your tablet."

"Thanks, Sherlock." She smiled and nodded at the waiter.

While Dianne was getting the check, I decided to call the Embassy in Prague and make my inquiry. Excusing myself, I walked to the cloakroom and made the call.

The Defector's Diary

"Good afternoon, British Embassy. How may I help you?"

"Yes," I started. "Could you put me through to Adam Denton, please?"

The line went silent for a moment. "Who is calling, Sir?"

"John Smith," I answered. I never felt guilty using another name for a general inquiry.

"I'm sorry, Mr Smith. Mr Denton is not available right now. Would you like to leave a message?"

"Oh, right. I take it he's there then?"

"I am sorry, Sir. Mr Denton is not available today. Perhaps try tomorrow."

I thanked the woman and ended the call. There was no confirmation that Adam was there, so I assumed he either left of his own accord or was genuinely unavailable.

As Dianne and I left the restaurant, she pinched my arm and steered me to armchairs opposite the lift.

"I Googled the sentence. The note will knock you off your feet." We sat, and she whispered, "The Club will start the first phase in London after the next general election."

My reaction was immediate. I could not help laughing. "Dianne, you're letting this get to you. The message is just a reminder of the next meeting for the Steerage Committee, or the planning for the next convention, perhaps in London." I held out my hands as her face clouded. "Darling, this is really getting to you, and I know how concerned you are, but really, you need to see this for what it is. Of course, there's a worrying side to Adam's note, but I'm sure I'm going to solve it as soon as I arrive."

I put an arm around her and ushered her to the lift.

"Listen," I said, "why don't you go back into the bar and have a quiet drink? I'll come back with my luggage and pick you up."

"You're a sweetie. Thanks." She kissed my cheek and waved me off.

The traffic had thinned, and ten minutes later, I was back home. After loading the luggage, I realized I left one of my chargers for the tablet upstairs on Dianne's dressing table. I raced upstairs and grabbed the lead. That's when I noticed one end of an envelope sticking out of the partially closed bureau drawer. There was an embossed emblem on one corner I recognized belongs to the clinic Dianne and I visited. Curious, I pulled the envelope out and read the letter.

My heart sank. I sat for a minute trying to fathom why she did not tell me straight away. An empty feeling and perhaps a little guilt overcame me. I put the letter back and returned to the cab. There was no way I could tell Dianne I knew, and I hoped she would find a way to tell me herself over the next few days.

There was a broad smile on my face when we left the hotel later.

"I was wondering," said Dianne. "After booking into your hotel, why not go to Adam's address tonight. If he isn't there, you can call Max later, right? We need someone else in the know just in case."

"Good idea."

After arriving at Heathrow, we pulled my luggage into the departure hall and made for the boarding pass machine.

"If, and it's a big if," I said, "but if Adam somehow got involved on his own, then he appears to be way over his head, especially if it has anything to do with the Bilderberg Club. We'll see."

I didn't want to alarm Dianne but I was worried I might be over my head too if the pieces of the puzzle fitted together. Hopefully, if they did, the Czech, or whoever it was, would be sitting at table twenty-two in the Da Capo Café and Cocktail Bar.

"You are aware, Pete, Max will shout and scream at you for getting involved." We sat near passport control. "How much are you going to tell him?"

"Everything. If this turns out to be something to do with the conference, every security service in the bloody world will get involved, and I don't want Whitehall hanging us out to dry. We need an ally we can trust. I'll call him and let him have the hotel number. He can rant while I'm sitting comfortably, but not while I'm at Heathrow. I'll tell him about Adam and the note. I don't have a choice. "

Dianne put her arms around me and we kissed. "Have a safe flight and call me when you get booked into your room."

Hugging her, I closed my eyes, hoping our dreams of having a family would come true despite the first medical. I also hoped she would talk to me. I needed more than anything to tell her that no matter what, we were as one.

"Oh, I forgot to give you this," she said and pressed a key into my hand. "It's the key to Adam's apartment. I forgot to give it back when we last saw each other." She lowered her eyes. "Don't read anything into this. Besides, it was way back when."

"I'll call you," I said. "Bye."

She turned and walked away, leaving me apprehensive, wishing I were not going to Prague.

Chapter Six

WITH THE RIVER VLTAVA dividing the city in two, Prague is one of the most beautiful cities in Europe. No dumping ugly glass structures here, there, and everywhere. Instead, the skyline stretched in all directions, a red carpet of roof tiles and countless spires, hence the nickname 'City of a Hundred Spires'. The distant roofs of red were masked by taller, more modern buildings that skirted the city's outer regions from the highway. There was no question that Prague would end up like London, though.

Hotel Brixen was thirty minutes from the airport.

As my cab sped along the highway, I took Adam's letter out of my pocket and read it again. There was nothing in it to suggest anything had already happened. I could not understand why he scribbled the note and tore it out of the diary without pointing attention to the entry on the reverse side. Possibly, he hadn't the opportunity to read anything in his rush to get the warning sent. Still, he appeared to reach out in a panic.

Adam was a diplomat, trained to be patient, understanding, knowledgeable of local culture, and above all, loyal to the Crown. As a member of an embassy abroad, he would also have been screened by SIS.

My thoughts had wandered elsewhere by the time I checked in. I knew Max would explode but given time to digest what I had to tell him, I knew he would calm down and let me follow the story. I called Dianne before texting Max.

"Hi, there, I just arrived and about to upset Max."

"Just remember to get over to Adam's place as soon as possible, or you'll upset me."

The Defector's Diary

I gave her my assurance and said goodnight.

A couple of minutes later, I sent Max a message and started to unpack. It was the only way to give him the full picture without getting shouted down before I finished.

My phone rang a minute after the text.

"Why can't you do as you're told? Every time you walk out of my office, I start worrying. If you're not insulting Number Ten or the White House, you're having a bloody fight with SIS and chasing across bleedin' Europe with bloody Russian spies behind you. Can't you have a normal life like other journalists? I'm sick of this—do you hear me?" The line went dead.

Upsetting Max or not, he had to know what was going on.

By the time I unpacked my case, the phone rang again. I knew the caller was Max when he coughed and didn't give him a chance to draw breath.

"Max, we're talking about information that might or could be changing the world as we know it. Not overnight, but gradually over a few years. Remember my article way back? Something about my research into the Bilderberg setup made me suspicious. I guess I got swept up by my colleague's conspiracy theory. Now those feelings are renewed. Maybe I'm wrong, but what if, huh?"

I gave him seconds to think about it.

"Even forgetting conspiracy theory and looking at facts, Max, if this Czech has a diary belonging to Novotney, the contents might reveal what is going on inside Bilderberg or reveal something about Moscow's Ukraine issue. Either way, we have a great story here. Dianne and I believe our friend Adam is accidentally or deliberately mixed up in this. All I want is your backup when security services come knocking on your door. In the meantime, I'll write the story for Tuesday and send it to the office tomorrow night."

There was a sharp intake of breath on the other end of the line. "You keep doing this, Pete, and I'm not going to be around for much longer. My heart can't take all this." He paused. "I want a phone call every day, so I know what's going on."

"Agreed," I answered. "Thanks."

"Don't thank me. There's something else you should know about the conference. When you start tip-toeing discreetly around, make sure you take your shoes off. Against my better judgement, I'm sending you a list of attendees because one of them is our owner, Richard Hart. Our Prime Minister is going too. I still don't think the Denton problem or Novotney has anything to do with that organization, but just in case you're right, I'll send it."

I winced at the name. The last thing I wanted was any contact with Hart. If he knew I was near, there would be trouble. "Okay, I'll do my best, Max. I'll be in touch tomorrow. Thanks again."

The call ended. My watch showed nine o'clock, so it wasn't that late to call on Adam. The guest phone rang.

"A mister Tosh to see you, Sir. He's in the bar."

I smiled but a little annoyed at the same time. Over the last five years, Tosh had been a useful source of gossip and general information on security matters, both domestic and international. The man always managed to surprise me.

He was or had been in the wrong profession. I told him many times, he should have taken to the stage. Of the many faces he wore, none were more appreciated than his natural face from the East End of London.

How the Secret Intelligence Services, previously MI5, conscripted him to start with was a mystery, and a secret Tosh never passed on despite my curiosity. Back then, MI5 recruited from high society and universities. Knowing the security service of old, I guessed he was approached for a particular task. That would be gathering intel from his contacts at home and abroad, and the criminal fraternity he called his family. The last time we crossed paths, his future was in doubt. The Cross housed the new breed of operatives, and Tosh found himself left in limbo. The fact that he made contact made me suspect he might still be in the business.

A pair of trainers jiggled up and down in front of a leather sofa. The wearer in jeans was hidden behind a copy of The Times. Only one person I knew would have no problem either standing out or hiding in a crowd. It was Tosh. Small in stature, normally unshaven and never smart, Dianne had nicknamed him 'penny-farthing'.

He was sitting with a beer and a wide grin. As was his usual unusual dress sense, he wore a brown leather bomber jacket over a green shirt. On his head, he wore a Tam O' Shanter.

"'Ello, guv, long time no see."

We shook hands warmly. I pointed to a hole in his jeans in one knee. "Don't tell me things have got that bad?" I quizzed.

"No, I'm just comfortable being casual, ain't I. Besides, I didn't have much time to pack me whistle and flute." He motioned to the bartender and ordered two beers. "You can pay for the beer, guv," he said cheerfully.

I nodded. "How did you know where I was staying? Are you still with the firm?"

Tosh didn't answer. We moved to a table. It was clear he was, but in what way? A staunch ally and a friendship that had matured over four years, I still knew that come the moment, his first loyalty would be to the Crown.

"You know as well as I do," he answered, looking around. "Whenever journalists travel on assignment, the Foreign Office and local embassies are informed. But, no, I ain't with the dirt factory anymore. The bastards tin-tacked me out on early retirement."

Tosh, or rather, Nigel' Tosh' Silsbury, and I went back several years. Son of an aristocratic stepfather, he joined SIS after leaving the Army intelligence service. Assigned to Berlin during the reunification of East Berlin, he experienced a particularly painful time when he lost an operative, he managed due to a traitorous double agent inside SIS. We met at a magistrate's court where he was being prosecuted for shoplifting. Due to an impassioned plea—Tosh was an excellent actor—he got a small fine. It was later that I realized he was there on purpose to snare me. SIS was looking for a conduit line into the EU for any information about gossip that might show a scandal or something not for public consumption. Who is better than a political correspondent with contacts inside the EU? Of course, I never knew this until a couple of years later, after I employed Tosh as a gofer and amateur—would you believe—sleuth to ferret around for me. He was very good and taught me a lot while feeding his office with general information he gleaned from me about Brussels' goings-on.

When his secret did finally appear, our relationship changed, of course. Now, two years later, he was still a little rogue from the East End, his birthplace, and we were joining forces again. In the back of my mind, I was still a bit suspicious about what he was doing. Nonetheless, if Tosh did turn out to be telling fibs, it would not surprise me. One thing I did know for sure. I could trust him entirely as a colleague and friend not to see me get into trouble.

"So?" I waited while he sipped beer.

Tosh rubbed the side of his nose and winked. "No further."

I nodded. "Of course."

"I have a friend," he answered. "Well, a sort of friend in the Foreign Office who got hold of me when he found out I was being pushed and asked me to lunch. I had a chat with him about EU corruption. That's something you might like to get your teeth into, although I guess Max could start spitting at you."

"Let me guess," I said. "Michael Myer. You're looking for him."

Tosh winked. "Specifically, yeah. There is, of course, the murder of the Commissioner as well. The two were friends, sort of."

I hesitated. Max had told me about Myer, but there was nothing to suggest anything else.

"Gay?" I asked.

"No. The two were close, though. My office got the jitters the moment Myer went missing, and that was a day before the Commissioner was found dead."

"Your office?"

"The Foreign Office. No need for you to know more, guv. The point is, when I found out you were on the list of visiting pen pushers, I knew I would get into things a lot quicker by grabbing your shirttail. I made inquiries and found out you and Dianne were coming here for a weddin'." He grinned. "Like old times, eh?"

I never heard of the department he was supposed to be working for, but knowing Whitehall after years, I kept an open mind. He had not mentioned Adam or the diary. If he knew about the wedding, he must have known who the bride and groom were. I decided to talk about Myer even though he was not there yet.

"Myer was a Member of the European Parliament for five years before the UK left the EU. He presently holds a position as our European trade secretary. Can you tell me if he's engaged in anything of particular interest before he went missing?"

"I can't tell you anything about his work, guv. I can say he had nothing or should have had nothing to do with Commissioner Novotney's dealings with Ukraine. Two days ago, we know he went to see Novotney and was not seen again. SIS started looking for him at once and, as far as I know, still are."

"He was under investigation then. For what?" I asked.

Tosh paused. "He was seen associating with several high-ranking EU officials and business tycoons over the last couple of months, and none of them had anything to do with his work. The first we heard of this was when the Foreign Office received a report from SIS."

"SIS? That's unusual."

Whitehall had a long history of bad feelings with the security services, particularly with matters abroad such as terrorism. I was suspended on one occasion by Richard Hart for a damning piece of work that embarrassed SIS so much, they wanted to charge me with contravening the Official Secrets Act.

"Not recently," replied Tosh. "They had their knuckles rapped a couple of times and now share some information with us." He waggled a finger. "Mind, they're not to be trusted. They still like to keep intel to themselves if it's useful to a current line of inquiry or exposes something they shouldn't be dabbling in."

Nothing had changed much. It interested me, though, that Tosh had moved to another branch of the security system. He must have read my thoughts.

"I can't tell you much, guv, but my department performs just one task in permanently investigating anything that smells ponky about diplomats abroad. SIS sometimes gets there before us, as in this case. Mostly though, we alert them. The idea is we keep each other in the loop like the FBI and the CIA…and we know how that goes, right? We keep an eye open to weed out anyone or anything that seems suspicious and likely to embarrass the government."

I still had to ask. Tosh was unique and not the face one associates with national security. "How do you play the game? You don't look the part, if I may say so."

"I don't have much to do with the target, guv. I investigate, report, and keep eye on things until the cavalry arrives from London. It's usually a white-collar job, nothing violent. I spend all of the time undercover." He grinned. "I got the job because of my contacts and knowledge of my playground. My misspent youth came in useful after all."

We looked at each other over our beers. Tosh had shared enough, and it was my turn to either trust him or go things alone. I guessed he had a few pieces of the puzzle missing or he would have mentioned Adam.

"So, what's on your agenda, guv?"

"Okay, before I start, I have information that, on the face of

The Defector's Diary

things, seems to show there might be a threat to national security. It might also be a big damp squid. Whatever you make of it, I ask one favour."

"How long do ya need, guv?"

Tosh knew me too well. "Twenty-four hours. Officially, I'm writing a piece on Novotney for Max," I answered.

"Interesting that I now know Novotney met the UK Trade Secretary in Prague before the Commissioner was murdered."

I pulled Adam's letter from my pocket and passed it across the table. Tosh read it, turned it over, then read the attached business card. If he was surprised, he didn't show it.

"I'll keep these, guv, if I may. I take it you have a copy?"

I tapped my tablet. "The information is safe."

He stood. "Let's take a walk, and you can tell me about Adam and Aurora. I'm assuming that's Dianne?"

"Yes, but that's old history," I said, joining him. "Give me a minute to fetch my coat."

I left him in the lobby and took the lift, feeling a little apprehensive. While I trusted Tosh, I did not doubt that depending on what I told him, he could decide my information was too important not to send back to London right away. The key to action lay with Adam.

Outside, the evening had turned cold as we joined tourists strolling on the sidewalk. The square still looked busy as it had on my first visit. Rows of green, leafy plane trees flanked the street outside shops, hotels, and nightclubs. The mouth-watering smell of cooked food and fresh bread hung in the air. In the central pedestrian precinct, well-wrapped tourists sat on benches watching the changing scenery. Others stood, admiring the views as the light faded and the city began changing its persona into a kaleidoscope of neon lights, illuminated bridges and castle. Prague was alive and open to all kinds of established businesses, from a storefront to dealers on street corners. A vibrant city like many in Europe, its two faces changed with ease at daybreak.

Tosh's first words confirmed my thoughts on Myer's connection with Novotney.

"Myer was or is up to something. The fact that we can't find him tells us he has some influential friends helping him to evade arrest. One of those connections was Novotney."

"Arrest? What for?"

"SIS. They've used the Official Secrets Act. Myer breached it by not officially reporting his association with a foreign diplomat."

We found a bench and sat while I filled Tosh in on what I knew about Adam. When I finished, we sat in silence for a minute. A knot began to grow in the pit of my stomach.

"Okay, Adam's gone missing, and like Myer, around the time of Novotney's death," said Tosh. "This note indicates action after the general election. That's four weeks from now, just after Adam's wedding. As you say, Adam's involvement with a Czech agent could be a separate thing. My worry, guv, is Myer. For all we know, he may have topped the Commissioner or, because of what he was up to, be on the run from the killer. I have to find him quick. With regards to Adam, I could check in with the Embassy to see if he's missing, and you can bet on it that SIS will be after him, especially if they know about a would-be defector." Tosh's face cracked into a wide grin. "Like old times, guv…like old times."

"So, we have a deal then?" I asked. "I want to find Adam, and tomorrow, I'm making contact with Novotney's secretary and the police."

"We both need to find Adam," said Tosh. "That diary is the one piece that all four have in common." He pushed hair out of his eyes. "My hands are tied, guv. My main man is Myer, but should either of us unearth him or Adam, we keep each other informed, yeah? Forget the time limit. We both know when to shout." He hunched his shoulders against the chill air. "You're solo, guv. I'll help all I can."

The Defector's Diary

With that, he got up and walked briskly across the square. I watched him go and could not help wondering how a man like Tosh could lead a life hiding in shadows, courting occasional danger, and having to hold hands with Westminster's bureaucracy. Retirement would have finished him. He knew nothing else.

My cell phone buzzed. I pulled it out and a text read, 'Give my love to Dianne'. I answered and sat thinking about her and the letter from the clinic. I desperately wanted to talk to her about it, especially if she thought I would be so upset if things did not turn out the way we wanted. The one thing to avoid, I told myself, was to create tension. It was a waiting game I had little stomach for.

I checked the time and was surprised how long my meeting with Tosh had lasted. It was too late to go knocking on Adam's door. I decided to find the Da Capo Café instead.

Dianne had found the address for me. I walked across to the other side of the square and found it quickly. It was not hard to find. I tried to remember the square as I had seen it.

The buildings were the same, but the shops and stores were mostly under new management. New additions included a McDonald's, but the one thing that brought back real memories was the smell of the place: aromatic hot red wine, coffee being ground, and freshly baked bread and rolls. There were more trees along the pavements than before and, of course, the relatively new highway that cut the museum off from the square. The people had not changed, though. There were more Asians and black people, yet it was not that I noticed, but rather the looks on faces as they passed me. They were smiling instead of the sullen and worried expressions etched on faces surrounded by communist oppression decades before.

A large McDonald's neon glared down at me from one side of The Da Capo. The café was fronted by glass, behind which two twenty-somethings sat looking at the street scene from high stools behind a long counter. Chill-out piano jazz spilled out through the open door. The faint hiss of steam from the coffee machine added to the noisy but comfortable atmosphere from the main bar. It was the kind of place Dianne and I liked. The clientele was not too young, and one could either relax with eyes closed or have an intelligent conversation with others. I stood outside for a moment, missing her.

I decided not to enter but wait until I had more time.

In the morning, my priority was to contact the police and Novotney's secretary. My promise to Dianne to look for Adam first thing broken, I hoped she would not ring me.

On the way back to the hotel, I had a strange feeling I was being watched. Spots of rain began to pepper my head. I pulled the collar of my coat up and, holding both ends tight, bent forward and began to walk briskly. The rain started to fall more heavily. I stopped and took shelter in a doorway.

Instinctively, I looked back in the direction I had come in and caught movement of something or someone disappearing into another doorway several doors down. My conversation with Tosh may have set my nerves on edge. There again, maybe not.

Chapter Seven

A PIGEON WADDLED out of the long shadows cast across Horse Guards Parade and into the bright sunshine that bathed central London. It stopped at the edge of a small puddle of rainwater before flying off to join a line of pigeons perched on the Horse Guards building roof.

Sir John Carlton sipped tea and looked down at a lone pedestrian walking along the avenue of trees to one side of the parade ground. His small eyes missed nothing. He struck an imposing figure, upright and fit, a short man of slight build that gave him an air of unquestionable authority.

Behind him, James Driscol stood nervously waiting.

"So, what have you done about the situation in Prague? Are things that bad that you should stand there peeing your pants?" asked Carlton without turning around. "I chose you to head the UK Bilderberg Club security force because of your Middle East experience dealing with those bloody terrorists. Are you telling me you can't handle the situation now?"

"Well, Sir, so far as I can see," answered Driscol, ignoring the insult, "we have just one more thing to clear up. You have already dealt with our target, 'Order' and arranged things. I take it you will be using Charles as the shooter?"

Sir Carlton nodded and turned. "Besides that, we're on schedule. Everyone is ready for the big day." The corners of Driscol's mouth twitched. He was about to speak but thought better of it.

"One more thing to clear up," repeated Sir Carlton. "Am I to assume the last thing for you to clear up is our wayward gentleman Myer, who decided to run away?"

"Yes, Sir. Our people are promising to have him found very shortly." Driscol ran a hand through his hair.

Sir Carlton placed his teacup and saucer carefully on the desk.

Driscol, towering above Sir Carlton, swallowed, and tried to smile. Two defections from the Committee had rattled everyone's nerves. The whole operation was balanced on a knife-edge. He knew if things got out of control, the plan would be cancelled. Heads would roll. Two already had.

"You've forgotten some other matters that, to my knowledge, have not been cleared up," said Sir Carlton Now sit, calm down, and let's go through things together."

Driscol eased himself into an armchair and sat biting his bottom lip. He hoped news of the latest development would not have reached Carlton too soon, but his fears were realized. The man had eyes and ears everywhere. There was no choice but to inform him about the diary.

He chose his words carefully and explained. "The Czech police were helpful, reporting to the Committee's SIS contact that Novotney's secretary had discovered a personal diary kept by the Commissioner, was missing. She suspected her junior secretary, whom she had caught looking through the diary the week before, claiming she was checking the official appointments one and picked up the personal diary instead. The junior secretary was also missing."

"Do we know what's in the diary?" Sir Carlton sat and drummed his fingers on the arm of the chair.

"No idea, Sir. No matter what, we have to get it back, though. We need to make sure there's no incriminating evidence."

"I take it we have people looking for her too?"

"Yes, Sir." Driscol hesitated and breathed deeply. "There is something else, Sir."

Carlton's fingers stopped tapping. His tone became aggressive. "I'm beginning to wonder if I made a mistake with you. What the hell has happened now? We're already looking for two

The Defector's Diary

people; please don't tell me there's a third."

"No, Sir. Our man in the Embassy reported this morning that a journalist is sniffing around in Prague. It looks like the press is after a story on the Commissioner. I'm sure that's all, but I've taken steps to have this particular journalist tailed."

"Do we know anything about him?"

Driscol looked at the floor, avoiding Carlton's stare. "Yes, it's Pete West, I—"

What? He is not just a journalist. He's a bloody columnist. Have you any idea what this means? That bloody man is like a dog with a bone when he gets his teeth into something. How long has he been sniffing around?"

"He arrived yesterday afternoon, Sir. The British Embassy have him listed officially as press. I assure you—"

"I don't want your bloody assurances. I want West back where he belongs, here in London, you idiot."

Driscol's jaw dropped. His face blanched. "I'm going to Prague to deal with this myself."

"No. You will not do any such thing. You're supposed to be here to coordinate all the parts of our plan during the next few weeks. You will speak to whoever you have over there and make sure the junior secretary, the diary, and Myer are found. If West gets in the way, you will warn him off."

Driscol shifted uncomfortably. "And if he does get his teeth into a bone, Sir?"

"You'll make sure he doesn't." Carlton glared at Driscol. "Do you realize what would happen if something compromising in the diary ends up being read here?"

There was one more piece of information, the worst possible kind that Driscol had found out the previous evening.

"The Czech agent…the junior secretary is a Czech agent. I am sure she has the diary. It's not got back into BIS - Czech Security Service, hands. According to our man in SIS, it looks like she's defecting but not through the normal channels. BIS has recalled her." His fingers fiddled with a wedding ring. "If the agent is caught, she would be handed over to the Czech security services and executed after a brief military court appearance."

"What the hell?" Carlton choked and sat rigidly, his face tight with rage. "Let's hope she is caught by us before her people find her. I don't care how you handle her. Just get the diary and find Myer. Now, get out."

Driscol left the office, pleased to escape Sir Carlton's temper. The man could be a real tyrant, but as a leader, he was brilliant. He would help change the corrupt world and bring peace and a sense of pride and achievement to all nations under one government. Driscol felt privileged to be given the position of head of the organization's UK security. He was determined to keep the position. Back in his office, he pulled the files on Myer and Pete West.

Dianne West was an interesting woman. She was married to West and, like her husband, a journalist. If West was in Prague, then she would be on her own. It would not be hard to send a warning. It would undoubtedly give West something to think about. He picked up his phone and called Rougeon. The man was dependable and efficient.

"Pierre, I have a little job for you. I'm going to e-mail you a file. I want you to persuade a lady that she should convince her husband to catch a plane home. I don't want her hurt, but one of your great car crunches might just do the trick." He ended the call and pulled another file marked Charles Cranthorp. The phone rang as he flipped through the pages.

"I was just looking through your file," he answered. "How are we doing?"

"I suppose I could say we're doing well, but that wouldn't be quite right. Our popular media man is going to be nosing around all over the place. However, I have my own man doing the right thing. We're following him. It appears he came to Prague for a wedding. His wife got an invite from Adam Denton who was marrying an innocent young Czech girl. I guess that means West is here to see Denton about the wedding arrangements."

Driscol gritted his teeth and clenched a fist. Cranthorp was frustratingly cool and laid back with little regard for authority. "Charles, you will follow him, and at the earliest opportunity, warn him that it's better for his health that he returns home."

"And we both know he's not going home. What do you want me to do? How about we throw him in the river, or maybe he drowns in his hotel bath?"

"If you had not messed things up the other night," said Driscol, "we wouldn't be in the position we're in today."

"That I messed up? It was you who gave the order and me that had to clean up after your men. Now, you have a real problem with West. There's only one thing we can do. Get rid of him."

Driscol thought for a moment. "No, that would be very counterproductive on the eve of our operation. We also have a problem with the girl. Anything on her?"

"Not yet, but the best way to find her is probably to follow West,." said Cranthorp. "If he gets a sniff of what is going on, he may well lead us to her. I take it you just want the back of her?"

"Yes. Only this time, please take care of it yourself. I don't like the people you use. I told you when we started you would have to get your hands dirty. The boss needs to know whose side you're going to be on when the curtain goes up. I am depending on you to make sure the Rosebud drop team are ready with their lighters on the day of action. We don't want any slip-ups. Remember, another team will be cleaning up the drop team. We only have one opportunity to get things right. By the way, what's the name of the man you have in charge of the snatch squad, as you call them?"

"Joseph Labrum. A real nasty piece of work, but he's outstanding. It wasn't him that messed up the other night. That blame goes to an outfit from Paris. I sent them packing afterwards. By the way, there are six in the drop team who will be at their destinations on time but how do I know your cleanup squad are going to be efficient? If one of them survives we will have a problem. Surely it makes sense for me to clean up.""

"Stop worrying Okay, Charles. The shooters are handpicked by the President himself. Call me daily while we have this diary problem. The boss is going mad here. I have to take his temper every day."

The conversation ended and Driscol looked through West's file. A popular columnist, he would be a dangerous thorn in the side if he got too close, but perhaps someone who could be courted and offered a very lucrative post within the organization. It was unfortunate that Operation Rosebud would commence with such drastic action but as the President had said, the world would turn to the New Order for guidance.

Chapter Eight

MY CELL PHONE RANG and woke me from a restless night.

Sleep evaded me. Mixed thoughts about Adam and Dianne's situation over the clinic's letter had me wrestling with the bed sheets until I finally fell asleep around three. I looked at my watch, annoyed it showed seven o'clock.

The caller was Dianne. Still half asleep, I dreaded talking to her. I yawned as I answered. "Good morning."

"Hi, there, sorry if I woke you. Did you find Adam?"

There has never been any point telling Dianne a harmless lie, even over the phone. "No, I'm sorry, but when I got here, I had the surprise of my life. Tosh turned up as I was about to go to Adam's address. I'm going there now, though." I held my breath.

"Great, Pete. By having an old boys' reunion last night, you might have missed Adam. Tell me, do you care at all?"

I recounted the conversation I'd had with Tosh and that we would keep in touch. There wasn't much else to tell her except that I would be at Adam's address within the hour.

"I can't do more than that at this moment," I explained. "Remember, I have to see Novotney's secretary and the police later today."

"Then I'll expect a call in a couple of hours from either you or Adam. Or perhaps it may be your sidekick who just happened to appear. I expect you'll add another housebreaking method to your portfolio. Just keep him away from me."

I was still tired and irritable. "Dianne, I'll do the best I can. If I don't call you, it's because I have not found Adam, okay?"

"No, that's not good enough, Pete. I need to know what's going on."

"Tell me something," I retorted. "How deep is this friendship of yours with Adam?"

"He's a good friend who needs my help, and I don't like what you're implying."

"Your help? How about my help I've been pushed into giving? I know nothing about this guy. You never told me anything about him apart from the fact you've kept in touch. Now he sends a wedding invitation after what…four years? You've practically got your arms around him, and I'm supposed to get him for you. Perhaps you'd like to explain."

There was a pause. I closed my eyes and thumped my knee with regret at being so stupid.

"I'm sorry," I began. "I'm tired, Dianne. I'm—"

"So am I, Pete, so am I. You're right. I should have told you more about Adam, but then, you have no right to ask or expect an explanation. I asked for your help, that's all."

"Adam asked for my help through you. I'll call when I have news."

I could hear Dianne's heavy breathing. "Don't bother."

There was a click, and the line went dead. I called back, but that proved pointless. Both of us were going to have a bad day. It was one of those moments I wished I had no tongue. I wished I had not heard of her 'good friend'.

As I showered, I thought of my conversation with Tosh about Myer. I didn't think that apart from Adam's scribbled note on Novotney's diary page, there was nothing to link him personally to the Commissioner's friend, Myer. Adam was possibly a missing person, in which case SIS would be hot on his tail.

With the police and security already involved in Novotney's death, there seemed little I could do apart from getting on with the article Hart wanted. I called reception to arrange a cab. Adam's apartment wasn't too far from the city centre, and I

The Defector's Diary

wanted to find out whether he was there or missing.

The receptionist was trying to call me at the same time.

"Mr West, a Mr Tosh is here to see you."

"Is he? Please send him up."

I knew my spat with Dianne wasn't Tosh's fault. I had to call on Adam before I did anything else. And then there were the police, although, from experience, they would give me little. The secretary was a much better bet at getting what I needed, plus possibly more on the Commissioner's murder.

There was a knock on the door.

"Morning, guv." Tosh walked past me and sat on the end of the bed as if he owned the room.

"I have things to do today, Tosh," I said. "First, I'm going to Adam's apartment to see if he's there or at work."

He looked serious. "If you don't mind, I'd like to come with you. This morning, I found out from a friend at the Embassy he's been missing since the day after the Commissioner's death. SIS is looking for him, as are the city police." He puffed his cheeks. "I think you should still go, although he won't be there, but something of interest might turn up."

"Such as?" I asked.

"Something SIS missed...or planted. They're not beyond getting their hands dirty."

I thought for a moment. Tosh knew enough from his own time with MI5 that the department could not be trusted in certain areas. Perhaps he knew something he was unwilling to share with me.

"Okay, I need to arrange an interview today, so time is short. First, I need to go to the police HQ."

Tosh said nothing, which I found a little strange. He followed me downstairs and out where guests had arrived by cab. We climbed into one and I gave the cabby instructions.

"You won't get much out of them," warned Tosh. "They'll be in a bad mood dealing with our bleedin' lot and the Embassy. A journalist is gonna' get shown the door."

Despite the feeling that Tosh was acting strangely, I ignored the remark and made some notes on my tablet. Ten minutes later, we pulled up outside the police HQ.

"I'll wait here with the cab, guv. I'll see you in about ten minutes after you've used up all your persuasive powers to see an officer in charge of the investigation."

"It's my job, so stop pushing me into changing my schedule to suit yours."

"Don't know what you mean, guv."

I grinned at him. "You forget, I know you well. I'm sure you have something you want to show me, otherwise you'd have told me right away."

I walked in through the main entrance and was met by an officer. My credentials were enough to stop me getting any further. I did, however, get the name of the officer conducting the investigation. Instructed to call for an appointment, which I knew wouldn't work anyway, I retreated.

"Don't say it," I said, climbing into the cab.

I gave the cabby Adam's address and settled back. Tosh pulled a paper flyer from his pocket and handed it to me.

"Take a look at what I found last night."

Across the top was the heading Da Capo Café & Cocktail Bar.

Below was an offer of a twenty per cent dinner discount, plus a free drink every Tuesday after seven o'clock.

"Tomorrow is Tuesday. I doubt it'll be the Czech agent, but it has to be someone in the know, which could be Adam. I think it might be a good idea if I go alone so I can keep an eye open and watch your back."

"I thought you were more interested in Myer," I said. "What are you keeping from me?"

"There's a connection. Myer, the Commissioner, Adam, and the diary." He looked at me and raised his eyebrows. "You could be right that these are separate incidences, but that's doubtful,

The Defector's Diary

guv."

"I can see what you see," I answered, "but Myer is still the odd one out. Something about him doesn't add up. Anyway, Richard Hart wants a nice piece on Novotney."

Tosh gave me a knowing look. Of the three missing people, Myer should have been the easiest for the authorities to find. The possibility that he could have been murdered along with the Commissioner was in the back of my mind, but if he had not, he would have to have some powerful friends keeping him safe somewhere. But why? Apart from being a friend of Novotney, there was nothing else to show any wrongdoing or political conspiracy involvement. The man was a mystery. He was also the story Max told me not to pursue. A missing politician was big news. A dead one was an obituary and a police investigation progress report. I hoped Myer would turn up and I could get involved.

"Why don't we go take a look at the café and work something out for tomorrow night?" asked Tosh. "We can also check out the apartment this afternoon."

I thought of Dianne. She would be waiting for my call, knowing I was smarting from her verbal slap and making her wait a little. That would give me a few hours. I told the cabby to take us to the Da Capo Café.

In daylight, the Da Capo looked a little different. From outside, the café boasted just one large window with a door to one side. A row of high chairs behind the glass looked out over the square. It appeared very non-descript. The surprise came as we walked in. Above us was the original curved brick ceiling. Below it, small and large tables covered with colourful art deco designs gave the place an ultra-modern look. The lounge went back quite a way, lined on one side with bright matching padded chairs, and against the wall all manner of comfortable grey lounge sofas covered with various cushions. Stairs at the far end led up to another level. The bar was just inside the entrance, and on the back counter, a sparkling espresso machine hissed and puffed wisps of steam.

As I stepped past it, the mixed aromas of coffee and vetrnik pastries mingling in the air made me feel hungry. I tried looking preoccupied to find an empty table but couldn't help worrying. There was very little I could do until someone showed up for a meeting. If nobody showed tomorrow, then I had to decide if I would wait another seven days.

I knew it wouldn't be long before SIS came knocking on the door, and Tosh needed to avoid them. As far as he was aware, his office had kept quiet about his visit.

Half a dozen people were sitting around, some reading papers. I walked to the far end and climbed the stairs.

Upstairs was a different matter. Two neat rows of numbered tables stretched to the far wall, and table twenty-two was at the far end. Spotting someone from the head of the stairs would be easy. Tosh and I sat and ordered coffee.

"If the agent is expecting to see Adam or another contact, then she'll turn up," said Tosh. "They would have agreed on a contingency plan if Adam didn't show for whatever reason."

Tosh insisted he go, and I agreed. He would arrive at the café at six-thirty and take a seat upstairs. The agent was unlikely to know him.

"I can remain hidden in plain sight a couple of tables away," suggested Tosh. "That way, I can spot any other familiar faces."

"Well, if it turns into a no-show, then that's it for me," I said thoughtfully. "Myer is my story. By the way, I haven't thought about what to do if the agent does turn up. I'm assuming that she'll have hidden this diary with its revelations somewhere safe until she gets what she wants. I can't afford to wait any longer than tomorrow night. According to Adam, she's going to give it to me. If she doesn't let me have it, then I'm going to report to SIS myself. I could be in trouble for withholding evidence as it

The Defector's Diary

is."

Tosh shook his head. "Don't be too fast contacting SIS, guv. If it comes to it, I'll report her. Besides, if you do get her on her own and she's uncooperative, you can let me handle her. A simple threat to contact her headquarters will do the trick. A shot to the back of the head is not something she would want to look forward to."

Tosh's answer reminded me that there was a more serious and darker side to him behind the cheeky chap from the East End of London. I would never underestimate him. With that in mind, I wondered if I had jumped too soon in revealing Adam's letter to him. It isn't often that I feel uncertain about something. When that does happen, I know where to go.

I decided. "Tell you what, I have to call Max and write tomorrow's obituary on the Commissioner. First, I have the secretary to interview. Let's meet up later this evening and look for Adam. I need to call Dianne too."

We grinned at each other. "Okay, guv. Give me a call when you're ready. Best of luck with the wife if she's talking to you yet. Give her my love."

Chapter Nine

DIANNE WAS NOT PICKING UP her phone. After two messages, I gave up and decided I would try again later.

I felt a little uncomfortable about deceiving Tosh, but I couldn't shake the feeling that somehow, he had a hidden agenda regarding Adam. He knew more, I was sure, about the defector.

I wanted to be on my own to clear my head and make some sort of sense of the situation. Adam and his problem were not my main worry, but apart from looking for him, there was little I could do to satisfy Dianne's fears. Max needed a story about Novotney, and I was already twenty-four hours behind schedule. I allowed my heart and not my head steer me off course.

Tosh and I parted company outside the Capo Café, and I waited a few minutes watching him disappear before walking in the opposite direction. Adam lived in New Town, one of the several municipal areas that made up the central inner city. His apartment was in the touristy part of the city—a side street off Wenceslas Square.

I strolled through the square's garden, sat down on one of the benches and watched as sightseers and the general populace strolled or hurried along the pavement. The day had turned chilly. A slight breeze blowing through the avenue of trees orchestrated a loud but soothing symphony of rustling leaves. For a moment, I remembered sitting in the central pedestrian precinct in the lower square where flower beds surrounded a grassed area. The scent of the flowers came back to me, igniting mixed moving pictures that flashed through my mind's eye.

There were images of fellow journalists sitting and eating

The Defector's Diary

lunch. These merged into scenes of chaotic violence as the same benches were used to lay the wounded in '78. The noise of public battle, water cannon, and gunshots raged all that day. I remembered how I felt when I finally stood looking at the torn battlefield of broken glass, ripped banners, and general rubbish strewn across the small park where Russian troops crushed Czech resistance. Two people were dead and hundreds injured. My anger at Moscow and my respect for the futile Czech resistance fuelled my heart and pen. I left the memory behind as I stood and looked around. I couldn't see Tosh, but that didn't mean he wasn't there. I hoped he wasn't, although I'd have to tell him about my deception later.

I turned left out of the square into a narrow street. Adam's apartment block was situated about halfway down. It was a quiet street lined by tall, grey austere buildings made before the First World War. It was a typical middle-class area.

A lift took me up to the fourth floor and, as the doors slid back, I found myself in a narrow hallway. I soon found Adam's door, one of six apartments on each level. I half expected the door to be taped by the police. After ringing the bell and knocking several times, an old lady with hair in curlers appeared from the next flat. She wore a flower-embroidered housecoat over a pair of jeans tucked into fur-lined boots. Waving a cigarette, she spoke understandable English.

"He not here. Has not been for three days. His young lady called other day, and she left before him. Now they both gone."

"You mean, Valerie?" I asked.

"Yes. The tart with her...how you say...air and grace. A real madame. She not good woman."

Before I could inquire further, she shrugged, placed the cigarette between her lips, and disappeared back into her flat, slamming the door shut.

I pulled the key from my pocket and rang the bell one more time to make sure. The key turned and the door opened enough for me to step inside. I closed the door behind me and looked around the apartment's main living room.

I noticed a partially open door into what I assumed was the bedroom. I stepped across the carpet and entered carefully. A non-descript lined pattern paper covered the walls. From the ceiling hung a small glass or plastic chandelier. A chest of drawers stood at the foot of the bed, and in one corner was a black suit on a hanger draped over an upright chair.

My eyes settled on two photos displayed on the top of the chest. The first showed Adam and, I assumed, Valerie smiling for the camera. The second made me look twice. Adam was sitting in the after-well of a small cabin cruiser, and next to him was a man. Both were holding fishing rods.

What interested me was a face in the shadows behind them, appearing from the cabin. A face I knew well, and it reminded me of other faces and darker moments. The face belonged to Charles Cranthorp.

Cranthorp was SIS, and although a reasonably friendly contact, I had not seen or heard from him in two years, just like Tosh, since my last brush with the dirty side of national security. I did not and never would trust him. Neither Cranthorp nor Tosh gave anything away for free.

What bothered me was the connection between Cranthorp and Adam. If SIS had recruited Adam, that would change the whole situation. I wasn't going to get tied up in that.

Not knowing how things would develop, I pulled out the photo of Adam and Valerie and put it in my pocket. At least I would have something to give Dianne that might turn out to be a memento. I walked into the living room and open kitchen area. Nothing looked out of place. Without thinking, I rested a hand on the kitchen worktop. Tosh had once jokingly reminded me in conversation that I should never touch anything if I went burglarizing unless I was wearing gloves.

I pulled my hand back instinctively and a small cloud of dust rose in the air. My palm was dusted white, and the realization sent a chill down my spine. The apartment had been investigated. Someone, either the police or SIS, had already called. That was that. I tried calling Dianne again and, when the answering service cut in, I left a message.

"Dianne, I have news about Adam. There is nothing I can do as he has absconded. Whether he is with Valerie or the agent, or both, I don't know. The embassy and security are looking for him. I'm in his apartment and found it must have been searched because it's been dusted for fingerprints. I—"

"Pete, what's going on?" Dianne cut in. "If he's not there, have you been to the police? What about Novotney's secretary?"

I waited for her to finish. "Dianne, there is no point in looking for him. I went to the police, and they'll not give me anything. I'm off to see the secretary next."

"I know you have a job to do, but that doesn't stop you from looking for Adam, does it?"

Her voice was cold and sharp. I thought of a compromise that would hopefully give her some peace of mind. "Do you know Valerie's address or surname? I can chase her up. Adam, might be with her."

There was no possibility he was with her, but I didn't want to tell Dianne that.

"I have no idea, Pete."

"I'm sorry about this morning. You caught me as I woke up. Of course, I'm as worried about things as you are, but I cannot think of anything else to do. The Embassy is looking for Adam, and so are SIS. Apart from that, I have a story to write, and Max will be on top of me later today."

I waited. After what seemed an unusually long pause, Dianne answered calmly.

"You had no right to question me about Adam. There are certain areas of our lives that we keep private. You have some secrets, I'm sure. For example, the scar on your face you won't tell me about."

Ignoring her remark, all I wanted to do was get out of the apartment. "I'm sorry. I won't make that mistake again. I hate upsetting you. Forgive me, but I have to get out of here in case someone comes back."

"You see what I mean? You cannot spare me a minute."

She was right, but not the way she was thinking. My reaction was to get out as soon as possible. I saw no end to the conversation. Dianne wanted the last word, as always. "Dianne, I have to go. I'm sorry." I ended the call and wiped the worktop. I couldn't see SIS powdering the place again, and if it had been the police, it meant they had a murder on their hands, or suspected one. All of a sudden, I felt alone and vulnerable. Something didn't fit. If the place was dusted, why wasn't there a police crime scene tape across the front door? So, Adam was on the run and the hounds were on his heels.

As much as I wanted to get out and away, I knew I could be implicated. The old lady across the hall had seen me. I needed an escape route. Despite my misgivings, I dialled Tosh's number.

He answered almost at once. "Yes, guv. Don't tell me. You're in the shit."

"Look, I'm sure you're not far away. I'm at Adam's, and the place has been gone over by pros. There's fingerprint dust everywhere, and a neighbour across the hall saw me."

"Have you touched anything?"

"Only a worktop, but I cleaned it. The doorknob I can wipe on the way out."

"No," said Tosh. "You stay there until I arrive. Have you looked all over the place and made certain there is nothing that connects Adam to Myer or Novotney?"

I pulled the photo of Adam and Valerie from my pocket.

"Nothing really, although I took a picture from his bedroom of a happy couple for Dianne. There's another photo of Adam and a friend with fishing gear in the back of a small boat. Behind them is Cranthorp."

"Okay, guv, here's what I suggest you do. Stay there and eyeball every corner. Visualize everything. I'll be there in fifteen."

"Tosh, I owe you an apology."

"Yes, you do, guv. Let's discuss that when we're having dinner on you."

I almost laughed at his cheek, but as was Tosh's habit, he was making light of a serious problem, namely me. The call ended and I felt better that I had someone on my side.

The kitchen was clean, as was the lounge. I pulled some towels off the roll above the worktop and carefully opened all the cupboards. Adam was a neat man.

Crockery and cutlery were stacked or placed in straight lines, and his larder was the same. I moved back into the bedroom and found nothing out of place. The floor beneath the bed had been cleaned. It was a little frustrating finding nothing. I felt guilty and wanted to find something I could wave in front of Tosh. Once again, I knew I might be putting him in an awkward position.

Adam had asked for help, and I all but ignored his letter until the message on the back of the note suggested something sinister was going to happen. Even then, it was only a maybe. My thoughts turned to Dianne. I sat on a stool, waiting for Tosh, thinking about her.

I was sure Adam was a genuine friend, no matter what their relationship in the past. It was more personal; she never talked to me as she had the last two days. I felt a deep sense of loss that the particular part of her love she showed every time she spoke or smiled was gone. This other person was a Dianne I had not known before.

I sat thinking things over, guessing that the clinic's letter probably had a lot to do with her feelings. There was a tap on the front door. I waited for another knock and opened it.

Tosh stepped into the room and glanced around. He put a finger to his lips. He took two pairs of clinical gloves from his pocket.

"Put these on and clean any area you touched, however slightly. While you're doing that, I'll have a look through the drawers."

"I apologize for getting you into this, Tosh. I hope you're not in any trouble because of me."

Tosh was kneeling on the floor, looking into the cupboard under the sink. "I'm afraid you and I are both up to our necks in trouble, guv. Adam Denton was washed up under the Charles Bridge this morning and SIS is everywhere. They're after Myer. They think he's the killer and a Bilderberg member. That doesn't make sense to me, but we'll see. SIS will hang a tag on anyone if they want a scapegoat."

I found it hard to speak. "Bastards," I eventually hissed.

Chapter Ten

I FROZE. MAYBE IT WAS THE WAY Tosh's matter-of-fact announcement was delivered, or the confirmation of something nasty that had happened since discovering the apartment had been dusted.

Tosh finished his search through all the drawers. "Keep the gloves on, guv, and put them in your pocket when we leave. You can dump them along the way back to the hotel."

"What next?" I asked.

"You behave as usual. Don't worry about the neighbour. The police will book this as suicide. Nothing like a tidy case, is there? I doubt they'll even knock on her door. Of course, there is something urgent you have to do before news of Adam's death is broadcast by the BBC." He gave me a knowing look.

My heart thumped. Dianne! I had to tell her.

Whether I liked it or not, she would get involved. I had a column to write, but Adam Denton had taken centre stage, and regardless of his involvement in the unfolding story, his killer or killers had to be found. My guilty conscience wouldn't let his death go, and neither would she.

Tosh motioned me to the door. "Come on, guv, let's get out of here. I suggest you have that interview and make up with Dianne, Max, or both." He grinned, but I didn't find anything funny in his words. "I should know more about Adam by tonight." He turned to me. "Seriously, guv, talk to her. She wants to hear your voice."

We parted company outside. Tosh hopped onto a passing tram. I walked to a small park and sat on a bench. Calling Dianne in her present mood was not what I wanted to do.

"Hi, there," I said as soon as she answered. "I have some news for you, but I'm afraid it's not good."

There was silence after I told her.

"Thank you," she said quietly. "Go and get that interview. That's why you're there."

The line went dead without another word. I knew we would talk again after she dealt with the news in her way. I breathed a sigh of relief, not that I was without feeling, but Dianne was more on my mind than Adam, whom I never met.

I decided to walk to the other end of the square and call Novotney's secretary, Vilma Bosko. I needed to breathe fresh air. Whatever way the conversation went, I knew Richard Hart would know about it within a couple of hours.

Treading carefully wasn't something I liked doing very often. It wasted time and usually involved a second visit. I reached the other end of the square and sat on a bench admiring the surroundings, listing my questions mentally by priority in case she hung up on me at any point.

Within a few seconds of dialling her number, she answered.

"Yes, Mr West, Richard told me you might call. I'm home right now. This situation has been a nightmare for me. Can you visit me rather than talk on the phone? I have two photos to give you. Richard said he would have an excellent story written about Jozef and a picture in the paper."

I wondered what Richard would think if Jozef turned out to be a corrupt politician?

"Could you give me your address and I'll catch a cab, Vilma?"

The aroma of hot red wine laced with cinnamon filled the air around me as I walked toward the cab rank. I reached for my wallet and stopped at one of the small stalls dotted along the street. Mulled red wine or cider was an instant cure against cold weather. I sipped as the cab drove out of the square. Vilma lived in the Vinohrady area, a couple of kilometres outside the city centre. Devoid of tourists, it was a quiet suburb with parks, clean streets full of trees, and an occasional pedestrian. Most of the buildings were apartments, and Vilma's looked out over a well-kept park. By the time the driver reached her address, the wine had done its job. I had a glowing face.

I buzzed the entrance bell and the main door clicked open.

There was no lift, so I was out of breath by the time I reached the third floor. I grinned to myself. Dianne would be giving me a lecture if she could see me gasping for breath. Number thirty-seven was at the end of the corridor, the door ajar.

"Come in, Mr West, come in, and have tea after all those stairs."

I stepped in and pulled the door shut behind me. Vilma was a short, slim lady with blonde hair tied up in a ponytail. Her pale green suit and horn-rimmed glasses made her look older than I guessed she was. Hart and Vilma were close, and that surprised me, considering Hart's lifestyle compared to hers.

She was handsome, though, and very quietly spoken. I took an instant liking to her as she poured tea from a pot instead of water onto the dreaded tea-bag rubbish bought by most people who ruined their palates. I warmed to her.

I followed her into the living room and sat next to the window. After a few minutes of small talk, she said, "I understand why you're here, and Richard asked me to tell you what I could. I have to say, Pete, that I have no wish to cast bad light on the Commissioner. He was a good man doing a thankless job. He worked long hours, sometimes through seven days, and that's as long as I worked with him for over twelve years."

Truth proved time and again that politicians the world over had hard-working people behind them who were loyal and believed in their boss and what he or she wanted to achieve.

My experience also proved that politicians were the best actors of all and could fool the people who supported them.

I chose my words carefully. "Vilma, I know the Commissioner had a few enemies who wanted him out of his job. Can you think of anyone in particular who may have wanted to harm him?"

"No, I can't think of anyone. In any case, Jozef had police protection." Vilma hesitated before saying, "Why weren't they there when he needed them?"

"Who, the police?"

"Yes, he always had one police officer with him when he was here in Prague. The officer and a chauffeur looked after him and took him to and from work and any appointments he had."

"Did he seem agitated or worried more than usual during the last couple of weeks?"

"Not really. Jozef was very busy with the EU deal involving Ukraine. As you know, Ukraine wants to be a member, and Moscow sees that as a threat. Jozef was on one of the EU committee trying to get the Ukrainian president to sign the Association Agreement. Still, Moscow forced the President out of it by threatening the country's national security."

"Were the police providing round the clock security for him?" I asked.

"They were supposed to," she answered. "After being dropped home, an officer was on duty outside his house until he was picked up in the morning. I went to work in the morning as normal, but his usual escort was nowhere around, and neither was the officer on duty." Her face clouded. "He was lying on the floor of his office, the place ransacked.

"I asked the police for an explanation, but they said the Commissioner sent the duty officer off for the night and cancelled his morning pickup." She shook her head. "He had never done that before. I'm sure the police are being very secretive."

I made a note and then asked, "I understand his attaché case was open and empty. Did you know what was in it?"

"If I did, Mr West, I wouldn't tell you. It would most likely be

EU papers of the utmost confidential nature."

"Of course. Sorry, but Richard just wanted me to cover all aspects of this tragedy for the Herald, so I have to ask a couple of delicate questions." I changed tack. "There was a British EU trade secretary named Michael Myer who appears to have had regular meetings with the Commissioner. I know they met in Brussels but wondered if he ever came to Prague. He was a tall gentleman who wore glasses and had a moustache. Any recollections?"

"Yes. Why is he involved?" asked Vilma. "He came to the office a week ago and dropped off some papers, then the two of them went out together. They met every week."

"His name came up in the course of my inquiries, Vilma, that's all."

She gazed around the room as though confused, trying to remember something. I waited.

"That was the afternoon he went out without his aide or anyone to drive him. I assumed the gentleman was a friend, and they were going to Jozef's favourite bar, the one in the square—the Da Capo Café and cocktail bar. I think they played chess. Jozef spent hours playing chess online in the evenings."

I suppressed an urge to jump up and down but felt a tingle of excitement run down my spine. "Jozef's aide seems to have disappeared too. What sort of man was he, and how long had he been with the Commissioner?"

"Oh, it was a woman. Forst. She had been with him for two years. The police asked me about her, but I have no idea what happened to the young woman. She didn't turn up for work—let me see—yes, two days before…" Her voice trailed off, and I noticed moist eyes. "I do know that there is a personal diary belonging to the Commissioner that appears to be missing. I think she may have taken it." Vilma sighed. "I suppose she'll be offering it to the highest bidder from the news media. That's what happens these days, isn't it?"

I knew differently but said nothing. The lady was upset and I let her remark alone. We spoke for a further thirty minutes, by which time, I had more than enough information for Max's story. I was about to leave when I remembered Vilma saying she had some photos of the Commissioner. She went into another room after I reminded her and came back with a large brown envelope.

I thanked her and left but got the feeling that she had a lot more to tell. I knew no secretary who had been with a diplomat for more than ten years who didn't know a few family secrets. What concerned me was the police activity or non-activity. An EU commissioner was pretty way up there in the hierarchy. I hoped Tosh was having luck at his end. With all the information we were collecting, I hoped our conversation later would give us enough parts of the puzzle to start building a picture.

It was mid-afternoon and still sunny. I crossed the road into the park, found an empty bench by a small ornamental fishpond, and opened the envelope. The photos were regular headshots and good enough for the paper. They showed Commissioner Novotney at a much younger age. I reached for my tablet and sat writing my story, referring to my notebook. A copy went to Wapping with a promise I would scan and fax a photo by teatime. As I put the pictures back into the envelope, my eyes caught a faded pencil scribble on the back of one photo.

I pulled it free and turned it around so I could see more clearly. The faded words read, 'Bilderberg' 78'.

I called Tosh to arrange for lunch back at the hotel if he had time. The day had started badly, and I needed Tosh's company. With a little time on my hands, I found a small internet café with fax services in the square and had them scan and send Jozef Novotney's photo to the Herald. That's when I noticed someone taking my picture as I left. It was a middle-aged man sitting on a bench. Dressed in nondescript jeans and a leather jacket, he looked like any other tourist until he looked directly at me and took another picture. I felt a little uncomfortable, particularly given what had happened to Adam and the mysterious diary note.

I strode off toward the other end of the square and took the turn that would take me to the hotel. After reaching a small cigarette kiosk, I stopped and faced a rack of newspapers. The man who took my picture was sitting on another bench, quite close. I pulled my phone out of my jacket pocket and took a quick snap of him.

Curious by nature, I debated whether to confront him and ask what he was about or wait and let him follow. I decided to let him follow. Within ten minutes, I turned into the road that led to a park and the hotel I was staying at on the other side. At the entrance to the park, I looked back over my shoulder.

I was still being followed. Two more men appeared from behind some trees and walked purposefully toward me.

Worried, I started striding along the perimeter path instead of cutting across the grass. As soon as they changed direction to follow, I began to run. Dianne's warnings about me not getting enough exercise ran like a recording through my head.

A small kiosk at the next entrance was busy with several noisy kids buying sweets. Within a few meters of it and breathing heavily, an arm went around my neck and pulled me backwards.

Then everything went black.

I felt a strange sensation regaining consciousness. To look into the eyes of a beautiful woman like Dianne was one thing, but looking into the eyes of Tosh was quite another.

"What the hell?" My head was spinning, and Tosh was grinning within inches of his face. Behind him, I could make out a ring of young faces.

"You need a snifter, guv. Let's get you out of here before a noddy arrives."

He helped me to my feet and handed me the small travel bag I carried everywhere. It housed a tablet, digital recorder, a spare battery, a notebook, and any manner of other things I needed when on the move.

"They took the brown envelope before I arrived, guv. Mind, the bleeders didn't get anything else except a thick ear from me. They ran off quick enough."

I sat on the nearest bench to catch my breath. "The envelope wasn't a real loss—but why the attack?"

"Depends on what you've been up to," said Tosh, brushing dirt off his trousers.

"There were three of them. What did you do?"

Tosh's face cracked into a broad grin. "Bawl and shout. Then I gave one of them a bloody good clout on the end of his bugle."

I rubbed my head. "Well, thank you. It's a good job they did run. God knows what would have happened if you hadn't scared them off."

Tosh sat next to me. "You've got to know when to be brave and when to be cautious. I'm not stupid, guv. I'd have had it away on me feet."

He hadn't changed a bit. I saw the funny side but didn't feel like laughing. The thought that Dianne was grieving the loss of her friend bothered me. I felt terrible enough at having upset her over him.

"Let's get back to the hotel," I said and stood.

We walked slowly past the kiosk to the park exit. Tosh's pace slowed.

"Certain powers that be know you came for Adam Denton's wedding, as well as looking into the Novotney murder. Richard Hart lost some brownie points from Number Ten over this. They officially want you to go home, guv."

"Unofficially?" I asked.

"Unofficially, there is no 'unofficially', and if you meddle, the Foreign Office would be duty-bound to report you to SIS and have you arrested. That's after you passed all the unofficial info you had to them—and not SIS."

"So, nothing's changed." I raised my voice as a motorcycle roared past when we crossed the road. "Something big is going

The Defector's Diary

on regarding the Club, and I guess that Novotney's aide is the would-be defector that SIS will want badly."

Tosh stopped on the steps. "Everyone knows Novotney is dead, but only our Embassy and SIS know about Adam's connection to the Commissioner's aide. They also know about the diary, guv." He walked to the top of the steps. "We—my department, that is, think the aide must have contacted Adam. That was probably by accident; we're not sure. What we do know is, he died hours after Novotney. Whoever gets to the aide first will have the diary. Whitehall is very desperate to have it and SIS kept out of the loop. I get the feeling that some of our ministers, past and present, know something we don't." He paused at the entrance. "No one trusts SIS. If they get the prize, they'll almost certainly keep half the information to themselves."

I pushed through the swing doors. "Number Ten will do the same."

"Yes, guv, but at least the government will have the diary and its secrets, not the security services who are great at making deals without telling Whitehall. That's scary."

Chapter Eleven

DIANNE SAT PONDERING the present situation while her phone rang for a long minute. When the ringing stopped, she looked at the caller's name. It was not Pete. She dialled back and the receptionist at the clinic gave her the date and time for a series of new tests. Relieved, Dianne took the shopping list reminder magnetized to the refrigerator door.

Moments later, as she sat in her car, engine running, she wondered what might be going through Pete's mind. They had never had a serious argument in two years. Although she felt it was right that she scolded him for making comments about her relationship with Adam, it was the intrusive manner in which he had not only read her mail from the clinic but kept it to himself. She guessed it was because he wanted her to tell him the contents without letting her know he read it. That didn't make what he had done right. A hint of a smile crossed her face. Pete was a neat man at home and work. She remembered the side of the bureau lid had caught one edge of the clinic's letter as she closed it. Later, she found the note inside the bureau neatly placed on top of other paperwork.

Her involvement with Adam brought back a memory of another deception. Why he did not tell of his move to Prague before inviting her to Spain meant there was an element of secretiveness about him. Perhaps she thought it could be a fault of her own in expecting too much.

Dianne bit her lower lip as she pulled the seatbelt across.

She had to talk to Pete.

She turned the ignition off and called Pete's number. There

was no reply. Messaging was activated, but she ended the call. Thumping the steering wheel, she started the car again and drove out of The Mews and onto the main road. It took her half an hour to get to the shopping mall. As she parked, a large off-road four-wheel-drive reversed close to her driver's side while another reversed into a space on the other side, its fender scratching her paintwork from one end to the other.

Unable to get out, Dianne wound down her window and shouted.

The driver of the off-road put a finger to his lips. "Lady, or should I address you as Mrs West or Dianne Paakkonen? Your husband is causing unnecessary trouble for some important people who think it would be a good idea if you persuaded him to come home. Mr West is a well-read columnist, and it would be a shame if he couldn't do what he does best anymore."

Dianne reacted. Clenching her fist, she let fly and caught the driver in one eye as her arm stretched through the windows. As he put a hand to his face, she struck out a second time, hitting him on his nose.

"The next time we meet, I'll make sure your pretty face gets some alteration, you bitch."

Dianne rewound her window up halfway. "Do you think my husband and I will be scared of thugs like you? Tell me, was it you who killed my friend Adam? You can tell your boss his days are numbered."

The driver signalled to his accomplice in the second vehicle and sneered at Dianne. "You have no idea. If I were you, I would get a flight to Prague as soon as possible. You might just be in time to see your husband float face-down under a bridge."

As he backed away, Dianne's car rocked with further damage inflicted by the off-road. She did not see the other vehicle until it was too late. There was a loud crash, and she was thrown forward, then back, by the impact. With a squeal of tires, both vehicles left the car park. Annoyed, she looked into the driving mirror. A trickle of blood was running from her nose.

She remembered one of the license plates and called the police to report the incident, a hit and run, she said. There was no point in trying to explain what was happening.

Thankful the car was still drivable, she finished her shopping. On the way home, she received a call from the officer investigating the accident.

"Mrs West, I have the details of the owner of the car involved. I'm afraid the driver was an employee of the owner, and so legally, you will have to take action against the employee for the damage done to your car. His details are sketchy, but I will forward them to you at your address."

Dianne pulled onto the side of the road. "Can you tell me who is the owner of the car? I can at least write him and let him know what a nasty piece of work his employee is."

There was a short silence. "Lord Basil Gresham, ma'am. Unfortunately, we have been informed that his lordship is abroad."

The name rang a bell, but that was all. She thanked the officer and drove home, trying to think where she heard of Lord Gresham.

After putting her shopping away, she phoned her father in Cannes and recounted the incident and asked about Gresham.

"That is one of the elite's nastiest pieces of work. Lord Gresham heads a racist political party that promotes private ownership of power and water. A real throwback to the thirties who, during the last three years, created a small army of thugs. His organization reminds me of Sir Oswald Mosely. Don't let Pete get mixed up with the likes of him."

"Too late, Father. He is mixed up with them, but we don't know how much."

"Well, I think you should come here for a few weeks. Let Pete know where you are. Come today."

Dianne quietly accepted the invitation. The visit would be a

The Defector's Diary

welcome break, and she looked on it as a chance to take stock of her relationship with Pete. She loved him but felt he had betrayed her—or had he? Was it her being too dramatic, asking too much of him? She spent an hour packing a suitcase and arranging a flight to Cannes. With that done, she settled down to lunch, deep in thought.

Chapter Twelve

I KNEW TOSH WAS RIGHT about all the backstabbing that went on in Whitehall. I tried unravelling some of the conundrums. There were plenty of questions, but not many answers. Valerie was missing, and the mysterious trade secretary, Michael Myer, was involved somewhere in the mix.

My head was beginning to ache.

Dianne booked what she termed as the second-best type of room in the hotel. A depressing dark room on the second floor that looked out onto branches of a tree, giving the room hardly any light. The walls glared bright green even in subdued lighting, and the bathroom only had a shower surrounded by cracked, ugly green tiles. Twin beds covered in red top covers and a nightstand with a lamp finished the décor of the 'fully furnished' room. Tosh pulled two miniatures of scotch from the small fridge. We demolished them in seconds.

Tosh stepped slowly to the window and looked down at the street. I bent to take another two miniatures from the fridge and felt his hand on my shoulder.

"Outside, guv."

I didn't ask why. He followed me through the door and up the passage to the fire escape door.

"Change your room now, guv, and then leave the hotel in the morning. Find a nice place in the square. There's a bit of snot on your windowsill."

"Excuse me?"

"Snot. Someone has wired your window. Stuck with a little

dab of green gel to the window is a small microphone and transmitter. In the trade, we call it snot. It can send a signal to anyone in a car or van below in the street. The smart thing is, it not only picks up your conversation but can also take stuff from your computer too. I could easily bug another newspaper office for you." He grinned and swallowed the contents of his bottle. "You remember Brussels in 2003?"

I did. In 2003, bugs found in the offices of the French and German delegates caused an international incident. The Americans topped the list of the accused, but nothing came of the find. I got into trouble for upsetting Bush and his administration by writing a column that slapped the President down to size.

Tosh's information was added to the already massive pile of security and underworld data he passed to me in the last few years I had known him, and his vocabulary of slang terminology was enormous.

We went downstairs and decided to change the room.

As we settled in the bar, I decided against calling Dianne until bedtime. At least that would give her time on her own to grieve her loss.

"Thank you, Tosh. So, who would have known I was staying here?"

"Could have been any one of half a dozen," he answered.

As we browsed the menu, I brought him up to date on my interview with Vilma.

"The agent, or whoever it is who wants to cross over, has the key to everything. We need to be at the café tomorrow on time," said Tosh. "I'm afraid we, or you, are at the point of no return. You can't walk away from this now, guv."

"I know, I still have an article to write on the upcoming general elections for our Sunday magazine. I'll rest a bit and get that finished before we meet. Let's be at the café half an hour earlier. That gives me time to get comfortable." I cringed as I felt the lump on my head. "I wonder who those men were."

"English," said Tosh. "They spoke English. That means Whitehall or several Bilderberg members are all on the hunt for the Czech agent, and you're in their way. What you got was a warning to bugger off or else. It should be an exciting night tomorrow." He grinned and tapped my arm with a playful fist. "Come on, guv, this is like old times. You and me like flatman and wobblin' against the nasties."

I ignored his humour. He was used to stepping into the rough side of politics and joking about it. It was hard to understand and one area I wanted to avoid. Adam's death meant little to Tosh and a warning to me that he should be a friend at a distance. Agents had no real friends, and I guess Tosh led a lonely life.

The hotel had a small restaurant on the ground floor, an extension of the cocktail bar. Small table lamps threw soft lighting onto lace-covered tables and across pale green walls. It was comfortable, and the surroundings were pleasant enough. It was also empty of guests, ideal for a chat without interference.

The slightly spicy aroma of goulash and knedlíky dumplings made from potato flour had my taste buds working overtime. Within a short space of time, my headache easing, both of us sat enjoying our lunch while I recounted my call to Dianne.

"I also have to call Max," I added. "I don't know what he's going to do, but I'll try to convince him I should be here. Dianne won't leave Adam's murder alone and neither will I. He tried to warn us about impending danger and I didn't take him seriously."

Tosh just nodded while he ate.

"Did you call the police at all? Was there anything useful?" I asked.

Tosh pulled a sarcastic face. "It was a short call. The chief investigator told me more or less what we already knew, although he indicated he thinks it could have been a suicide. The police here appear to be very lax, and I got the impression they wanted Adam's death neatly filed out of the way. And by the way, he confirmed that none of his people had been to Adam's apartment yet."

"So, we can assume the thugs from Bilderberg were there," I said. "They couldn't find what they wanted and dusted everything to see if they could ID anyone who might have the diary. They must have members within law enforcement or SIS."

Tosh stopped eating as though he read my thoughts. "What?"

I had a sudden thought that I had not shown Tosh the photo I took from Adam's flat. He knew that Adam could have been involved with SIS, as the other photo revealed him with Cranthorp, but Valerie was someone he might not know. It worried me that she might have suffered the same fate as Adam.

"Here, look at this."

I removed the photo and looked at two happy people, still assuming the girl was Valerie. Adam had an arm around her shoulders as they stood outside a restaurant. "Tall, isn't he?" I remarked. "Do you see what restaurant that is?"

It was Da Capo Café. I caught a quick movement of Tosh's head and a jerk of the shoulders, but he said nothing and continued to look at the photo. I ignored him for a moment.

"Well, we at least know that Adam and Valerie visited the café, as well as the Commissioner and Myer. The agent must know it too."

Tosh pulled the photo toward him. "I don't know if this is your Valerie or not, but what I do know, she's a BIS agent, that's the Czech secret service. Her name is Forst."

I stared at the photo. "Novotney's young office aide. You already knew her? Why didn't you tell me? Vilma Bosko spoke of her as Forst and suspected she took the diary."

A few scraps of information began gelling together.

Forst was Valerie, and I was sure now that she was the defector. Adam may have been serious about getting married, but my gut feeling was that he rather amateurishly used Dianne and me. He knew the girl's surname, which was certain. After the Profumo and Christine Keeler affair Kim Philby, Burgess, McClaine and Blunt's political scandals in the '50s to late '60s, lessons should have been learned. Attractive women foreign agents netting diplomats for information would go on despite stricter security.

Whatever was in the diary, Adam wanted it revealed and wanted to help Valerie defect. Trusting SIS or not, the man should have reported to them and walked away. Now Dianne and I were involved too. If Tosh knew about Forst, his Whitehall office, and not the Cross, had to be, I guessed, in Downing Street or the Palace of Westminster. .

Despite his outward appearance with a lack of social graces, his qualifications must have been impeccable.

"Why didn't Forst come to you for help?" I asked.

Tosh leaned back and took a deep breath. "Okay, I'm sorry, guv, but you can understand my position. I had no idea Forst knew Adam until I saw this photo. I've never met the woman. She reported to SIS, not my office, so that would explain why Adam warned you against contacting SIS or the Embassy."

I waved a fork full of meat above my plate. "What about the diary and the Bilderberg conference?"

"As far as Adam and the conference are concerned, I had no idea about all that until you showed up," answered Tosh. "The Embassy did tell me about Adam's death, but I genuinely came here to check on Myer before Commissioner Novotney's death." He fingered the photo. "Mind, I wouldn't put it past the department to know more but keep me in the dark."

"How come the Embassy told you about Adam?" I asked. "Wouldn't SIS be keeping everyone quiet about that?"

"SIS knew my department was investigating Myer and knew about his meetings with Novotney. Once they connected two dead bodies to Myer, whether through association or direct contact, they asked my people to contact the Embassy and get in touch with me, their man on the ground." He tapped the table. "Someone who stays hidden from SIS view. Much better to let somebody else already involved poke around for them. Typical Cross watching brief policy. Remember, Myer was in contact with Novotney, who was in contact with Forst, Adam's lover. I would think SIS went looking for Adam at the apartment, and when they found it empty, went in looking for evidence of his whereabouts." Tosh almost spoke in a whisper while looking apologetically at me. "Perhaps they knew something before they got there. Funny how they rubbed the place clean and left a little evidence that pros had dusted the place."

I was silent for a moment. What Tosh suggested was too incredible. "They wouldn't dare."

"It depends," answered Tosh. "We have no idea what's in the diary or who in the government is with the Bilderberg Club. We have to get to Forst and find out. The Club could even have someone inside SIS." He shook his head slowly. "Guv, can you imagine what information is in that diary? What if it reveals some power conspiracy to create a new world council organization controlling stock and money markets, for example? What if it got into the wrong hands? Just as dangerous, what of the conspirators who want the diary back? They won't stop at anything."

We sat looking at each other, deep in thought. If a member of the security services was a member of Bilderberg's New Order and killed Adam, the conspirators wouldn't hesitate to eliminate others who were threatening their plans. The two deaths were nothing compared to a nightmare scenario across Europe. Some world or European domination plot set carefully in place over several decades involving the world's most powerful and influential industrialists and politicians. A lot could have happened since the Bilderberg Club was first formed in 54."

"When you transfer to another hotel, send your suitcase by cab and have it away on your feet. You can cut through the square and lose yourself from anyone following that way. Just be careful and keep an eye out for Barney."

I laughed but looked lost. Trying to master Tosh cockney language was worse than learning Greek.

"Trouble. Blimey, guv, trouble." Tosh looked at me with a rather hurt stare.

"Of course," I said. "How could I forget? Barney Rubble, Toil and Trouble."

Chapter Thirteen

DRISCOL SAT LISTENING to Le Clerc. "...and then she poked my eye out, the bitch. I'll get her back for that."

Driscol laughed. "Okay, well done. What's the verdict on Mrs West? Will she have a word with her husband, you think?"

"I don't know. She's pretty tough. That type always has to get a good slap before they do as they're told."

"Well, I hope things won't go that far," said Driscol. "I'll call you later if need be. In the meantime, have you set things up for next Friday? Sir Carlton will want a security plan, and I need to know how many men you have for that evening."

"The list will be ready by tonight. Is the big man himself coming? I can't believe it's finally happening." Le Clerc's voice became excited. "By the way, when do we get armed?"

"In plenty of time for the big day. I hope your men have been training every weekend." Driscol tapped the desk blotter as he spoke. "When we move, we have to be quick, and all buildings on the list must be secured. Sir Carlton will run through things with you when the time comes. The demonstrations are planned for each city on the day, and no-one is to carry arms – not until phase three."

The call ended, and Driscol closed his eyes for a moment, deep in thought. There were few in the New Order who knew how action day would really start. The President had made it quite clear that only those who were directly involved should know about the drops. All the delegates knew they would be moving into new positions they had been assigned in governments as and when the time came for phase three of the greater plan. Driscol took a deep breath and looked down at the folded file with West's name printed across the top. He reached for the file and opened it. Dianne West's picture was pinned to the top sheet of notes next to Pete West's.

* * *

Cranthorp took the earpiece out and switched the small listening receiver unit off. Annoyed at not arriving a few minutes earlier, he just managed to hear two words that signalled a warning. He replayed the digital recorder.

Listening intently, he heard the words 'outside, guv'. He had been too late. The Cross knew where West was staying, and Driscol had sent a 'maintenance man' the day before. West was not on his own. He listened again but could not name the speaker. Whoever was with West knew his stuff, and it could only mean the security service, or a clever technician was involved. Driscol would have to know. This new situation would have to be dealt with as soon as possible. The meeting on Friday was one he could not miss. West was on the loose, and if he got wind of anything, he could jeopardize the whole plan.

Cranthorp pulled a cell phone from his pocket and scrolled to Driscol's number. He waited a minute before ending the call, and call and texted instead. When finished, he backed his car further up the street and under the shade of some trees. The front entrance to the hotel was visible. He sat waiting, his thoughts on the last meeting with West. It had been three or four years since they last crossed swords but ended up lukewarm friends. As he lit a cigarette, he realized there was something about the voice he recognized. He played the recording again, but no one that he could think of came to mind. West had to be followed and dealt with quickly. Driscol could not afford to hang around and wait for Carlton to agree.

Cranthorp watched a group of guests leave the hotel as it

started to rain. A couple of taxis arrived and left. Then he spotted West leaving. As he pulled out from the curb to follow, his front tire ran over a plastic drink cup in the gutter. There was a loud pop, and he watched West turn quickly to look behind him. Cranthorp smiled. It was obvious that West had been schooled by whoever had found the transmitter in his room. He hit the steering wheel with a clenched fist as West walked from the street and cut across the car park to the main square. There was no time to park, and Cranthorp watched with frustration as West disappeared into a crowd of tourists and shoppers.

As he stopped at the traffic light, his phone rang. It was Driscol.

"What's up? Where is West?"

"Nice one, covering your rear before starting the conversation. I always said you were a fair -weather friendly bastard."

"Cut it out, Charles. What's going on?"

Cranthorp reported what happened. "I lost him as he walked across the square. I'll have the hotel covered tonight. I don't expect he'll be back before then."

"Any idea where he might be headed? The boys could comb the area."

"Not after their meeting in the park. West would recognize them right away. There are two or three possibilities, and I'll check them out. The first place is Denton's flat. The old girl will know if he's been there."

Driscol sighed. "Okay, keep me informed and let me know the moment you find West. Sir Carlton is hopping mad that the one correspondent he hates is running loose in our meeting area." There was a pause. "Remember, the meeting is at nine p.m. Don't be late. I hear that our commander-in-chief will be bringing half the committee with him, so it should be an interesting insight into what is going to happen during the first year of occupation."

"Don't you mean the first year of rule, James? You make it

sound like we'll be winning a great victory and enjoying the spoils of war."

Driscol chuckled. "Well, it will be a great victory, and the likes of you and I will be enjoying the spoils, I think."

Cranthorp ended the call and pulled away from the intersection.

West was going to be a problem, and the longer he stayed in Prague, the more danger there was of the group being uncovered. The man had an uncanny knack for being in the right place at the wrong time. His wife was a dream but equally as tough and annoying as her husband. Driscol had made a mistake having the French guy try to shake her up. He only succeeded in making her want to fight back. The answer was to win both of them over. Give West a position within the media and public services division where he had a voice to win over the people. He was already a popular voice, and the public would listen to him.

Cranthorp looked at the clock on the dashboard. The Cross would be expecting him to call in. He looked for a suitable place to stop and turned off the main road onto the main railway station car park. The bays were mostly empty, and he called in, reporting that West was in the city but could not be found.

He smiled as he finished his report. Both organizations were looking for West, and both wanted West out of Prague, although the Cross wanted anything West had picked up that could help find Forst. He breathed in deeply. The other problem was Myer who turned traitor. He had to be found and dealt with, although not in the same way Denton had been dispatched.

Chapter Fourteen

TOSH LEFT ME AFTER LUNCH, and we agreed to meet again around six. I was a little surprised that he chose to share so much knowledge about his mission, and I appreciated that he could face prison for passing information to me, a newspaper columnist. I'd probably share the same cell.

Nonetheless, we both realized the broader and more critical implications of the situation, that Valerie Forst had to be found, and the diary handed over to Whitehall. We needed to tie up one last loose end.

Charles Cranthorp was a devious man best suited to the cut and thrust of political turmoil going on at any time inside SIS. He could not be trusted. A nice enough man, but the discovery of the photo linking him to Adam Denton needed an explanation. Then also, Michael Myer, the man Tosh came to investigate, who visited the Capo Café at least once with Jozef Novotney. Every person involved in the investigation ended up being linked in some way to the Bilderberg Club.

There were too many coincidences.

I strolled, taking a casual look through glass fronts and over my shoulder. I was wary since the park attack and worried that the meeting in the café might be unsafe. It was a futile concern. There was no way a stalker would be so close to me again. If anyone was taking an interest, it had to be further away on the other side of the square.

It was late afternoon and I decided to call Max, who needed convincing that something dreadful on an international scale was about to happen, and the starting line was London. Max drummed into all journalists that a story should make sense, and facts stand alone on merit without support from a supposition or the journalist's creative mind.

I smiled. That was why Max sometimes gave me a rocket. Calling politicians nothing short of stupid was one example, even if I was right. I sat on a bench in the central reservation and called him.

It was mid-afternoon in London, and as always, Max would be getting ready for a daily news briefing. The phone rang for several seconds, followed by a loud click. A gruff voice answered. "You're bloody early. What d'ya want, Pete?"

"Max, whatever else, don't shout. Let me talk, and then you can cry later."

"Why, what the hell have you done?"

"Nothing yet, but something will be happening at 7.00 p.m. tomorrow. In case it all goes wrong, you need to be up to speed now."

"I'm taping this conversation just so's you know."

I was amazed. Either Max knew something I didn't, or he wanted to cover his rear. There was no pre-conversation warning or light-hearted insults. That was suspicious, and I didn't have to wait long to find out why.

"Richard called and asked me what the hell was going on. He's had the bloody security service telling him you're mixed up in Bilderberg stupidity and that he should order you back home at once."

"But Max—"

"Shut up!"

I did. It was always best to let Max empty the rhetoric until he ran out of breath.

"Not only that, but the Foreign Office sent two chinless wonders to my office demanding I don't print any column by you until Number Ten's press agent sees it first. You're treading a fine line from now on. Unless you have a positive story about political conspiracy, or conclusive proof of murder times two, then you're coming home." He drew a breath. "Do you bloody hear me?"

"Yes, Max. So did all the people in Wenceslas Square. Now listen, because we have the makings of an incredible story, but at the moment, no substantive proof."

I spent the next ten minutes giving him everything I had but left Tosh out of it. If Whitehall was already onto the Herald, then Tosh might be in trouble with his office. Then again, maybe not, but I thought it was prudent to appear solo.

"So, you're meeting a person we're not too sure is a woman or a man who may or may not be an agent who wants to defect and who may or may not have a diary letting us into the secret as to when we can expect the end of the world. Then there is the possibility that SIS might have killed Dianne's friend, and Bilderberg thugs killed Novotney and are now stalking you. Have you any idea how bloody stupid you sound, Pete?"

It did seem far-fetched to me, but so did the Watergate scandal before the truth came out. I needed to have the meeting. I waited while Max chewed my report over.

"Okay, let's see what happens tomorrow night. There's no point in cancelling, seeing as you're there. If anything goes wrong, I need to know right away. Why not have Tosh sit somewhere else in the café and he can call the cavalry if necessary."

"Tosh? What's he to do with this?"

"I'm the editor with a finger on your pulse. If he isn't with you, he'll be close by."

Neither of us said any more about Tosh. Max knew Tosh and I went back away, and Max knew there was more than a possibility the little guy was with me or in the city for SIS. My association with Tosh was frowned on because of his connections with SIS, but Max was always ready to take risks for a story that deserved to be in print.

"Maybe SIS has a finger on my pulse, too."

Max coughed. "Not SIS. They're too busy trying to pull a finger out of their ass."

I agreed without letting him know I had everything in hand. Tosh would be there, keeping an eye out for anyone else of interest.

"What are you going to do if the person you meet is the defector?" growled Max. "Where are you going to take him or her if she or he hands over the diary, and how are you going to get the diary to Whitehall? I assume you're not going to give it to SIS so they can cook up one of their great deals that end in disaster."

With all that was going on, I hadn't given much thought to that problem. The obvious place was the Embassy, but Adam had warned against that. The American embassy was no good either. With over one hundred and fifty powerful men attending each year, the Bilderberg Club had fingers in many influential US industrial and political pies. Finding a pair of hands to trust was going to be a problem, not just to give the diary to, but also what to do with the defector.

"I have no idea," I replied. "The best idea will be to wait and see if anyone turns up. We're assuming it will be Forst, but maybe Michael Myer, the missing EU trade secretary. What part he's playing in all this is a mystery. There are so many questions, Max, but I'm sure something big is brewing."

There was another deep breath at the other end of the line.

The last thing I needed to do at that moment was to push Max. I let him think. A chill breeze had sprung up, and I shivered. I had left the hotel without a coat, forgetting how cold the evenings in this part of Europe could be.

"Okay, Pete, whatever happens, you must get back to me. If no one turns up, I want you to go to the Embassy and talk to someone. I don't want Richard Hart jumping all over me. I'll speak to him in the meantime and tell him there is a link between the murder of the Commissioner and the Bilderberg conference, and you're just interested in that case and nothing else. That should keep him quiet for a few days. As an afterthought," he added, "there shouldn't be any reason to go to the castle, so stay away from it unless it's necessary. I'll tell Richard you're not considering upsetting his glorious bloody weekend."

"It's a little less than four weeks away, Max. It coincides with our general election for parliament. I hope we'll have this other business sorted by then so I can be back in London for that. I'll ring you later tonight."

"Pete, I called Dianne and told her to stay home today. She was distraught, of course, but I could tell she was very close to Adam. Take my advice and call her when you can. I was going round tomorrow to see if she was okay, but she was going to stay with her father in Cannes for a few days. Oh, before I forget, I've sent a fax to your hotel with a list of attendees that we know of at the Bilderberg do. Remember what I said about them."

My heart sank. Dianne going to Cannes meant she was not only upset at the loss of Adam, but still angry with me.

I sat, thinking. Max was going out on a limb for me once again, and I didn't want to let the man down, but the thought of talking to an Embassy official wasn't on. That would mean the end of any involvement I had in the affair. I mentally crossed my fingers and hoped. With time to get my last article off in the morning, I looked forward to an afternoon nap before the meeting at seven p.m.

* * *

A few spots of rain pattered off the pages of a discarded newspaper lying next to me on the bench. Almost as one, the knowledgeable locals opened umbrellas across the square. I walked briskly to a small kiosk and stood under a canopy.

The rain fell more heavily, creating an increasingly noisy protest from fluttering leaves as it lashed the trees. My cell phone rang—it was Tosh.

"Hi, there, I'm on the move. I just had an idea. I'll turn into the square from the National Museum steps, and you wait for me at the Wenceslas statue. When I get to the statue, I'll carry on down the central pedestrian area until I get to the café. Shout if you see anything. Otherwise, you follow me in and take your seat. I'll give you ten to get into position before I start from here." There was a short pause. "It might be in our interest if you get a cab and let our target wait outside the café. If we're meeting Forst, we'll need transport."

I quickly told him about my conversation with Max. With that done, I spotted what I needed in the kiosk. A couple of minutes later, I was striding along the pavement under a gaily colored ladies' umbrella. Reaching the statue, I hung with a crowd of young Japanese students, keeping an eye on the museum steps Tosh told me to watch. At six-thirty, he appeared, and I changed position. As he walked past, the pavement was clear behind him. My phone beeped. I stopped and pulled it from my pocket. It was a text from Dianne, giving me a number to call as soon as possible. Meeting or not, I called the number as I walked.

"Pete, I need to tell you something important, but I don't want you doing anything stupid."

I stopped as she recounted her meeting with the thugs who ran into her that morning and the message they gave her to get me to go home. Assuring me that she was well, she ended by saying that she was with her father and would be there if I needed her.

Angry and concerned, I said nothing.

"Apart from this meeting, what else is going on?"

I told her what we planned, and that Max was aware. It was good to hear her being so calm, but I was anxious not to upset her again. "I'll ring you directly after the meeting. Tosh is going in now and I have to follow. I just wanted to know how things are with you." I hesitated. "I'm so sorry—"

The line went dead, leaving me still wondering how I should

deal with the business of the letter and my comments about Adam, all of which were left in the air. Telling her I had found the clinic's results would be a mistake, even though we had always been honest with each other. I also realized that she had not asked how I was.

It wasn't hard to find a cab. As in all cities, particularly at night, cabs roamed the streets looking for pickups outside bars and nightclubs. I hailed one and, arriving at the café, asked the driver to wait. A quick look at my wristwatch told me I had two minutes to get to table twenty-two.

Inside, the place was full of students, visitors, and three police officers sitting at the window bar looking out through fogged windows. Two girls dressed in holed jeans and T-shirts with rude messages printed across the bust stood at the counter, both shouting down cell phones as piped jazz filled the seated area. One of them had pins in on her lip. I walked past them and made for the stairs at the far end, pushing through several people standing in the aisle chatting.

It wasn't hard to spot Tosh. He was sitting half-way down with his back to the wall, his head bent forward, napping. A free newspaper and a steaming cup of coffee lay on the table in front of him. I shouldered my way to table twenty-two and took a seat. Almost right away, the waitress arrived. I picked up the café menu.

"Sir, Sir were you expecting your girlfriend to join you?" she asked as she held a pen ready to take my order.

Something told me to say yes. A message was one thing I hadn't expected, but it was evident since the waitress was asking at a particular table. I nodded.

She handed me a folded note and left. I glanced at Tosh before reading the message.

Tomorrow morning at 10.00. Charles Bridge. Meet me opposite the fourth statue on the right, crossing toward the castle.

I pocketed the note and rose to leave, ignoring Tosh. By the time I was at the bottom of the stairs, he was close behind. Outside, we climbed into the cab and told the driver to drive around for fifteen minutes. As soon as we moved off, I read Tosh the note.

"This was meant for Adam's stand-in. Forst must know he's dead and was hoping a new contact would appear," Tosh said. "Whoever wrote this knows you received the torn page and business card for the Café from Adam. I'd say this is definitely from Forst."

I took another look at the note. "Okay, same arrangement tomorrow. If I go for the meeting and stand a little way off to one side, and you do the same across the way, we can keep an eye out." It suddenly occurred to me I was trying to order an agent around. "Sorry, Tosh. I'm caught up in this."

"That's all right. I think you're doing fine." He grinned. "I'll arrange an interview for you when we get back home. In the meantime, make sure you touch the statue of St John of Nepomuk, and you'll return to Prague. That's the statue she's talking about."

"Let's hope we don't suffer the Saint's end and get thrown into the river," I said. "Poor Adam did. Do you think you could get a picture of her or him, whoever turns up? I thought we could also take some pictures up and down the bridge. You never know who's in the crowd."

I dropped Tosh off outside a gay nightclub, The Red Stocking. His taste in out of town accommodation was always the same: a room over a nightclub that sported topless women or gay clubs. He was not short of friends in strange places.

I arranged to pick him up at nine in the morning and then walk onto the bridge separately. What happened after that, we agreed, would involve on-the-spot decisions.

The cabby pulled up outside Novotel, my new hotel. I changed hotels after Tosh's discovery and booked into one on the square. By now the rain had stopped, leaving puddles everywhere, and fallen leaves stuck to the pavements. My mind was on Dianne and the call I was about to make.

I reached my room after checking for messages at reception. With my mind made up that I would call Dianne before dinner, I sat on the edge of the bed and rang her number. It took several rings before she answered.

"So, what happened?" she asked.

Her voice was strangely detached, cold and aloof, which surprised me. I had never heard her speak like that before, but then, I had never upset her so much.

I took a deep breath. "Before we talk, can you please not hang up on me?" I said. "I know you are upset and mad at me, but we must talk. If you need to know, I am upset myself that I'm seriously thinking of calling Max and coming home."

"I can't see you doing that, Pete." Her voice was a little sarcastic.

"I have already been told that I should return."

She ignored my remark. "What's going on about Adam's death? Have you found out anything from the Embassy or the police?"

"The police only want to look at suicide. The Embassy is being tight-lipped. I'm trying to find out what the arrangements are for Adam's return home, but he'll be subject to a post-mortem before being moved."

"He was murdered." Her voice had softened.

"I know," I replied. "I didn't take Adam's note seriously, and I'll not forgive myself for that."

There was a long pause before she spoke. "What happened at the café? Did your date appear?"

"No, but I did receive a note arranging a meeting for tomorrow morning on the Charles Bridge," I replied. "I guess I'm being checked out."

I quickly recounted the day's activities before tackling the prickly task of apologizing. Dianne stopped me short.

"Exactly what are you apologizing for, Pete? For asking questions about my relationship with Adam, or is there something else that you have not mentioned yet?"

My chest heaved with a thumping heart and my face flushed. She knew. "When I returned for my cases, I—"

"Stop! I don't want to hear some feeble excuse that you just happened to stumble on my letter. I waited since Monday morning to hear from you about it, but nothing, just nothing."

"Dianne, if you would just let—"

"No, Pete, I trusted you. I trusted and believed in you."

She began to sob, and all I could do was listen to the woman I loved. I betrayed her trust. My mind was full of failure—first Dianne and then her friend Adam.

"I'm coming home," I said at length. "You're right, of course. What happened between Adam and you has nothing to do with me. I'm sure if things had worked out, the two of you would be together today. He was clearly the love of your life, and I tore a hole in your memory of him. I do sincerely apologize, Dianne. I hope I can put things right. I love you. You know that."

"Do you? You have a strange way of showing that. I did not tell you about the results. I was hoping to go for another test and either have the clinic confirm what they suspected or give me good news. I was then going to tell you everything so we could plan ahead. You're not coming home," she declared. "I don't want you here. I want you to find out who killed Adam. As far as the Czech agent is concerned, I don't want to hear any more about her."

I started to say I would call every day, when she interrupted me and said, "If Adam had asked me to marry him, I would have said yes. He was a real gentleman, Pete."

My heart sank, and I tried to speak but remained silent. Dianne hung up, leaving me with tearful eyes. I tried calling her back but got the answering service. I tried to sound positive, but my words stumbled lamely from my mouth.

"Dianne, I am so sorry. Please let's work this out. I'm shattered and can only tell you how much you mean to me. I want us to be together, and I don't mind being second best. Forgive me. I love you."

I sat on the edge of the bed for quite a while afterward, emotionally drained, wondering what I could do to resolve the situation.

The morning was clear and bright. The bridge would be full of artists sketching, and musicians playing. A couple of little stalls would be open, and there was a jazz band that entertained passersby. It would be busy. It was a tourist attraction.

After a hurried continental breakfast, I took a cab to The Red Stocking. I found Tosh in the middle of the pavement saying goodbye to a tall dancer in fishnet stockings, a very skimpy black dress with a slit up one side, and pink hair that had to be a wig. It wasn't until I got closer that I realized the dancer was a man.

"Morning, Pete. Say hello to Petra. She's a dancer here. This place is open day and night—ideal for diving into when you want to hide." He laughed at the expression on my face.

'Dive,' I thought, was a suitable word to describe the gay Club. I shook limp hands with Petra, who grinned at me through heavy make-up and large, glossy red lips. He must have been fifty-something and reminded me of a pantomime dame.

"Well, hellooo, Pete," he cooed. "My little friend here told me such a lot about you. If you get the chance, you must visit and catch my show." With that, he kissed the top of Tosh's head and sashayed back into the Club.

"Handy man to know." Tosh smiled. "He's been here for ten years now, and now and can get you anything you want off the black market—even guns."

"Useful for you perhaps, but not to me, Tosh. Now, can we get to the bridge?"

We climbed into the cab and, a few minutes later, arrived

along the approach road.

"Okay," said Tosh, shrugging off the chill air. "Now wander around and keep me in sight. I'll walk to the other end of the bridge taking pictures as I go."

"Hopefully, you'll get a good shot of the person I'm here to meet," I said.

We parted company, and I stood against the balustrade.

I was five minutes early and decided to arrive at the statue a minute late. That way, Tosh could get a good look at the contact. The bridge was already busy. I walked through the archway of one of the ancient towers that spanned the bridge entrance on both ends. Several artists were sitting on their collapsible chairs, and one musician was playing the accordion. I tossed a few coins into his hat as I passed by.

Tosh was on the other side of the bridge opposite the fourth statue, looking down at the boats below. At least a dozen tourists were all having photos taken as they touched St John's figure. I couldn't see anyone who looked as though they were waiting for me.

At half past the hour, thoroughly fed up with the cold, I'd had enough. It was a no-show. Disappointed, I walked to the bridge's castle end and bought a cup of hot cider wine. Of Tosh, there was no sign. He told me he would visit the Embassy to find out what the funeral arrangements were for Adam. Whatever he said, he would find me later.

Very disappointing, I thought. Without making contact, I could not think what else to do. Dianne was another matter. My pending conversation with her would, I hoped, be more conciliatory than the last.

I stopped to take a photograph along the length of the bridge behind me. My phone rang.

Tosh's voice was calm. "Forst contacted you and may well be checking you out to see if you can be trusted and will genuinely help her. Let's be a little more positive and wait. She'll contact

The Defector's Diary

you again."

As I was on the castle end of the bridge, I began to walk up the hill, ignoring Max. If Dianne was with me, we would most certainly make for the castle. Fifteen minutes later, I was in the first of four courtyards and spent time admiring the Archbishop's Palace. It was strange but exciting to think that court shoes, horses' hooves, and German jack-boots had stood, walked, and marched on the grounds around me.

My feet ached, and it was a welcome relief to sit at the back of St Vitus's Cathedral in the pews next to the nave.

"You need to go jogging more often," I could hear Dianne's soft voice in my ear.

At that moment, Tosh appeared and slid into the pew next to me.

"Look at that fantastic work up there," I said. "Can you imagine what it was like to put all that carved wood into place?"

Tosh jerked his thumb toward the entrance. "I don't know anything about the woodwork, but we have a problem. I spotted him on the bridge, and then again as you entered the castle. He's been following until you came in here. I followed him back out and he'll be waiting outside, or one of his colleagues will be waiting to follow you."

"Who are you talking about? The picture taker or the thugs who attacked me?"

"Neither…Cranthorp."

"Bloody SIS." I sighed heavily. I had to lose Cranthorp before I met Forst. Whether Cranthorp knew we were on to Forst or investigating Adam's death didn't matter. "Did he see you, Tosh?"

He shook his head. "No, he only had eyes for you. We need to sort something out."

I agreed. The whole situation surrounding the two deaths and a mysterious defector with information about a secret club had attracted an awful amount of attention from all sides. None of it is friendly.

"The problem is Forst," I said. "I have a feeling that no one knows about the Novotney diary she has except maybe certain members of the Bilderberg Club—hence the thugs and, unfortunately, SIS. My guess is it was the Club who killed Adam. The Czech security service must be hopping mad that one of their own wants to defect and must be linking her to the Novotney death. SIS is looking for a missing EU trade secretary who was meeting Novotney. Then, of course, they're also involved in Adam's death." I looked at my watch. "It's 3.30, so how about going back to my hotel for tea and then sort out a timeline to make sense of everything?"

Something suddenly occurred to me. I had forgotten that Max had sent a fax to my first hotel. While Tosh walked back to the Novotel, I took a cab to collect the Bilderberg attendees' list.

Deep in thought, I took no notice of the car pulling up behind my cab as I arrived. I told the driver to wait, entered the lobby, and walked to the reception desk. The clerk recognised me and reached into the letter rack behind the counter. I was handed two envelopes, one large and the other small.

"The smaller envelope was handed in just a few minutes before you arrived, Sir."

"Can you describe the person who handed it in?" I asked.

"It was a tall man. Middle-aged, I'd say, and very distinguished-looking looking."

Curious, I took a seat across the lobby and opened the smaller envelope. My heart leapt. It was another note from Forst, or so I assumed.

Central railway station—listen to the piano player—be alone—now.

That was it, I was sure. If anything went wrong, Forst could use the railway to escape. I stuffed the envelopes inside my coat pocket and walked to the entrance. That's when I noticed the car. It had pulled up within inches of the rear of the cab, its engine still ticking over. I wasn't about to take any chances. I climbed into the cab and passed one hundred euros to an amazed driver.

"The car behind is going to follow us. I need to get to the station. Do you think you can drop me off near it without the car seeing me so that he follows you instead of me? I've done nothing wrong, and I think they may be your secret police. I'm a journalist. I write about politics and normally get into trouble," I mumbled to myself rather than the driver.

The cabby spat out the window and looked at me through his driving mirror. "Secret police are no better than the Russian bastards. Hold on."

With that, we lurched forward, mounted the pavement, crashed down the curb, and back onto the road. We took off in the opposite direction with squealing tyres, leaving the follower to reverse out of the hotel slip road.

At the end of the road, I saw them just as we took a right. Light was fading and all I could see were headlights behind us.

The tires squealed again, and the cab juddered. I was about to tell the driver not to get stopped by the police when we lurched into another turn on what felt like two wheels.

"Very superb, very splendid, yes? We take the highway for a minute and then come back on another side—you then jump, yes? Excellent."

Confused, I had no idea what he would do but wondered if my cabby knew a similar driver called Tosh. They both drove the same way. I clung tightly to a broken hand strap while trying to remain on the seat. We came to a junction and slip road that took us out onto the motorway. The engine was screaming, and my driver was saying something I didn't hear or understand. He had one hand on the wheel and the other waving around as he spoke. I clung on for dear life.

Within seconds, we were racing down the next exit ramp toward the traffic lights.

The cab approached them at red and raced across the intersection, missing two cars and a tram, all of whom blared horns and shook fists. My driver waved back at them while turning the wheel. There was a loud bang as we braked and pulled onto the curb. I slipped forward and fell onto the floor.

"You get lost here," the driver shouted over his shoulder. "You near railway here."

Frightened that my driver might take off again, I opened the door and stumbled out into the cold night air. As I stood up, the cab was off in a cloud of dust and smoke. I ran across the pavement into what looked like a small park. Seconds later, I crouched behind a tree. The car following the cable shot past. My only problem now was finding the railway station.

I could see the clock towers of the original Art Nouveau rail buildings against the skyline through the trees. Unmistakably, they reminded me of London's public buildings before going through a massive power wash program back in the seventies. Black grime covered the towers, a remnant of an era of smoke and smog back home.

After entering the main building, I walked across the concourse, dialled Tosh, and read him the note.

"So, I should meet you there or at least follow you."

"I guess," I replied. "I'm here now, and there are only three other people near the entrance to the booking offices. I'll go and find the piano player. I'll be in touch as soon as possible." With that, I hung up.

I started to walk across the ornate building's oval concourse toward the main terminus on the other side of the two mainline tracks. A pedestrian tunnel at the bottom of an escalator brought me to the other side within earshot of a piano playing a classical music piece. I walked along the extensive precinct of underground shops. A group of a dozens of or so onlookers were listening to a young girl playing a small concert piano that had been donated for the public's enjoyment.

The Defector's Diary

"I already have our tickets."

The distinctive male voice came in a half-whisper from behind and startled me as I stood there.

"Don't turn around, MrMr West—just walk toward the entrance to the booking hall and platforms."

It had to be the one man everyone wanted to meet. He was taking a hell of a risk. That made me think. He wouldn't risk being out in the open if he was a murderer.

"Mr Myer, I presume."

"Platform seven, please. Just follow the signs. I will be close. Here's your ticket if we get separated."

A ticket slid into my hand from behind, but he ignored my assumption of his name. As we separated, I looked sideways. Despite the turned-up collar and a flat cap pulled low, I could tell it was Myer, proving my suspicion of his involvement with Bilderberg was correct. The man had attended one conference years beforehand, which made me wonder why he would appear to be breaking the Club's secrecy rules. I followed him at a distance, rode an escalator and took in the vast area's layout. There were crowds of people throughout the terminal. Most were on the move, sitting in cafés or shopping.

The new Prague station was huge. Electronic boards listing arrivals and departures from all platforms, served by escalators and lifts, hung from the vast curved roof.

Platform seven did not appear crowded. Cleaners were inside the train. Myer stood behind a group of noisy backpacking students with his nose in a railway timetable. I felt a little conspicuous, pulled the ticket out of my pocket and looked at it, reading my destination twice and wondered what Dianne was going to think. Berlin and change for Amsterdam—a long journey of thirteen hours, and I had a sleeper ticket. At least I could have something to eat aboard and sleep. I called Dianne.

"Hi, there. I just wanted to let you know that Tosh confirms there will be a postmortem, so Adam will remain here, probably for two weeks."

"How is your inquiry going?"

I didn't remind her that she told me she didn't want to hear any more about that subject. "I received instructions to go to Amsterdam, and that's where I'll meet Valerie. When I got to the station, I met Myer. We're travelling on the same train. I guess I should be finding out a lot more, perhaps how Adam fits into all this. Let Max know all this in case my phone runs out of juice."

A whistle sounded almost in my ear. Passengers were stepping into onto the train.

"I have to go," I said. "I'll call you in the morning."

"Yes, do that. I need to talk to you."

I was unsure, but I got the impression that she sounded a little calmer, although maybe the calm before the storm. Whatever, I deserved what I got for being an idiot.

I hoped Tosh had made it to the train. He was only a short walk from the station. A plus was that Myer didn't know him, which meant Tosh could keep an eye on both of us.

The train's klaxon blared out, announcing it was time to board. The departure time was 6.30 p.m., and arrival in Berlin was early morning.at 6.15 a.m. A change to another train there would take me all the way to Amsterdam in one hour. In between, I was determined to grill Myer as much as I could.

After finding my sleeping couchette, I walked through two carriages to find the dining car. There was no service for an hour. I thought it a good idea good idea to grab a table and window seat. If Myer appeared, we could at least have a drink and start to talk. I looked out across the tracks to the next platform.

The door at the end of the carriage slid back and Tosh moved quickly toward me.

"Hi, there. What's up?" I asked. "Myer could show at any minute."

"Yes, I know, guv, but you need to know something, then I'll disappear." He seemed short of breath. "I've been looking at the

The Defector's Diary

pictures from the bridge and castle, and in two of them, I spotted Cranthorp. In a third, I could see Myer standing no more than ten feet away from you. Nothing unusual about this, but it does prove you're becoming famous as a target. Of course, Cranthorp may have spotted Myer, so be careful, guv. You might be travelling with a few dubious characters. Cranthorp could be following Myer, or the two are part of the same group. Watch your step."

"I will, don't worry."

"By the way, did you manage to pick up the fax?"

I had forgotten all about the fax and felt for it under my coat. Removing it from the envelope, I looked at the list of attendees and spotted Hart's name.

"Now, let's see if there are any surprises," said Tosh. "Nothing unusual." He ran his finger over the proposed schedule of discussion points and then froze, finger resting on one name making up the Steerage Committee.

"What's that? You found something?" I said, leaning over him.

"Yes," he said. "Guess who's on the Committee?"

"Who?"

"Michael Myer."

"Wow."

We were both silent. Whatever doubts I had about this story being a huge scoop vanished. A member of the Committee involved in whistleblowing was more than huge.

"If I were you, I'd get on the phone to Max, guv, and tell him everything. Suggest he talks to Hart and dissuade him from going to the conference. If this diary blows the lid off some political scandal or worse that affects the stability of Europe, he should be on the outside."

"Okay, I'll phone him now. This whole thing is starting to get dangerous, and we're right in the middle of it." He nodded and walked out of the compartment.

After bringing Max up to date, I sat back, closed my eyes, and dozed off, thinking about Dianne.

"Would you like a menu, Sir?"

I woke up with a start. I nodded and asked the steward for a beer as well. The train had been travelling for an hour, and Myer had not turned up. There was, however, a text on my cell from Tosh. It just said, 'I'm in 2nd class.'

Dinner was pleasant, and I didn't have to share the table.

I spent several minutes looking down at the conference list again. Included were the Prime Minister, Angela Merkel, and several big hitters from the industrial world. It was the Steerage members who interested me. These men arranged and attended each conference and were more knowledgeable about the overall strategy, aims, and plans the Club discussed at the meeting. What made the general public wary of this particular Club were the very people who attended—the world's most influential leaders, heads of state, and industry.

More worrying for me were the real power brokers who sat on the Committee, including Myer. Most of them I had never heard of before.

My ticket was for a single bed compartment. In absence of any meeting, I decided to rest and take things easy. That thought quickly evaporated when I opened the door to my cubicle. Michael Myer sat at the end of the bed, reading a newspaper. Folding the paper, he stood and offered his hand.

"Pete, it's nice to say hello at last."

Chapter Fifteen

MYER STOOD AND WE SHOOK HANDS. "It's a bit cramped in here, but it's private and we can talk."

"That's a good idea," I replied. "At the moment, I'm looking at a giant puzzle whose parts don't fit."

"That's a good way of putting it," Myer agreed. "First, let me explain myself."

I was already getting a little annoyed with his matter-of-fact attitude. "Yes, why not. It's a shame Adam Denton isn't here to listen to your tale of woe."

Myer loosened the buttons on his jacket without replying. He settled back before commenting. "He got himself into a situation from which he couldn't escape. I'm genuinely sorry, but there was nothing I could do but warn him. He refused my advice. I was not surprised at what happened to him."

"I was," I said. "So was my wife, and I would think everyone who knew him at the Embassy and back home."

"I'm sorry, Pete, but we're looking at something more significant than the death of two men. If that sounds arrogant, then…" He shrugged. "What I'm about to tell you will prove my point."

I didn't want to annoy the man. I needed to hear his story.

"I've been an EU trade secretary for the last few years and made many good friends in Brussels," he continued. "That includes Jozef Novotney. I'm sure by now you've found out that Jozef attended the Bilderberg conference way back when. However, what you don't know is that the same year he attended, he was approached by the Steerage Committee to become one of them."

I was listening intently, my recorder on the nightstand, reassuring Myer our conversation remained unrecorded until he decided otherwise.

"At first, Jozef told me he accepted the honor, and for two years, things went well. However, shortly after my first meeting with him, he confided to me certain irregularities taking place within the Committee members. They met every six months."

"Shortly after your first meeting?" I quizzed him.

Myer paused as though trying to find a way through embarrassment.

"Our first meeting was at my inauguration into the Committee. Jozef proposed me to them. Positions only come up when someone dies or retires, and Jozef and I worked closely together in Brussels at the time. He used his influence to get me in."

"So, what were these irregularities?" I asked.

"Jozef was aware that the chairperson and about half the other Steerage Committee members were having unscheduled meetings in Prague, Amsterdam, and London. He found out accidentally after overhearing a conversation between the men and asked me if I would help him find out what was going on."

"What did he overhear?"

"Not a lot, but enough to raise suspicion that the discussion centered on how the EU needed to change with regards to membership rules. They wanted to relax certain criteria so that Turkey could join, despite a ruling that many issues and human rights had to improve in that country first. That's when we came up with our plan."

I was getting more interested as Myer spoke. My first impression of him was not good. The man had gone missing, which put Brussels into a spin, not to mention the security services, and he made secret meetings with the Czech EU commissioner. Despite that, he talked to the press, knowing his career would be over once we reached Amsterdam.

"What plan was that?"

The Defector's Diary

"Jozef was contacted by the president of the European Council just before this happened and offered a place on the EU Foreign Affairs Council, a pretty powerful position, and one we thought would help him keep an eye on the members of the small group inside the Club. I was to stay on the Committee, and we would meet every so often to pool any information we gathered. You can imagine my surprise when the Club's chairperson, Sir John Carlton, approached me shortly after and asked me to attend a meeting at his home in London."

Outside, the light was fading fast, and poplar trees were turning into tall, black shadowy fingers by the side of the line. The sun had disappeared below the horizon, leaving a dark landscape illuminated in flashes from the carriage windows as we rushed along. With all I was getting involved in, I felt my surroundings matched the mood of the conversation.

"So, what happened at this meeting? I take it you accepted the opportunity to join?"

Myer hesitated for a moment. "I'd rather not go into details at this time. Much better to hear the rest of my story first, but yes, you're right—I did accept the offer to attend."

I wanted to ask him about Adam, but focused on the Commissioner. There was more to tell, and it was much better to travel down one road at a time. "And what about Jozef's death? What happened?" I asked.

Myer averted his eyes to the floor and clasped his hands in his lap. "I've been worried since the last meeting with the—shall we call them the New Order group—and I needed to talk to Jozef. The New Order was, or is, putting a plan into action that would see drastic changes to the way our society runs, and this is a long-term plan for the next ten years. There is nothing intrinsically wrong with the plan's goals until we realized that members of this group, including myself, all stand to gain tremendous wealth and power." He waved a hand as I opened my mouth. "You need to find out more details from the diary Forst has when you get to

Amsterdam. Jozef was a meticulous record-keeper, but there is a lot of information from his last two meetings with the group I never saw. She will also explain how Jozef died."

"Okay." I changed tack. "Can you enlighten me on how Adam Denton got involved?"

Myer stood and faced the window. "Bloody SIS, that's how he became involved."

I knew I'd touched a nerve. Myer spun around and glared at me.

"Jozef had an invite to some social event at the Embassy, and because he was a bachelor, he took his assistant Valerie with him."

"So that's how Adam met Valerie Forst, or Valerie as she introduced herself to him. Was he aware that she was a Czech agent?"

"No, of course not, and neither was Jozef. The EU security services had cleared her before she accepted her post."

I was galloping ahead of him. "Valerie was a plant whose sole purpose was to look over Jozef's shoulder and pass back EU titbits to her HQ in Prague."

Myer pushed the glass vent open at the top of the window, then took a pack of Du Maurier from his jacket pocket. "Do you mind? I'm gasping for this."

I waved a hand. Much better, the man would talk with settled nerves.

"Yes, Adam met Forst at the reception," said Myer, lit the cigarette and crushed the packet. "Forst, as I found out later, had been looking for a way to leave for some time. You can imagine how she felt when offered a job working within the EU. She waited for an opportunity and took one as soon as Adam came along."

I clicked my fingers. There was something odd about that statement. "Forst knew about the diary before she met Adam?" I pushed.

The Defector's Diary

Myer took a long draw on his cigarette before answering. He blew a long stream of smoke at the air vent.

"No, but she convinced Adam that she had information in exchange for asylum. Adam reported to SIS Forst's request for asylum a little later. Of course, that was after she became Adam's lover and his proposed wife. She's a beautiful girl and Adam was a pushover. He had to convince SIS she was a real prospect, so they spent some time as lovers with SIS's blessing. She told her people she had a contact at the Embassy and started passing her office useless information supplied by SIS. This was while SIS were pressing her for a sample of the info, she promised them in return for asylum." Myer flicked his cigarette stub out of the glass vent, sat down, and pulled a pack of cigarettes from a soft leather case at his side. "All this Adam told me when we met on the day of Jozef's death. Bloody SIS messed up and gave Forst some info to pass on the Czechs would know was not something she would be able to get firsthand."

He lit another cigarette from the new carton after tapping the end on the lid.

"So, her masters learned she was cheating them," I said and reached for my tablet. "I want to make some notes. I can't remember all this. Do you mind?"

Myer nodded. "Of course, neither Jozef nor I had any idea this was going on. We only knew one day before Jozef's death after receiving a directive from Brussels telling him that Forst would receive a decommission message. He was not to say a word to her. She would be ordered back to Prague on returning to Brussels that week. It didn't say why, but we guessed. We knew about Adam by then through a conversation Forst had with Vilma. Adam told the rest of the story himself when I met him."

I stopped him here. "How did you get Adam to give you all this information? Surely, he would have been pretty scared after finding out who you were."

"Actually, it helped. He knew I lost my career and reputation and probably faced a term of imprisonment. There were things about Forst I knew, so it was not too hard to convince him I wanted to help. I also gave him a heads-up on SIS and guessed it was them who deliberately gave her the information that got her recalled."

I could understand that. Forst was a foreign agent and knew the risks she faced if caught.

"That would have made him angry," I said. "I take it then that the last two days of Jozef's life, and Adam's, is when everything happened?" I was busy typing and raised my head when Myer didn't answer.

"It was the last four days before he died," he said.

There was a tap on the door. Myer touched my elbow as he got up and put a finger to his lips. He slipped into the small toilet closet.

"Any drinks before you retire, sir?" The steward stood in the passage with a little silver tray and order pad.

"Yes, could you bring me two scotch on the rocks, please? That'll save me going to the bar for a second." I thanked him, and as he closed the door, I caught a quick glimpse of Tosh standing by the passage window.

I closed the door and tapped on the toilet. "All clear."

Myer reappeared. "I need to tell you the rest. If I'm not with you for some reason, don't worry when we reach Cologne or Amsterdam. Forst will collect you."

The thread of the story was getting lost again. I wasn't interested in whether Myer would be with me in Amsterdam or not. SIS would be scooping him up soon enough. I guided Myer back, although the warning made me realize we both faced a dangerous situation. If the Czechs or SIS caught us together, there could be grave consequences for Europe and us if the New Order group was not exposed. Apart from that, the Order had men who would stop at nothing to eliminate us both.

"Okay, so give me a rundown on what happened in those four

days."

We were disturbed again and Myer disappeared into the toilet. I opened the door and took the drinks. Tosh was gone. The smell of scotch brightened my evening. I had no idea why, but the sound of clinking ice on glass had a calming effect on me. I passed Myer a drink and sat down.

"Well," said Myer and sipped. "I went to see Jozef and we discussed the situation regarding Forst. We decided that whatever else, we had to warn Adam. Far better for him to distance himself from her before SIS knew of her decommissioning and came looking for him. I would imagine no one except Forst, Jozef, me, and SIS knew of his involvement. That way, SIS could keep their house clean and point at Adam if things went wrong. Then, Jozef gave me Adam's address—we didn't have a single telephone number for him. As far as we were concerned, we needed to lose any ties he had to us and act normally. Our mission was focusing on the New Order within the Club."

"Right, I understand things so far, but how did Forst get her hands on the diary?" I asked without looking up.

"The day before I went to visit Jozef, he caught…no, maybe that's the wrong word. He or Vilma- I can't remember who, found her going through his diary. She said she was looking for a specified date and event—I can't remember what. The diary is full of our information, but most of it is about initials and times. To the right eyes, it is not hard to decipher. In particular, it has information that Jozef picked up at the last meeting of the New Order, and it is that information we have to find. Do you have anything that Adam may have sent to you?"

I ignored the question. "I suppose Forst would be able to decipher the notes?"

"Yes. That's what worried us." He squeezed the end of his cigarette between two fingers and flicked the stub out the window. Loosening his tie, he gulped the rest of the scotch. "The following morning, after our meeting at the café, I went to contact Adam. I'd never met him before, but I told him I needed help with a passport issue. That was around lunchtime. I caught up with him at the Embassy and we walked into the nearby park where he sometimes had lunch and met Forst. We had a long chat—that's how both of us found out what else has been happening. You can imagine how worried he was about the whole situation with SIS, and then my warning to him. Neither of them had a clue that a decommission order was in effect. Adam left me, saying he would see Forst. A short while later, he called me to say she had the diary and was at his flat."

"Did Adam say whether he knew what was in the diary or not?"

"I don't think he knew too much, but hinted it was to do with the Bilderberg Club. I tried to convince him not to take it to SIS and pleaded with him to let me have it back. Unfortunately, they wanted to keep it as a ticket to London for Forst, and I was in no position to make threats."

"I take it your objective was a little different to Forst's?"

"Yes, we wanted to expose the New Order, but in such a way as not to damage the reputation of the Bilderberg Club. All this I explained to Adam. Forst just wanted out and was prepared to offer the diary to anyone in London."

I was tired and longed for some rest, but as long as Myer wanted to talk, I was happy to listen. It was an invisible threat hanging over him that he may not reach Amsterdam that convinced me he wanted to tell me everything. It wasn't the security services he was mostly worried about, but the New Order thugs. I thought for a moment before my next question. Something wasn't right about Myer's relationship with Valerie Forst.

"Correct me if I'm wrong, but Forst was at Adam's apartment with the diary the day you met him and after your last meeting with Jozef the previous day. That's when she and Adam must have sent my wife that letter. Jozef, by then, was dead in his office just hours after your meeting with him. When did you know?"

"I was supposed to see Jozef that afternoon after seeing Adam before I returned to Brussels. Things were getting complicated by then and I was going to suggest to Jozef that we contact a couple of trusted members on the Steerage Committee to get Forst safe passage in return for the diary. When I approached Jozef's office, I saw all the police activity and heard about his death in the late afternoon news. In the position I was in, I knew it was the end of my career and decided to hide until I could preserve the integrity of the Club."

"And Adam?"

"At the same time, Forst went into hiding. Adam told her how to get in touch with me, and the next day, I got a frightened Forst Skyping me from an internet café. I gave her a number to reach me and she called me later. She told me Adam had sent you a letter. She would give you the diary in return for asylum. Adam had assured her of that. I believed what she told me and agreed to help. As far as telling Adam that Jozef was dead, I would imagine she probably did tell him before disappearing, or he could have heard about it on the news." Myer lit a cigarette. "That poor kid is looking at a bullet in the neck. Her people won't hesitate."

I wanted to believe him, but he was evading one question.

"She was at Adam's apartment with the diary on the day you met him in the park. She saw him after he returned home. She could have killed him."

"No, she killed neither man. How would she get rid of the body and dump it in the river? My guess is some Club soldiers did it." He blew a cloud of smoke up at the ceiling. "Please take my word for it and wait until you meet her. She'll explain." Myer must have read my mind and sighed. "I didn't kill anyone either."

"Does Forst know who killed them?"

"Jozef, yes, but not Adam." He sat back and rested his head on the wall, looking utterly exhausted.

I looked at my watch and said, "It's nearly midnight, and we'll be in Berlin in a few hours. You look done in. Have you got a berth?"

"Yes, I'll collect you in the morning after breakfast. You'll find me here waiting. I have to be careful, and I'll have a continental breakfast in my cabin."

I saw him out and texted Max, letting him know of my conversation with Myer, along with an urgent request that it was in the best interest of the Herald that Richard Hart went sick before the conference. I hoped Dianne would draw some comfort from the update, too. I brought up her number a few minutes later, explaining with a text that I would call after getting a few hours of sleep. Just as I finished, there was a single tap on the door. It was Tosh.

Too tired to read through my report again, I gave Tosh the tablet and told him to read. We were now all on the same page. All I needed to do was meet Forst and decide whether I would stick my neck out further for her.

"Very interesting," Tosh said. "Do you know what's happening in Amsterdam?"

I shook my head. "No, but I hope you'll stay close."

As he reached the door, I stopped him from opening it. "Two things. I need two or three throwaway cells. We can't afford to have someone hacking into my reports. I texted Max and told him I'll call him tomorrow and dictate the report to his secretary." I paused. "Do you have a gun on you?"

Chapter Sixteen

I WAS UP EARLY WITH ONE AIM in mind. I had to talk to Dianne. I had to make her understand how important she was to my life and how much I regretted causing her anguish, particularly now that Adam was dead. I sat in the dining car and called her.

"Good morning," she answered my call right away. "I read your message. It seems you were right all along that these thugs from Bilderberg were responsible for Adam's death. I contacted our Embassy in London and my father. He's pulling a few strings to get Adam home as soon as possible. A second post-mortem will show the cause of death."

"Well done," I said. "Unfortunately, the chances of naming the actual killers will be remote, but I'm going to name names whether Richard Hart likes it or not. Max is going to try and get our illustrious leader to go sick."

She cut in. "I won't ask how you feel, Pete, but our issue is on the waiting list until you get home. We do need to talk. I said something I regret. It must have upset you and, selfishly, that's what I wanted to do. I cannot take it back, but we should talk about it. I know how you feel, and I never doubted your love. As for now, I have to tell you what I found out about the men who gave me that message for you. The owner of the car that hit me is Lord Basil Gresham. I met him several years ago at a garden party at Buckingham Palace just after my father was awarded the MBE."

From the tone of our conversation, I knew she was no longer angry with me. I sighed and leaned back with relief. I interrupted her. "Dianne, Max told me you were going to Cannes. Are you okay?"

"I'm fine, and yes, I'll be there tonight. I spoke to Max who is furious as always. He didn't exactly send you his love but changed his tune when I told him about Basil Gresham. Max, like my father, wants you to be aware that Lord Gresham is someone who leads the United British Legion."

"I am aware," I answered. "That would not surprise me. There will be a lot more members of the House of Lords involved in this sorry mess. I wish I could get onto those thugs."

Dianne hesitated. "Don't worry about me. Just stay out of danger until you get home."

"The good news is that Tosh and I will have Valerie Forst by tonight, so things will soon be over, fingers crossed." I caught sight of Myer entering the dining car. "I have to go. Myer is coming. I'll call you soon. I love you."

Myer joined me, a rolled newspaper in one hand. "Morning, Pete. We have ten minutes before our next train the Amsterdam shuttle service leaves. We'd better hop to it."

As we left the train, I suddenly realized what Dianne had said and smiled. I was going to be 'in for it' when I got back. A period of naughty boy punishment awaited, probably including a morning jog that Dianne knew I hated.

Berlin Hbf railway station was enormous, noisy, and had a large shopping mall. It was one of the leading transportation hubs in Europe and not somewhere I wanted to stay for very long. Unlike Prague, the station was devoid of a welcoming atmosphere.

We left the train and made our way to the train for Amsterdam. By the time we reached it, the doors were closing. I turned, but Myer had gone. Planned or otherwise, he was out of the picture, and I was in the hands of a young woman looking for asylum with a diary full of secrets.

"Morning, guv. Myer went as soon as you hopped on." Tosh

slid into the seat beside me. "He's probably on his way to Brussels, but I told London I found him, and they'll be there to meet him. Don't worry; they think I spotted him in Prague and followed him as far as Cologne. You're not in the picture yet, but my guess is you will be shortly."

I knew he was right. Whitehall had already told Hart to send me home, and Max would eventually have to let them know I saw and spoke to Myer. Unfortunately, SIS knew through Cranthorp, but that didn't mean they told anyone. They were being their usual devious selves to scoop all the glory or find someone to use as a pawn. I hoped that wasn't going to be me. I needed more time before that happened. We were on the verge of uncovering the whole story, including who killed Adam.

"If Forst is meeting you and all the bits fit, where are you gonna take her?" asked Tosh. "I can't get involved in any of this officially or they'll throw me in jail."

"I have no idea," I answered. "First, I need a safe house until things are sorted out."

"Well, that's a breeze. I know this beautiful lady who runs a tea shop—specializes in spiced tea and cake." A broad grin spread across his face. "She's got a soft spot for me."

I laughed. "Yes, of course. Forst may have arranged a place, and if she has, I'm sure it's somewhere safe, if that's okay with you."

Tosh smiled. "You're on your own, remember?"

He was right. If I was found out, or worse still, found with Forst, even Max would not help. Thinking about that, I much preferred whatever Dianne had in store for me.

Thirty minutes later, we were on the outskirts of Amsterdam. Memories erased the present situation as the train gently rocked back and forth. Amsterdam was a great capital city that, like New York, never slept. I remembered happier times when Dianne and I visited on a couple of occasions and enjoyed canal sightseeing trips and seeing the museum district by bicycle. As the water came into view, I recalled that Amsterdam had more bicycles than Oxford and Cambridge put together. The nightlife was pretty good too, with many nightclubs and restaurants open twenty-four hours.

Tosh nudged me back to reality as the train slowed. "I'll get lost until she picks you up, and then I'll keep my eyes on you. When it's okay, I'll contact you. In the meantime, do you want me to give Dianne a ring?"

"No, I'll get hold of her later, but thanks." The last thing I wanted was Tosh calling Dianne. He wasn't a diplomat as far as ladies were concerned and the last thing I wanted was Dianne hearing "Mornin' missus W."

The train came to a squeaking halt, and Tosh was first through the door.

I stepped out and walked toward the ticket barrier. If Forst was close, she would have to be waiting there. There was a small bench seat halfway down the platform. I reached it and stopped, but after five minutes, it looked like another no-show.

From an earlier visit, I knew the exit through the old turn of the century red brick station led out onto a vast concourse, an area where thousands of travellers used the tram and coach services. It was a place that hummed with life and where bicycle parks replaced car parks. I half smiled, remembering Dianne and me using bikes to get around.

"Number five tram from the far end of the station concourse, please, Mr West. Here is your chip card; it's valid for five days."

A small hand sheathed in leather wound its way under my arm and held on. I took the ticket, looked sideways, and was surprised. Valerie Forst was a stunning young woman. The photo I obtained showed a brunette, but this Forst was a blonde. Dark red lips, a little rouge, and a dab of powder on a small dainty nose was all I could see. A tall collar on her cream raincoat hid most of her face, apart from a small gold cross earring that jiggled on a chain from an earlobe. I didn't care for the scent; too heavy, I thought. Her hip brushed against mine as we strode through the early morning crowds. I enjoyed the experience for a brief moment but realized she was too close, maybe weakening my resolve or defences. I gently pulled away my arm.

The blue and white packed trams moved slowly.

Impatiently, we stood waiting for ours to arrive. Forst wasn't talking and stared straight ahead. If she was nervous, she didn't show it. A little while later, our tram arrived and we boarded. With the coach packed from end to end, we stood pressed together. It was then, looking down at her, that I noticed the bluest of eyes.

"We get off at Spuistraat, which runs by the side of the Singel canal," she said. "I have a room at the Van Cleve, a short walk from the stop." I saw the hint of a smile at the corners of her mouth. "We'll be walking through the red-light district, but you probably won't notice."

The first thought that came into my head was Tosh. The man would be right at home. It was probably a good place for Forst, though I needed somewhere quieter. Thinking of Tosh, I tried looking for him, but it was impossible in the crush.

A few minutes later, I pushed my way toward the nearest exit as the tram trundled to a halt by the side of the canal. My first impression was of trees on either side of the water and several brightly painted barges moored beneath them. A small barge passed by under a footbridge that led to the other side. Beautiful and serene, the landscape was a postcard rather than a red-light district.

Forst led the way. As I mounted a couple of stone steps to the bridge, I smelled the unmistakable odour of fried fish and, mixed lightly with it, cinnamon, used in most pastries, but especially my favourite, lattice apple pie. Apart from marijuana, these were two of the most familiar smells around Amsterdam. I felt hungry and hoped the hotel would offer early lunch.

The hotel was a small five-story red brick and grey stone

building with green wooden shutters on all the windows. Guests in the rooms that faced the front had an excellent view of the canal and barges. Entering Reception, Forst stopped by the lift and pointed to a double glass door.

Eat, Mr West. I'm in room thirty-two." She smiled. "Don't worry. I'm not going anywhere just yet."

With that, she stepped into the lift and was gone. I entered the restaurant and found a seat in one corner. A waiter pounced on me and left the menu. As I trawled through it, I thought of Myer and the situation he would have to face. Tomorrow morning, there would be a story concerning his sudden reappearance and expected resignation because of secret meetings with the murdered Commissioner. Whitehall wouldn't look after him.

I ordered my lunch and spent an hour hoping the job of getting Forst and the diary to London would be simple.

Room thirty-two was on the back of the floor, looking out across the roofs of buildings that fronted the adjacent canal. I knocked lightly and the door opened almost at once, but just a crack. I pushed it open. Forst stood in the middle of the room with a small pistol in her hand pointed directly at me. If I had ever thought she didn't look the part of a security agent, my mind changed at that moment. The eyes never moved, and the pistol was held steady. Her stance, legs slightly apart, arms held straight out in front, oozed defiance.

"Come in, Mr West. I do hope there is no friend downstairs from SIS...or will it be the thugs from Bilderberg?"

"Neither" I answered. "They're all thugs as far as I'm concerned." I was getting uncomfortable looking at the muzzle end of the pistol. "Can we do without that thing?"

She lowered her arms and motioned to a chair. "While you were eating, I was looking out of the window at the rear courtyard and saw something very strange."

Her English was perfect, but she couldn't hide the slight accent, that edge to the voice that identifies a foreign tongue.

The Defector's Diary

I stood next to the chair and flipped the curtain back. The back yard was a small area full of empty beer crates and a large gas tank. A little tree grew in one corner next to an overflowing waste wheelie bin. In the other corner, a wooden gate opened into the opposite yard.

"I saw this little man expertly open an adjacent gate to the garden of the other hotel. He then came inside this hotel, but I have no idea where he is now. Someone acting so strange had to be something to do with you. Then I remembered where I had seen him before—Da Capo Café."

"You were there? Where?"

"Close enough to give you a slip of paper." She raised her eyebrows. "Your little friend was fooled too."

"Incredible."

"You never looked at me when I spoke to you, but at everybody around you."

I was impressed, but still felt uncomfortable while she held the pistol. Sensing my feelings, she laid it on the table next to her chair.

"He won't be bothering us," I reassured her. "Indeed, before we get down to business, let me tell you I am nothing more than a journalist, and if you get to the UK, you'll have to answer to SIS."

Forst relaxed a little and sat as I showed her my press pass and offered my business card. She paused, looking undecided before continuing.

"Before we get down to how things have happened that led to the present situation, I want to tell you about Jozef Novotney and who killed him. I had no choice but to hide because of the diary, not the man's death."

"You'll still have to answer to SIS," I said.

She gave me a hard stare, and the corners of her lips drew back. "I will be shot if I go back to Prague."

There was a long silence.

"Okay," I said. "Tell me about Novotney. Myer told me a lot but said you would explain his death."

Forst crossed her legs and brushed some long strands of hair before her eyes. She seemed to hesitate again. "I will tell you the whole story. Six months before his death, I met Adam at an Embassy function. He was a nice man, and I knew he was ideal as someone I could rely on to help me get asylum in the UK."

"You mean, he was easy to manipulate. So, you used him?"

"I'm sorry, but yes."

She was a beautiful girl, but her beauty belied her aggressive, no-nonsense attitude. I could see her using the pistol without turning a hair.

"I spent the last two years hoping to find a way to live in the West. Despite our faked good relations with Moscow, they still influence our security services, and it's almost impossible for people in the Service to obtain travel permits. I told Adam I planned to marry him with my department's blessing and move to the UK and work from there for BIS. Of course, I wasn't going to do that, wanting to give myself up to SIS. The trouble was, I had no information to give. SIS and your Whitehall would not have allowed me to stay."

"I take it Adam was not aware of your BIS position apart from being Novotney's assistant?"

"No, not at first. I waited until we were lovers, then I told him who I was, and wanting to get to London. He contacted SIS and they arranged everything. I found out about the diary later. That was before Jozef Novotney died."

I started making notes. "Back to Novotney. What happened?"

Forst got up and walked to the small drinks' fridge. "I was taking notes for Novotney. He was due to attend a meeting in Brussels over the deal with Ukraine. I wanted the time for the meeting and a list of those attending. I was late sending in my weekly report to BIS, and I knew he kept important notes in his diary. I went to his case and pulled out the wrong one. After going through several pages, I realized what I had uncovered. Unfortunately, Novotney caught me with the diary. I made an excuse, and he accepted it."

"Then what?"

Forst helped herself to a couple of small scotch bottles from the fridge. Twisting the cap off one, she poured the contents into a glass and handed it to me. She drank half her scotch and crossed her legs, showing far too much thigh. My respect and concern for her dropped, but then, I reasoned, what did I expect? Security services employed people with hard skin and massive egos. Valerie's real makeup was beginning to glow through the powder and lipstick, and I wasn't impressed.

For the next ten minutes, she explained how she and Adam realized that to convince SIS that certain individual members of the Bilderberg Club were posing a threat to the Western world and, in particular, the European Union, they would have to have proof, the diary. It was also necessary for her to hand the diary over in return for asylum, but she would only do that in London. The problem was, they needed to steal it first without anyone knowing, and then negotiate with SIS through Adam for a ticket to London.

"If that was the plan, why was I brought into this?" I asked. "Surely, you could have sent the diary to London by courier addressed to anywhere you liked, then delivered it after completing the deal for asylum."

"Because after I took the diary, SIS knew I had it, and now everyone is after me. I had to hide. It was safer for me to keep the diary, a kind of insurance. Adam said he found out I couldn't trust SIS, but then he spoke about you and your wife and sent a page to you."

"Who are 'they'?"

"The Bilderberg people."

I was writing as fast as I could. The more Forst spoke, the

more I wanted to know. She wasn't worried about the contents of the diary. She just wanted a bargaining chip.

"So, what came first—the diary or Jozef Novotney's death?"

Forst shifted uneasily in her seat and downed the rest of the scotch. "Both together. I wanted to get the diary and told Adam early morning on the day all this happened that I would return, hopefully with the diary around noon. I was going to hide the diary and he would contact SIS while I went to work as normal."

"But something went wrong," I suggested. I pressed the record button on my digital recorder while she got up to fetch another miniature. Things had gone wrong, all right.

She said she checked Novotney's calendar, and he was due back in Brussels the following day. There were tickets booked for a flight for both of them. That gave her one day to take the diary. Novotney's office in Prague was below his apartment. Vilma worked every day, and both women had keys to the office and his residence in case of emergencies. All she had to do was enter the ground floor, disable the alarm while Vilma went to lunch, and take the diary. She knew where he kept it.

As I listened to her, I began to get the feeling that her story was too neat and tidy, even though she hadn't got to the end yet. I wanted to know what she knew about Adam's death and just how involved he had become.

"I got to the office and waited outside until Vilma left. Novotney was upstairs in his flat. Normally, if time and work permitted while he was in Prague, he took an afternoon nap. I entered and went to his office. After searching through his desk, I found nothing and panicked. Novotney could have taken it upstairs with him. I searched everywhere until I looked in Vilma's desk. The diary was in the bottom drawer, where she kept her personal things and a first aid kit. I grabbed it, knowing Vilma would be back soon. As I was leaving, I heard two men talking outside and hid behind the toilet door in the outer office. They were Czech, also looking for the diary. One of them mentioned

The Defector's Diary

the diary was in a case, probably be with Novotney upstairs. After that, it was quiet for several minutes until I heard the muffled crack of a small pistol. It sounded as though they used a pillow. Anyway, the men came rushing back through the office and out into the street. As they did, my name was mentioned. "One of them said, 'Forst must have it'. I waited for a few minutes and left. There was no point going up to the apartment. I knew Novotney was dead."

I held up my hand to stop her. "Who knew you were going to steal the diary?"

"Adam and the man he saw after I left his apartment that morning. They were the only two who knew."

"What man?"

"Adam didn't tell me about him until I got back with the diary. He said he already had a quiet word with him. I was mad at him, but it was too late to do anything about it."

"What man?"

"Michael Myer. They met at the same time I was at Novotney's stealing the diary."

I felt satisfied Myer had told the truth, although I knew he had a lot more to tell. In all probability, a story I or anyone else would never hear. One question remained unanswered. How did the thugs know about the diary?

Chapter Seventeen

DRISCOL SAT LOOKING AT THE MESSAGES that came in overnight. One in particular was worrying him.

Cranthorp was playing a casual game. His bridge appearance in Prague had nearly ended in disaster. West turned twice at one point, and each time, Cranthorp was able to dodge behind a tourist. A close call that Cranthorp had included in his report. Driscol admired the man but couldn't stand his arrogance.

He had a different opinion of the man sitting opposite him.

Lord Basil Gresham had an army of zealous followers who supported his United British Legion. A pompous and arrogant person, Driscol despised him.

In the upcoming general elections, the UBL was expected to win two or three seats. Gresham had more than a fledgling political party. He had a huge following of members, some of whom wore a security guard's party uniform. This small army would be useful, according to Carlton, as soon as the new ruling party took control of Britain and Europe. The president and senators of the New Order had a meeting in Paris, and Sir John Carlton ordered to accept Lord Gresham's offer to police the streets of Britain.

He sat listening to Gresham as he boasted what he was about to achieve. Grossly overweight, his double chin flapped over his shirt's collar, as did his stomach over his trousers. The most visible feature that caught the eye was his eyebrows. Big untrimmed bushy things that grew in a mass. His head was bald, and an old wound had left a long white line over his left ear and around the back of his neck, something he liked to refer to as his war wound.

"We'll show those monkeys in parliament. I can't wait to

The Defector's Diary

march across Westminster bridge flying our flag. You wait, Driscol, the people of this country will follow us once they learn about the New Order."

Driscol agreed. "You have all the men ready, and did you remember any speech you give from now on must be about supporting the New Order and not the UBL? Once we take over, you'll be a British Senator in the European Order with special responsibility as head of Sir Carlton's security detail. You'll only answer to me."

"Absolutely, old boy. I cannot wait."

Driscol showed Gresham out as his phone rang. "Driscol here."

"Well, I'm glad you're in a good mood. I guess I'm going to put you in a bad mood now." Cranthorp's tone was, as always, sarcastic.

"You know your arrogance and stupid humour are going to get you sacked."

"That's alright, James. I still have another job. Do you?"

"Quit Shut your mouth, Charles, and let me know what happened."

"We found the girl, but she got away in Amsterdam on a crowded bus with West, would you believe. It also looks like West is hot on the trail of the diary. My men are following. I have another source of information. Whatever you decide, I think it best we act as soon as possible."

"Okay, leave that. Follow them, and the first chance you get, grab the girl. The possibilities are that West has prised the diary from her. We might get it back if he thinks she is going to be shot."

"She will be anyway."

"Just follow and grab her when the chance comes along, and it will. Ring me when you have her. Time is short now with just a couple of weeks left until we strike." As an afterthought, he said, "Will you be attending the meeting in London before the

Othello night?"

"Yes," answered Charles. "I suppose all of us important people will be there."

"And you would do well to take things a little more seriously. The New Order president will be flying in from Paris, so no humour or stupid behaviour. He's going to address us, then fly straight back to Paris for the start of our offensive there." Driscol ended the call.

The upcoming meeting was a risk the President was prepared to accept. All top executives were going to be there. The security arrangements were a nightmare involving fifty of Basil Gresham's men and another ten security staff travelling with the President.

Driscol glanced through the files again. Cranford was right, he thought. West was a dangerous man armed with political knowledge and a great insight into Westminster's workings, admired by a strong following who read him daily.

A copy of the Herald lay on the desk in front of him. He picked it up and threw it in anger at the waste bin.

"Damn you, West. Damn you."

He picked up the file marked Pete West—the Herald, and the name, Richard Hart—owner, was typed across the top.

Driscol looked at the name. There were two possibilities that might save a lot of time and aggravation. In the eventual change of power, someone like Richard Hart could control media that would dwarf Rupert Murdoch's empire. Another scenario could be Pete West, the official editor of the New Order newspaper. With a huge salary and shares in the paper, he would be a fool to turn that offer down.

Chapter Eighteen

A LIGHT TAP ON THE DOOR sounded like a thunderclap in the moment's silence following Valerie's story. I shot out of the chair while she grabbed the pistol and stepped smartly behind the door. "Pete, it's me."

The soft rasping whisper was unmistakable. I opened the door and pulled Tosh in, closing the door quickly behind him.

"What the hell's going on?"

Tosh inclined his head sideways at Valerie, who was pointing the pistol at him.

"Perhaps you can tell me who you are, little man?"

Tosh stepped in front of her. "I'm ex-SIS and I'm helping Mr West tell the world about you. I don't have any ID. Do you?"

Valeries' eyes focused on me, then back to Tosh.

I nodded. "He's one reason you'll get to London. Give him the gun."

She hesitated and gave up the weapon.

"Her friends are outside in a car, guv," said Tosh pocketing the small pistol. "They've been there for the last half hour. There's also another stranger looking very agitated in the lobby. My guess is they're waiting for a couple more before they pounce. We have to move." He walked to the window and pulled the curtain back with one finger just enough to look down into the rear yard. "We'll have to climb down the fire escape and through the gate to the other property."

"I doubt that she can climb down anywhere in that outfit," I said, one eye on Valerie.

Tosh turned to her. "Take that bloody skirt off and get your ass in a pair of jeans. If you don't hurry up about it. I'll do it for you." He thumbed at me over his shoulder. "He might be a gentleman, but I'm not where you're concerned—now get your finger out."

I was a little surprised at the way he spoke to her. Tosh turned to me as Valerie undressed and winked. "If you make a woman angry, have you ever noticed how much quicker they move around?"

Thoughts of Dianne and little instances that had happened between us in the past came to my mind, and I raised an eyebrow and nodded. Without a doubt, Tosh was a truly incredible character, a great expert on criminal behaviour and life in general. I wondered at SIS's stupidity at letting him go.

Valerie was in a pair of slacks within seconds and opening the sash window situated above the fire escape.

"I'll go first, then her, and last, you, Pete." He pushed the window as far up as possible and climbed out. Holding Valerie's arm, he pulled her after him, and they started down the metal stairs.

I followed them rather heavily, and once again wished I listened to Dianne. By the time I reached the bottom of the stairs, I was out of breath. I remembered to pick up my leather case but wondered about Valerie. She was leaving without taking anything. The wooden gate closed with a loud squeak behind them as I trotted across the yard. Concentrating on the gate and not where I was going, my foot caught on the side of a beer crate and I fell forward, dropping to the ground. Some empty bottles rolled across the concrete paving, announcing my presence. I picked myself up and lunged for the gate. As I stumbled again on cracked concrete, I looked back over my shoulder and saw the back door of the hotel kitchen open.

Ahead of me, there was no sign of Tosh or Forst. Afraid of being captured by the thugs I had already met, I ran across the lawn and into an alleyway. At the far end, I could see the next canal and trees. Of Tosh, there was no sign. A passerby collided with me on the canal pavement, and a cyclist wobbled past trying to avoid us.

"C'mon Pete, over here!"

I saw an arm waving frantically at me from the stern of a brightly coloured barge moving away from its mooring along the canal. I ran and jumped the three feet gap of water, landing in a heap next to Tosh.

"That was damn close," I gasped.

Tosh did not answer. We both watched four figures appear from the alley and stand by the side of the canal. One was on the phone. I brushed myself down. "Where's Valerie?" I asked. "And where are we going?"

"She's inside, and we're going to a safe house. My mate here is taking us to another boat. This is Jan—he's a boat builder, and that's all you need to know, guv."

I shook hands with Jan, a heavyset Dutchman with a barrel chest and a shock of red hair covered by a corduroy peaked cap. He was a giant of a man with one eyelid that flickered continuously from below bushy eyebrows. Dressed in jeans and worn navy roll-neck jumper, he was a fearsome sight. I could smell beer on his breath. His large, calloused hands pushed and pulled at the tiller while the barge maneuvered into the centre of the canal.

"I'll go and catch up with Valerie," I announced and left Tosh sitting with Jan, both enjoying a smoke.

I entered the living room down three steps and through a small blue door—the wooden walls painted blue halfway up from the deck and the top half pale pink. A three-piece suite covered in a chintz fabric and an Indian carpet on the floor made the room strangely warm and cozy. A dresser stood to one side next to an old oak dining table and chairs. A single Oil of landscape hung from the walls. At the far end, a side opening revealed a walk-in galley painted yellow and green. Sitting in front of a coffee table was Valerie.

I sat opposite the dining table. "Now, let's finish our conversation before I decide what to do next."

She sighed and shook her head. "What you decide and what we do are two different things, Mr West. I decide what happens next."

It was the look that did it—a haughty look down the nose with half-closed eyes. A red flag dropped in front of me. Bad guys were chasing me. I was avoiding SIS, and used by this girl so she could live in the West. I missed Dianne. I exploded.

"You'll decide? And why—because you have the diary? My wife lost a friend because of you. An influential politician ends up murdered because of you. Security services across Europe are on alert because of you. Now you want to decide what happens next?" I stood in front of her and bent forward, shaking with anger. "I'll tell you what I'm going to do," I snapped. "I'm washing my hands of your sordid little escapade and having a word with SIS, something I should have done right from the start. I'm reporting to the Czech authorities with a copy to the Press Association. Then I'm going to the British Embassy in Prague with your statement I recorded back at the hotel. There's enough there to hang you, you supercilious little bitch."

I spat the words out and turned away from her. Dianne wanted to know who killed her friend. My best guess was the New Order. SIS would not kill one of their own unless he or she was a traitor. Until then, the Czech authorities had not been involved. The last thing I needed was a diva agent. I was annoyed that I even bothered with her.

The door opened, and Tosh stood on the bottom step, a wisp of smoke rising from a cigarette between his lips. "Looks like you could do with some fresh air, guv." He motioned me to step out with the wave of a hand.

"You're right." I strode past him. "Valerie is going to tell us what we have to do next."

The door stayed ajar as I joined Jan by the tiller. There was a

The Defector's Diary

loud sound of a slap. Jan's hand pulled me back into my seat as I rose.

"You're too much a gentleman," he said. "This business we're in is not good. Most of us are not what we seem." He pointed to the cabin. "She's just a tart."

There was another slap and the sound of Tosh's raised voice.

"You see that gent out there?" Tosh demanded loudly. "He's your ticket to the lights of bleedin' London. He's also a very famous man that millions of people read. He's stuck his bloody neck out for you, and you treat him like a lump of dirt. He could go to prison because of you. Why then is he doing all this, because you asked him? I don't think so, you stupid little bitch. That man cares about the world and all the people who don't know what's going on. He's letting them know about the dirty, bloody things you and I are involved in, and what some scheming snobby politician is trying to do behind our backs." There was a moment's pause. "And another thing. When he speaks to you again, you bloody listen, and you tell him what he wants to know. Other than that, you keep your trap shut. If he buggers off because of you, I'm going to put a bullet through your stupid head myself. Now think about it, darlin'."

The door swung back, and Tosh reappeared, his face creased with fury. He sat and lit a cigarette without looking at me. Jan struck a match and cupped his hands over the bowl of his pipe. Smoke drifted up from both men in silence. I could see the canal widening in the distance as we approached the main North Sea Canal leading to the dock area for ships coming and going to the North Sea.

"Thank you, Tosh," I muttered.

He and Jan said nothing, but both glanced at me and puffed smoke. As we slowly moved out into the canal, I had time to reflect on all that happened over last week. I had a choice, and despite the unresolved situation with Dianne, I knew, as she did, the story came first.

The air was fresh, and despite a chilly breeze, I enjoyed the salt air as we neared the main Ijmuiden lock area some two miles ahead. We were heading for a small canal called 'side canal C.' Jan had a trawler there we would take out into the North Sea on a journey to England when safe.

I decided to wait until we were on the trawler before tackling Valerie again. I had to know what happened the day Adam died and where she had hidden the diary. Valarie needed Adam to help get her to London, so it was obvious she had nothing to do with his death. Tosh needed to call his office, and I had to call Dianne and Max. I was going to do that before tackling the young woman in the cabin.

As darkness descended, it got colder. By the time we moored and transferred to the trawler, light rain was falling. Tosh suggested that I sit with Valerie and get as much as I could out of her, particularly the diary's hiding place. He seemed impatient when I told him I would wait until we had eaten and got comfortable in the trawler.

"You need to tackle her as soon as possible before she has a chance to change her mind again. I'd question her myself, but she'll trust you more than me." He was rubbing his hands together and stamping his feet against the cold. "Jan's stoking the boiler. It'll be warm enough in a short while. I'll go get us something to eat."

"She'll feel a little more secure if we're comfortable," I replied, nodding in agreement. "First, though, I have to call Dianne."

I left the trawler and walked along the dock to find a spot out of the blustery wind. I sheltered in the doorway of an office.

Dianne answered almost at once. "I take it you're on the move? Where are you going today?"

After I told her what had happened and where we were, she agreed to talk to Max and asked me to call her as soon as I had any more news.

"Be safe, Pete, and remember to call me the moment you

reach the safe house."

I put a hand to one ear to drown out the sudden noise of the trawler's big diesel engine. Thick black smoke rose from the stack and was caught in a downdraft that blew it down and along the deck. I was soon coughing. "Love you," I managed to shout, and then Dianne hung up.

Tosh, as always, was one step ahead. On reaching Amsterdam, he had arranged for two train tickets to go back to Prague and leave Valerie with Jan on the trawler where she was comparatively safe. That was if the diary was in Prague.

I was sure it was not in Amsterdam. Another thing bothered me. I had snatched two newspapers from the rail station and the hotel, but nothing appeared about Myer. I couldn't help thinking, 'Whitehall conspiracy.'

The crew's quarters on the trawler were dirty and smelled foul. I wrinkled my nose at the mess. The cabin was just below and forward of the bridge house. Six bunks occupied the cramped place. A table and two bench seats strewn with old newspapers was the only furniture in the other cabin—the galley walk-through led off that, an area no bigger than the inside of a car. White walls were speckled with red rust all over, and the stench of engine oil was overpowering.

I found enamel mugs in the galley and a battered tea-making kettle and bowl of sugar in a cupboard. There was no milk but plenty of tea.

The deck started to vibrate as the engine began heating the small radiators. I made the tea and stepped into the small eating area. Valerie sat quietly, smoking at the table. I pushed a mug in front of her and sat opposite her.

"I'm sorry about what happened earlier," I said. "I don't like seeing women hurt."

She smiled briefly. "Tosh was right about you. You are a gentleman."

"Let's get something clear," I said and took a sip of hot tea.

"You haven't told me much about the contents of the diary yet, but if you're right and something that affects our way of life is about to happen, then it's of paramount importance that you let me deal with it. For my part, I'll do all in my power to see you safely to London. After that, it's up to you."

She drew deeply on the cigarette and blew a long line of smoke into the air. "Okay, I understand."

"Good. So, let's get back to where we were before our falling out."

The door opened with a bang, and Tosh appeared in oilskins. "There's going be a storm, but not to worry. Jan's got us tied up neatly." He squeezed past me and shuffled into the small cubicle that served as a toilet. "Sorry. Got to see a man about a dog." With that, he closed the door and started whistling.

Valerie's mouth was open. A mystified expression on her face said it all. I put a hand to my mouth and muffled my laughter. We waited for Tosh to reappear.

"All, okay?" he asked.

I smiled. "We're fine, Tosh. Thank you."

Valerie's eyes followed Tosh out through the door.

"Okay, Valerie." I snapped my fingers at her. "Let's concentrate. I want to tie up all you know about Myer and what role he played in all this."

She wrapped both hands around the tea mug and shivered.

"Here, just a minute," I said. I stepped into the bunk cabin through an interconnecting iron door, pulled an old blanket from one of the bunks, and tossed it to her.

She stood, pulled it around her and sat. "I got to the flat after leaving Novotney's office. I was very upset. When Adam returned, he looked at the diary as I told him what had happened. He was very anxious and said he had to tell Charles Cranthorp. He said he was arranging for me to go to London, but I would have to see Cranthorp first and hand over the diary. We argued because handing it over meant they would not have to let me go

The Defector's Diary

to London."

Knowing SIS as I did, I did not blame her for thinking that way, or maybe she knew what would have happened if it had been her in Cranthorp's shoes. Wherever they work or play all agents are strange bedfellows, and from lessons learnt, I trusted none of them. Unfortunately, that included Tosh, even though he was a friendly contact.

"So, you argued," I prompted.

"Yes. I told Adam the killers had mentioned my name and I had to get away and hide, but I wasn't giving up the diary."

She seemed relieved to be shedding information. I sat listening, trying to interrupt as little as possible.

"Adam said he would go with me. I refused and told him he had to go to the Embassy or security would come looking for him. He became frightened and said the diary was a bomb waiting to go off, and that I should give it to Cranthorp. That's when he suggested we compromise, or at least let someone know about the diary apart from Mr Myer."

I stopped her there. "Myer. Tell me about Myer."

"I don't know a lot. Adam met him during lunchtime I stole the diary, as I said. Myer said he would help sort things out and that we should not give the diary to Cranthorp, or even let him know I had it, and I agreed. Myer wanted to have the diary, but I refused. Then I let Adam send a page to you. He had your address. He said you would help me get to London if anything happened to him."

"After you two came to an agreement, what happened then?"

"I left Adam at the apartment and went to a safe house with the diary."

"He was going to meet you at the café?"

"If he could, but we both knew different."

"How did you know to contact Myer?"

"Adam gave me Myer's details. He said he never met the man before that day, but Myer told him to stay away from me when they talked that afternoon. He also told Adam that Cranthorp would be after both of us because Prague had recalled me. Adam said if I needed any help in dealing with the diary, I should contact Myer." She sat smoking, occasionally warming a hand on the hot water pipe running to the radiator.

She stubbed the cigarette out in her mug. Good looking, she may be, I thought, but a lady—never.

"One last thing, Valerie. Who told you that Adam was dead?"

"Myer. He told me when I spoke to him the following day. He said the Embassy told him when he called to talk to Adam."

I could imagine how Adam must have felt. Caught in a web of deceit, he was a pawn of SIS who could easily manipulate him for other purposes. BIS knew he was ripe for plucking and was aware of his affair with Valerie and association with SIS.

Myer, on the Steerage Committee of Bilderberg, was beginning to look like a bad guy again. I wondered if it was just coincidence that Tosh snapped him on the Charles Bridge. But why was he there? I knew what Cranthorp was doing there. Either Myer was following him, hoping to find Valerie, or was Cranthorp following Myer?

"Okay, so you contacted Myer."

"Yes. I told Myer that Adam sent you a card with the letter arranging where to meet. Myer said he would collaborate with me to make sure I got to London. We met later and arranged the first note I gave you in the café, and then the second at the hotel after we aborted at the bridge."

"Why was that?"

"I spotted Cranthorp."

"Did you also see Myer?"

"No."

I thanked her for the information and told her to catnap for an hour. I needed to think. Myer was lying. No embassy would give that kind of information to an EU trade secretary, no matter who he had an appointment with. I left Valerie curled up and pulled the iron door open. The cold wind caught my breath, and salt spray stung my face as I stepped over the curved metal lip of the door coaming and out onto the deck. The door, captured by the strong wind, crashed shut.

I stood at the top of the ladder leading down to the engine room, letting the wind clear my head a little. The more I got involved in Adam's death, the more I realized that unless the New Order's ambition to create a world governing body was stopped, the world could experience a collective dictatorship that would have a firm grip on the population.

Adam may not have realized this, or maybe he did, but I was determined to at least warn Westminster. That was if I could get hold of the diary.

Chapter Nineteen

I LOOKED AT TOSH AS I STOOD NEXT TO HIM on the bridge.

"Well, we know quite a bit more now, and who we can trust."

There was a green glow on the small bridge from the control panel.

"No one, guv. We trust no one. That's where people make mistakes. I know you don't trust politicians, especially the kind we're dealing with." He chuckled. "You'd be out of work if you trusted the buggers."

The door slid open and Jan entered, bringing with him a cold blast of air. "Eats are on the table," he announced with a wide grin. "I think the woman wants to talk to you. I told her I'd get her smokes only if she wanted to talk." He held up a packet of cigarettes.

"Now that's convenient. I wonder where those came from," I said.

Tosh had introduced me to Jan, and that was all. I learned in the past not to ask but to trust Tosh's judgement. For all I knew, Jan was someone to be relied on because Tosh said so.

"Things seem to be looking up," I remarked. I put a hand on Tosh's shoulder. "Everything is nicely arranged, but I'm thinking too well arranged."

Without turning, Tosh said, "As soon as we got on Jan's boat, I figured London will be looking for Myer to arrive in Brussels. I've also filled them in—not SIS—on the reliable info you gave me to keep them happy. It won't be too long before we have to start spilling the beans—and not only to my office, but SIS as

The Defector's Diary

well."

"I can't do a damn thing," I said, "until we have the diary, and Valerie won't reveal its whereabouts until she's in London. That's the first problem to solve. We also can't tell anyone where she is. We don't know who the bad guys are in the New Order. We have to get her back on our own."

"I hear you. We'll sort something out, guv. Don't worry." Tosh turned his face sideways. "I know you hate me for what I did to her, and I'm sorry about that, but she needed to know who was in charge, and quick too."

"I don't hate you. I understand, but I'd appreciate it if you could use some psychology on her first if there's a next time. We're not SIS."

Tosh shrugged. "I'm ex-SIS, and I used psychology. The imprint of my fingers on her pretty cheek is proof of that."

We left the bridge to eat and check on Valerie. A bowl of steaming stew greeted us. She was already eating. Jan tossed the cigarettes onto the table.

"Okay," I said, "I can help you, but I can only do so much sitting here on a barge. Say we look at the diary and you do some unravelling of the code I'm told the entries are written in." I turned to Tosh. "I'm sure he has some plan to get us back to London as well, and he can explain it to us."

Valerie stopped eating and looked at me to Tosh. "I trust you," she said, looking at me, "but I do not trust Tosh."

"Is this going to lead to another problem?" I asked. "Where is the diary?"

"Burnt. I burnt it after copying it onto a stick. I have it safe."

"How the hell do we know that for sure?" Tosh glared at her. "Of all the tricks in the book. A copy. Why did you burn the thing? If I were in your shoes, I would keep the diary in case SIS did the dirty on you. Here's another thing. If SIS got hold of you, they would assume you still had the original and make you tell them where it was." He looked at me. "Guv, the original is still hidden. You can bet on it."

Valerie shook her head. "That's what I should have done, but I wasn't thinking. I was scared after hearing they killed Adam. I can only tell you the original is gone, and I have a copy."

I believed her. "Let's calm down. After eating, Valerie and I can run this through my laptop. She can have the stick back, so she has insurance that gets her to London. In exchange, she can help me decipher the important stuff we're looking for."

Tosh nodded. "I'm doubtful about what she did with the diary, but yes, I agree we should work on the information as soon as possible."

We finished the meal in silence, and Jan got a powerline fixed from the jetty facilities hut. With the setup complete, I was about to tidy up with a few more questions before getting onto the diary when my phone rang. It was Dianne. She got straight to the point.

"My phone has not stopped ringing. Richard Hart for once is on your side and said to thank you for sparing him a lot of embarrassment, but only if you succeed at getting the diary, of course. He didn't seem too concerned about the girl."

"Of course not. What about Max?"

"Max, I'm afraid, had no choice. The Cross descended on his office, and they've been with him all day trying to find out where you and the girl are. He did bring them up to date without telling them where you are, though. Apart from harbouring a fugitive wanted by every security service and police force in Europe, you're in the clear."

"Oh, gosh," I joked. "I still get a life sentence, though."

"Yes, and someone with a Whitehall number called to let us know they knew we were friends with Tosh. If we don't let them know where he is, we'd be charged with perverting the course of justice."

"Looks as though they're ganging up on me, but Hart can talk to his friend at Number Ten and get me a 'get out of jail free' card."

"Stop joking, Pete. You're at the sharp end again, and you'll have to do some fancy step-dancing to avoid the fallout from your escapade." There was silence before she realised her mistake. "Pete, I'm sorry. I should have said, 'my escapade'. Sorry."

"Okay, Tosh and I will put our heads together and come up with a way to get Valerie back home." I ended the call and looked at her.

She rose, and I stopped her. "You heard we're planning to get you back to England, so I need you to keep to your side of the bargain. Where is the copy?"

"No, the arrangement is that I give it to you when I reach safety."

She looked nervous but defiant as Tosh leaned over her and grabbed both arms of her chair. He lowered his face to hers.

"Tell you what, darlin'. You wanna' keep the stick, that's fine. I'm gonna call my colleagues who have nothing to do with SIS and tell them where you are. The Guvnor here and me will bugger off and leave you here. I guarantee you won't get off this barge before they've caught you and beaten the crap out of you for the location of that damned diary. After that, you won't be worth a penny piece to anyone except your people, and I'll call them at the same time. Okay?"

Valerie's eyes flickered. "How do I know you'll get me to England?"

"You don't know, dear, but Pete's a gentleman who's risking his bloody life for you. I'm not a gentleman." Tosh leaned over her. "Stop acting like a schoolgirl and tell him what he wants to know or I start rearranging your teeth."

Fight drained out of her, and she looked dejected. "I can't go back to Prague. My people will kill me," she said softly.

I gave Tosh's jacket a little tug, and he stepped out of the way.

"Valerie," I said gently. "Listen to me. There is little chance that your secret service is going to get you back. I know you're worried, but you have to trust me. I'm not putting myself in harm's way to help you if you continue being uncooperative. Tosh and I will sort out how we're going to get you to London. I'm on the run too. SIS is looking for me as well as you, so we both need to trust one another. Tell me. Did Myer or Adam recommend that you copy the diary?"

"No. Adam suggested I send the diary to a friend who could keep it for me. He said it should be someone I knew well and trusted. That's what he said about you, that I should trust you. I kept the diary and copied it. I put it into a bucket and burned it when I finished."

Tosh and I exchanged glances. Perhaps poorly trained or a good actress, she should have known that her handler fully logged every minute of her life and those of the people she knew, all listed in a file with her name on the cover.

"Where is the stick?" I asked. "We need answers now if we're to stop these people from doing whatever it is they have planned in a few weeks' time."

"You'll have to let me go to the powder room." She smiled. "I've had it on me all the time."

Tosh's reaction was one of anger. "You think that will satisfy SIS or anyone else you talk to about asylum? Where is the original?" He stood over her threateningly.

"I told you, I burnt it," she replied, looking at me.

"Liar!"

I moved in front of Tosh as he took a step forward. "That's not going to get us anywhere," I said. "Why don't we look at what we have and worry about the original afterward. If she has copies of the diary, we can at least work out what Novotney knew about the meetings just before his death."

For the second time, I asked myself if Novotney and Myer were the only two who knew that Novotney kept secret notes on the New Order's meetings. How did the New Order know of the diary's existence? Cranthorp came to mind, but I kept the

The Defector's Diary

thought to myself.

"I told you," said Valerie firmly. "I burned the diary at the safe house in the Jewish quarter after using the internet café equipment. I stayed there until it was completely gone."

"Bloody liar," Tosh protested. "Pete, she's lying. You can bet the original is hidden somewhere as her insurance. I'll swear to it." He turned to me. "Let me get the truth from her. Five minutes is all I need."

Valerie excused herself and went to the bathroom.

I glared at Tosh. "No," I said. "We do this my way. And I think it might be a good idea if you went and had a smoke with Jan and calmed down. I know you're the intel agent, but as I see things, both of us are in trouble over this diary. If we're to avoid a spell at Her Majesty's pleasure, I suggest you listen to me. In our situation, it's me who has the contacts to get us out of this predicament. Don't you think?"

Without a word, Tosh stomped out of the cabin and slammed the door after him.

I turned to Valerie, who just returned. "Now, let's start again," I said.

She held out a memory stick. "It's all on there. Thank you for intervening." As she sat and looked at the stick in my hand, I could tell she was frightened. Everything she had to exchange for asylum had gone. The diary was in my hands, and she had nowhere else to go, and no one else to trust. I felt sorry for her. No more than in her early twenties, she was looking at the prospect of being shot as a traitor. I kept my feelings to myself. There was still something out of place about her.

I pulled out my laptop and set it up. After inserting the stick, I waited. "Okay, let's see what we have here."

The entries for each day were quite straightforward, some in English, but most in Czech.

"When was the last entry?" I mumbled more to myself than to her.

"It would perhaps be one day before Novotney was killed because as you know, this diary does not have entries every day like his business diary."

I ran down the pages to the day before Novotney died. "Tell me," I asked her. "What was it you saw when you first opened this diary that made you realize this could be your ticket to England?"

"An entry for the seventh of August. It says there will be a bomb in the house. That is all it said, but the Commissioner was an honest man and I believed what he had written about a bomb. When I told Adam, he thought it might mean the Houses of Parliament."

I figured that was the point at which Adam had laid his life on the line. He knew about the entry before Valerie stole it. The fool had fallen in love, and despite arguing with her after she took it, she refused to give the diary to SIS or the Embassy. He had given in to her and let her walk away.

"Well before that, of course, you told Adam who you were. Where did Charles Cranthorp come into the picture?"

"Cranthorp met me after I contacted SIS through Adam, offering them information in exchange for asylum. Cranthorp suggested I start feeding my own side little unimportant bits of information. He suggested that Adam and I pretend we were getting married, although Adam wanted that for real. So that is what we did. Charles met Adam at weekends for a month socially to keep an eye on us. I promised I had something for him, but I did not have anything. Charles got angry and said he would report me to my station. It was a day after that last meeting with him that I found the diary. When I told Charles, he told me to get the diary and I would be sent to London. What I did not know was that he had already arranged something for me to feed my station. Material I would not normally manage."

"He did the dirty on you, and that's why we have your people chasing us, as well as SIS and the New Order."

The Defector's Diary

"I'm afraid so. But Adam should have gone to his Embassy. I told him to do that before I left. I think it was the New Order that killed him."

"I don't think, Valerie. I know." I refilled my cup with tea while she scrolled to the page she was referring to. The entry was in Czech. There was a curious doodle next to the date: A1 to B2."

"There are quite a lot of those figures and letters," she said as I looked over her shoulder. "I don't know what they mean. They're in the back of the diary."

Sure enough, they were. I sat trying to fathom what the entries meant. I pulled the tablet in front of me and scrolled back to the week before the Commissioner died. There was an entry on one page written in Czech that read, The King of the House will amend his speech," I said. She looked at me and shrugged.

I returned to the page I had first seen A1 to B2 and then back to the list at the back. Letters and digits ran in lines, and every so often, the A1 to B2 was inserted in brackets. Each set consisted of a letter and a number, then the word 'to', followed by another letter and digit.

"This is a crude code," I said, "I'm damned if I can make heads or tails of any message, but I know what the clues are constructed from."

The A1 to B2 was written next to a little drawing of what looked like a castle turret. "Chess!" I exclaimed. "The man played a lot of chess. Vilma, his secretary, told me he played a lot of chess, particularly online. Of course." I snapped my fingers.

"And A1 to B2 is a move that happens more than any other," added Valerie.

I made a note of all the listed groups at the back of the book and pulled up a chessboard picture. Across the board, the squares were notated from A to G and vertically 1 to 8. I was still mystified. A1 to B2 was a key, I thought. However, A1 was a castle. It could not move to B2 because it was not allowed to move diagonally. In any case, the pawn on B2 would be in the way.

"Perhaps we should play the game," suggested Valerie, "using the moves Jozef has written down."

Our conversation was interrupted by Tosh, accompanied by Jan. They both looked cold.

"A bit too drafty for me, guv. Any luck?" Tosh stood over me, hands in pockets, while Jan walked into the galley. "Sorry, I was a little short back there," said Tosh. "This whole thing is turning into a nightmare. I've got my people on my back now."

I acknowledged the apology but said nothing. While Jan was making tea, I filled Tosh in.

"So," I concluded, "we're just about to play a game using the group of moves Novotney wrote down."

Valerie had drawn a chessboard in my notebook, numbered and lettered the squares.

"White plays first," she said. "I move A2 to A3."

I replied, "Black A7 to A5."

"A3 to A4." she came back.

The next move was in brackets. A1 to B2. As A2 had been moved, it meant that A1, the castle, could move into that square, but that was an illegal move. "That has to be a stop…a full stop…the end of whatever those three steps meant. But what do they mean?" I sat studying the three alternating moves. As in chess, the white moved first and then black. Something puzzled me.

"All these moves go up and down. Some move two spaces and others one. It doesn't make any sense."

"A bomb will explode in the House," Forst reminded me. "Maybe I'll save a lot of lives, and they'll let me have asylum."

Chapter Twenty

Tosh shook his head. "I don't think you should let Max know what you have here just yet. Maybe Novotney was guessing. After all, this information is now almost three weeks old."

The thought there was a bomb threat sent shivers through me. I had no choice despite Tosh's argument. I called Max right away.

"This entry is weeks old, Max, but if security is informed, at least I'll get a few handshakes."

"Leave it with me. I'll call you back shortly."

Within ten minutes, Max was back. "Pete, this is from the Cross. As you have the diary and no one knows who from the government or industry is involved, they want you to hold onto Forst until an agent contacts you. I told them I didn't know where you are, and you're using those throwaway phones. It's up to you, but you should contact them so she can be picked up. Forst will be brought to London and will spend a long time in a safe house being debriefed. Have you got all that?"

"Yes, but I have Tosh here already."

"I was referring to an agent from the Cross. Tosh retired a year ago. Someone I trust in SIS and with whom I had a long conversation gave me one piece of information once she knew Tosh was involved. She is linking Tosh to the United British Legion Party. He's off the rails, Pete. Watch your step."

Tosh was standing behind me, and I hoped he hadn't heard Max. The hair went up on the back of my neck.

"That's fine, Max," I replied, trying to sound businesslike. "In the meantime, I'll try to sort out more information in the diary."

Max's contact within SIS was well known to a lot of media people. Sarah Burns was Deputy Director of SIS and someone Max had known for many years as she moved from Blair's cabinet to security at the Cross some eight years earlier. It was clear I had a 'get out of jail free' card, but I had not gotten out of trouble yet. Tosh was now a worry.

"What's happening, guv?" asked Tosh.

I looked concerned. "Well, we started to unearth the Commissioner's entries, but I have a feeling we're going to be at this for most of the night."

"Max said something about me?"

"I told him you were with us and helping with decoding the diary, and that got the two of us some brownie points."

Whether Tosh was working for another department, despite Sarah Burns' warning or not, I was wary. Whitehall was good at playing hide and seek between different departments.

"We're waiting for an agent buddy of yours to come and pick up Valerie. Meanwhile, you and I can continue. I think we should maybe look for another safe place that's a lot warmer than this tub. Right now, I don't think it a good idea to tell anyone where we are." I grinned at Jan. "Sorry, I wish I was warmer, but the tea was my brand."

Jan grinned back, and I downloaded a copy of the diary to my laptop.

"That's all very well letting Max have information, guv, but suppose the New Order finds out that he and Security are alerted. Their plan might be brought forward. You could be playing straight into their hands. Max could be in danger, and so could Dianne."

I was well aware of the risks. Dianne was in Cannes and Max would have Security looking after him.

Valerie still seemed apprehensive, especially when Tosh appeared. He might have been correct in his assumptions, and she may well have hidden the diary instead of burning it. It would

The Defector's Diary

most certainly be an essential piece of insurance if the stick she gave me missed some intelligence we needed. We would not know that until the contents of what we had were deciphered.

"I appreciate your concerns and your advice, Tosh. You're the expert, and I hope you're wrong, but we have to start working on what we have."

He thumbed his nose at me. "Okay, what you have there is beyond me. I have never played chess, so I guess you should figure it out."

I caught a relieved look on Valerie's face as Tosh left us. He had not threatened or looked at her, so why the reaction of relief, unless she was guarding the truth and had nearly been found out.

"Valerie," I said and reached out to touch her hand. "I am hoping you know by now that I can be trusted and that if I say you're going to get to London, you will." I squeezed her hand. "Let's do this together and we'll get to London a lot faster."

She sat quietly, thinking things through before she answered. "Tosh will lose his temper, and he might report me or even shoot me himself." Her eyes told me all I needed to know. Frightened but determined, like many other people in the Eastern bloc, she was prepared to risk her life for freedom and democracy in the West.

"No, he won't," I answered. "I'll go see him now if you tell me the diary is hidden somewhere. I'm sure he'll be pleased to know he was right not to believe you."

She shrugged and took a deep breath. "Yes," she whispered. "I have the diary. Please talk to Tosh."

"I'll do that right away," I said.

"Not all of the information is on the stick. You'll need the diary." She lowered her eyes and looked uncomfortable.

I snorted and shook my head, annoyed at being played by her.

Jan brought a blanket from the other cabin and wrapped it around her shoulders as I got up to find Tosh.

Smoke drifted from the bridge window and disappeared as

gusts of wind caught it. Tosh stood inside the door as I entered.

"Okay, so it's time for me to say sorry once again. I'm getting fed up getting things wrong, so I hope I can redeem myself by cracking that code tonight."

"You're kidding me, guv." His face mellowed into a wide grin.

"You was right, but I don't like the way you're treating her. She's scared of you and what you represent. That might not be in your favor later on. Anyway, I told her we're going to London. In the meantime, we need to break that code. I suggest you sit in with us. That way, I don't have to go through it all again."

Tosh dug me in the ribs. "Okay, I'll play mister nice guy, guv. Would you Adam and Eve it," he said with a wide grin.

Outside, the weather had gone from bad to worse. With the wind growing stronger, the rain fell like a whip stinging my face. On entering the main cabin, Tosh held his hands up apologetically and half smiled.

"I'm sorry I was so rude, Valerie. I promise you, I'll be with you going to London."

I wondered if he meant that as I turned to her. "What happened to the diary?"

"I put it in the left luggage locker at the Prague railway station. The key is with Ivan, a friend who lives in Amsterdam. He said it was the best thing to do."

Tosh and I looked at each other and sighed. Whoever the friend was, he was in danger if the New Order found out.

"Write down the address and name of your friend, and if you can remember, the locker number," said Tosh.

I had Jan make our coffee. It looked like we were going to be up all night. A short while later, I had the list of moves written neatly in the order Novotney jotted them. I had also drawn a larger chessboard and numbered and lettered the squares.

I completed seven sets of moves. Some sets involved three or four moves, while one had just one move. At the end of each set was that puzzling move, A1 to B2.

The Defector's Diary

"Don't make any sense," said Tosh, looking over Valerie's shoulder.

It began to make sense to me.

"The Commissioner played chess every day and, by all accounts, was a good player. He played online. What we need to find out is what two squares or only one represent."

"How about writing down next to each move the number of squares involved." Tosh put a hand to his mouth. "Blimey, I think I've got it."

With the group of moves I already completed, I wrote against each step either one tick or two.

"My dad taught me something after the war," Tosh remarked. "He was a bigwig with the RAF, and his hobby when I was a lad was to tune into the ships in the Thames waiting for a pilot to take them to the docks. He would listen for ages to Morse code and write dots and dashes, and then write them into words." He pointed with excitement at the list. "Go on. I'll bet I'm right. One move is a dot, and two is a dash." He turned to Jan. "Each line going down the board has two or more moves of dashes and dots that spell a word ending with the false move, meaning full stop."

I turned to Jan. "Fetch a copy of Morse if you got one on the bridge."

I hoped Tosh was right and, at the same time, knew it was unlikely he was not of the New Order, even if he had some strange ideas about politics. Maybe his experiences in the old MI5 had given him a twisted view of democracy, but I was sure if he had ideas on what we were doing, he would keep them to himself.

With the manual that Jan came back with, we went over the sets. Each set, according to Tosh's guess, spelt a letter. When I finished, we all looked at one word: ROSEBUD.

"What a clever old geezer Jozef was," said Tosh.

I agreed. I looked at Valerie. "You're tired. Why not get some sleep? Tomorrow, Tosh and I will have a plan of action."

I waited for her to leave and set about discovering the other sets of letters. Although I did not want to contemplate it, if Valerie was to be taken, she would know nothing about the code except the one word: Rosebud. It took another two hours. By the time we were finished, we had the words, but nothing that made sense as a message. There were four words and one number: Rosebud, Dedham, Sept 17, Fast.

Seventeen had been written next to the moves spelling Sept. We also had the original message on the back of the letter Adam sent me, and the message Valerie pointed out, a bomb in the house. We needed more. All I could do at that moment was guess. And what on earth did Fast mean? It could be a name or something that had to be done at once. The one thing that did stand out was the date. Could that be the date the bomb was going to explode in the House of Commons?

I sat with Tosh for some time afterwards.

"I'm supposed to let my people know where I am, and they're obliged to tell the Cross." Tosh sighed. "Whatever we do, it has to happen in a few hours."

"Let's sort out the best way to get the diary and Valerie to London," I said. "You can bet on it the Czechs will be falling over themselves to get her back."

"I should go to Amsterdam and collect the key," said Tosh. "You could watch my back for a change, guv, and take over if I'm caught or diverted for some reason. I'll sort some details out later."

I didn't like the idea. It was too risky, and besides, the New Order knew what I looked like up close.

"I hate to suggest it, but we need someone to give the key to who can open the locker and take the diary for us. That should be Dianne."

Tosh thought for a moment. "That won't work. She's as well-known as you."

"Not if she's disguised. A different hairstyle, a pair of jeans and a stupid T-shirt with a slogan. The only thing is, I'm not exactly in her good books right now."

Tosh wrinkled his nose. "Mrs W will say yes, guv. Women love being part of a dangerous plot." He winked. "Especially crackers like her."

I wanted to laugh, but it was ridiculous to ask Dianne, especially with our home life the way it was.

"I'll give her a ring in the morning," I said. My thoughts turned to Forst as I tried to get comfortable.

She lay asleep in the trawler cabin. That one so young held a diary having secrets that might one day be the cause of catastrophic political upheaval was a sobering thought. Not knowing how many different groups were involved in chasing the diary added to the danger and confusion. We both dozed off, sitting in our chairs.

The aroma of coffee and the sound of heavy rain battering the cabin roof woke me from a light nap. Tosh, yawning, was standing by the table cutting bread. A faint sizzle from the stove announced the arrival of eggs and bacon. Valerie sat at the table drinking coffee. I threw off the blanket someone covered me with and stretched. My body ached from the awkward position I lounged in the seat.

"Good morning, Valerie," I said and grabbed the offered coffee.

Valerie mumbled something and stared into her cup. She had managed to sleep well. Her hair was a mess, and the half-closed eyes were fighting to stay open.

Tosh had cooked all the bacon and made some omelettes. Although the weather outside was bad, the breakfast put us all in a good mood.

"So, what's the plan to get me to England?" asked Valerie.

"You don't have to worry about that," replied Tosh. He went to the window. "Jan'll be looking after you. I talked to him last night." He turned, his head inclined. "You do as he tells you, but most important of all, stay inside until we're ready to move you."

I joined him at the window. "Bloody weather. I've just checked my tablet," I said, looking at the sky. "It's supposed to get worse before it gets better."

I got into the habit of turning my tablet off and only turning it on for a couple of minutes at a time since Tosh obtained some throwaway phones. I reminded him we only had two left.

Black clouds hung low in the sky as far as the eye could see, and the dockyard outside was littered with large pools of water. I planned to leave as soon as possible after I shaved, relieved to find that Tosh, as usual, brought everything we needed, including a gun. I hoped it would not be used. Ten minutes later, I ran through the pouring rain to a small service hut to call Dianne.

"Hi, there," I said cheerily. "We have a plan to get Valerie and the diary to London. There's one problem, though. I—"

"You want me to do something. You do know I'm in Cannes, don't you? It's where Father thought it a good idea I stay out of danger, and you agreed."

I sighed. "Well, yes, you're right, and I wouldn't ask, but I don't think you would object. I want someone to buy a key to the left luggage lockers at Prague station. Then with another key that I'll give you, retrieve the diary from one locker and put it in the locker you paid for."

"Am I to be disguised?" asked Dianne. "And when is this scene from a James Bond movie going to take place?"

I couldn't tell whether she was joking or being sarcastic.

"I'm taking a train to Amsterdam to get the key today, and then I'll be at Prague station at seven-thirty in the morning. As we bump into each other in the left luggage hall, I'll pass the key to you, and then you buy a locker before making the switch. What do you think?"

"And what do I do with the key to the new locker hiding the diary?"

"Tosh will be watching your every move, and you give him

the key as soon as you leave the luggage office."

"If all goes well, what are you going to do about Valerie?"

I explained that I discussed this at length with Tosh, and the only solution we could arrive at was to get her to the ferry terminal hidden in the trunk of a car, then smuggle her through the port of Dover.

"Well, that might work, and it doesn't matter too much if you get caught. She would be in safe hands of UK Immigration. You and Tosh will have Whitehall save your skins and you give Downing Street the diary."

I waited, knowing she had more to say. Two years of marriage taught me women like having the final word and Dianne had not finished – yet.

"I won't have much time to do this, so I guess I'll pack," said Dianne. "I can get a taxi flight this afternoon. One day, preferably sooner rather than later, we might have a proper conversation on the telephone. And before you say anymore, I feel a lot better, but we'll have a long talk when you come home, and it will be without the phone ringing or listening to Max. Talking of Max, make sure you let him know what's going on."

"Of course," I said.

"Right, then. I'll see you in the booking hall at seven-thirty tomorrow morning."

"Thank you," I said quietly.

She hung up, and that was that. I was pleased, though, that she seemed to be in a good mood and was agreeable without any reservations about being part of our plan. Now, all I had to do was have a last-minute talk with Tosh and Jan before we started.

Valerie was sitting smoking in one corner, no longer self-assured, but looking like a bored teenager. She had changed into baggy jeans and a thick woollen jumper that must have been Jan's.

"Let's have five minutes together and make sure we all know what's going to happen." I looked across at Valerie. "You too.

We all need to know what we're about."

"I've got the address of her friend," said Tosh and looked at Valerie. "If he isn't in, we might have to break in. If you can raise him in the meantime, you have to let him know that we're friends and just need the key. Also, let him know not to mouth off to anyone about you or the key. Nothing, right?"

"I'll try to call him every thirty minutes," she said. "I did tell him to hide the key in his house and not carry it about."

Tosh had given her a phone but took the precaution of letting Jan hold onto it.

"Then let's run through the timetable," said Tosh sitting at the table and grabbed some tea Jan set down. "Pete and I will travel separately from the local station to catch the train to Amsterdam. When we arrive, I'll work alone. The idea is that if either of us hits trouble, the other one will execute the rest of the plan. We hope that Ivan, Valerie's friend, will be in and we'll have the key. Whatever happens, we have to have the key by tonight, as Dianne will meet Pete in the morning. With luck, we'll then have the diary and be on the way back here."

"I'll make sure we're safe here until you return. The girl will be ready to move as soon as you call me," said Jan. "She'll need water and food for the journey. Shall I go out to get something?"

"No." Both Tosh and I said at the same time. "I'll get some stuff on the way back," said Tosh.

A car horn outside sounded. "Our cab," said Tosh. "We'll see you two tomorrow night or the following morning."

With that, we were both off the trawler and down to the quayside. The wind was bitter, and I wished I had gloves. Seconds later, my nose and earlobes were red from the cold. We sat in the rear of the cab rubbing our hands and pulled up collars.

The drab area of dockyards and canals on such a dismal day made me yearn to be home with a woman I loved so much. Someone I dearly wanted to hug and have her forgive me. I looked at the passing collage of bony tree fingers pointing rigidly up against the grey buildings into a black and grey sky.

I thought of Dianne and the colour she brought to my life. It was hard to believe that in a day, I would see her for a brief moment, and I wished I could forget Valerie, the diary, and go home.

I concentrated on the day's plans and called Max.

"It's me. I wanted to know what was going on at your end. Has Hart been to see the PM yet?"

Max sounded excited. "Yes, he has, and the dung has hit every fan in Whitehall, but strangely, SIS is quiet. Richard told the PM only about your discovery that Novotney died for a diary that holds information relating to a secret group within the Bilderberg Club. He said nothing else, so give the man his dues. He's hoping you'll hit the jackpot. Of course, Number Ten is duty-bound to call in the Cross, and spookies are running around everywhere."

"There are some spookies, Max, who already know the whole story. Everything is confusing. That's why we're trying to get Valerie and the diary back by ourselves, and then decide who the right guy is to hand it over to."

"Well, Hart and I think you've got hold of something huge. Officially, go for it, but be careful. Unfortunately, a story like this will be watered down if it ever gets into print. By the way, what's happening with Dianne? Is she with you now?"

The cab swerved onto the railway terminal slip road and pulled up outside the main entrance. I handed a couple of notes to the driver and got out.

"She'll be with me in the morning," I said as the cab drove away. "I'm boarding a train now for Amsterdam."

"One interesting thing, Pete. It looks as though the bloody CIA is running a joint operation with SIS and the Czechs, so be very careful. Hart warned us to keep our mouths shut. Whatever's in that diary is something your Joe public can never know, certainly not the whole truth.

"Our embassy sent Downing Street a report on Michael Myer's disappearance and Adam Denton's death. It will read a lot different from the one you've given me. A couple of hours after the report reached Number Ten, there was a total clamp-down on press inquiries regarding Novotney's death. That means all our competitors are wondering what's going on and are joining the race for information. Hart is collaborating with our lawyers to find a way around the Official Secrets Act to at least get a hint of a connection between the Bilderberg group and Novotney's death."

I stopped at a small kiosk and bought a paper, the phone held precariously on my shoulder. "Okay, Max," I said. "One last thing. There have been two related deaths, and I don't believe our security services are involved even if they have mucked up the police investigations. I'm now sure we're dealing with thugs hired by a secret group within the primary Bilderberg organization."

"Then take double care of yourself. For Christ's sake, don't take any risks. Have you still got Tosh with you?"

"Yes, we're going to find the key to get the diary and then make the switch in Prague."

With that, I walked briskly to the platform and boarded the train. It was full, but I managed to squeeze into a window seat. Two minutes later, the train left for Central Amsterdam. My eyes were shut.

Chapter Twenty-One

AN HOUR LATER, I STEPPED OUT onto the platform and walked to the exit. It still rained. I caught a glimpse of Tosh as he headed smartly toward the trams, hands in pockets and looking like a local. I called him as he boarded a tram.

"There could be anyone following you, but I don't see anything suspicious. What do you want me to do? Incidentally, I only have one more phone in my pocket, and that's it."

"No worries, guv. Leave that to me. Here's what I'm going to do. I'll take a taxi to Ivan's address and, if necessary, break in. If you can, grab a taxi to that address, but stop short of the block he lives in, and try to find a vantage point where you can keep an eye on my back. When I have the key, I'll call but don't hang around. Get the hell out, and I'll see you back at the hotel."

I could imagine Tosh inside the apartment getting caught by his old SIS mates. His instruction to escape quickly made sense, but that could also be a double-edged sword. While I ran for cover, Tosh could easily take the diary and have me and Valerie captured. I gave the situation some thought, but decided if Tosh was going to do that, it would probably be later when we were back with Valerie and Jan.

I didn't spot him entering the rundown block of apartments twenty minutes later. A sad sign that hung over one of the balconies advertised apartments for rent. At the entrance, cracked concrete steps—small weeds poked between the cracks—were worn. In a couple of places, they looked spattered with white paint. I wondered how anyone could live in such a dirty place. A large KFC box in the gutter was dragged noisily under my taxi as it pulled onto the curb. My thoughts were with Tosh, and I willed him to get out of the apartment as quickly as possible.

My phone rang. It was Tosh. "Hi, there, any luck?"

I have no idea how extrasensory powers work or why one has premonitions. All I know is that they do occur. I felt something extraordinary and unpleasant while it took Tosh several seconds to answer.

"Hello, guv." His voice was strangely soft, and I could hear a bird chirp in the background. "Got here about fifteen minutes ago," he continued. "Bad news. He's a stiff, and the place is ransacked. He's got one in the chest and another in the head. Pro job, guv."

I looked up at the apartments and slowly shook my head. Three bodies and I began to understand why SIS would send an active agent back to their people even though they knew what would happen to the agent. It was a dirty branch of security and not in the least romantic. Valerie had a wish to live in the West, but were three deaths acceptable? As Tosh said, if they had the diary, Valerie would be looking for a bullet from her own side. I took a deep breath and realized that SIS would be on my tail, and I'd have to tell Max about this death. I pushed the thought out of my mind.

"Oh, bloody hell, Tosh. Our friends have called again, but did they leave empty-handed? Have you found the key?"

"No, guv, and it should be here. Even if they found it, I doubt they would know what it was for unless it's marked. I'll keep looking, and when I leave, I'll call this in via London. They can update the police. That way, London stays in the loop and know you're not involved—sort of."

"Thanks." I half smiled. Whether London knew or thought I was somewhere else, they would know I was involved, and of course, so did Tosh, but he was trying to give me a mental hug that showed we were all in the soup together.

"Get out of there as quickly as possible. It could have been

The Defector's Diary

them watching or following you earlier."

Tosh suddenly cursed as something crashed.

"What's going on?" I asked.

"It's okay. I just tripped over a computer cable and pulled over the monitor."

"Are you—"

"Hey! Guess what? The damn key just dropped out of the back of the monitor. It was taped inside the back cover."

Out of the corner of my eye, I noticed a car pull onto the sidewalk. The way it came in at some speed made me turn and look. The front door opened and out jumped a man I did not recognize, but I knew from how he looked and acted, he was no salesperson. He was someone Tosh did not want to meet. I called Tosh.

Without giving him a chance to speak, I hissed, "Get out now. There must have been someone watching."

Without waiting for him, I took my own advice and started to walk quickly down the road. I dodged beneath an awning of a small kiosk and strode to the newsvendor on the other side of the street. There were no stories on the front page of any newspaper, but one showed Novotney's face and a short article about his death.

I bought the paper and resumed my walk. Again, a sudden feeling that something was not right made me look over my shoulder in time to see Cranthorp jump out of a second car outside the block. I began running along the street to a trolley stop. The line there ran into the city center, and all I could do was hope that Tosh would get out of the apartment without bumping into Cranthorp.

I did not have to wait long for a tram, glad it wasn't full. Thankful for a seat, I sat and tried to regain my breath. Sweat and prickly heat under my layers of clothing made me feel very uncomfortable. My chest heaved and thumped as I loosened my coat. Five minutes later my worries disappeared as I walked down the street from the trolley stop to the hotel Tosh said we were to meet after getting the key.

Almost predictably, Tosh was leaning against the wall, wearing a big grin. "You're getting used to all this, guv. I can tell."

My hands were shaking. "If I could, Tosh, I'd throttle you just for the sheer satisfaction."

He laughed. "Well, we have the key, guv, so don't get all upset. You did a good job warning me, and that's all you had to do. I missed the buggers by seconds, thank you. Let's have something to eat and talk about tomorrow morning." He waved a hand up the road. "Don't worry, they'll be looking for the diary, not a key. A quick search and they'll leave thinking we or the New Order have it, especially after finding a body. Cranthorp knows the only way to find the diary is to follow us. We have to lose him."

As always, Tosh seemed oblivious to the danger. But at least his mind was working how we would bypass those following us.

"What do you think we should do in the morning?" I asked as we found a table. "Do we change our plans?"

A waiter came with menus and took an order for drinks.

Tosh sat sideways with legs crossed, a curious habit, but he always ate like that. I once asked him about it. He told me it was quicker to get out of the chair and get away than having both legs under the table. He was taught this by a tragic incident in the Middle East when in the Army. His company sergeant-major was killed while they were eating in a restaurant. A terrorist walked in and pointed a gun at them. He managed to kill the sergeant-major, who took too long to get his legs out from under the table. Tosh had developed several strange habits, but all of them made sense.

"I think we start as planned. Dianne is going to be on the platform at seven-thirty, and we'll let her have the key." He paused briefly. "I know you want to be with her and make up, but not tomorrow. You walk toward her and drop the key in her bag. That's it, then you walk away from her. She walks to the left locker counter, and we know what happens then. Myer won't chance to have you or Dianne hurt or attack in public. SIS is the same, although in their case, they'll just wait until someone else gets the diary for them. No, the New Order are the ones we have to watch."

He was right. "Cure my curiosity and tell me exactly how we keep attention off Dianne?" I asked.

He pulled a key from his pocket and placed it on the table.

It was a locker key. "I assume," I said, "that's from the station. How did you get it?"

"Boy Scout's motto, Guv. Be prepared. Before we left Prague, I bought it at the station."

"And the idea is?" I quizzed.

Tosh put the key back in his pocket. "There is a parcel in the locker I rented. Inside is a diary similar in the size to Novotney's original, an A5. As soon as Dianne goes to the counter to get a new locker, you'll go to my locker and take out the parcel. While you're doing that, Dianne will be opening Valerie's locker with the key you passed to her and remove the real diary. She'll then put the diary into the locker she just bought and walk away. She'll walk past me and I'll lift the key from her. Don't worry." He held up a hand. "She'll be fine with these arrangements. I'll be watching her from the left luggage exit, and you'll be attracting attention if anyone we know is there. They know you and will see the parcel you'll carry. Dianne will be on her way back to Cannes. Daddy will be waiting for her, so all's well. In the meantime, you'll be strolling around with the dummy diarydiary, and you'll be if I read the situation well, confronted by Myer. He isn't violent. He just wants to preserve his precious Club reputation. SIS will not go near you…they may follow. They want Valerie as well. The New Order? I'm sorry to say, but you just have to hope they don't grab you. Mind, if they do, they won't harm you. The last thing they want is bad press involving one of the media's most popular political columnists."

"Thanks, Tosh," I replied sarcastically. "That makes me feel much better. By the way, what are you going to be doing once you've got the diary?"

"I'll take the first train back to Amsterdam as fast as I can. You're going to have to wait for the second train, but with an hour or more to wait, it might be a good idea to hide in a loo or, dare I suggest it, one of the brothels hereabouts." He fumbled in his jacket pocket. "I think I've got a card here somewhere, guv. Hang on a mo."

"No, thank you, Tosh," I said. "Nice of you, but no."

"You're looking a bit annoyed, guv. What's up?"

"If you were married," I said. "You would understand why I'm a little pissed. I'll be seeing my wife tomorrow after I've upset her badly, and I'll not even be able to speak to her or hug her."

Tosh shrugged and looked at the menu. "Well, now that we have that sorted out, how about ordering something to eat? I hear the duck is delicious."

"Bollocks! Buy your own bloody duck."

The waiter arrived with drinks, and I ordered dinner.

At twenty-five euros, plus drinks, plus tip, I let Tosh think about the duck and ordered chicken schnitzel. The man had no feelings.

After our hurried meal, we left separately for the station. As normal, Tosh had already arranged tickets, mine with an attached sleeper token.

Chapter Twenty-Two

THE EVENING WAS AS THE DAY, drizzling. People walked under umbrellas and drove in long queues of traffic, each a string of stoplights going on and off like Christmas tree lights.

I was tired. I thought more about Dianne than what I was about to do. Tosh left me with a suggestion I get to the station a few minutes before departure. He was already watching my back. Cranthorp was a problem. If things worked out the way Tosh had it figured, Cranthorp would be duped by collecting what he thought was the diary everyone was after. That would give Tosh the chance to get away with the genuine article so I could decode the rest of the chess moves. My other worry was Dianne.

I stood shivering under the electronic board, looking at the departure time for Prague. My train was due in thirty minutes, but instead of finding warmth in one of the bars or fast-food outlets, I decided it was best to wait on the platform away from the crowds. Snacks and drinks on the overnight train would be preferable.

I couldn't help feeling a little paranoid, especially about being followed. I felt a strange urge to look around. As I moved off to find a bench, I caught a glimpse of a figure I knew well. Michael Myer had disappeared shortly after our first meeting on the same train. I was sure it was him climbing the stairs at the end of the platform. I realized the man had lied when saying he had to report to Brussels.

I followed, but at the top of the stairs, there was no sign of him. Returning to the platform, I paced up and down until my train pulled in. It irritated me that Myer and Cranthorp were flitting in and out of my life long enough to be seen, but not heard. They were keeping a watch on me, so it seemed.

I climbed aboard and found my compartment. I tipped the steward and ordered something to drink. After settling in, I called Tosh.

"Everything okay? Myer might be with us. I think he was at the station," I said.

"I'm on board. Don't worry about him. It's Cranthorp you need to think about. Get some shuteye, guv."

After a large scotch, I tried, but sleep evaded me. Apart from the clattering of wheels and a rattling window I could do nothing about, I was sick to my stomach. I had been involved with Tosh in a few escapades but never in one that threatened my life so much.

In the early hours, a hot breakfast did nothing to raise my confidence. I wanted the next hour or so to go quickly so I could be on my way back to Amsterdam. As the train pulled into Prague, the locker key was safely held in my palm under my right hand glove. As the doors opened, I decided to remove my gloves and have the key ready for the drop. As usual, the station was bustling, which made walking across the platform an easy task. I kept an eye out for Dianne and hoped she was looking for me. When I did catch sight of her, I couldn't help smiling.

Dark glasses hid her eyes and a white beret worn on a slant made me think of pictures I had at home of her when she was still a teenager. They were a prize possession of mine. She turned down a modelling career because photographic journalism held more excitement for her.

She was sitting on one of the many benches by the left luggage counter. As she rose from the seat and strolled toward me, I tried hard not to smile or look directly at her. Dressed in a long flower-printed dress and pink jacket, she had a large open bag on her right shoulder. All I could think of was Cranthorp. As I reached

The Defector's Diary

her, she stopped and turned a little away from me as I bumped her and deposited the key. I needed to know she was on the train home and safe.

"Apologies, ma'am," I said, smiled and added, "Text me."

I watched her walk toward the locker counter, concerned for her safety. My part in this charade that Tosh orchestrated was nearly over, but Dianne was at risk.

While looking for Tosh's locker, I spotted her walking away from the locker counter. So far, so good, I thought.

Tosh's locker was, I noticed, at the end of a row that was visible to anyone walking the precinct. So much for his concerns and reassurances. I opened the locker and nearly put the dummy diary back. It was of no use now. I had parted with the other key, tempted to find Dianne and disappear.

I left the key in the locker door and watched Dianne open and remove the real diary package from Forst's locker. I wanted to watch her put the diary into the locker she rented, but I couldn't stand there. I had to move. With the dummy package under my arm, I returned to the precinct. My main concern was Dianne. I hoped she would catch a cab straight to the airport.

As for Tosh, I was not worried about him. By the time I got to the precinct, he would have removed the diary and be on the train to Amsterdam within minutes.

There wasn't any point looking over my shoulder or stop to check reflections in shop windows like furtive spies do in the movies. Cranthorp was a real pro, a man with a gun. As I passed the booking hall, I looked up at the arrival and departure board.

My train was leaving in an hour and fifty minutes. I noted the platform and decided to find a seat there and wait. If Cranthorp or whoever watched me, I might as well save my energy and rest. My phone rang. Dianne texted she was getting just about to catch a cab to the airport.on the train, and I breathed with relief.

After reaching the escalator to the pedestrian tunnel under the main line, someone called my name. I froze and my heart

169

pounded. I looked up at the overhead footbridge leading to the station exit in time to see two men staring down at me. I panicked and dropped the parcel, then ran.

Just as I reached the bottom of the stairs to the footbridge, a figure appeared from nowhere, and I felt a foot tap my shins. I was falling to the ground when strong hands caught my arms and pulled me back up. One looked like a bald boxer. A flattened nose, puffy lips, and thick chin stubble that hid a couple of scars, boasted the battles he had endured. His menacing dark eyes squinted at me beneath unruly eyebrows. The rest of him was covered with a long, black leather coat. His accomplice was a different matter. Tall and thin, his hair was long, black, and greasy. A drooping moustache and pointed nose and tanned skin. I guessed meant he had a Mediterranean air about him. Perhaps Italian or Turkish.

One whispered in my ear, "You do as you're told, Mr West, and your lovely lady will be unharmed. If not…"

I remembered a similar line from Raymond Chandler's The Big Sleep, or was it Farewell my Lovely. Whatever. Under different circumstances, I'd have enjoyed the moment and aimed a famous literary line back at him. All I was concerned with was Dianne. We stepped onto the escalator, going up to the exit.

We reached the top of the escalator and walked across the concourse and out. Two large white Mercedes waited behind a line of cabs, vapor drifting out of the exhaust pipes. I kept looking around trying to find an enquiring face as I was marched along, but no one seemed to care what happened to me. One of the thugs thrust me into the rear car.

Both vehicles shot off, swerved around the cab rank, and headed between coaches and general traffic to the north-south bypass through Wenceslas Square. With my knowledge of the local infrastructure, I guessed we might head for the D1, the main motorway connecting Prague to Brno.

I kept craning my neck back and forth as the car in front sped on. Sure enough, within minutes, we were joining the D1 and heading out of the city. The rain fell in sheets and it was hard to see anything through the windscreen except blurred red lights and the occasional passing lorry.

We were on the city's outskirts when the driver indicated a left turn and took a slip road leading into an industrial estate.

"Where are you taking me?" I asked.

It was a pointless thing to say, but I wanted to get them talking if I could. They remained silent. We drove past a few warehouses and small industrial units. We turned onto a short driveway that led to a large dilapidated green warehouse fronted by an enormous concrete area, cracked, and scattered with paper and cardboard rubbish. The double doors closed behind us with a loud, echoing bang as we drove in. I struggled out of the car and shouted, "Who's in charge here? I'm a journalist, and you're in a lot of trouble if anything happens to me."

My two minders pushed and shoved me toward an office.

"You touch my wife; you'll spend a long time regretting it!" I shouted.

"Very touching, Mr West. A gentleman to the end. Let's not get nasty with each other. I can assure you your wife will come to no harm." The smooth voice came behind me.

I turned to see the smiling face of a man in his thirties. Dressed in a black suit with a Crombie-style coat draped over his shoulders, he looked suave and very Continental.

"Shall we?" He pointed at the office. "Just a few words and we're done."

"And if there are none?" I stared defiantly at him. "You have a very London voice, but I don't think you work anywhere near Whitehall."

"Please, Mr West, let's not start being a drama queen. Your choices are limited. You can talk to me and walk out of here, or you can be a hero and get carried out cold."

He followed me as the thugs pulled me on. I tripped on some

loose banding wire still attached to one of the broken wooden pallets that lay around on the floor. The warehouse looked as though it was once used to store wood and building materials. Two large electric motors were still on the roof's moving crane framework from which dangled lengths of heavy chain with hooks. As I walked into the office, the rain beat a staccato rhythm on the corrugated metal roof.

The office surprised me. Someone had gone to the trouble to equip it with a desk and chairs and a small table on which stood an electric kettle and all the necessary tea-making items. A car battery and a coil of electrical leads were also on the table. That was worrying.

I tried a little humour to lighten the situation. "Tea first, I think, and maybe you have some bourbon biscuits?"

My head took the full force of a firm hand, giving me a slap from behind. Unprepared, I fell forward across a chair. I held my head. The pain, although brief, made me cry out.

"We don't want comedy either."

The smooth talker sat and motioned me to a chair. I sat and a hand rested on my shoulders, while another pair of hands tied me down.

"First, my name is Joseph Labrum, and I work for some very influential people who are annoyed with you. You have or know the whereabouts of an article that belongs to them. They realize that a journalist like you gets excited stumbling on a great story, especially through Adam's sad death, something we regret. He was becoming a useful player until he wanted to restore his reputation."

"Not quite with you," I said. "Who do you represent; SIS or the secret squirrels club within Bilderberg?" My sarcasm earned me another slap across the head.

"You'd do well to remember your wife instead of cracking silly witticisms. We already got to her once, and now we have her again. A beautiful lady. It would be a crime to hurt her good looks."

Labrum sneered at me, and I smiled. She was on her way home and safe.

Reaching into his jacket pocket, Labrum pulled out a light brown box with the legend 'Al Capone cigarillos' on it and took out a small cigar. "I'd offer you one, but these are my favorites," he said. "They're dipped in cognac."

I thought better of it and remained silent. Labrum crossed his legs as he lit the cigarillo with a gold Dunhill lighter. A highly polished, hand-cut Italian leather shoe jiggled in the air. Labrum was used to the finer things in life and, I guessed, not been contracted solely for security reasons. He had to be part of the inner Bilderberg circle that Novotney had warned about with chess moves in the diary. I got the feeling he would be a ruthless adversary if necessary. His thugs certainly showed him a lot of respect.

"I have no idea what you're talking about, apart from the fact that Adam Denton was a close friend of my wife. We want to find out why he died and who killed him. Was it you?"

Labrum puffed on the cigar before blowing a stream of sweet-smelling smoke across the office. "No, it wasn't me. Mr Denton, I can tell you, was playing a dangerous game."

"Like what?"

"I haven't got all day, Mr West. Don't let's get into a debate about who did what. I want the diary. Where is it?"

"I don't know," I replied.

A fist smashed into my jaw and I felt enormous pain as I fell to the floor still tied to the chair. No hands caught me this time. My head hit the concrete, and I saw a burst of stars and a bright flash. Then I was hauled upright.

"We can play this all day and night if we have to," said Labrum. "I know Denton took the diary from Forst, who stole it from Novotney. You're an intelligent man and I'm sure you know where it is." He sneered again. "You probably know where that bitch Forst is too."

As he spoke of Valerie, I realized something interesting. I remembered Adam's warning. Trust no one. All roads led back to Adam. Was he used as Labrum suggested by someone hiding some dark secret? There was no one I could trust. They all wanted the diary, and any one of them could have killed Adam and Novotney.

"I have no idea where Forst is. With regards to the diary, you should look to the security services. Last I heard, SIS was looking for her. I heard a rumor she worked for them." I shrugged. "It's all so confusing."

Labrum held his cigar in a raised foppish manner and, with his other hand, drew a small pistol from his jacket.

"I think it's time to show you how painful it can be to play games with me." He waved the pistol in my direction. "This is a small calibre gun that can cause a lot of damage to one's extremities or kneecap."

I took a deep breath, my eyes locked on the pistol. He slowly stood.

"Oh no, West. The bullet isn't for you." He looked outside and turned to one of the men. "Go and fetch Mrs West."

My chest heaved. I couldn't see how Labrum could have Dianne. She texted she was all right. I decided to play along, just in case.

"No! Leave her alone. She knows nothing. Please leave her alone."

A sudden, terrifying panic, accompanied by a thumping heartbeat, coursed through me as the man left the office and closed the door behind him. Labrum said nothing.

"All right," I said. "Forst hid the diary in a locker at the station where you caught us. I dropped it, but your guys didn't see that. I hoped to go back later and search for it, but my guess is, it'll be gone." I looked at him, trying to display a look of real panic, not that I had to work very hard. "She told us where it was when we met her at the café in the square. She gave me a key."

"How did you know to meet her in the first place?"

I quickly told him about the wedding invitation and a little white lie that Adam wanted us to meet Forst at the café where she worked. It was then we found out she wanted to get to Britain and in exchange, had something of high value—the diary. There was no point lying to him, so I kept to the facts he must already know or worked out for himself.

"We were on our way back when you caught us. I assure you, I'm no hero. I'm after a story, but SIS and the Czech authorities and our Embassy threatened me with a trip back to England unless I stop snooping around. I only got so far with my investigation, and then all the doors shut in my face. You know how it is."

Labrum rubbed his chin with the barrel of the pistol. "Let me tell you what's going to happen. Your wife will stay here while we go and look for the diary. If we don't find it, she will suffer."

"For Christ's sake, man, we don't even know what's in the diary," I pleaded.

The sound of footsteps came from outside. As I looked out the window, I heard a faint cracking echo. I felt a sharp pain in my leg and closed my eyes momentarily. My chair tipped as something heavy fell against me. When I opened my eyes, I was aware of a small piece of glass sticking out of my leg and the large bald thug lying on the floor beside the chair.

Labrum crouched behind the door.

Lying on my side, I could see Dianne's boots through a crack at the bottom of the door.

"Your wife is dead, West," were the last words I heard from Labrum before a shot rang out.

Chapter Twenty-Three

THERE IS NOTHING WORSE than a combination of pain and total confusion after regaining consciousness. Dull pain seared through my head, accompanied by a sharp stabbing throb from my knee. A hand held my head above the ground, and I could recognize the smell of gardenias. It took several seconds to come out of my confused state, but I knew Dianne was with me.

"Oh, thank Christ it's you," I uttered.

She bent and kissed my forehead. "Of course, it's me. The bad guys are gone, thanks to this gentleman."

As I breathed heavily, Dianne helped me sit and untangle myself from the chair. The bald man and Labrum had disappeared, and looking down at me with a somewhat dispassionate eye was Michael Myer.

"Hello, old boy." He nodded toward the door. "Time we were not here. I'll explain all while we drive to Amsterdam."

He had a lot of explaining to do. As much as I needed to hear him, my thoughts were on Tosh. I hobbled behind Dianne as Myer held one of my arms for support.

"I surprised the two men," Myer explained, "and they ran as soon as they saw the gun. They come from a dubious security firm in London. Labrum, on the other hand, is a different matter. He's part of the Bilderberg Club and dangerous. I fired a couple of warning shots above your heads. Unfortunately, he saw me as he ran, so the Bilderberg Club will now know where I am and will be after me. I suspect they already were anyway. By the way, sorry about your leg."

I ignored the apology and climbed into the back of his car. "I

The Defector's Diary

need a phone," I said. "Incidentally, thanks for saving my ass."

Myer slid into the driver's seat. "Not a problem, old boy."

Dianne poked a recall number on her phone and handed it to me. "It's ringing," she said.

As I placed it to my ear, I smiled at her. Tosh answered almost at once.

"Hello Pete, I've been trying to get you for a while."

Aware that Myer was listening, I simply asked, "I'll explain later, but for now, tell me what you've got."

"I managed to catch the train on time, and I'm headed for a different station short of the city to confuse whoever might be after me. A friend of Jan's is picking me up. Forst is fine by all accounts. All we have to do now is look at the book and try to figure out the puzzle."

"Okay, good. I'll see you tomorrow, probably in the evening."

As I spoke, I was thinking of Myer. I still had a hard time trying to trust him. I needed to be with Tosh on my own.

I turned to Dianne. "Why aren't you on your way to Cannes?"

She smiled. "I cannot trust you to behave yourself. I was about to board my train when I saw you run, which is unusual for you. Then I saw the two men pushing you along. I recognized the big one. He was the thug who hit my car. They caught me before I could move."

I squeezed her hand. "Well, you're safe now…I think. We are meeting Tosh on a trawler docked near Amsterdam. The skipper is a friend of Tosh called Jan."

Dianne pulled a face. "Not exactly the Hilton then. Never mind, I'll survive as long asTosh Fish keeps his trainers on."

As we drove back to the highway, Myer said, "Let me tell you a few things, then we'll decide what should happen next. I take it that was Tosh. How is he these days?"

"So, you are SIS, then?"

Myer laughed. "No, Pete. I knew Tosh from my Army days in

Berlin. He loved the intelligence world, while I got into government. As I recall, he was approached by a colleague with connections in Whitehall. I do know he was sent to check me out, though."

He was silent for a moment, and I remembered Tosh telling me about a friend of his father offering him a job with SIS after returning from a tour in Cyprus.

"I guess you know where he is then and why, right?" I asked.

"Actually, no, I don't, although I can imagine he's teamed up with you somehow. You should be careful. You're his friend until you serve your purpose. Let me guess, he turned up when least expected and was ready to help with your quest."

"You're half right," I responded. "We're useful for each other—"

"Maybe it would be better for me to start by giving you a little background on what's been going on," Myer interrupted, "and you'll see how Adam came into all this."

"Talking about Adam," I said. "How did you find out he was dead?"

Myer was silent for a moment.

"I told Forst that the Embassy informed me he was dead, but then I guess you already know that and wondered why I lied, right?"

I was happy he wasn't going to try and convince me otherwise. "Right," I answered.

We overtook a coach and moved back to the inside lane before he answered. "One of the reasons I never went back to Brussels to clear up this mess was because the Czech police and SIS want to question me in connection with both murders. Although mostly circumstantial, the mountain of evidence they have against me is so impressive, it would see me in jail for life."

"So, how did you know about Adam? He died sometime between Forst leaving him early evening and the following morning."

The Defector's Diary

Myer flicked the windscreen wipers on as the rain started hammering on the car. "Jozef had a communique from Brussels telling him of Forst's decommissioning. I agreed with Jozef to contact Adam and convince him to stay away from Forst for all our sakes; separating us, the Bilderberg Club, and the British Embassy from a real diplomatic mess. Jozef and I needed to stay focused on weeding out the New Order from within. Adam was very protective of Forst, who by then was involved with SIS. It was then he shocked me with the revelation that Forst called him minutes before I arrived for our appointment to say she was at his flat with Jozef's diary."

"The New Order knew where Adam lived, I'm sure," I said. "But how did they know? Only you and Forst knew where Adam lived, apart from the Embassy. SIS and Adam knew where Forst lived. Diplomats' addresses are not listed or given out under any circumstances. They found Adam and silenced him. Then there was just Forst to deal with - until they found out I was poking around."

Myer pulled sharply onto the hard shoulder. "Who the bloody hell do you think you are? I just saved your life." He was poking a finger at me, and I pushed his hand away.

"How did they know where either of them lived?" I demanded.

"How does any intelligence agency find your address," he snapped. "For someone who writes so much about government, you amaze me. Think, man. They've been organizing and planning for years. Don't you think they would have infiltrated SIS by now? We're facing dangerous times, and the New Order is ruining an organization that, although secret, has been doing great work for the last few years. It's about time you stopped trying to point a finger. Adam died because he was a fool who fell for another fool who is bloody lucky to be alive. I wish I had never heard of her or met her."

"I suppose you would agree with Tosh that she should be sent home to be shot."

Myer's eyes looked at me in the driving mirror. "That little girl is responsible for the deaths of three people. Do you remember Philby and his nasty colleagues? How many of our agents died because of them? You have a heart that's too big, and an opinion that's way off course."

Dianne interrupted. "Enough! You two are tired and tempers are getting frayed. I think we should find somewhere to stay for the night and meet Jan tomorrow."

We drove on and I called Jan, letting him know I would meet him at the boat by noon the following day. A huge neon sign ahead advertised a motel just off the highway. As we pulled onto the slip road, Myer slowed and stopped. "I didn't tell you how I knew Adam was dead."

"No, you didn't. So how did you know?"

"I went to his flat."

"When?"

"After I saw him, I went back to Jozef's in time to see the police activity. I got out of there quick and went back to my hotel. After thinking things through, there was only one thing I could do—go back to Adam's place, speak to him and Forst, and try to make them see sense by explaining what was going on and get them to give me the diary. I could have helped Forst get to London, but she trusted no one."

"You got to Adam's place when?" asked Dianne.

"In late afternoon. I rang his doorbell but got no answer. I left and waited until after dark. By then, there must have been at least three agencies looking for me. It was past midnight when I arrived at Adam's block of flats again. I couldn't see any light and assumed he was asleep. Then all hell broke loose in a quiet way."

I motioned Myer to drive into the car park. The last thing we wanted was to draw attention to ourselves. "Then what?"

"A car pulled up and Labrum with two thugs got out. They went into the apartment block. A minute later, the light went on

The Defector's Diary

in Adam's flat, and after five minutes—no more—they came out and drove off in a hurry. I couldn't walk away. The chances that Adam was alive were pretty slim, but I had to look for the diary, although I had no idea whether Forst left it with him or not."

Dianne squeezed my hand, but when I glanced at her, she was facing the window.

"Then what?" I pushed.

"I went up to Adam's floor and found his door ajar. I looked in and found him in the kitchen. The place was a mess. Everything was turned out. Papers and clothes scattered all over the floor. I spent ten, maybe fifteen minutes searching but found nothing. When I left, I made sure the flat was as I found it." He sighed loudly. "Just as well I left when I did. That's when the heavy brigade turned up."

"What do you mean?"

"SIS without a doubt. Their lead capo was Cranthorp. I'd recognize him anywhere."

"So how the hell did he get there so quick? Someone had to tell him."

Myer nodded. "I have no idea, but it could have been Labrum's thugs. Cranthorp was with the cleanup squad. That's probably how the body was removed, and the apartment cleaned and dusted. There's something else. I did notice a photo in the bedroom that showed Adam with Cranthorp. There has to be a tie-in somehow."

From the expression on his face and how he described everything, I realized he was as genuinely surprised as I was to find the photo.

"You're right," I answered. "Maybe Adam fooled us all."

Dianne looked rather glum and nodded. "I agree. Something is very wrong."

"Where do we go from here?" said Myer and climbed out of the car. "May I suggest we go and find Tosh and see if he's been successful?"

"I'm all for a good night's sleep," I replied. "I'm in touch with Tosh, and as soon as he has some news, I know he'll call me. In the meantime, let's book in and get something to eat."

A little voice at the back of my head kept telling me not to say anything to Myer about where Tosh was. There was no possibility he was going to be with me either. It would make sense for him to go with Dianne and Forst back to UK. He might be on our side, but he wanted the diary for different reasons than mine. Besides, I reasoned, better for him to appear before Parliament, having returned from a mysterious disappearance holding the hand of an asylum seeker and defector SIS failed to capture.

Whitehall would forgive him, and Number Ten would reward him once it was revealed what secrets the Bilderberg diary held and the part he played to retrieve it. His wish to preserve the Bilderberg Club's integrity was his problem.

Later, as we ate dinner, I decided the following day's plan had to be changed if I met Tosh on my own. It meant making sure Dianne travelled safely to Amsterdam and Jan's boat. First, I had to slip away unnoticed. After midnight, a cab arriving at the motel might attract attention, and Myer had the key for his car. I could hardly ask for it. There was a small, fast-food transport café across the other side of the car park. It would be easy to find a driver going part or all of the way to Amsterdam for a hundred euros.

"Do you feel comfortable travelling alone with Myer?" I asked Dianne a little later as we lay in bed. "I've written the address of the dock where Jan is tied up at and his number, but don't let Myer have it. You'll have to use the train."

She took a scrap of paper I gave her and looked at it before putting it in her purse.

"I have no problem with that, Pete, but it's you I'm worried about."

"I'll be fine," I answered. "I'll call Jan when I'm out of here, then Tosh so he can meet me somewhere."

The Defector's Diary

I set my tablet's alarm and dozed off. I couldn't sleep. There were too many scenarios playing out in my mind. Mixed with them a great sense of danger, especially where Dianne and Myer were concerned. Myer was wanted by two, maybe three secret services, and Dianne by SIS. Once on Jan's boat, they should be safe enough.

Although neither of us had said a word about our earlier conversation, I could not sleep next to Dianne without at least trying to let her know how I felt.

"Listen," I said. "I cannot pretend anymore. I have to tell you that this week has been the most emotional ride ever, and I never want to go through something like this again." I turned sideways and looked into her eyes. "Dianne, I am truly sorry for the hurt I caused you. All I can do is promise I'll never do anything like that again."

She reached with one hand and touched my cheek. "I'm furious at you for another reason, but I forgive you because of your feelings at the time. You said you didn't mind being second best. That's an insult. How dare you accuse me of settling for second best. You're the best, and I'm glad I didn't marry Adam. You were worth the wait. However, you're still in trouble when we get home. Now get some sleep."

With that, she rolled over, and I lay there with a silly grin on my face. At two o'clock, I kissed her goodbye as she slept and slipped out of the room. Fortunately, the night clerk was not in the front office, and I managed to walk out of the glare of a halogen lamp at the entrance and into darkness. I hurried to the café across the car park, planning to get a lift to Amsterdam in a truck. That way, I stood little chance running the risk of being recognized. With no one I could completely trust, apart from Dianne, I really felt alone.

Chapter Twenty-Four

AMSTERDAM IN THE RAIN is still a vibrant city. It's alive, and in some parts boisterous, as clubs and bars stay open around the clock. The driver who gave me a lift dropped me off outside some docks, and a cab took me to the quayside and Jan's trawler as dawn started to break. I was disappointed to find Tosh had not turned up. I gave him a ring.

"Anything happening at your end, guv? I gave Cranthorp the French Connection wave as my train passed him standing on the platform. He's a great example of how SIS works as long as it's past nine in the morning. Bleedin' limp wrists, all of 'em."

A moment of light relief brightened up a grey day and had me smiling. Tosh intended to be with me in an hour. His train was held up, but back on the move. My next call was to Dianne, but Myer answered.

"Pete, I thought we trusted each other."

"That's right," I replied. "You thought. I never agreed. You should thank me. You're going home with the star of the show that SIS failed to catch. When the diary is delivered to Downing Street, you'll be hailed a hero with reputation restored."

"I was afraid you would do something like that. You must not give the diary to Downing Street, Pete. On no account should you let them have it." He paused. "I haven't told you everything. We need to sit down with the diary and look at the entries. Jozef gave me a warning that the New Order will would engineer some catastrophic disaster, but before he could tell me, he was murdered. On the day we went for a coffee, he said he was going back to Brussels the next day, but he made a discovery that would

The Defector's Diary

shake the world. We agreed to meet at the airport before his flight, and he would show me entries in the diary and what they meant. I was to have the diary and get it to the Home Office—not Downing Street or SIS. He was most specific."

"Let me speak to Dianne, Michael."

Dianne answered. "Hi, darling, I'm driving, so be quick."

"Okay, what do you make of that? Is he genuine?"

"I would say so."

"All right, tell him to hurry up and get to Jan's boat and join me. Tosh will be there shortly with the diary."

She sounded positive about Myer, and I decided to carry on as planned. to change our plans again.

Tosh had someone waiting in Whitby to take the women to a safe house and wait for us. Myer was still holding back, and it was time to make him talk—after we had the diary.

* * *

I sat next to Valerie Forst and asked for her help.

"You know, you said something the other night I think we should consider with care. If there is a genuine bomb attack on the Houses of Parliament, then for that alone, I'm sure the Prime Minister and the Home Office, and all the other departments involved in terrorism, will grant you asylum."

Her face lit up. I was pretty sure she would get asylum. Tosh and Myer had been in the game for years. Their hard-bitten attitude came from many political incidents and government security policies.

Jan made tea and cooked some hard biscuits.

"I'm afraid there is nothing else," she replied. "Tosh said he would be back with food for our journey."

I nodded as Valerie and I sipped tea and nibbled biscuits.

A loud clang announced Tosh's entrance a short while later. He greeted me with a huge smile and placed a package on the table along with food.

"I haven't looked at it yet."

I unwrapped the diary and opened it, an A5 with two days per page. Valerie was right. The last two months' entries were mostly initials and numbers. Apart from that, everything written was in Czech. I closed the diary.

"The secrets here are getting people killed. I'm hoping Myer can make sense of the words as we decode the initials. I'm curious to find out why he doesn't want me visiting Downing Street."

Tosh gazed intently at the diary and took the mug of tea Jan held out. "If you think about it, guv, Myer must know someone in the New Order…or maybe there's more than one."

It was possible, of course, I mused. If the New Order had people in our government cabinet, then there had to be someone planted in other EU governments as well. If the Bilderberg Club was planning for a single European governing body, regardless of whether it was a right or wrong thing for us, the splinter New Order group had grossly undermined that work. I could understand Myer's frustration but trying to protect the Club's integrity while exposing the people responsible for murder was not something I would condone if it meant putting more lives at risk.

As Jan started cooking a meal, Myer and Dianne arrived. It was starting to get a little crowded. Myer came straight to the point.

"What are your plans for our return to London?"

"You're going to give yourself up to some SIS staffer who will transport you all to a place in the country where you will be held for a minimum of three months and debriefed," Tosh said and turned to Valerie. "You may be there for a year, and even then, they may throw you back, so you'd better tell them everything you know."

Valerie looked across the cabin at me. I winked.

"But first," I said, "we're going to decode this diary. Whitehall has the information we gained from the memory stick Valerie

The Defector's Diary

gave us. However, we don't know who we can trust with this information. We should understand the entries so that any plan to disrupt the government or cause a catastrophic incident will give us time to broadcast a warning."

I handed Myer a hot sandwich from a stack Jan was making. "Michael, it's up to you to deliver the warning and take with you the diary. No one is going to believe anything you say without proof, and that means the diary. You cannot afford to get caught until it gets into the right hands. SIS is supposed to be sending an agent to collect Valerie, but—"

"No, not SIS," interrupted Tosh. "It will be my side, and you can take my word for it; my colleague is straight."

I exchanged a glance with Myer. All day, I had a strange feeling that things were not quite right. I wondered how Labrum had turned up at the station and grabbed us. Where was Cranthorp? I kept my feelings to myself and decided to talk things over with Dianne later.

"If any of these groups who are searching for me recognize me, they could arrest us," said Myer, "but I don't think so. We're being allowed to run. Have you noticed anyone following us in the last forty-eight hours, apart from the New Order?"

"Simple." Dianne had made herself comfortable in the corner on a couple of cushions. "What do they want the most? You or the diary? If they arrest you and you don't have it, they lose the one person they know will lead them to it."

"I don't like the idea," said Myer. "I'll be with you and Valerie and the diary. Surely, it makes sense to give Valerie up so I can—"

Valerie sat upright and looked at me.

"Don't worry, we are discussing all the possibilities."

"Can what?" said Tosh.

"We do not give her up after all the trouble we've been to. Someone with a lot of power has squashed the alert on us. That, someone must work in Whitehall or Downing Street."

"Well, it wouldn't have been SIS," I replied. "It has to be the Home Office."

"Or the Prime Minister's office," said Tosh. "We have some dangerous people looking for us."

Dianne held up a hand. "We're working against one another, and all of us are putting our necks out. Neither Tosh, if I understand his situation, nor Michael will have a job when this is over, and Pete's reputation is at stake. If things are as bad as you say they are, then I say forget the Bilderberg Club. Let's get the guys ruining the Club's future and stop whatever catastrophe is about to happen."

Myer's fingers gripped the mug he held tight before he spoke. "We'll agree to disagree about the Club, but agree we need to work together."

"Good. Thanks for calling order, Dianne," I said. "Let's take a look at the entries in the diary, especially those around the time of the general election. We have tonight to contact Max, my editor, and Richard Hart. I want them to know everything that's been going on. If we're to expose this group, the paper has to find a way to get around the Official Secrets Act. We can't just go and publish a story. I think our best bet, Michael, is to write the story on the linked deaths with a couple of finger-pointing hints we might be able to get away with, and let the establishment take care of the rest. Nothing unnerves Whitehall more than a scandal involving a minister or one of their own."

"There's one thing we should be careful of at all times," said Myer. "What if someone was watching Adam's place to see if any of us turned up?"

Tosh clicked his fingers. "If someone was watching, they could have taken a photo of any of us, guv. The problem is, we have two or three interested parties on our tail, so your guess is as good as mine—that is, if someone was watching."

"Well, it doesn't matter. I suggest we take turns tonight to keep watch outside the boat for any unwelcome visitors." I looked over my shoulder at Tosh. "I take it you have a gun with you?"

He nodded.

"Okay, then let's get cracking on the diary."

I waited until we were all settled before bringing up a point that had been bothering me ever since my earlier conversation with Myer.

"Why did you warn me to stay away from Downing Street?" I asked him. "Surely, you're not telling me the Prime Minister is involved in the New Order."

Myer forked a pork ball and held it mid-air before popping it into his mouth. It seemed to me that each time I asked him a question, he took several seconds to answer, probably part of the make-up of a diplomat that had been formed during his years in office.

"No," he eventually replied, "but there is someone in his office who is. At this moment in time, we can't tell the PM much, so we can't tell him to keep his mouth shut. Everyone at Number Ten knows what's going on at any one time, from the PM's daily schedule to what he's going to say in the House at Question Time, or about current issues at home or abroad. His press secretary and private secretary have their fingers in just about everyone else's pie. That's how he keeps up with what the Russian president says, sometimes before the president has said anything." Myer looked across the table at Tosh. "You know more than the rest of us about Downing Street. SIS will have a man inside there right now, and as always, he or she will be reporting back to the Cross on an hourly basis. They had staff on hand there ever since the country went on amber terrorist alert."

"Correct," said Tosh. "So, who's the mole?"

Myer hesitated and sighed. "Hugh Muscott, the Private Secretary. He's been involved with the New Order for some time. It was Jozef Novotney's belief the man manages recruitment and placement."

"Placement?" I queried.

"Yes, recruiting someone for a particular job in the New Order, and then placing them in a position within the government from where they can step into a New Order position once it takes over."

For a moment, I thought the full impact and the implications of what Myer said were creating a very dark and ominous picture. "How does anyone know the Bilderberg Club you're trying to save is just as evil as the New Order within it?"

"You don't, but I assure you the Club's members are all good men and women who want nothing but a peaceful and well-ordered world to live in."

"That's rubbish," I replied. "It sounds to me like you want the new world order created in secret, and populations everywhere to accept it whether they wish to or not. What is happening to democracy? There will be protest groups springing up and forming their movements. For Christ's sake, man, you already have one in your midst before you've even got very far. Three men are dead."

Myer shrugged. "I think this is not the time for a political debate. As agreed, let's stop fighting each other and get to grips with the present problem."

I agreed, and the conversation turned to other matters while we finished dinner. After clearing the table, I produced the diary, and Myer started writing notes while Tosh and I got working with our chess moves and conversion into words via Morse code. What intrigued us were single words grouped with two lots of initials during the election week.

There were also five dates spaced a week apart, starting with the Bilderberg meeting in Prague. Each date was marked UK, FR, and DE respectively, with numbers and letters plus three more, RU, SAWH, and HP. The UK date was the 21st of Sept, the first day after the elections. The initials, we assumed, represented individuals or places involved. It was the best we could do so far.

The Defector's Diary

"The one that interests me is this one," said Tosh, thumbing through the pages. "This is the day before the election and the start of all the different entries, apart from the torn page Valerie sent you, guv. That was dated last week. The Order will start the first phase in London after the election."

I tapped the diary. "Let's take a look at the first entry and concentrate on that. My guess, this is the trigger that will start the ball rolling. What the message is and what is going to happen is unclear, but we know from the way the New Order is chasing and murdering those in their way, it has to be something that will get world headlines."

"Like nine-eleven?" Myer scratched his head.

"Not that bad with the loss of life, but certainly involving someone or something affecting the way we live, like finance or trade on the stock markets. Don't forget this group we're dealing with wants to impress the world, not wage war on it like a bunch of terrorists."

"Valerie did hint that what she saw, she recognized from previous entries in Novotney's business diary," said Myer. "Like the initials of political figures in Brussels and individual words, she was always transcribing from his shorthand scribbling on notes prepared for reports."

We all looked at Valerie, who was half asleep. She nodded. "Do you need my help?"

"Perhaps," I said, "but for now, we're okay."

I pored over the first entry and had an idea. "Listen, we already have a few words that at the moment mean nothing. These copies Valerie took are scattered, but do run in date order. What say we look through the diary and find pages where those words were written down? That would be helpful later when we start putting all the pieces together."

There was a general buzz of agreement. "The date of September seventeen is significant. Let's find that first and see if the surrounding pages have more information."

I looked at Dianne. "Could you start searching the clues we have? Maybe with a political slant like the place name we have: Dedham. I'm sure that's in Essex. Could be a politician's home there."

Dianne held up her tablet. "I'm already on it."

I was so glad of her company but afraid for her safety. She should have been in Cannes and safely with her father.

We went through the diary from the first notation chess move to the last dated a week after the general election for the next two hours. Myer made a list of our findings, and at one a.m., we sat looking at it. Against the dates, we wrote the day, but there were no times, except with the one date before the election that was part of a sentence that read, the king will die on Sept 17, as does Othello, but not by the same hand. The dialogue was then split—as on the final curtain.

"We need a list of dignitaries," I said. "It looks obvious that whoever the victim is, he or she will be assassinated on the final curtain of Othello."

Chapter Twenty-Five

THE REST OF THE DECODED LIST consisted of other two sentences about the 'bomb warning' and the 'first phase'. Neither of which were dated, apart from the diary pages themselves, and sets of six initials against four headings—UK, HP, SA, RU, DE, and FR. A question mark had been written after the last set separated FR—? Even putting the whole conundrum in chronological date order, we had a message that still meant nothing.

At the top was FASTNG—Rosebud—Dedham (diary dated the 15th of June)

Next was, 'The king of the House'. (diary dated the 15th of June)

Then the sentence about, 'the king will die'. (diary dated the 20th of June)

The warning about a bomb that we had passed on. (diary dated the 22nd of July)

The last five lists of four initials against five countries or cities (diary also dated the 22nd of July). The five symbols were repeated on the last page, dated the 17th of September.

Myer was adding to his notes. He stopped abruptly, which made us jump.

"Of course!" He looked at Dianne. "About that date and Othello? I've had that at the back of my mind and it suddenly came to me."

"I got it before you," she said, "but I've been getting other information we can add as well."

I looked at both of them. "Will one of you explain? Tosh and

I are falling asleep."

Dianne moved to the table. "Okay. The 17th of September is the day the starting pistol is fired, and someone is going to die."

Myer grinned and touched her arm. "Very good, Dianne."

I felt a little annoyed at his stance, but even more so when Dianne smiled back at him. I realized that smile innocently acknowledged 'two great minds and all that', but I still didn't like it.

"What have you found, or are you going to keep another secret?" I remarked a little sarcastically. As soon as I said it, I knew I lit the fire again. Dianne turned, and a dozen arrows came my way. "I am sorry. I'm tired, Dianne."

The look lasted a second longer and then creased into laughter. She looked at the others. "Sorry, that was a private joke." She gave me a hell of a wink, pulled Myer's notes toward her and placed her tablet on the table. On the screen was an advert for Shakespeare's Othello at London's Royal Opera House. Opening night, the 17th of September.

Dianne explained, "This is the first catastrophe we have uncovered, and by the looks of things, there are five more acts of violence or specific acts of sabotage. You can't take over a continent unless you cripple critical industries, such as finance and trade structures—hence the other five countries, HP, SA, RU, DE, and FR."

"And what has that got to do with Othello?" Tosh was suddenly awake.

"Opening night at the Royal Opera always means a list of dignitaries, many from the political arena," I said. "Well done, you two. Are we looking at a protest or what?"

"No, Pete," said Myer. "We're looking at assassination in full public view. I mean, what a great opportunity to send a message to all the right people. That list is like a who's who in Debrett's. What bothers me, who or what is FASTNG? What is Rosebud? We're working on it.

The Defector's Diary

"However, the assassination date is also the date notated next to the groups of initials under three of the countries. The killing of the king is going to coincide with something nasty taking place in these countries, and the initials of four people could mean certain politicians who will take over control."

Dianne nodded. "Finance, agriculture, stock markets, and trade."

Myer nodded. "I say you're good at this," he said. "You should try the Times crossword, Dianne."

Myer was getting on my nerves.

"The initials FASTNG," said Dianne. "That's what part of it stands for, at least that's a really good guess. But I have no idea what NG stands for. Maybe I'm wrong."

The puzzle was beginning to come together. "We have to find out who the target is and have to see him or her ourselves," I said. "Again, we cannot afford the chance of telling the wrong person."

Myer, who had been looking through the diary, slapped the table and cursed. "There's more here. Three pages stuck together. Probably Jan's bacon sandwiches." He gently prised the pages apart and found one more set of moves on each page.

Another hour and we had the final moves sorted into initials and times, and the 17th was noted again.

17th, WB 11.30—HP 12.00—ET CG DIV—MED EX SCHED 10.00 —Order

Tosh had a go at deciphering, "Okay, how about this? WB could be a place, like West Barsford, and HP another place half an hour later. It's like a route map, each place or person half an hour apart. Then ET, CG and DIV could be three people. There's something scheduled for 7.30. Could be a departure time or a place where they're going to meet." He looked up and grinned.

I grinned. "Not bad, Tosh. Let's keep at it."

We spent the next two hours coming up with various solutions, but nothing made sense without the names.

It was four o'clock, and Tosh got ready to watch outside. With that, he pulled a pistol from inside his coat and left us to continue.

Jan had spent some time in the engine room. When he appeared, he stepped through the cabin and caught Tosh as he was leaving. After a whispered conversation, Tosh gave me a wink and I joined him outside.

"What's up?" The bridge was bitterly cold, but I noticed the engine's control panel was fully lit up and the radar screen was operational.

"We can be on the move in a very short while, slip through the canal and into the North Sea. We can make the Whitby coast by around 4.30 tomorrow morning while it's still dark. Jan can get close in and lower the inflatable, and you can all get ashore quickly. It's a deserted part of the coast, so there shouldn't be any trouble. I've organised a car for us. It'll be waiting on the coast road. Jan has the coordinates."

"Okay, but we haven't finished the diary yet. We'll need somewhere to work."

Tosh smiled, his face glowing green from the control panel in front of us. I should have guessed, and neither of us said a word. He had already organized a place. A small fishing smack would not arouse too much interest with a coastguard or fisheries inspection.

"Tell them I'm sorry for keeping them up." He thumbed the cabin steps and nodded at Jan.

The engine started with a roar, and the trawler shook. It was hard to hear anything above the clattering diesel. The bridge door opened with a crash, and Myer appeared.

"What the hell are you doing? We never discussed this. We need to work on the diary."

Tosh ignored him and peered through the bridge window as rain beat against the glass. I patted Jan's shoulder and ushered

The Defector's Diary

Myer back down below. Myer turned on me the moment we were back in the cabin.

Dianne and Valarie were standing by the table.

"What's going on?"

Myer looked angry. Unshaven and with dark rings around the eyes, his appearance was a far cry from the man I first met on the train.

"We're going to be landed at Whitby sometime in the morning. From there a car will take us to a place organised by Tosh. There, you can work on the diary while we decide who does what. It may get a little rough once we get out of the canal, so find a place to curl up and try to get some rest. I would like to get on with some more work myself."

"Typical bloody SIS. Don't tell anyone what the other hand is doing," Myer growled.

"That's right," retorted Tosh. You bleedin' political types love moving the goalposts when it suits. That's why I don't tell you zip!"

"Can you two shut the hell up?" I said firmly. "If you want to fight each other, wait until all this trouble is over."

"I'll stay up with Pete," agreed Dianne. She smiled at Valerie, who was already curled up. "You can take my blanket if you like and we'll swop in a couple of hours. Okay?"

I spent the day with a strange feeling in the back of my mind and couldn't shake it off. I had no idea why I felt like that, but perhaps it was something or someone I needed to deal with as soon as possible. There was a definite uneasy atmosphere in our little group. Myer and Tosh seemed to be at odds with each other, while Valerie had completely closed down. As for Dianne and myself, we were holding hands again, but I suspected her hand would grip mine a lot tighter when we were back home.

"We need to talk," whispered Dianne in my ear.

"Wait until we get clear of the canal and are at sea," I suggested. "We can talk in the galley."

I spent the next hour poring over the diary, Dianne and I thinking Tosh had the right idea to move us out. Despite the continual clatter and thump from the engine below us, Myer and Valerie were sound asleep. Dianne and I stepped into the galley and closed the door behind us.

She pointed at the door. "What's with Myer and Tosh? I know you get along with Tosh, but you know I don't trust him. He has changed, and I think he's lying."

"Don't be sorry," I answered. "Tosh has changed. He lost his job, and when I asked him about his present position, he sounded a little bitter. After years of faithful service, I'd still be surprised if he engaged with the New Order. No, thank you for your service, and the future looking lonely at the age of fifty plus. Then you get offered a position with a group of powerful men who have world domination in mind. No, I can't see Tosh accepting that, but there is something he's hiding, and it may have to do with Myer."

As I said that, I visualized Tosh being made that offer by Cranthorp and smiled. Tosh did not like the man. The situation was confusing all around.

"You know what?" I said. "We have to keep an eye over our shoulder."

"But why would Tosh help us if he's involved with the New Order? He could have handed all of us to them."

Her comment clicked my thoughts into gear. "Suppose Myer and Cranthorp are both SIS and with the New Order? What then?"

Dianne shrugged. "Well, the only worry we have at the moment is decoding the diary. Whatever game any of the others are playing will not be known until they have no further use for us."

That was a worrying thought as we sailed home to Whitby.

Chapter Twenty-Six

SIR JOHN CARLTON STOOD ON THE STEPS of Chatsworth, his country house in Surrey. Behind him stood Driscol and Lord Gresham, flanked by Cranthorp and Labrum. Another fifty executives of the New Order waited patiently in the lobby.

Driscol nodded to a couple of guards standing to one side as three headlights turned one after the other onto the drive. The guards slipped through the front entrance to await the cars pulling up in front of the steps while Sir John Carlton moved down to welcome the President.

Driscol shivered as a chill breeze caught the waiting men unawares, blowing hair in all directions and causing a door in the reception area to close with a bang. Startled, Labrum jerked sideways and looked over his shoulder.

As the door of the first limousine opened, the waiting party clapped. Carlton shook hands with the President of the New Order.

"Mr President, it's a great honour to finally greet you. We're all eager to hear what you have to say."

"And eager, I hope, to shake up the world and show we're creating a better place for all, the President replied in a deep voice."

"My chief of security, James Driscol, Mr President."

Driscol shook hands and introduced the heads of departments. The last introduction was Cranthorp.

The President chuckled. "So, you are my man inside SIS. Good to meet you, Charles. It is Charles, isn't it?" He looked at Driscol with a mock frown. "Or has he got another name? He could be the PM in disguise."

Everyone laughed except Cranthorp, who managed to put on a weak smile. "Let's hope there are no more members in disguise, Mr President. They have a habit of slipping through our fingers."

Carlton winced and looked warily at Driscol.

"That's my man, Mr President, always on the job and one step ahead. Charles is one of my best," said Driscol with a grin.

The party made their way up the ornate stairway and along a passage to a banqueting hall. On entering, a waiting crowd of delegates gave the President a thunderous applause.

Minutes later, with dinner served, the President turned to Carlton.

"From Cranthorp's quip, I would say you haven't found that damn fool, Myer?"

"That traitor," replied Carlton. "We'll have him soon. Cranthorp is good but needs reigning in."

The President tapped the table. "No, let him run. Besides, anyone who can hide in two jobs at once has the brains to survive and satisfy two masters. That's the kind of man we need." He inclined his head nearer Carlton. "Talking about Myer, Charles, I take it we have target 'Order' taken care of?"

Carlton nodded. "Yes, Mr President, I have someone keeping an eye out."

"Your best man will be carrying out the task?"

"Actually, yes. Our problem is not the target, but someone who could be more dangerous—Pete West."

The President settled back into his chair. "I know about West, John, and the diary. I also heard that the Czech is on the run. What have you done? You have a few days to sort things out. I take it Driscol is taking an active part in tidying up?"

Carlton nodded again. "Yes, Mr President, he is, and I'm sure the diary and the Czech agent will be in our hands shortly. Myer will be taken care of by SIS, but it's West who is a worry. I would like a directive about him."

The Defector's Diary

The President looked around the hall. "You know, John, I'm quite envious of you. A country seat and a knighthood, and soon a bulging bank account." He sighed deeply. "I don't think you need a directive from me. You make sure West is not a player on the day - or the Czech."

Carlton said nothing. The dinner continued with talk of plans until the noisy hum of conversation stopped.

"My lords, ladies and gentlemen, if you please, pray silence for our leader, President George Graham," barked the Toast Master.

Graham stood to address the delegates. He looked around the hall and waited for the applause to stop.

"Delegates, at last, the time has come to help the world step into the future instead of languishing in the darkness of poverty, sickness, and war. In seven days, all of you will help me and the Committee control the start of a smooth takeover of power in Europe. We call it a soft takeover, gradually controlling world finance, pharmaceutical, industrial, and agricultural industries. Our friends in Russia will implement a program we agreed upon. They will control all previous Iron Curtain countries along our guidelines, but control will be in their hands as decided at the last Council meeting. Within a few days, the first phase of the operation will begin.

"This world has become a utopia for rich industrialists who consider themselves our saviours. For most of the population who suffer bad health, poor diet, and the inability to support their families, their lives have become a dark journey like that in Dante's Inferno, a journey through hell. We are going to change that. The industrious workers deserve to enjoy a better standard of life. The rich need to learn a lesson. We will teach it to them."

Thunderous applause erupted, and delegates rose from their chairs. Despite the President holding up a hand, the audience continued to applaud for a minute before settling.

"Across Europe, we will change the face of capitalism and

take control of major industries that have grown too big. Industries, I might add, who have shied away from taxes through legal loopholes, foreign production units, and cheap labour. They will no longer be able to do that. We're taking over."

Carlton applauded with the delegates, who were on their feet again. Cranthorp caught his eye and signalled he was leaving. Carlton nodded. If anyone could recruit or eliminate West, it was Cranthorp. A useful agent, Carlton, had Cranthorp tapped for promotion as soon as the first phase was over.

As the applause lapsed, Graham continued. "And how are we going to do this? The answer is simple. We will achieve our aim peacefully. We already have many people from government and industry in positions who will influence decisions that will start to change living standards for the poor and the needy, not just in third-world countries, but worldwide. It will take time. It has taken fifty years from the time the Bilderberg Club was formed to get to this point, but we are on the threshold of putting our well-laid plans into operation. You have all been given your orders for next week's standby. I want participants to be in position by next weekend. The overall details cannot be given for security reasons but be assured that we cannot succeed without you conducting your part of the plan. One thing I can promise, though. If we all work hard, every one of you will have a seat in the Global Council we're working to create."

There was more applause.

"Gentlemen, apart from a couple of traitors, we're solid in our resolve to get this world back on its feet. Fifty years in the making, we're on the threshold of the most significant social change worldwide. The general election takes place next week. The following day, our plan starts with a peaceful parade as Lord Gresham leads his men across Westminster Bridge. The parade will end at Westminster Palace, and his Lordship will speak to the masses about our intentions. This march, of course, will become a trouble spot, carefully orchestrated.

The Defector's Diary

"And then, the involvement of law and order will assure plenty of publicity. There will be similar demonstrations across Europe and the Middle East, all of which are a smokescreen that will cover our carefully planned soft takeover operation. I predict we will be forming a Global Council within three years to bring stability and an end to heavy investment in nuclear weaponry instead of medicine, agriculture, and other humanitarian projects."

Graham held up both hands above his head, acknowledging the applause. As the ovation subsided, he looked sideways at Carlton with a fixed smile.

"Okay, get the Committee into the conference room and let's go through the program one last time. I have to leave as soon as we're finished."

The two men left the hall, and Carlton nodded to a committee member on the way out. As Graham followed Carlton into the conference room, he turned and closed the door.

"You haven't told the Committee what we're going to do?"

Carlton shook his head. "Part of me is scared stiff. The thought that so many will—"

"Stop thinking about that. Start thinking about what your life is going to be like in a couple of years from now." Graham breathed deeply. "As soon as the drop team have done their job, they will be eliminated. No one except you and me and a couple of our staff will know anything about it. All we have to do is put our public plan into action."

Carlton sat and drummed the table with his fingers. "Are the drop team delivering at the same time? Do they know how to deliver the lighters?"

"Yes, and the beauty of the plan is that the eliminators have no idea what the drop team have done. We have the UK, three cities covered in Europe and two in the Middle East." Graham stopped talking as the Committee started to walk in.

Lord Gresham was the last to arrive and beamed as Graham called for order.

Graham paused before continuing. "We're about to commit ourselves to breaking many international laws. With that in mind, let us get down to details."

* * *

"It looks like we're all ready for the big day. Well done, John. Now let's get rid of the four problems." Graham eased back in his chair as the last Committee member left the room.

Carlton looked worried. It was okay for the President to look at the big picture, but any of the four he talked about could bring the whole thing down.

"Order will be taken care of before the new government sits. SIS is hunting down the Czech agent, the diary, and Myer. Even if they get a chance to open their mouths, no one will listen to them, and the papers will be gagged. It's West who worries me. That man has a reputation for causing trouble. We have to silence him."

Graham chuckled. "You're rattled about him. Relax, John. Offer West something that appeals to his ego. Tell him he can run our world news and broadcasting stations as broadcasting and media director with a few million a year."

Carlton couldn't raise a smile. Graham had no idea what West was capable of doing. He decided to do things his way. West had to be silenced for good.

Chapter Twenty-Seven

JUST AFTER THREE in the morning, a few shore lights sparkled in the distance. The trawler rolled slowly, pushed amidships by waves as Jan cut the engine to a slow speed and manoeuvred to lower the zodiac safely over the side.

Despite that, the engine was still loud, and the noise would carry to the shore. Worried that an inquisitive fishing boat might come to investigate, I grabbed one of the ropes and helped Tosh swing the inflatable over the side. We had no navigation lights, and the wheelhouse lights were turned off by Jan.

"As quick as you can," said Jan, his head barely visible as he leaned out of the bridge window. "Myer first, then the ladies, and then you and Pete, Tosh."

Myer surprised me with his agility, sitting on the gunwale and turning before lowering himself into the zodiac. Dianne did the same, but Valerie panicked. As she made to lower herself, she slipped and dropped with a short gasp that seemed to echo into the black sky. Tosh's attempt to 'shush' her was even louder.

"Come on, guv, you next." Tosh helped me over the side and followed closely. As I sat, I made out Jan, pushing us away from the trawler with a boat hook. As crowded as we were, Myer and I managed to use paddles to get us away from the boat. Seconds later, the trawler's engine roared as it moved off. We sat looking as the dark outline of the ship disappeared into the night.

Tosh sat in the stern with one hand on the outboard control arm. Myer whispered, "The noise from that will wake the whole of Whitby. How about we get within a quarter mile, cut the outboard, and paddle the rest of the way?"

I agreed. "While we're about it, Tosh, do you know where your mate is with the car?"

Tosh raised a torch from his side. "No, but we'll know in a minute." He pointed at the shore. "Watch for a light after I flash. I should be answered with three flashes."

After he signalled the shore, we waited for a long time.

"There it is," said Valerie and pointed. No one saw anything.

After another attempt, we saw a tiny light flashing from the shore.

"Okay," said Tosh. "Keep your heads down. Guv, you and Myer have the paddles handy. That last stretch is gonna' be hard. When we get to the shore, there's a cliff, but some steps will take us to the top and the car."

With that, the outboard started at once. I looked over my shoulder and saw what I hoped was the trawler's navigation lights that Jan had switched back on. Jan had served Tosh and us well, but I doubted I would ever see him again.

With all of us in a crouched position to reduce our silhouette against a bright moon, it took another fifteen minutes before Tosh cut the outboard, and Myer and I started paddling in earnest. Tosh was right. It was hard work. Every two waves we went forward, it felt like we were returning within sight of the shore. Myer signalled to stop. Voices echoed across the water from the beach.

After a moment, Tosh nodded. "It's okay. They won't see or hear us. They're too busy havin' a good rumpy-pumpy. Let's go more to the left of them. I think they're right near our landing spot."

The voices turned out to be a lot of groans. I was glad I could not see Dianne's face, nor she my grin. As we started paddling again, a strong beam of light lit up a couple on the shore, who quickly got up and ran along the beach.

"Thank you, George," said Tosh. "Come on. Get us in."

As the boat beached, we scrambled and pulled the inflatable

The Defector's Diary

onto the sand.

"Have to make sure it's safe for the collection boys. Her Majesty would not be pleased if I lost her boat."

Exhausted, Myer and I climbed the steps to the top of the cliff and stood with the rest of our group, catching our breath until Tosh arrived. He walked ahead of us and came back with our driver.

"This is George, ladies and gentlemen." He introduced us and moved up front as we got comfortable in the twelve-seater.

George proved to be another man of few words, and I wondered if all of Tosh's contacts were underworld members. None of them dressed smartly, and none smiled, but they were all tough. George, a thick-set man of middle age with a no-nonsense air about him, had a quick chat with Tosh before moving off.

"We're going for breakfast at a cottage I arranged, and George is cooking. He's a fast-food chef."

There was a chorus of approval that at least we would have a decent meal and a drink to warm our flagging spirits.

Twenty minutes later, it was six o'clock, and dawn had broken. We came to a roadside sign that announced a welcome to Staithes. Ahead, I could see the start of a row of cottages and shops. We turned into a lane and came to a halt.

Tosh's safe house was a small, whitewashed cottage standing in a cobbled area leading down to a footbridge that spanned the Upper Beck. The cottage backed onto the tidal river. A varied collection of colourful dinghies and small clinker-built fishing boats lay moored to buoys on the mudflats within a few feet of the untidy garden.

"Your home sweet home," announced Tosh, pointing at the cottage. "We'll eat first and then settle in."

A few minutes later, we sat and looked at a hot meal and a mug of tea. The conversation was minimal, and I spent the whole meal thinking about our situation. I wanted to see Dianne away to her father in Cannes, but her help was invaluable. With a puzzle to unlock quickly, I was deciding whether or not to suggest that she leave us.

Myer got up with Valerie as the meal ended and announced he would get some cigarettes.

"Then I go too," said Valerie.

Myer shook his head. "No, you stay here and I'll get the cigarettes for you."

Valerie was adamant. "We're in England and nearly in London. The little row of shops we passed when we arrived is a short distance away."

"No," said Myer. "You stay here."

He left and banged the door after him. Before anyone could move, Valerie rushed for the door and ran after him.

Tosh joined us in the lounge. "That girl is a load of trouble. The sooner we offload her, the better."

I waited until we sat comfortably, then told Dianne of my concern. "You should seriously consider returning to your father's place. He must be worried about your safety as I am."

A sudden crash on the cottage door made us all jump. Myer staggered into the cottage. Blood ran down the side of his face from a head wound. "She's gone. They were waiting." He waved at the door. "At the newsagents. Someone hit me from behind and threw me to the ground. One of the men hit me again while a big bald guy pulled her into a car as I got up. She was screaming, but I couldn't get to her in time. I'm sorry. I'm so sorry."

Tosh bent over Myer as I wiped the side of his head. He looked dejected.

"I told her to go back, but she was so insistent. We walked to the top of the lane, turned left on the main road through the village to the newsagents, and that's when it happened."

Tosh handed me more tissues.

"It's all right," I said. "So, what happened next?"

Myer winced as I touched his forehead. "A big brute grabbed

The Defector's Diary

Valerie and kicked me. I tried my best, but I fell to the ground, and they raced off."

I looked at Tosh, but there was no reaction. Something about the way Valarie filled me with anxiety. Getting the diary to London was essential, but getting the girl there was now more critical. We had to have Valerie backing up the diary and SIS confirming her identity as a Czech agent.

"They must have gone back to the station to look for the fake diary you dropped and know we still have the real one, guv," said Tosh. "What bothers me is how they found us so quickly."

"Only Cranthorp could have found us so quickly," I answered. SIS have all sorts of satellite surveillance data, covering land and sea worldwide. Labrum has nothing like that. Cranthorp must be considered part of the New Order. He would have passed the information on to Labrum, who returned to London a day before we set sail."

Labrum was only too aware of our situation, and as long as he had Valerie, he had the upper hand. I didn't doubt he would want the diary in exchange for the young woman's life, but that had little chance of happening. Whether we gave him the diary or not, Valerie was most certainly looking at being shot.

Dejected, we sat around in the cottage, knowing time was running out, and we still had no idea where the planned assassination would take place or who the victim would be. There were also the four cities where an attack of some description was to occur on the same day.

"Well, we still have the diary," said Dianne. "Come on. We can't just sit here."

Myer almost jumped out of his chair. "What the hell is wrong with you all? The bloody girl is gone and you'll not get her back. She's as good as dead, and you know it. I agree with Dianne. Let's find out who the target is and where the assassin will be."

Despite Myer's rejuvenated enthusiasm, I felt terrible, and Tosh looked defeated. It was as though we had hit a wall. It would take a miracle to solve the problem and save a life with just a few days to go.

We spent a very gloomy evening after desperately attempting to look at all possibilities. No one spoke through dinner, and I had an early night, leaving Dianne and Myer scribbling and discussing the diary entries. I fell asleep, hoping for a better day come morning.

Tosh had been quiet throughout breakfast, and I kept looking at his facial expression. He showed no emotion as he ate breakfast. By contrast, Myer was talking animatedly with Dianne.

"Was Labrum involved again?" observed Tosh. "Did you see him in the car, Michael?"

Myer shook his head.

I turned to Tosh. "You're the expert. What next?"

"Well, they'll take her somewhere safe and question her. They know we have the diary, but Valerie has a lot of information about other dealings with SIS and her people that could be useful to the New Order. That's why debriefing takes months. Labrum will be back and won't rest until they have the diary. It won't be long before they start following us again. There's probably someone out there right now. The first thing we have to do is get out of here and relocate."

"Supposing it was Cranthorp who snatched Valerie?" I suggested. He wouldn't try and take us all. That would be too public and cause a problem for all who want the diary – namely publicity. Neither Cranthorp nor the New Order want publicity."

"You could be right, guv,

so let's make a move and shake the buggers off." +

"Where are we going?" said Dianne.

"Valerie said Westminster."

We all looked at Myer, head in hand.

"She was screaming at me, something about Westminster."

Tosh tossed the house key to George. "Clean up here and go home. You'll have to grab a lift to the station. I doubt they'll be

The Defector's Diary

back but be as quick as you can. I'll call you later if we need you. Thanks, George."

We left George and, within a few minutes, drove out of the village.

"I think we should head for London," I suggested. "We need to alert someone in Whitehall— someone who is a true royalist."

"Home Secretary," said Myer promptly."

"Do you know him well?" I asked.

"I do," replied Myer. "We were at Eton together."

"Good," interrupted Tosh. "You can go talk to him and tell him your story. Well, most of it anyway. You know the man. You're a diplomat. You have more knowledge of what's going on inside the Bilderberg Club than we. You're more believable than us. We're on the run and wanted in connection with the murders. You can, at least, warn him about the New Order members you know. Name them and get them watched."

"We need time, Michael," I said. "Whatever's going to happen is now only a few days away. Somehow, we have to decipher the diary, and before you suggest it, no, we're not going to hand it over."

Dianne stirred from a catnap on my shoulder. "Michael, we'll be arrested on sight if we try to see anyone. It's you or nothing. SIS will be all over you, and you can tell them we have the diary and why."

"What?" Tosh and I said it together.

"We have a few days," she answered. "Whether they believe you or not, they'll start looking for a mole or two. We know that. They're paranoid, and with a bit of luck, Cranthorp will be caught. If he takes part in whatever goes on and gets nabbed before the time is up, the New Order plan may fail. We have to try something."

"I'm going to end up in jail." Myer sighed as we entered the motorway.

I decided to call Hart when we stopped at a services rest area.

It would take about five hours and over 250 miles to get to central London via the A1. Then, I needed to hide Tosh and Dianne so they could work on the diary. I was half expecting the phone to ring and hear Labrum's sarcastic voice giving me an order. Then I realized he didn't have our mobile numbers—or maybe he did. There was one he might have.

"Valerie shouted Westminster to me. She shouted it twice," reminded Myer. He went through the clues again.

"17th, WB 11.30—HP 12.00—ET CG DIV—MED EX SCHED 10.00—Order."

"What the heck has that to do with Westminster?" I asked.

Myer gunned the car to seventy. "Okay, so what's associated with Westminster?"

"Government, tradition, the cathedral, Big Ben, River Thames, House of Lords," recited Dianne.

"More precise," I said. "Think politics."

"Government, House of Lords, MPs, the Speaker, the Prime—"

"No, no," I interrupted. "Landmarks. If this entry is to do with a meeting, surely the letters or some of them will refer to the place where the meeting is to take place."

"Good thinking, Pete."

We reached the outskirts of York and continued for Leeds. The rain was relentless, falling from a dark, grey sky, giving the landscape a Dickensian feel.

Dianne poked me in the ribs. "Okay, Mr Smarty, let's hear what you're thinking."

"Westminster Palace, Big Ben, the Terrace, Royal Gallery, Peers' Lobby, Westminster Hall—"

"Hold it, Pete. You said, Westminster Palace?"

"We're looking for a WB," I corrected.

Dianne stopped me. "How about Westminster Bridge? And what's at the end of the bridge?"

"HP, the Houses of Parliament," interrupted Tosh.

The Defector's Diary

I tapped my forehead and gave Tosh a wink. "Well done."

We were all in a good mood at last, a moment of triumph that encouraged a more active and enthusiastic approach to the problem.

"Rest stop coming up," announced Myer. "Time to have something to eat at a café and pick up petrol."

Myer turned onto the A1(M), and the services were three miles further on. Although it was a welcome break, I was anxious about getting to London.

Tosh had indicated that he knew a place—when didn't he—that Myer and Dianne could use as a safe house. According to him, the place was empty and due for demolition. I couldn't see Dianne liking that, but we had no choice for now. My other concern, of course, was for Valerie. I felt it was right to get to London. Labrum would not keep her up north.

He would want her near as a bargaining chip and as the diary interpreter once he got a hold of it. He would need to know how much Jozef found out and if it was correct. If it were, he would want to see if we had passed anything on to the authorities. He must have known we would head for London, particularly Whitehall.

After filling the tank, we drove into the service centre and parked near the exit. Mindful that we were all wanted people, we found a corner table and sent Dianne to order food for us all. She returned with four plastic cups full of steaming, hot tea.

From under her arm, she dropped a newspaper onto the table and sat. "Headlines, gentlemen."

Myer's face stared at us from a story headlined, EU trade secretary wanted in connection with two murders. The story was much the same as published a few days before in the European press. What was annoying was the photo.

"At least you look a little different now," said Tosh, sipping tea. "You haven't shaved, and your clothes are dirty. You'll do for now."

I choked on tea and laughed. "He means well, Michael."

"On a more serious note, we need to hide as soon as we get within striking distance of Westminster. In a few days, something is going to happen, and we have no idea what. We need to be there." Tosh looked at each one of us in turn as he spoke.

I excused myself, leaving them to sort that problem out, and called Max. He answered almost at once.

"Bad news, I'm afraid," I replied. "Valerie has been kidnapped."

It took me another five minutes to bring him up to date. I also gave him the entry from the diary and asked him to get a paper crossword expert to decipher the rest of the initials.

"By the way, Max, can you urgently get me a copy of the dignitaries attending the Othello production at the Royal Opera House on the seventeenth? It's important."

"Okay." There was a loud sigh. "Well, at least the Home Secretary will know, and that will get the authorities off your back. Be very careful tonight. I take it Dianne is going to be left out of all this?"

"Max, I do believe you have a soft spot for my wife."

"Sod off, Pete." With that, he was gone.

I rejoined the others, and we left as soon as we gobbled lunch. The rain had abated, leaving puddles dotted about on the potholed tarmac. Several cars splashed past us as we tried to avoid the holes.

Tosh was the first to spot something as he looked around the park, worrying about his trainers getting dirty. A piece of paper stuck to the screen under a wiper blade of our car.

"Can't be a parking ticket," Tosh joked as he pulled it off the screen. He took one look and gave it to me. "Bastards!"

Myer pushed the engine into drive, and I read the note as we got underway.

Forst will die, and so will you, unless you bring the diary to the address below at one a.m. No police and no SIS.

The Defector's Diary

Give us the dairy, and you can have Forst. Remember, as you may have already found out, we are everywhere in positions of authority.

Your death will be an accident.

I turned the paper over. "The address is a boatyard in Norfolk."

Chapter Twenty-Eight

MYER HAD A QUESTION. "What happens to my trip to Whitehall?"

Tosh answered him. "You still go, Michael. We get you to meet somewhere without Labrum finding out."

"How do you propose doing that? Labrum's been following us all morning, and he'll have others follow us when we get to London."

"Leave it to me."

"You'll be letting him have the diary, though?" asked Dianne. "He will know we have a copy, but all he wants to know is how much Jozef knew."

We were on that same wavelength again. "Yes," I answered, "but we'll not be letting him have the diary."

"Why?"

"As we agreed, without the diary, we have nothing concrete to show the Prime Minister that he has traitors in his camp, and that SIS, or some of the staff there, are taking part in destabilizing the European government and murdering anyone that gets in their way. Then, of course, he has to know about all the other members of the Bilderberg Club's inner circle in EU governments and the USA. Remember that Valerie probably has a lot of information that will be very useful for our security services." I took a breath. "We also have another problem. We can't scream for help without getting arrested and put in jail."

We were all silent for a moment. Valerie's life lay in the balance. Myer switched on the headlights as the rain started to fall again.

The Defector's Diary

"There's only one thing for it, guv. We'll have to rescue the girl."

Myer shook his head. "Are you kidding, Tosh? That would be suicide. Look who we're up against."

"There is another way to rescue her that does not involve violence," said Dianne. "Pete, do you remember the file switch you did on the News of the World expose?"

"Yes, I switched one with rubbish notes for their one with the incriminating evidence on phone tapping. What are you proposing?"

"Will Labrum know what the diary looks like? If not, let's call in at a stationery office and gift wrap a diary for Mr Labrum. Inside, he'll find all the information Jozef knew about. The trouble is it won't be anything like the notes in the original."

"I don't think he does either," I replied. "If Jozef kept secrets in that diary, he's not likely to have shown anyone. Well thought, darling. We'll make it look well used. Fold a few pages over and tear a couple out. It will look genuine enough."

"Okay, who's going to the meeting? It can't be Dianne, and it can't be me," said Myer. "I'll be making arrangements to visit the Home Secretary and give myself up."

Tosh caught my eye in the rearview mirror and grinned.

"Blimey, guv, it's down to the dynamic duo again. Got your cape, have you? I'll do the business and you can cover me. Labrum doesn't know me, does he?"

"I don't think it matters who he knows or doesn't know, Tosh. I'm sure he does know you if he's been following us." I eyed Dianne's concerned face. "I know you said that for her sake, but really, you want me handling a gun? That's what she's concerned about—me with a gun."

We all laughed and got stuck into the initials puzzle again. In the back of my mind, I was sure Cranthorp was working with Labrum and the New Order.

***

"Can you write Czech, Michael?" I asked as Dianne got back into the car.

We had driven off the main road to visit a shopping parade in Cambridge. Dianne found the stationers and bought a diary—the same size and colour as Jozef Novotney's book.

"I'm not too bad at it. Why?"

I waved the torn page that Valerie sent me.

"Oh, right. Yes, I see. Well, I'll have a go. Should be enough to fool Labrum for long enough."

"There's always a chance he's going to follow us anyway, just in case—that's if he lets us go at all."

Tosh was right. It wasn't just the diary Labrum was after for his masters. Labrum would have instructions to get rid of us or keep us captive until after the event, in which case there wouldn't be any need to stop us from telling our story. Without the diary, it was the end of our mission.

We got no further with the initials game and decided to rest our brains until we got to the house Tosh arranged. Dianne started to write initials and other entries into the new diary, apart from anything written in extended Czech. Outside, the weather had not improved. When we reached the main road again, it started to rain again. We drove on in a sombre mood, with Tosh calling his contacts and Myer and me discussing what he would say to the Home Secretary.

We pulled outside a tenement block of flats in Brixton an hour later. Tosh did his best to be cheerful after noting the look of absolute displeasure on Dianne's face but failed miserably.

"It's all right, Mrs W, you'll be safe here. Even the police won't venture around here at night. After six, it's a no-go area for the blues. They come here, and these buggers throw petrol bombs at them. It's happened a couple of times. I remember—"

"Thanks, Tosh. Now, can we get into the flat?" I asked.

The Defector's Diary

Dianne said nothing. We climbed out of the car as quickly as possible and entered the building's hallway. We took the stairs littered with cigarette butts, beer cans, takeaway food cartons, and a variety of other rubbish scattered everywhere.

The flat consisted of two bedrooms, each with one bed with no bedclothes, a sitting room with a three-piece suite, a dining table and chairs with the sixties written all over them, and a clean bathroom with no running water. The kitchen had an electric kettle and crockery but no tea or food in the cupboards.

We had only been there a few minutes when a knock came, and Tosh opened the door to a stranger carrying a large box of food, milk, and two bottles of water. We could also smell hot Chinese food.

"Thanks, Tosh," I said as the man disappeared. "We eat well even though we don't sleep well."

The remark brought laughter from Dianne, who thought it funny, and I was pleased she could see the lighter side of our situation.

"All right let's eat. Dianne and Michael can then have a go at the diary while Tosh and I go do business with Labrum." I turned to Myer. "Michael, why not call the Home Secretary at home in the morning rather than tonight in case he decides to have SIS pick you up. That way, you will stay with Dianne until we return."

Myer nodded as Tosh left to talk to the delivery man.

"Another thing," I said. "If we're being followed, I'll call you, and you can either get downstairs and wait for us to pick you up or, if the bad boys are close behind, agree on a meeting point later on. Let's play this by ear. If we don't get to you, it means we have run into trouble, and you, Dianne, must go with Michael to see the Home Secretary tomorrow. Okay?"

They both nodded.

Tosh returned and thumbed over his shoulder. "He's gonna look after you tonight. Him and a mate." He looked at Dianne. "Three men to look after you, Mrs W. What more could you want?" He chuckled.

"My husband," replied Dianne. "I want him back, and if he has a scratch on him, you'll be wearing one too after I've dealt with you." She glared at him.

I smiled, but that faded as her glare settled on me. I still wasn't forgiven. It was not the fact that we might part; there was no chance of that. I know how she felt about me. I worried that trust had been thrown out of the window when I opened her letter and said nothing. Would she still want a family if further examination proved good? I said goodbye, but there was no smile, just a hand wave. I felt awful.

Chapter Twenty-Nine

TOSH DECIDED it would be good to get to Norfolk as early as possible and stake out the boatyard where the meeting was to occur. Our destination was Beccles, a traditional casting-off place for holidaymakers wanting to mess about on boats on the Broads—mostly during summer.

The journey across the flat landscape of Essex and Suffolk before reaching Norfolk was uneventful. With night drawing in and a black, cloudy sky threatening a thunderstorm, Tosh drove around in several patterns after reaching the small town, checking we had not been followed.

I took the opportunity to question him. It was time to test our friendship.

"Why haven't you told me what's going on with you?" I asked. "You may not be with SIS anymore, but you're still with security regardless of what government department you're working for."

Tosh's face revealed nothing except a blank stare on the road ahead. He worked for SIS for many years, and as far as I knew, there was only one real tragedy he'd endured when he lost a colleague. Apart from some of his family history, I knew nothing else about him. His story about investigating the disappearance of Myer was, at the very least, weak. And why, after finding the man, did he not escort him back to Britain, or at least Brussels? Why was he still involved in something he claimed had nothing to do with the department he worked for? He had once told me there would be no answers or discussions on his work, and I respected his wishes. Now, it appeared he was no longer part of SIS. With the warning from Max and the relationship between him and Myer, I wanted answers.

I looked sideways at him and said, "I think you owe me."

He bit his bottom lip, and his eyes caught mine. "I guess I do owe you an explanation, but if you use anything I tell you, both of us will end up in real trouble," he said at length. "The truth is, my office has been investigating the Bilderberg Club for some time now."

"Okay, so where does Myer come into this?"

"Myer is my agent," said Tosh. "I've been running him for the last eighteen months."

"What! You're attached to SIS then?"

"No, I'm attached to Number Eleven Downing Street."

I took a deep breath. "The Chancellor's office. Now that's a first."

Tosh flicked the heater switch and turned up the heat. "No. There have been Treasury agents for quite a few years now."

The conversation came to an end as we approached Beccles. Satisfied no one was following, we found the boatyard two hours before the meeting and left the car near the car park exit.

"Ready for a climbing exercise, guv?"

"Not with you, Tosh. What climb?"

He pointed at the long boathouse roof with a grin. "I'll teach you somethin' here. It's called the 'Bye-bye drop.'"

"What?"

"Guv, pick up some bricks and follow me up the ladder."

Something told me he was about to extend my knowledge of tradecraft that might be outside the law. I looked around and grabbed a couple of bricks from a pile against the fence.

"There's another boatyard to one side of us and on the other, a car park. Behind us, we have the river, and in front, the main road. The roof is a good vantage point to see if Labrum places men around us. We have a ladder at the back and front of the shed for access for escape. There's also this." He produced a pistol and patted the grip. "It's fully loaded."

The Defector's Diary

I've never been happy about guns, but after a couple of dramatic episodes in the past with Tosh, I was pleased that we had some security, knowing that Labrum was capable of killing.

"We're going up on the roof?" I asked as he pocketed the pistol.

"Yes, and if no one comes up here, you can stay until I signal. Then you go down and insist you do the business where the car is. You're not going inside the boatshed. By the way, don't forget to call Dianne."

"Okay, let's climb and then I'll call to let her know we arrived."

I looked at my watch. We had another hour and a half before the meeting. Labrum was sure to get to the yard early, and I was thankful for Tosh's directions and thinking. At that moment, we had the upper hand.

After reaching the roof, we found a channel between the two halves of the roof with a row of duckboards we could walk on.

"Listen, guv, you go and sit at the other end and cover the rear and river. When they come, I'll give you a couple of flashes with my torch if it's safe, and you climb down the back way and go and meet him, okay?" He chuckled. "If I see anyone hiding at the bottom of the ladder, I'll flash the torch, and when you're above the ladder, drop the bricks one at a time. If you don't knock him out, you'll at least get him to retreat."

For the next hour, I sat watching the river and several people sitting outside a pub on the other bank having a drink.

Dianne seemed pleased when I called. Before I left, she had scribbled all the entries inside the pad, and it did not take long to transfer everything into the new diary. Myer had written some longhand about meetings at the coffee shop, making the notations look like private chat notes. Not knowing what they meant, she had written every other one correctly, and the rest were made up or changed slightly, including the one we were trying to understand. Myer had devised a new solution: ET stood for the Elizabeth Tower, Big Ben's home. We now knew that whatever was going to happen involved the Tower. I hoped my assessment that the New Order was not contemplating terrorism of any kind was correct, but my instincts said otherwise. I sat going through all the scenarios I could think of, including the Tower's use.

When Tosh flashed his torch, it took me unawares. I was deep in thought and missed the first flash. At the end of the duckboards, I found the top of the metal ladder attached to the rear wall and swung a leg over the guardrail. Halfway down, I heard a faint conversation and Labrum's loud voice.

"If you're there, West, show yourself or the girl will be shot and left here. I do hope you're going to be sensible. Your wife would want that, wouldn't she?"

By then, I was on the ground and started to walk along the side of the boatshed. I reached about halfway when I heard footsteps behind me.

"Keep walking," said a gruff voice.

Labrum stood beside his car a little way from mine as I appeared in the open car park. Next to him was a thug, but I couldn't see Valerie. Hands touched my back as my follower patted me down.

"He's clean."

In the half-light, I could see Labrum's smirking face.

"If you think you're getting the diary without handing over the girl, you can think again," I snapped. "In case you want to get rid of me, you should know a story will appear in my paper exposing your sordid little group and its activities, including the murders of three men."

Labrum laughed. "My dear West, the last thing on my mind is causing any undue distress to you or your friends. I want the diary so you cannot wave it in the air to prove your silly story of lies. We're setting up a single worldwide government that will deal with terrorism by using strict security and create a sound economy by controlling industry."

I was astounded. The man seemed as though brainwashed—

maybe he was.

"You look confused, West. The public will soon lose confidence in the present government, and journalists like yourself will be pushing for a referendum on our new proposals."

I shook my head. "You're mad, totally off your head. Do you honestly believe other countries like America will applaud this stupid pipedream?"

"We already have many Americans in the Order."

There it was again, another reference to terrorism. Whatever their plan, it would be an act of violence. I was now convinced of that.

"Where's the girl?" I asked.

"She's safe, and unless you hand over the diary, she'll be killed, I assure you. I think you call it collateral damage."

"You bastard," I muttered. "You're not going to get away with this. Tell me whereabouts in the Order are you? If you're so proud of your organization, tell me who sits at the top controlling thugs like you?"

"You'll know soon enough," said Labrum, holding out a hand. "Nothing is happening overnight—no coup or dramatic mass resignations. There will be a slow swing to the idea of a new form of government. Now give me the diary."

"I take it you have members of our security services as well," I said, reaching inside my coat.

"Of course. Loyal and very efficient, they are, too. That reminds me," Labrum said, his hand steady on a small pistol pointing at me. "I have been asked to make you an offer to become director of media communications at three million a year."

I laughed as I handed over the fake diary. The full impact of what he proposed was frightening. "If you think I'd be impressed, you can think again, and tell that to the idiots running your stupid show. Stick your offer."

He used the word 'control', suggesting less democracy and more heavy-handed authoritarian ideals. Even more worrying was that industrialists and politicians with vast knowledge who provide utilities such as oil, gas, water, pharmaceutical production and the Midas touch in investment and money markets could become huge sharks in a sea of cartels, leaving the public at their mercy. We had to stop them, but how?

Labrum raised a hand, and the thug beside him walked to the car's rear. Moments later, Valerie appeared and pushed forward. Labrum held the diary in front of her.

"Is this the correct book, or have they tried doing something stupid?"

Valerie looked at me and then at Labrum and hesitated.

"After putting her right, she decided to join our side, especially as we offered her sanctuary in London. You see, West, you cannot win."

I held my breath.

"It's the right one," she answered.

I played along, not wishing to have Labrum think she was fooling him. She must have told him something, but whatever it was, I was glad she did not appear hurt in any way.

"You'll go to jail, Valerie. They won't keep their promise. You should know that. When they're finished with you, they'll throw you to the wolves—or worse."

"I'll take my chances," replied Valerie.

"Now, get in the car." Labrum waved the gun and motioned me toward his car.

I was trying to think quickly, wondering how I could escape, when our meeting broke up with a loud bang, thanks to Tosh. A shot rang out from behind me, and a bullet ricocheted off the roof of Labrum's car. Everyone ducked. Without thinking, I ran to the back of our car.

Valerie ran toward me as Labrum returned fire.

"I didn't tell them anything," she shouted.

She seemed to stumble and fall between Labrum and me, who

The Defector's Diary

had shielded himself behind the open car door. Valerie lay motionless, and I was stunned. Another shot rang out and was returned by Tosh, who hit one of the thugs in the leg. The man fell and then crawled into the back of the car.

"You murdering bastard," I shouted. "You'll suffer for this."

"No, West!" Labrum cried out. "She confirmed you had the right goods, and that was all we needed from her. Now you'll suffer. I know where your wife is. I would think by now we have her in custody, along with Myer. You open your mouth and she's dead."

All the time he was talking, he was edging into the car.

Tosh ran to join me.

"Don't worry, guv. I called Mrs W after we got on the roof and told her to get out and take a cab ride around London for a couple of hours until we phoned. I couldn't take the chance they followed us and were going to lift her."

"Thanks." I looked at Valerie lying in front of us and cuffed a tear from an eye. That she had tried to do the right thing hurt. All I could see was a frightened face and eyes that closed before she hit the ground.

Labrum shouted. "I'll be going now! Don't try anything stupid. If you want to blame anyone for what has just happened, blame Tosh. I guess you could say it was a usual SIS cock-up."

"Oh, I see," I choked, trying to shout. "It was him who pulled the trigger and killed this young woman. You had a choice…you killed her, you bastard!"

Labrum slammed his door, and the car sped away, wheels spinning for grip.

"He's right in a way, guv. If I hadn't taken the first shot, he wouldn't have shot back," said Tosh. "I'm sorry, but I couldn't let you be taken."

I put an arm on his shoulder, and he helped me to my feet.

"No, you were right, Tosh. He didn't have to shoot her." I took a deep breath. "I'm going to make sure he spends the rest of his miserable existence in jail, or worse."

Valerie lay face down on the wet tarmac, her hair a tangled mess. Tosh stopped me from touching her. "Crime scene, guv. We have to leave her there. There could be DNA from that swine on her clothing. I'll call the office and have things dealt with."

It felt so wrong to leave her there, but Tosh's advice made sense once again. Our DNA would not be found, although Tosh would make a full report to his people. I got into the car and called Dianne.

"She's dead. Labrum shot her in the back. I'm now as sure as I can be that he was responsible for the deaths of the others, including Adam."

Dianne was distraught. Eventually, she explained that another car had pulled up with three men inside as they left in a cab.

Tosh spent the next few minutes on the phone talking to his office. From how he spoke, I knew he kept in constant touch with them, informing them as I did with Max.

I wanted to talk and not think about Valerie. The thought that she lay alone during the time it took the services to reach her made me feel angry.

Chapter Thirty

IT WAS STILL DARK by the time we reached the outskirts of London. A faint glimmer of dawn pricked the horizon.

Bread delivery vans with open doors and bright interiors illuminated rows of freshly wrapped bread, and trays of pastries were everywhere, parked on pavements or double-parked on roads outside supermarkets and small corner grocers. The new day was already alive, but there would be no more mornings for some. Valerie was dead. The vision of her running toward me, shouting she told that bastard nothing, played on my mind. I promised her she would get to London. I felt I let Adam down, and now Valerie. Just twenty-something. What a waste.

I continued my conversation with Tosh about why he became involved in the events surrounding the Bilderberg conference. It was understandable why the Chancellor of the Exchequer would be concerned if rumours spread that a breakaway group within the society was planning something that would upset our very foundation. It was worrying that those involved were top-level government officials and industrial masterminds from all over Europe who could change the world in a concerted effort, provided they had surprise and people in the right places at the right time.

"They got wind of what was going on way back before I joined the department," explained Tosh. "Four years ago, Jozef Novotney made some private remarks to a colleague in Brussels who just happened to be the Prime Minister's press officer. The conversation was overheard by someone sitting in the interpreter's box at the back of the auditorium. Novotney said the best thing for Europe would be a centralized government controlling a European single currency market from London.

"The Prime Minister was pissed off when the interpreter leaked the conversation to an American reporter. Even more embarrassing for the PM was that the Number 10 press officer didn't bother to mention anything to him because he didn't think it was that important. Of course, a new press officer was in place within days."

"Sounds like a typical cock-up situation," I said.

"It gets better," replied Tosh. "The guy who was replaced had an offer of an excellent position with SIS. After all, what better recruit for security than the PM's old press officer."

"I take it this guy has to do with our present situation, or you wouldn't be talking about him."

Tosh overtook a bus and then slowed as we approached Blackfriars Bridge. "He most certainly has. It's Cranthorp—a real nice bastard if there ever was one. He came in over my head and is pencilled as next in line to make assistant to the Director."

I was amazed. SIS trawled in the most unlikely places and employed some strange bedfellows. "He's one of the New Order thugs too."

"Yes, we have a pretty extensive list, but we must be careful and choose the right time to whisper in the PM's ear."

"The time to whisper is upon us," I muttered. "You still haven't told me about your part in all this, not that I'm supposed to know. It might help both of us if we are at the same place in this mess."

"Pretty simple. I was assigned to look at Novotney, keep an eye on his contacts and friends, and see if any of them had any dealings with other names we had on our list. Unfortunately, I only recognized two of the initials you're decoding in the diary."

"Let me guess," I said. "That's when you found out about Michael Myer and became his best friend."

Tosh nodded and turned the heater down a notch. "Yes. I

The Defector's Diary

wouldn't put it quite like that, guv. It took me three months to talk Myer into working for Number Eleven. He did a good job too. We knew within hours when Novotney became a member of the Steerage Committee, and that's when we came up with a plan for our mole."

"You engineered an offer Jozef Novotney couldn't refuse. Of course, by then, Myer was convincing Novotney that he had his feet in the wrong camp."

"After the second or third meeting, he began talking to Myer. Although he agreed with the principles of a world government, it was the realization that members would be wielding enormous personal power and gain untold wealth that changed his mind."

"I take it Myer and Novotney then came to an agreement—orchestrated by you and your office—that Novotney would nominate Myer to take his place while he accepted a position that would later help the New Order. Very neat."

"I thought so, guv. The two would meet and discuss things over a coffee, and Myer would report back to me. Then things started to go wrong. At their next meeting without the usual security, Novotney appeared to have a change of heart and told Myer he should consider working for the New Order's benefit. Myer was bloody annoyed and ended up arranging another meeting without police security. That's because I wanted to be near to eavesdrop. As you know, that meeting never took place because Myer found the police crawling all over Novotney's house."

"I take it Myer then contacted you because he heard from Novotney the day before that Valerie had been decommissioned, meaning she was working for the Czech security service?"

"Yes, of course. Only SIS knew, along with Adam, who she was. When Myer told me, I instructed him to go missing, but see Adam first and convince him to drop Valerie and distance himself. His career was finished anyway. Myer, too, was much better missing than in the Czechs' firing line. They knew through Forst's reports that he regularly met Novotney. Myer couldn't go home either, or Special Branch would have nabbed him, and we could not be seen verifying he worked for the Chancellor's office from inside a secret society. The whole thing turned mucky, and no one wanted dirt on their doorstep."

"And when Adam refused to give up the girl he loved, he put himself in harm's way." I sighed. "That was the day you, SIS, and the New Order found out about the diary—and me the day before.

"Adam must have told Cranthorp, who was running him. As we now know, Cranthorp is the New Order and high up in SIS." I paused before asking the next question. Myer had never revealed he knew Tosh or was doing anything except holding office as an EU trade secretary and supporter of the Bilderberg Club. "How come you and Myer haven't let on you know each other? In his talks with me, he never let on he had a handler. I got the impression he was working alone after Novotney's death."

"I'm glad to hear that, guv. He's not supposed to tell you anything and should only do what he's told to do. The reason he's not let on about his relationship with me is simple. He doesn't know me at all. We have always communicated by text or through other contacts such as Jan—and Myer doesn't personally know Jan either. If Special Branch or SIS question either of them, they have no one to point the finger at."

"You're unbelievable, Tosh."

"You learn a lot from other people's mistakes, guv. SIS was a good training ground."

We pulled into a parking spot on the Embankment. Dawn was breaking now, and early morning traffic was getting heavy. Across the pedestrian pavement, a small kiosk selling newspapers and cigarettes was open. Light from a single bare bulb cast a tapered shaft of brightness down onto the vendor sorting magazines and papers on a large counter.

Tosh left the car and walked across to the vendor. A cloud of smoke rose as the man exhaled, the cigarette hanging from his

The Defector's Diary

lips. They knew each other, which didn't surprise me. After a couple of minutes of conversation, Tosh returned. In his hand, apart from the usual packet of cigarettes, were four pay-as-you-go phones.

"There you go, guv," he said. He shivered as he closed the door. The dawn had brought frost in the air and a promise of more bad weather.

"I'll call Dianne," I said. "Let's hope she's somewhere near and we can all get breakfast, unless she's on the way to the meeting."

I tried her number twice but without a reply.

"She could be in a bad signal area or even at the meeting, so don't panic," said Tosh. "Let's give her another ten minutes and try again. Give Max a call and let him know we're back in town."

Max was available. He had been up all night and was putting the final touches on an article about rumours surrounding the latest Bilderberg conference that Richard Hart had composed, carefully avoiding any reference to the Conservative Party's involvement. It was a wise move. Other editors would avoid following an 'old chestnut' that did the rounds each year as protest groups made their voices heard.

When the real story hit the public, the Herald would be first to print it, two steps ahead of the rest.

I spoke for five minutes and told him about the previous night's activities and that he might have the story before the day was out, but I warned him that all Hart could do was talk to Number 10 and hope we could write the piece without revealing names. Too many top people were involved, and exposing them and their plans for the future to the public could have a counter-productive effect. An article presenting the diary of a man with ridiculous ideas about a world order would be of varied interest to people. Still, to members of the New Order, it would spell the end of their plans and the careers of all those involved. Jozef Novotney would be a scapegoat, but he would have approved as long as the integrity of the Bilderberg Club was maintained.

"That's a great line, Pete, but we need the diary, and you've given it to the government."

"We have to trust someone, Max. Look, there's something else I just found out." Tosh poked me in the ribs and put a finger to his lips. I nodded. "I can't tell you right now, but someone at the top of the government, excluding the PM, is seeing Myer and Dianne at the moment. That's the person who's looking at the diary at the moment, I hope."

"What do you mean, you hope?"

"I can't raise Dianne right now."

"Christ, Pete. And she's with Myer? Can you trust him?"

"I have to. I'm sure she's okay. Probably in a blind spot or at the meeting."

"Okay, what about the initials? Anything there? Our boy at this end came up with a good idea. Go to Westminster and look at all the buildings, statues, and places of interest around Parliament and see if you can match the initials to a building or reference a historical event. Oh, yes. Check the timing of TV interviews to see if anything is happening around one of those times you have."

"I have a feeling Tosh was about to suggest that. We're on the Embankment right now."

"Okay, Pete, keep me informed. Richard is standing by to drive to Number Ten, if necessary, although the PM is expected in the House today for Question Time."

"I'll bear that in mind. Thanks, Max. Did you get me that list of dignitaries?"

"Look at your tablet. It's nothing that would be kept from the general public."

Max ended the call, and I tried Dianne's number again. It rang and rang. Frustrated, I slapped the console in front of me.

"It's not like her not to pick up," I said. "Can't you call someone and get them to check with the Home Secretary's number?"

Tosh shook his head. "No, but I'll call my office in an hour if

The Defector's Diary

we can't raise her by then."

"Anything could have happened to her. She could be hurt. I can't wait an hour."

Tosh's lips tightened, a look of disapproval and frustration as he pulled out his phone. "This is one reason most of our people stay single."

"I'm not one of your people," I snapped. "It's because of you we're chasing a secret society full of bad guys who want to murder us for a bloody diary."

Tosh snapped back. "Correction, guv. It's because of your wife that you're involved at all. If you'd ignored the note from Forst, the invitation from Adam, and taken them to the authorities as you should have, you wouldn't be in the shit you're in at the moment, and I could have got on with my job instead of having to look after you."

We were both silent as he tapped a number into his phone. When the call was answered, he told the listener that he was concerned about Dianne and Myer and why. That done, he ended the call. He held a hand up as I started to speak. "Don't apologize. Let's just get on with it."

Parliament Square was two minutes up the Victoria Embankment, and we drove there in silence. It was the first time I could recall Tosh being so annoyed. He was usually calm. Pulling a card from his glove box, he put it in the window. As he placed it, I noticed the official coat of arms for the House of Commons. We turned onto College Street and then took the ramp to the two-level underground car park. I recalled trying to find a parking spot here several times. It was the closest to the parliament buildings, but finding a place with less than two hundred spaces was rare. Tosh pointed to the sticker as we reached the bottom of the ramp and found an attendant. We were waved through and found a spot next to a small van with a BBC legend. As I climbed out of the car, it hit me.

"College Green."

Tosh locked the car.

"Yes, it's on top of us. College Green—the park. It's on top of the car park."

His face suddenly creased into a grin. "You clever sod. College Green, of course."

CG—College Green. It was another moment of triumph.

Now, we had several pieces of the puzzle. We climbed some stairs to the small park. It was named a park, but it was a small triangle of grass that TV stations used to interview MPs and a nice little spot for the public to picnic or admire historic buildings. With the House of Lords in the background, it was an ideal venue.

We reached the park, and Tosh's phone rang. He listened rather than talked and then pocketed it without acknowledging the caller.

"The office. Valerie was pronounced dead at the scene, and the body will be buried at an undisclosed cemetery in the UK, a privilege awarded by the Home Office. Her next of kin will be informed."

I was pleased. At least, Valerie would rest in the country where she sought asylum.

"They're waiting for a call from the Home Secretary's office. Should be back to us within the hour. I'm sure Dianne and Myer are all right."

We walked to the park's centre and sat on one of the benches. I pulled my small writing pad from my pocket and turned to the set of initials.

"We have the Elizabeth Tower over there." I pointed to the clock tower. "We have College Green we're sitting on, and something scheduled for Houses of Parliament at noon, Elizabeth Tower. That leaves DIV MED EX SCHED 10.30 and ORDER. What the hell can this mean? There's also NG. Dianne was right about the first part of those initials, FASTNG. Labrum let loose some rhetoric about the industries that would be taken over, and

The Defector's Diary

he was talking about oil, gas, water, pharmaceutical production and the Midas touch in investment and money markets."

We both sat, slowly looking from the Tower, the House of Lords, then the other end. After several minutes, Tosh pulled out his phone again and went online. I looked over his shoulders as he Googled Westminster Palace. A list of historical facts and figures about various palace sections was displayed. One obvious and yet literary attraction hidden in the puzzle was the time 12.00 that had eluded us. Prime Minister's question time was from twelve to twelve-thirty.

"We're nearly there, guv," smiled Tosh. "The best thing to do is contact my office and get them to check with all TV stations if any of them have an interview booked for either of the other times on the 17th. If they have, we will hopefully find out who the interviewee is—perhaps DIV. Now let's assume the worst and say someone is going to be assassinated."

"I think that's a little far-fetched, Tosh," I said. "They want people to be on their side. They won't get that if they kill someone on TV."

"Not at all, guv. It depends on how clever they are. There are a few ways to get rid of someone, but have someone else do the dirty work, and then point the finger at them. These people are intelligent. They're working within an organization the public is already wary of. It will be easy to perpetrate something that will shock the world and then lay the blame firmly at the door of a secret society. The New Order will already have something planned that will make them heroes in the eyes of the public and start the process of gaining support for their movement."

That was the most worrying scenario that faced our country and, indeed, Europe. There would be no sudden coup, no dictatorship. Whatever the New Order planned could be a continuous program across Europe of public services disruption, infrastructure of power and transport, health service, and money markets. The thought of terrorist atrocities or assassinations might not be beyond the New Order's capabilities after all. With the leading decision-makers in place wielding power, I could see the day when the community, having suffered falling living standards due to the New Order's covert activities, would vote by referendum for a European government. It was a scary thought.

Chapter Thirty-One

TOSH SUMMARISED THE SCHEDULE. "There isn't anything listed for that day until 6.00 p.m. The House will be debating the doctors' pay claim for the National Health Service amongst other things—a lively discussion and one that will attract a media circus for sure," he said. "Whatever is happening at 2.30 p.m. is something unofficial, private, or Novotney made a mistake about the time. I did check the rest of the week and the following week, but nothing showed up. With Novotney and Valerie dead, we've hit a blank for the time being."

We were sitting in a small café across the way from College Green. Tosh's remark about an assassination started to take root in my mind. The Elizabeth Tower overlooked the park. Several parts of the green would be ideal places for sniper crossfire. Of course, if that were the plan, a shooter would have to access the Tower. With security tight, how would he achieve that?

"They would have to have a pass from a member of parliament to tour the Elizabeth Tower and be British residents."

As we discussed the issue, I kept an eye on the time. We talked for over an hour, but no message came from the Home Secretary's office. Dianne had not phoned, and it was time to do something other than sit and wait.

"We have to do the unthinkable," I said and rose. "One of us has to go to Whitehall and knock on the door, or you have to go and see your boss. Do you trust him?"

Tosh joined me outside after paying the cashier. "I don't trust anyone. We have no idea how far the New Order has infested the government. Could be half the Westminster Palace for all we know."

We returned to the car park and decided which of us would do what. On reaching the bottom of the steps leading down to the car, Tosh pulled me roughly to one side. Our car could be seen clearly from where we were, and two men who stood beside it were peering through the windows. A third stood at the front, looking up and down the access road.

"Cranthorp—bloody Cranthorp. I never trusted him at all."

My heart started thumping. How the hell had Cranthorp found us? I could only think of two reasons. He caught up with Dianne and Myer as they tried to get to see the Home Secretary, or they were handed to SIS by the Secretary himself. If so, was the man a New Order member or just doing what he thought was best? The point was that I needed to know if Dianne was safe or if Cranthorp had spirited her away.

My phone rang as we rushed up the stairs and onto the main road. Out of breath, I answered as I ran with the phone to my ear. "Myer." but at first, he made no sense. His voice cut in and out as I moved. "Myer, slow down -."

Tosh snatched the phone from me and answered. "Myer, the Cross is after you. You're a target, and with Mrs West in tow, there is in all probability a chance she could become a casualty. Now, where are you so I can pick her up?"

I heard Myer shouting something as we walked quickly past Westminster Abbey.

"Never mind. The point is, where do you want to go, hell or home?"

Tosh nudged me across the road into Parliament Square. "Okay, so where are you, and let me talk to Mrs West."

A moment later, Tosh handed me the phone. Before I could say anything, Dianne spoke.

"I'm okay, Pete. Mixed up he may be, but Myer's a gentleman. We're having tea at a small country pub a few miles from his country seat."

The Defector's Diary

"What the hell happened? I take it you still have the diary?"

"Yes. Myer drove straight here, and it appears he is beginning to realize there is only one way out for him, and the best way to achieve what he wants. I think he's ready to stop thinking the impossible. However, I'm glad we're here and not in Whitehall. We have solved, well almost solved, the riddle."

"Okay, give me the name of the pub and we'll head there right away. That's when we can get a car. No, I'll explain later. Tell me, why can't we go to Whitehall?"

"The Home Secretary's office is involved. Just get here as soon as possible. We may move to another pub to be on the safe side. It doesn't look as though we were followed. Don't forget, Labrum thinks he has the real diary."

"He may well do," I answered, "but the New Order still wants to get rid of Myer and us."

Tosh took the phone out of my hand. "Dianne, I know the pub you're at. Drive about five miles further up the road and you'll see three large green refuse bins and a dirt track. There's an old, empty caravan site there. Look for a dark green caravan. The key is under the mat of the next caravan along. Wait for us there." The call ended.

After turning onto Bridge Street, we walked down the Victoria Embankment to avoid Whitehall. If SIS were lurking around, their agents would take us to the Cross. If the New Order were around, we would end up on the banks of the Thames. It was not a happy situation.

"Here we are, guv," said Tosh, stopping by a BMW parked illegally outside the small park grass strip fronting the Ministry of Defence. "Courtesy of all the Whitehall clipboard carriers walkin' around in mummy's knitted pullover."

I could not help laughing. I half expected to see an office-type sitting in the back with a pile of sandwiches and coffee.

"Okay, guv, we'll be speedin', but don't worry about that. We can shift the Sunday drivers out the way."

Horrified, I looked at Tosh as he stuck a blue lamp onto the roof above his head and laughed. Under normal circumstances, he was the worst driver I ever sat next to, but a blue lamp giving him a license to break speed limits would give me a heart attack.

"Do we need to put our lives at risk, Tosh? If we crash, we won't get to Myer and Dianne at all."

Without looking behind us, Tosh pulled the car out onto the road, and we were hurtling along the embankment within seconds, blue light flashing.

"Relax, guv. I've driven in emergencies like this a hundred times, and I'm still here, ain't I?"

I shut my eyes and held onto the handhold above my head. Tosh, as normal, was his usual calm self.

"We'll be turning left up ahead depending on traffic and then link up with the A-ten. That'll take us out of London and not far from where they are."

As he said that, my phone rang. I grabbed it from my pocket and answered. Dianne's voice calmed me a little.

"Hi, there, are you on the way yet?"

"Well, let me put it this way. If we continue as we are, you might see us fly past. Tosh is very good around corners on two wheels."

"Let me talk to him."

I chuckled. "Are you kidding? We're doing eighty along Farringdon Road and you want him on the phone?"

"I'm going to kill him."

"No, we've had enough of that, but you can beat him up. He's scaring me with this expert rally driving. We'll be there soon."

Tosh spun the wheel, and the car screeched around a circle, narrowly missing a bus and two cyclists. I looked behind and caught a rude salute from one of the cyclists.

"Well, the Home Secretary... Who'd have thought?" Tosh nodded as we roared past a lorry. "Are we surprised?"

"No," I replied. "We should concentrate on the victim and

The Defector's Diary

worry about how much of Whitehall is involved."

As we sped through the countryside, I still had kaleidoscopic visions running through my mind's eye of Valerie pointing a gun at me, being slapped by Tosh, and then lying dead on a wet roadway. It was an awful feeling I shook off by engaging in conversation.

"Tosh, do you ever have any feelings toward others like Valerie Forst?"

"Yes, once upon a time, but I told you about a colleague I lost in Berlin. It took a long time to get over that, and when I did, I promised myself I'd never make friends in the business again, and I never have. People die every day, and others survive in this business. I guess I'm lucky not to have too many friends. You're a friend but not a close one. That's the way it is."

And that was that. It was more a statement than a conversation piece that came to a complete stop, defying further enquiry.

Twenty minutes later, we arrived at the caravan park, and I breathed a sigh of relief as I opened the door. Dianne approached with a determined look on her face as she confronted Tosh.

"I suppose you didn't give it a thought that maybe you were putting Pete's life in danger?"

Tosh looked surprised. "Mrs W, he's as safe as houses. We missed everything on the way." He laughed but stopped short. "Sorry, but you did say get here quick." He held his hands out in apology.

Myer joined us, smiling.

"Let's start and make plans for tomorrow," said Dianne.

We all stepped into the caravan. "So, what's going on?"

"Let's wait until we get settled." Dianne patted me on the shoulder. "You're going to be pleased and surprised."

Myer nodded. "Dianne solved the biggest problem." Then he asked, "Why are you getting involved in this, Tosh? I thought you were investigating me?"

Tosh pulled a card from his inside pocket and gave it to him.

"I'm Nigel Silsbury, your handler. We've been talking on text for eighteen months."

Dianne looked at me with wide eyes, and I winked.

Myer's face paled as he sank into an armchair. "What the hell?"

"Yes, what indeed. You and I are going to have a serious chat after tomorrow, however it ends."

"Okay, so what are you thinking?" asked Dianne.

"Home Secretary, what happened?" I asked. "Is there any office in Whitehall that's not infiltrated?"

"If you think about it, as I already said, practically every department will have someone placed or in a position to become part of the New Order's administration. People who love the idea of being part of world government." Myer's chin jutted out. "And yes, I was one of them until I realized my mistake."

Tosh looked angry.

"Don't have a go at him, Tosh. Michael realized that one of the office managers he was talking to was avoiding our enquiry and asking where we were, and if they could arrange for a pickup." Dianne frowned. "Okay, what have you got?"

"I'll start," said Tosh, looking through a shopping bag.

"Courtesy of me," said Dianne.

Tosh nodded a thank you. "First, noon on the seventeenth will be PM Question Time in the House. Remember, the House sits until a couple of days before the elections. Put the other times and places together, they all lead up to noon. Then Elizabeth Tower and College Green and then DIV."

Myer and Dianne were still none the wiser until Tosh walked his fingers across the table.

"A march route. A demonstration to Westminster to arrive and disrupt Question Time. I worked that out, but the Office worked out most of the rest."

"Then DIV makes sense, given what will happen later. MED, media attention on the disruption, and DIV equals diversion.

The Defector's Diary

Something is going to happen in five cities at the same time and it will go unnoticed. Look at the timing. Parliament will 'wash up' two days before the elections, starting on the seventeenth. All the bad things start together, including the assassination."

"Okay, so we have to find out who the king is. I'm assuming the bomb in the House will refer to the king's home?" I said. "And the king will amend his speech. That suggests a speech he was going to make is now rewritten. Why?"

"Right. And I have a feeling that my man here knows who." Tosh sat next to Myer. "You were quick to work out a couple of things with Dianne. You already knew the answers, I'm sure. After running you for eighteen months, I know how you think. I have all our conversations on text, and I only have to hand that over to the authorities and you're fried, matey." Tosh bent over him. "For the last eighteen months, I've been your contact and the only person in the world right now who can keep you from spending the rest of your life in jail. Unless you want serious time and a damn good hiding, I suggest you tell me who the king is."

"Dianne knows." Myer jumped up.

Dianne and I sat quietly. She saw Tosh in his natural role for the first time.

Tosh stood with hands on hips. "Who is the king of the house, and where does he live?"

"I told you, Dianne worked it out, Tosh. Is that your real name?"

"Never mind my name." Tosh turned to us and took a seat, indicating that Myer should do the same. "Okay, we must work this together. So that you know, SIS rebels have a contract out on Pete, you, me, and the king of the house."

"Have we all forgotten something Myer is trying to tell you?" Dianne prompted.

Tosh ran a hand through his hair. "Sorry. I guess I'm mad at this idiot."

"Well, who is the king of the house? My bet is the Prime Minister. Who better to become world news and a diversion from what is going to happen across Europe. A protest rally and assassination on the last day of Parliament. The thing is, he can't be killed in Downing Street, so it must be at or near the houses of Parliament or the House itself. Maybe a New Order member is an MP who will pull the trigger. The speech will be after PM Question Time and he must have something really important to say before the House breaks up for elections. The only puzzling thing is, he is supposed to die at ten-thirty p.m. on the final curtain of Othello tomorrow night."

"We don't have time to figure out what's going on across Europe," I said. "If we can stop the assassination and hand the diary over to the Prime Minister, the New Order will be finished."

Dianne left us holding the kettle, saying she would return with water.

"I think someone from Downing Street is keeping them at bay, but that won't stop the rebels closing in," answered Tosh.

He was right. "Let's get back into London," I suggested.

"We can at least be near the Westminster Palace or the Opera House."

We all agreed. As Tosh started going through the shopping, a sudden scream outside made us all jump. Dianne was running towards us, shouting incoherently over and over. "Order, order! I say Order. Would the honourable gentleman please refrain from name-calling across the House? Order, order! It's the Speaker!"

Despite a serious situation, we felt like applauding her.

Out of breath, she laughed. "I just kept repeating the word and it came to me." She placed the diary on the table. "Staring us in the face and none of us got it. I thought it was referring to the New Order."

"One of us got it," said Tosh, pointing at Myer.

Chapter Thirty-Two

MYER LOOKED TIRED and unsure.
"Come on, man, what do you know that we don't? You're not helping by staying silent, and you could be aiding the thugs kill a friend and colleague."

Myer sighed deeply. "It's a hell of a secret that Novotney and I shared. We had another way to expose the New Order without showing the diary to anyone. We had to reveal the intentions of the Order by having a trusted voice in the House that would be believed. You won't find his name on the Bilderberg list anywhere, not as a member nor Committee member. He insisted on secrecy from the start because of his neutral position in the government."

Tosh was pacing up and down, fists clenched. "And you didn't think the word Order was anything significant? You're not that stupid. You deliberately withheld information while our lives were put in danger. All you cared about is your bloody secret squirrel society. I've a good mind to hand you to SIS."

"Tosh, I am sorry." Myer held his hands out.

"Don't say sorry to me. Say sorry to Valerie. How about saying sorry to Pete and Dianne. You bloody fool. Surely it occurred to you that the New Order has found out about the Speaker, so why stay quiet?"

"They learned about Sir David Grant-Bowers and decided to make his end very public," I added. "Novotney found out, and it is that information, I'm sure, he was going to tell you the day he was due to go to Brussels. The diversion tactics are either to cover that, or some other event they have planned. Don't forget something is going on across Europe at the same time, and there are still one or two unsolved clues."

Myer held his hands up. "I already knew about Sir David and what he intended to do. Like me, he spent time on the Committee and kept up the pretence that he supported the New Order. Then that bastard Cranthorp followed Sir David and spotted him having a meeting with Novotney. Sir David was told the next meeting was cancelled but would be rescheduled. He knew the game was up and made me promise to keep things to myself. He intends to make a speech to the House tomorrow and then resign."

Tosh gave Myer an angry look and waved a finger at him. "So help me, if we're too late and this thing blows up in our faces, you are gonna' regret it."

"The thing is," continued Myer, "if anything were to happen to him, it would be me who made the speech to the House, whether I had the diary or not." He looked at me. "I'm of the impression, as I'm sure you and Dianne are, that by staying in Prague, you put yourself on the hit list."

"He's right, Tosh." Dianne placed cups of tea on the table.

"I insisted Pete look for Adam, and as you know, once a story presents itself, Pete is a dog with a bone. Michael's loyalty to Sir David went too far, but his plan was a good one. The point is, what now?"

"There's a problem here," I said. "If Sir David is killed tomorrow night after Othello, he would already have made the speech. That doesn't make sense." I took out my tablet and studied Max's list of attendees. Sir David's name was on the list. "How about letting Michael call Sir David, so we know he is safe and give him a warning?" I looked at Tosh, who was still angry but nodded.

Myer picked the phone up and made the call. "We must get Sir David into the House tomorrow to make his speech."

We all waited as the phone rang, but there was no reply.

Myer put the phone down. "Now you can see why I wanted

The Defector's Diary

to keep the diary. Sir David's word will be enough to stop Order's mad plans. The diary's only use to Valerie was to get to London, and now it's of no use to anyone. I was hoping you would let me have it or maybe burn the damn thing."

"You must be joking," said Tosh. "That diary is going to Downing Street so the PM can read it while the Speaker addresses the House and then resigns."

I took a cup of tea from Dianne. She handed another cup to Tosh. "I don't suppose anyone has thought of the possibility that a bomb in the House might mean the Opera House and not Sir David's house?"

Dianne faced Myer. "Maybe Tosh does not quite understand how you feel, but I do. I can see you're trying to protect an idea that has been fifty years in the making, and now you're looking at it being destroyed by ambitious men with only political power in mind."

"I don't understand. Is that what you—"

"Shut up, Tosh. Let Dianne speak." I winked at him.

"Look," she continued. "I'm sure Sir David is a personal friend. I like him, as do many others who understand politics and have a great hand in running our country. But there comes a time when we have to compromise in the best interest of others. Sir David is in danger, and as you pointed out, he's the right man to expose the New Order. The last thing any of us want is his death on our conscience when we're so close to success. Michael, the diary is lost to you, but not your friend. We need to know where he lives. Surely, you know someone who knows where he lives, perhaps in Dedham?" Dianne looked at us. "Time is running out fast. As we know who the target is, I suggest we forget the other clues that pertain to somewhere in Europe and concentrate on saving Sir David."

We all nodded in agreement.

Tosh sat down and looked into his cup of tea. "Blimey," was all he could mutter. He rose and stepped out; I assumed to call his office. After a few minutes, he returned.

"I called my people. They put the bomb squad on alert, and the Opera House will be searched after the dress rehearsal. I don't think there's a bomb there."

Dianne and I looked at each other. "That's it!" I exclaimed. "Sir David could die on the final curtain, but Novotney got the date wrong by thinking Sir David would die during the performance. His name is on the list of attendees."

Tosh nodded. "Of course, the dress rehearsal. But the Speaker lives at Westminster Palace. It's going to be hard to get at him with a gun, let alone a bomb. Time the date and work out the timeline for the rehearsal."

"I have to make a call," said Myer. "Sir David divorced a couple of years ago, but his ex should know where he is. I'm sure, like a lot of the Westminster peers, he has a little bolthole somewhere he can unwind on holidays."

Tosh handed Myer his phone. "Don't panic her. Tell her the PM wants to talk to him about arrangements for tomorrow and Sir David can't be contacted. Maybe he has a private number or address for this weekend cottage. You never know. She might have both. I take it you know her?"

Myer smiled and tapped out a number. Margaret answered almost at once. "Hello, Margaret. It's Michael. Sorry to bother you, but I was wondering if you had David's private number. The PM needs to talk to him."

Tosh handed him a pen and a small notebook.

As he jotted down a number, Myer asked, "Margaret, did he go to what we call his weekend hideaway? I know he's going to Othello tomorrow night, but it looks like he's taking a night away from Westminster. Tomorrow is a busy day for him." After making another note, Myer thanked her. "Are you going to Othello tomorrow? No? Would you like to? That's wonderful. I'll pick you up at six p.m. By the way, I'll have Dianne West with me, the wife of Pete West the columnist. It should be a wonderful night,

The Defector's Diary

and I'll treat you ladies to an after-show dinner at the Savoy… You're welcome…Look forward to it. Bye for now."

"That was a brilliant idea," said Dianne. "Well done, Michael."

"I take it that your plan was to make sure both women were safe," said Tosh. "Yes, good idea."

"Well, it looks like the two caped crusaders are at it again," I said, looking at Myer's note.

"We used to know each other quite well before she got married. Her family are connected, I believe. Anyway, I thought I would take the ladies there, and hopefully, we'll be celebrating your success over dinner. All of us, I hope," Myer added and looked at Tosh.

I started to get anxious about him with Dianne again, but I doubted he would do anything besides what he said. The note gave us a number and an address, and I was relieved to see the address was within twenty-odd miles from our position.

I looked at Dianne and smiled. "You better start for home and have plenty of time to get ready for the performance. By the way," I said and glanced at Myer. "Everyone there will know you. You could be arrested."

"Not if you're successful, Pete."

"In the meantime, I cannot go home," said Dianne. "Labrum and Cranthorp know our address."

"I'll fix that." Tosh made a call. "Just a minute," he said after a short conversation. He turned to Dianne and handed her his phone. "This is one of the ladies who works in the office. She's booking two rooms at the Dorchester. Tell her what you want, and she'll go shopping for you."

A few minutes later, Myer had the car outside.

I kissed Dianne. "See you later."

Tosh looked at the note. He smiled and glanced at Dianne and Myer. "Goodbye, and let's hope we have a great day tomorrow. If not, we'll meet again in HMP Brixton. Before you go, I'll be keeping this." He picked up the diary. "The only person we can trust is the man we're saving. He'll carry the diary into the House tomorrow."

Myer drove out of the park, leaving us to sit and mull over the option to get Sir David safely to Parliament.

"All right, guv, here is where I have to say that you don't have to get involved anymore. It would be best if you weren't. I'm assuming you don't like that. I know this is gonna be one hell of a story. The thing is, if we don't pull this off, we'll spend time in Brixton, and that's no joke."

I looked at his face and saw tired eyes. Until then, it never occurred to me that he hadn't slept much over the last three weeks. He arranged a lot in the background to help things run smoothly and keep his office up to date.

"How the hell do I leave you to be the hero? I want some glory too, you know." I punched his arm. "Don't let's think about Brixton. Of course, we could be wrong about Sir David, although I don't think so."

"Thanks, guv." He looked at his watch. "Right, let's see if we can raise Sir David. At the same time, we'll go to his cottage or whatever it is that Mister Speaker has for the weekend."

We tried several times, but the answering service was all we got. I realized then that I had not called Max, even though Dianne kept him in touch. I rang and got the usual response.

"Where the hell have you been, Pete? Good job Dianne knows her priorities." He coughed. "I'm up to speed and I don't like what you're up to. You're a bloody newspaperman, not a bloody hide-and-seek pinhead from SIS."

"I say, Max, you're getting better at name-calling. Listen, all we have to do is get Sir David to Westminster tomorrow and that's it."

"That's all? Have you thought about what happens if you fail? Your name will be mud. Everything will be covered up, you'll be under arrest and there's nothing I can do about that."

"What does the boss think? Is he still on my side?"

The Defector's Diary

"Pete, he only knows what I tell him about you. Yes, he's pleased with what's going on. He sees glory for the Herald and probably a knighthood. What the hell, Pete? You're getting too old for all this running around. Poor Dianne must be worried sick."

"Quite the reverse. Dianne's in her element. Look, Max, whatever way this goes, it will be over by this time tomorrow or ten-thirty tonight. I'll call you whenever I can."

"Make sure you do. I'll be in the office all night. If you get the Speaker to the House, I'll make sure we have something out before Downing Street sticks a gag in my mouth, and your name will be in the editorial. The public may not know what's gone on, but your peers will. Just take bloody care of yourself." He coughed and hung up.

Dianne was far from her element, and I looked forward to getting home and sorting out my problem with her. Another medical examination could show a good result, but if not, I wanted to reassure her nothing had changed between us.

"It won't take long to get there, so I'll drive slow," said Tosh, jogging my thoughts back to his driving techniques.

I hung onto the handhold as we pulled out of the gate and swerved to avoid oncoming traffic.

"Assuming we find Sir David and manage to get him to safety; how do we get him to the Commons tomorrow?"

"That shouldn't be a problem," said Tosh. "Remember, there's a protest rally, so there will be plenty of police activity. I'm also guessing his bleedin' Lordship Gresham is being used by the New Order. The police will arrest him anyway and all his henchmen before they can get to Westminster." He grinned. "My office decided to have a word with the Police Commissioner. Gresham's gonna be stopped as he and his thugs are marching across Westminster Bridge."

Chapter Thirty-Three

CRANTHORP SAT COMFORTABLY in the kitchen, looking out at a well-kept garden, admiring a large flowerbed backed by a high brick wall. A mixture of Iris, Lupin, and a clump of Forsythia shared the bed with Delphinium, Phlox, and several hardy Geraniums. The plants were carefully planted, and what colour was left in September blended well.

The cottage was cold. Cranthorp hated the cold, remembering what winters were like in Berlin and Prague. His posting back to London two years ago had been a welcomed change. SIS had been good for him, and promotion meant he had more control over specific operational details.

His phone beeped. "Yes?"

"It looks like they're on the way," answered Labrum. "I'll deal with them as they join the main road."

Cranthorp thought for a moment. Killing Tosh was nothing. West was a different proposition.

"It has to be an accident. No shooting."

"What if Tosh shoots at us?"

"Duck out of the way, you idiot. I repeat, do not shoot at them or at the tyres. You have to crash his car."

"Okay. Myer has gone with Paakkonen back to London, I'm guessing."

"That's fine," answered Cranthorp. "Myer will be staying in town. We can pick him up in the morning when he mourns the Speaker's death."

In the quiet that followed, he focused through the scope of the rifle fixed to a tripod in front of him. Tosh and West made

The Defector's Diary

an exemplary team, and he was sure they would arrive despite any attempt by Labrum to crash them. Tosh knew how to drive, but West needed to improve at deception. When he saw the diary Labrum had brought him, he knew it was a dummy. West would have the actual item with him. It had to be destroyed.

Cranthorp heard an engine and saw a large Bentley in the telescopic sight pull slowly into the drive through the wrought iron gates. He moved the rifle with gentle fingers until the driver's head lined up with the crosshairs.

"Welcome home, Sir David."

Cranthorp moved out of the chair and stood, his back to a wall beside the open hallway entrance. From his inside jacket pocket, he pulled a Baretta and held it up, ready to point at the victim as he swung around into the hall.

He listened as a car door slammed. His Downing Street contact had been right. Sir David was spending the night alone, and local police would patrol past his cottage every two hours.

The crunch of pea shingle underfoot, followed by the jangling of keys, sharpened his nerves. The victim had to step in before he could act. Control was an instant necessity. The door closed with a bang. Cranthorp entered the hall and confronted Sir David with a pistol.

Shocked, the man stood open-mouthed, his coat halfway down one shoulder, then raised his hands.

"Good afternoon, Mister Speaker," said Cranthorp. "It is always with some satisfaction that one catches a traitor."

Sir David dropped his arms and took off his coat. "I think you have that the wrong way around, don't you?"

"Sorry," answered Cranthorp. "I don't have time to come to order or listen to you. I'm here to say goodbye on behalf of the President of the New Order. In three years, we'll see the start of a world governing body formed in Britain. You'll not be here to experience such a momentous occasion."

Sir David shook his head as Cranthorp ushered him into the

bedroom at the far end of the hallway.

"Sit on the chair over in the corner."

Cranthorp used rope to tie Sir David's arms.

"It's like this," explained Cranthorp. "I cannot shoot you. Your body must not show foul play when they find you. You're going to have a terrible accident. You see the two gas cylinders? A small charge of Semtex will set them off, which will ignite the gas. Simple but wonderful. I'm going to enjoy seeing how well it works. Oh, yes. I forgot to say your two friends will join you momentarily. You'll all be going together."

His phone beeped again. He answered irritably. "What!"

"We're right behind him and he's seen us. Here we go."

* * *

Sir John Carlton rose and stepped across the office to close the door.

"George, Lord Gresham is getting too excited. One of my staff has been looking after him until tomorrow. The man has a big mouth. Several times, he nearly said something that would embarrass us. I guess it's too late to do anything about him now, but I never liked the man. At least we can be rid of him tomorrow."

"John, you panic too easily. You're right. It is too late to do anything, but if your man is doing his job, he should keep the idiot quiet for one night. You worry too much." There was a pause. "On a more important note, have you sorted out Myer and Order yet?"

Carlton slid into a chair and ran a hand over his forehead. "I heard from Charles Cranthorp that the way he has it organized, Myer will be with 'Order' tonight, and both will be dealt with. That being the case, we don't have to worry about Pete West anymore. Without the diary, which Charles will also obtain tonight, West doesn't have much of a story."

"Driscol was going to write to him with an offer. Did he?" asked Graham.

"As far as I know, he did," replied Carlton. "Unfortunately, the only way we knew he would get our letter was by sending it to his address."

"Well, he may come round after tonight or tomorrow."

Carlton nodded. "Has our first lighter carrier been left in place? I take it he knows how to do it?"

"Here you go again, John. He knows, and so does the man who'll deal with him when the job is done. Stop worrying."

"I guess this is where I say I wish you all the success in the world for tomorrow and a smooth transition over the next three years. All the very best, Mister President."

"Thank you, John. We'll be celebrating in a week, you'll see. Bye for now."

Carlton sat for several minutes, going over arrangements for the morning. It was going to be a day full of action and a lot of tension. Everything hinged on Charles doing his job. He called Driscol.

"Any news?"

"Yes," said Driscol, sounding upbeat. "Labrum is on the hunt, and Cranthorp is waiting at the cottage. I'll keep you informed. If it comes to it, I'll get involved to secure the bloody diary and Myer."

Carlton thought for a moment. "Gresham will be arrested tomorrow, along with his ragtag army. The press will jump on that. If and when you or I talk to the press, our position is one of ignorance. We have nothing to do with Gresham. Pass that on to all delegates."

Chapter Thirty-Four

I SWUNG MY HEAD BACK after taking a glance to the rear. "There's a large black Mercedes just turned onto the road and is following us," I said matter-of-factly.

Tosh looked in the mirror and put his foot down. We shot forward, the engine screaming. In a narrow country lane, the thought of meeting someone coming the other way was frightening. Our wheels left the road each time we hit a bump. I looked back nervously and gasped. The Mercedes was right behind us.

"He's gonna try to crash us," Tosh said. His hands worked the steering wheel, and his eyes never left the road.

Ahead, I could see a left-hand bend and a raised grass bank to the right. As we came to the bend, our wheels scuffed the bank. The Mercedes was now level with our rear door.

"He's coming up our left side, Tosh."

"I see him. Don't worry," said Tosh calmly.

As the Mercedes advanced, we suddenly lurched into the car, which knocked it across the road. We moved back as we neared the end of the bend. The Mercedes came at us again but had to draw back for an oncoming car. By now, we were hurtling along at over eighty miles an hour, and another bend loomed ahead.

"This is where we lose them," said Tosh. "Hold on tight, here we go."

Our car squealed around the bend on two wheels, or so it seemed, the Mercedes right behind us. Too late to slow, the other car hit the bank, catapulted into the air, crashed into two large trees, and burst into flames.

I looked back and saw one man fall from an open door as we

The Defector's Diary

sped on.

"The cottage is about two miles ahead. The problem is, guv, Cranthorp will probably be there, and if he is, Sir David may well be there too. We have to be careful."

Tosh, unmoved, slowed to a stop and pulled into a small field entrance about a mile further on, hiding the car behind hay bales. I remembered his words about his feelings and now saw them firsthand. I wasn't sure I liked the feeling he instilled in me, but I accepted it as he had become. Maybe it was a good thing for him.

"Right, here's where we find out what's what at the cottage. No point charging in if Sir David is there with Cranthorp. If Cranthorp is on his own, we can engage. Unlikely, but if Sir David is on his own, we pull him out right away. Best thing to do is take a look first but be careful. Cranthorp is bound to have a rifle covering the entrance. He's a dead shot."

We left the car and walked another mile before leaving the road, stumbling through a wooded area. After another quarter mile or so, Tosh called a halt.

"Right, get your breath and rest for five minutes. Then we edge forward until the cottage wall comes into sight. According to my office, the place is surrounded by high walls and sits back from the road. The nearest building to it is a farm a short distance away."

"Your office?" I quizzed.

"I gave them the address and they texted back the info." He gave me a funny look and smiled. "What? You expected me to go in not knowing the layout?"

I was still feeling sick after watching the car crash, no matter who the occupants were. "Tosh, are you reporting the accident at all? I know you have little feeling for those thugs, and neither do I, but surely, we report to the police?"

"The next driver travelling down the lane will do that for us, guv." He took a deep breath. "Let's get goin'."

We crouched behind some trees a few minutes later, looking

at the cottage wall. We moved slowly toward the gate and could see the rear of a Bentley.

"I can't see any other car. Do you think Cranthorp is there?"

A twig snapped with a loud crack. "No, he's not there," answered Tosh. "He's right behind you."

I felt a cold shiver run up my spine.

"Gosh, you heard me, damn it," came Cranthorp's sarcastic voice. "You've not lost your touch, Tosh, but I got you this time around."

I turned and looked into the muzzle of a large pistol with a silencer at the end.

"Well, hello, Pete. We meet again. What's it been, two years?"

With a helping hand from Tosh, I got to my feet and faced Cranthorp.

"And there I thought, what a stinker you were, but at least a stinker on our side. You're now a traitor," I said.

"Not only that," said Tosh, "he's due to sit in the second biggest chair at the Cross."

Cranthorp smiled. "Let's get in the warmth, shall we? Then you and Sir David can die together. Of course, Pete may not have to after I make an offer he can hardly refuse."

"I'd rather die," I said flippantly. "By the way, you do know that the Prime Minister is aware of what's going on, don't you? He has the diary. Myer and my wife took it to him this morning."

A shadow of confusion crossed Cranthorp's face for a brief second. Tosh stood next to me, nodding slowly.

"Good job she convinced me to let the bloody thing go. A great girl, is Dianne."

Cranthorp's smile returned. "Come on, gents, let's walk. Oh, and by the way, gun please, Tosh."

Tosh handed over his gun, and we walked to the cottage gates. I felt pretty glum that capturing us had been easy.

"Here," said Cranthorp, handing me the keys. "You open up and walk to the cottage."

The Defector's Diary

"You must be joking," said Tosh. "You've got backup up in there."

"Well, yes," replied Cranthorp, "but he won't shoot you. He's quite looking forward to meeting you again, Pete. He made it back to the cottage a lot quicker than you. While you stumbled through the woods, he walked the road. He's very upset with you."

Cranthorp stepped to one side, covering us with his gun. "Labrum, it's me," he shouted. "We're coming in, Pete first."

I nervously put the key in the lock and turned until it clicked. I pushed the door back and saw Labrum, gun in hand, standing at the other end of the passage.

"Well, I say, old boy, nice to meet you again. Shame that beauty of yours is not with you today, although I would hate to harm her in any way."

Tosh and Cranthorp followed me in. As I reached Labrum, he raised his fist and crashed it against my jaw. I fell back against Tosh.

"That's enough," ordered Cranthorp. He glared at Labrum. "Trust you to do something stupid."

Labrum said nothing and opened the door to the bedroom.

Waggling his gun, he ordered us inside. Relieved at finding him alive, Sir David winked at me as we entered.

He and I met a couple of times, although the last time was about three years ago when he and I crossed swords over NHS funding. It was hard to imagine that Sir David, knowledgeable and loyal to the Crown, could be convinced that the New Order was right for the UK, let alone the world.

"Hello, Pete. It looks like you're just in time for the party. Who's your friend?"

"He's an ex-SIS agent, but on the wrong side," said Cranthorp. He stood in front of us and motioned us to sit. I looked at Sir David and sat beside him on the bed. "This is Tosh."

Tosh sat on the other side of the bed, and Labrum began to tie our hands and ankles.

"Nice to see you're all getting acquainted. It's a shame that two of you will die soon," Cranthorp added.

"He means you and me, Sir," joked Tosh, looking at Sir David. "Pete is gonna' be the new media chief for the New Order."

"Stop joking, Tosh. That's not funny." Labrum looked up as I addressed Cranthorp. It was apparent how we would die, looking at the gas cylinders next to the lit gas fire. One had a timing device attached to a small charge taped to the gas governor.

Cranthorp took a pouch from his pocket. "Syringe filled with something that will put you to sleep for a couple of hours. I'll untie you before I leave, and you'll die in the explosion. Can't leave evidence of foul play. You'll be blown to pieces. There will be nothing left for forensics to discover." He grinned at Tosh. "Shame to see you go, old boy, but you're over the hill now, aren't you?"

Ignoring him, Tosh looked at me. "Listen, guv, whatever he has to offer, take it. Think of Dianne. You'll be able to carry on the fight to expose these idiots."

Labrum clapped. "Good little piece of advice, but your famous columnist wants to be a hero."

"Shut up." Cranthorp's voice stopped all conversation. He sat on the arm of Sir David's chair.

"Pete, in all seriousness, our offer is for real. You can be head of media broadcasting and have all the incentives that go with it. I hate this situation more than you. I don't give a damn for these two, but you're different. Listen to Tosh. He's been around and knows the score. What do you say?"

I was thinking of Dianne and what she would think if I gave in to the temptation to live. It was a tempting offer, but one I could not accept. I dedicated my whole working life to helping the public understand the politics of everyday life and uncover wrongdoings by those in public office trusted by people who voted for them.

"No," I replied. "I predict that this great future you're planning for the world is going to fail. Not because of any fault on your part, but because the world doesn't want to live in George Orwell's 1984. You're done, Cranthorp, and so is the New Order."

A shadow of doubt crossed Cranthorp's face. "I'm sorry to hear you say that, Pete. I'll leave you until last so you can have time to change your mind."

I watched as he unzipped the pouch and took out a syringe. After removing a plastic tip from the needle, he looked at Tosh. "You first."

Tosh closed his eyes. "Cheerio, guv. You ain't gonna feel a thing."

"Good job Dianne can't hear you," I sighed.

We both laughed.

Chapter Thirty-Five

As CRANTHORP BENT OVER TOSH, a noise outside the window distracted him, and he looked up. Then came an ear-shattering bang. An expression of surprise froze Labrum as Cranthorp staggered backwards and fell at his feet. Labrum ducked, but Cranthorp's hand grabbed his ankle and sent him crashing sideways against the open door.

Confused and dazed, my ears ringing, another shot rang out, and I flung myself to the floor. In seconds, the situation changed. I caught a glimpse of Cranthorp's head from where I was lying as he crawled from the room.

A small cloud of smoke accompanied a third shot fired from outside the window. Deafened by the first shots, I heard nothing but saw splinters flying across the room from the doorpost. My ears popped, and Tosh's voice sounded in the distance.

"Stay down, guv." Tosh coughed as he breathed the smoke. "It's bleedin' Myer, and he can't shoot straight. He's the only one who knew where we were."

In any other situation, I would have thought the remark funny, but it wasn't funny at that moment. I saw a penknife tossed through the window. It fell onto the floor beside me. I managed to grab it between my fingers and cut the binding.

"If Myer has enough sense and ammo, he'll keep those two busy. They must have got out."

I could hear Labrum cursing outside and then more shots.

Sir David, who had been quiet, tapped me with his toe. "I don't wish to interrupt you boys, but it's now three minutes to ten."

The Defector's Diary

"We're doing our bleedin' best, Mister Speaker," Tosh snapped. "We'll have you out of here in a minute."

"That's about all you have, Tosh," I said.

My hands were suddenly free. I quickly untied myself, cut Sir David loose, and then turned to Tosh.

"Never mind me," Tosh yelled. "Don't wait for me. This place will blow! Run for it!"

Sir David grabbed a blanket, threw it over the windowsill to cover the broken glass, and scrambled out.

"Keep low and run like hell across the field," shouted Tosh. "The grass is tall. No matter where Cranthorp is, he won't get a clear shot at you even with an infrared scope. He may have gone into the woods at the front of the cottage."

I followed Sir David out the window, ran along the garden path, and into the field without looking back. It was pitch black, but I ran and half-stumbled several times. Tosh was right. The grass and weeds had burned in the summer sun and stood at shoulder height.

I caught up with Sir David just as the ground shook, accompanied by an almighty explosion. Both of us dived to the ground and lay there. We watched as bricks and shards of glass flew over our heads. The kitchen door landed feet from us, smoking. The smell of smoke drifted around us. Above us, the air, illuminated by firelight, was filled with dust, paint chips, and swirling pieces of cloth and paper blown in all directions. It was a frightening moment, and both of us turned our faces to the ground with hands over our heads, breathing heavily.

Sir David turned to me as more paper and dust settled on us. "I do hope that fellow Tosh is all right. We should go and find him."

"No, Sir," I replied. "That's the last thing we should do. Believe me, if he's okay, he'll find us. We have to get to London."

We got to our knees and peered cautiously back at the cottage. It had gone and was now a pile of burning wood and general materials. Nothing but smoke rose from the foundations. Such was the blast that the front road wall was rubble. Parts of the Bentley lay scattered across the road, illuminated by the fire.

A single shot rang out, and Sir David reacted at once. "Get down!" he shouted. "It's probably Cranthorp.

Another shot followed, and I could hardly breathe. My stomach churned when another shot hit a clump of hawthorn bushes to my right. We remained flat on the ground for several minutes. Cranthorp had been very clever. If we'd been in the cottage as it exploded, we would have disappeared without a trace, and the whole thing classed an accident.

Gunfire sounded from the woods, and both of us ducked instinctively. There was a brief silence, then another shot, followed by screaming tires as a car hurtled away.

"I have second thoughts about looking for Tosh and Myer, "I said. "Perhaps we should make a quick search." I stood and looked toward the woods. There was no movement, and I began to worry that Tosh and Myer were shot in the exchange. Sir David joined me, and we stepped over debris until we reached the foundations.

Water gushed from broken mains, and we avoided the electrical wiring.

"We dare not shout in case Labrum or one of his thugs is still around."

"Well," answered Sir David, "how about throwing a milk bottle onto the road. The only trouble is, it would announce our existence."

I thought for a moment. It wouldn't be Tosh driving away. The question was, did they all leave?"

We picked up two bottles and threw them across the road and got an immediate response.

"You both all right, guv? We're okay. Bit deaf but that's all."

Tosh and Myer strolled across the road to join us. I smiled at Myer. "Thanks, you saved our lives again. That was courageous.

The Defector's Diary

Well done." I patted his shoulder as Sir David added his thanks.

Tosh just grinned. "You should look at yourselves. What a bleedin' mess." He glanced at his watch. "Time to get out of here quick. Fire Brigade and police will be here shortly, and so will Cranthorp with reinforcements."

"Was anyone injured?" Sir David was brushing himself down.

"Cranthorp got it in his left arm," said Tosh. "He'll have a quick repair job. His two bosses must be hopping mad. The one on top of the New Order bonfire, and the one sitting on Cranthorp's new chair."

We started walking down the road. There had been no activity at the farmhouse, so it was safe to assume no one was there, not that it meant the police were not on the way.

Something dawned on me about Tosh's remark.

"You're right, Tosh. There has to be a point at which the New Order leader has to give up to fight another day. After all, he and his top people don't want to be found out. They'll resume normal duties, as it were, and only those such as Lord Gresham who have spoken in public will be punished."

"In your opinion, then, Pete," asked Sir David. "When do we reach that point?"

Tosh interrupted us. "Unfortunately, while the boss will probably call a halt sometime in the mornin' if you're not caught, Cranthorp will disobey and keep after us as we are the only threat to his future job, whichever one that turns out to be."

He reached inside his jacket through a rip in the lining and held a mobile phone. "Just gotta spare dog and bone. I never leave for work without it. Excuse me, gents. Gotta make a call to a lady who hates me. I'll give her the good news that she'll get the sack tomorrow when Cranthorp points the finger at her failure to bring Myer in."

Neither Myer nor I said anything. Tosh had lost his job at Number Eleven. SIS had had words with his boss. He deserved the privilege of telling the boss of SIS what he thought of her.

Chapter Thirty-Six

SIR JOHN CARLTON SAT LOOKING at his mobile phone, then the clock on the office wall. It had been several hours since Driscol called to update him on the hunt for the Speaker and Myer. He jumped as the mobile rang. It was a very excited Driscol.

"Look at the news, look at the news! Turn the TV on. Cranthorp called earlier to report he had the Speaker."

Carlton flicked the control box on his desk, and the wall screen came alive. A picture of utter devastation met his eyes, and he smiled.

"Well done, James. I knew I could rely on you. Have you heard from Cranthorp since? His last report indicated West and Tosh might find the Speaker and spirit him away to safety."

"No, but if they made it to the cottage, they're dead, and the official story would be about a tragic accident. I'm sure Cranthorp got away okay, but I haven't heard from him."

"And Myer?" Carlton hesitated.

Driscol laughed. "Acting the gentleman in London tonight with Dianne West and Sir David's ex, attending Othello although I guess they will not be going now."

"We need to deal with him. He could have been given the diary and go to parliament himself to make a statement. Make sure of him."

"I will."

Carlton ended the call and sat with his eyes closed. The plan was going well with one loose end—Myer. The mobile rang again. Carlton looked at the screen and leaned back in his chair, pleased with himself. President George Graham would remember who smoothed the way to victory. He tapped the screen.

"Good evening, Mister Pres—"

"Don't you dare play with me, you stupid bastard."

"But we—"

"Shut up. Because you did not succeed in everything you promised, I'll have to call the whole thing off. Tosh called the deputy head at the Cross, Sarah Burns, and told her that he, Sir David, and Pete West escaped the explosion by seconds. He then implied that she and Cranthorp would be named in the press, meaning a bloody column written by West, the one thing I didn't want."

Carlton stayed silent.

"The only thing I'm pleased about is that the Rosebud lighter operation will start as scheduled. As far as what was to happen in Westminster is concerned, Gresham will be arrested. While that's happening, you'll inform all three hundred delegates that the operation is cancelled until further notice.

Carlton breathed heavily. "I think we should stop Rosebud completely, George."

"Stop!" Graham spoke slowly, "Carlton, I swear, if you do anything stupid, I'll have you shot. Let Driscol know that too. Now stop getting cold feet. You're losing your grip, so keep calm and sit back. Our time will come again in three years. Incidentally, Cranthorp let us down as well as you. As far as lighter drop is concerned, we go ahead. Three years from now people will listen to our plans and vote for our Global Council to be formed. Rosebud, the real takeover will shock and cause those in power to think. They are not prepared even though the warnings for preparedness have been many. All have been ignored. Once the world has learned its lesson, the population will rise against their governments. Politicians will quickly get the message."

"Mistakes were made, so let's learn from them for the future. The next annual Bilderberg Club meeting will be bigger, with more supporters and delegates attending. I'll call a Committee meeting for next month, and I want all our top people there. You have lots to do, so get on with it."

Carlton sat for some time, thinking of the enormity of their achievements. He thought of what was about to happen and bit his lower lip. Thousands of people worldwide would be affected by the hollow plastic cigarette lighters decorated with a rosebud emblem. Worried that he failed to change the President's mind about going ahead with phase two, Carlton punched the contacts key on his mobile and called Driscol.

Chapter Thirty-Seven

LABRUM HAD DOCTORED our car. Two flat tires and the fuse housing smashed. Scattered across the ground were all the fuses.

I looked at my watch, surprised to see it was only ten-forty-five. Tosh was talking on the phone to his office, his face angry. He could hardly contain himself.

"I am officially retired from the Service at Number Eleven," he announced as the call ended. "It seems there was a report sent to my office from Cross headquarters, and another from the Police Commissioner. I've been warned I'll face charges relating to the Official Secrets Act unless I go quietly and keep my gob shut."

"I'm sorry, Tosh," I said. "I think we'll all get the same speech, but I assume that won't matter to Sir David."

Sir David nodded. "They cannot stop me from making my speech, although I'll have to tread carefully when informing the House about the explosion—a terrible accident that I'll take responsibility for."

Tosh clicked his fingers. "And all the Bilderberg Committee will resign from their positions and rejoin the main delegation to allay public fears. The bleeders will still have influence and power, though. The bloody press will have a field day." Tosh was looking up the road in the direction of the farmhouse. "They also want me to give myself up to the nearest police station with you two gents." He finished shaking his jacket and put it back on. "I guess we won't be doin' that." He turned his back on us. "One last call."

I started to get impatient. It was cold, and I was shivering. We only had jackets to ward off the frosty air. Tosh eventually rejoined us. A sudden pang of panic hit me.

"We won't be doing anything," I said, "if we didn't have the diary. Where did you hide it?"

"Under the car." Tosh bent and recovered the diary from behind the rear wheel.

Sir David slowly shook his head. "We were lucky Cranthorp didn't see you. He must have caught up with you a couple of minutes later."

We were lucky. There had been too much violence over the diary; losing it when we were close to Westminster would have been tragic.

"We have one last hurdle, Sir David. It's a pity your car is ruined. We have to get transport on the quick before the bad guys return." Tosh started running toward the farmhouse. "You two stay here. You're too bleedin' old to run."

That was a funny remark from a man in his fifties.

The weather was changing. There were little gusts of light rain, and the breeze started to get stronger. Leaves around us began to spiral around the trees. I pulled my collar up, and Sir David looked uncomfortable. He was suffering, I thought from shock. The sooner we had transport and warmth, the better. We didn't have to wait long. The sound of a diesel engine broke the silence around us as Tosh returned with an old Land Rover that had seen better days. As if reading my mind, he shouted while opening the door.

"I borrowed this. No one was at the farm. Get in, gents. It's not comfortable, but we have a good bleedin' heater. C'mon, jump in."

True to form, Tosh was off when we closed the door. Sir David sat in the back seat while I held on for dear life at the front.

"Does he always drive like this?" asked Sir David, pointing at Tosh.

The Defector's Diary

"Always," I answered.

Sir David settled back, and I sighed with relief as we turned onto the main road to Dedham. So far, we had not seen anyone who might be following, but knowing Cranthorp, anything was possible.

Our advantage was our transport. Labrum should have left our car intact. It had to be his work before driving off to get medical help for Cranthorp, who must have been more than angry at Labrum's stupidity. Now, Cranthorp had no idea what we were driving. I could imagine Labrum thinking we would hide in the woods, but Cranthorp knew better. He knew Tosh only too well.

"We ought to change transport as soon as possible," announced Tosh. "This thing can just about do sixty." He slapped the steering wheel.

"Good idea," I agreed, although I didn't look forward to speeding again.

Chapter Thirty-Eight

TOSH LOOKED THOUGHTFULLY in my direction. "You ever been on a river cruise, guv?"

I glanced at him and recognized the sly look I had grown accustomed to. We stopped on a side street and spent a few hours catnapping at night.

"Okay, so what is going on? What have you got in mind?"

Sir David yawned. "Is there a change of plan?"

Tosh looked serious. "Let me tell you something. I learned not to trust anyone in all the years I worked for our Queen. I was gutted yesterday while talking to my office, but I sensed the anger in my boss' voice was just a little out of tune. I feel that Cranthorp knows what we are about today, and he'll try to get us before we get to Whitehall. The New Order will have retreated by now, apart from that idiot Gresham. Cranthorp wants the chair of SIS and looks at us to stop him. He's gonna try every trick in the bleedin' book."

Tosh was right. Cranthorp would have several men looking for us. We were so close, but taking unnecessary chances would be foolhardy.

"You obviously have a plan, Tosh?"

He grinned. "No, but I think Sir David might have one, even though he hasn't thought about it."

"I'm not sure I completely understand," said Sir David.

"What happens if the Commons catches fire while all the snotties and guests are having tea and lunch on the terrace?"

"They can use several exits or, as a last resort, jump into the Thames," replied Sir David. "Snotties, eh? I like that."

"Jump into the Thames?" Tosh shook his head. "I don't think the ladies would like that."

"Oh, oh oh. You mean the fire escape ladder." Sir David poked Tosh on the shoulder. "Only trouble is, we need someone to let the ladder down. It's a wooden affair that is swung over the wall and lowered to the water. Of course, we never used it except the fire brigade who test it now and again."

"You have a deputy," I said. "Can you trust him? What time will he be at the House this morning?"

"He'll be there now, and yes, he is very trustworthy and loyal to the Crown. Today is one of the most important and busy days. The House has to get through a lot of business, and then there's the Royal Opera House tonight. It's all happening today."

I looked at Tosh. "Okay, I have a plan. We get the Deputy Speaker to lower the ladder as we approach in a boat. Sir David is up the ladder and grabbed by the Deputy. They're in the House then. No one is going to be stupid enough to try anything there. Cranthorp is more worried about us than the Speaker, who can't name names in his resignation speech, but we can in the press."

"That place is wired for security with cameras and infrared equipment. We won't get up that ladder before security is on to us," said Tosh.

"Sir David will, though," I replied, "but we're not going up the ladder."

They both looked at me. "If Sir David got into the Palace, we have achieved our goal. From the moment his feet were firmly on the ladder, we would be off and on our way with Cranthorp's men in pursuit. If they were not patrolling in a boat, we would have enough time to find an escape route."

"That would work, guv." Tosh turned to Sir David. "If you give him a shout, someone might be checking your deputy's phone. We're okay; we've got some burners our end."

Sir David snapped his fingers. "Of course, the code."

Tosh groaned, and we both pulled a face. I had enough codes

and clues to last a lifetime.

"What code is that?" I asked.

Sir David got excited. "We named each room, or part of the Palace with a number. The Terrace Pavilion is number five, and the river is number two." He stopped and looked a little embarrassed. "I know it's a bit daft, but we thought it might come in handy in any emergency."

I didn't think it was daft at all. "Good idea, Sir David. We want to call the Deputy and tell him he needs to lower the fire escape at the right time and help you onto the veranda."

Sir David thought for a moment. "Okay. I say I'm in a right two and eight and need a leg up on five in five, which means, I'm in the river and need the fire escape in five minutes." He looked triumphantly at me.

"It'll work," I said. "It has to. We must ensure the Deputy is called at the right time, but how do we know he'll be there?"

"Reliability," replied Sir David. "He'll be there. He is always there before me to deal with non-urgent items I don't have to worry about."

I turned to Tosh. "Where do we get a boat, and where do we go when the job is done?"

"Westminster pier. There's a zodiac they slide under the pier near the bridge. There won't be anyone around, so we should be lucky. All attention will be up on the bridge and the crowds. As far as what to do after?" He held his arms up. "No idea, guv. We'll think of something."

"Well, before we do anything, I must call Dianne and Max." My call to Max was short, letting him know where we were and what we intended to do. Dianne was a little more concerned. I had spent time talking to her after our adventure the previous day. It was hard to convince her that I was safe, that the Speaker would be in parliament in a matter of hours, and that I would be meeting her later.

"You call me when you have the Speaker safe and you can

The Defector's Diary

warn Tosh I have a score to settle with him."

After driving through a few side streets, we found ourselves on Northumberland Avenue, heading for the Victoria Embankment. The bridge and the pier were only a few minutes away when Tosh swerved into a U-turn and started back, pointing at the sky.

"Drone! The bastards have a drone. They found us or are looking at us as we go for the Palace." He stopped the Rover and pulled a pistol from the glove compartment. "We don't need that. The pilot will be on the bridge or nearby. This means we can't afford to waste any time. We have to go for the boat even if people are around."

Stepping onto the side of the road, he aimed at the drone. One shot, and it disintegrated into pieces.

"Out, Sir David," I ordered. "We can't use the Rover anymore. They know what we're driving."

Tosh ran onto the avenue as a black cab turned the corner and came towards us. "Westminster Pier," shouted Tosh. "As fast as you can, mate."

A few minutes later, we were outside the pier. We followed Tosh, jumped over entrance gates, and ran past two river cruise boats to the end of the pier. I was worried someone might be up on the bridge waiting to take a shot at us. There were plenty of people making a lot of noise already.

Tosh found the zodiac, and I helped pull it out. A couple of people on the bank above us had taken an interest in what we were doing. We climbed in with unsteady feet. Tosh pulled the starter cord on the outboard engine, and we headed away from the pier.

"Call the Deputy now, Sir David. We won't be more than two or three minutes getting to the palace wall."

Sir David was answered quickly by his deputy and the message passed on.

As I looked forward, I could see more and more people up

on the bridge. Someone started beating a drum and the crowd noise level rose.

Chapter Thirty-Nine

GRESHAM FINISHED HIS SPEECH to the three hundred men in black shirts and a noisy crowd of supporters. Formed into a double column, he led his men onto Westminster Bridge at the south end, flags flying and a solo bagpiper leading ahead. A young man joined the jostling crowd and walked with a group of students. As they reached the centre of the bridge, he stopped and leaned against the parapet.

The crowd now blocked the entire width of the bridge as they moved slowly to the Victoria Embankment and Parliament Square. Above the bagpipes and the shouting throng came a chorus of whistles.

A line of police officers in riot gear was moving forward to meet Gresham. More whistles came from the column's rear as police blocked the bridge behind them.

Corralled in, Gresham brought his men to a halt. He shouted, "We're here to take over the rule of these islands and make this a country you can be proud of. Before he could say another word, he was surrounded by officers. Fighting spread quickly as Gresham was hustled away to a waiting police van. More arrests continued as other protesters arrived at the bridge's north end and attacked the police from the rear.

In the middle of the bridge, the young man looked anxiously around and lit a cigarette, shaking the small plastic lighter several times before the gas ignited. He threw the lighter away and joined the protestors. Seconds later, he fell as the fighting intensified around him.

A small trickle of blood escaped a clean hole in the side of his head as he lay face down. Several fighters and a police officer tripped and stumbled over him before someone realized he was dead. The lighter he had thrown shattered as someone's foot cracked the plastic fuel holder, splitting the image on it of a rosebud in half.

Chapter Forty

WITH TOSH STEERING, we were emerging on the other side of the bridge and clearly visible in the dawn light. The House was in gloom with the Elizabeth clock tower high above it, the clock face illuminated. Thoughts flashed through my mind of all the events we had gone through in such a short time and the deaths of four people. I gripped the boat's rope rail tight. We had to succeed, the wall within a few hundred feet. My heart was thumping, and I noticed Tosh's firm, determined look as he turned us to face the wall.

"A little more to your left, Tosh," ordered Sir David.

Caught off guard, I stifled a laugh while the other two gave me strange looks. Call it my weird sense of humour. I thought of an old BBC radio series, The Navy Lark, and a catchphrase, 'left hand down a bit.'

Tosh altered course while Sir David looked anxiously at the top of the wall. Behind us, I could see people on the bridge and a couple of flags.

"No ladder yet," observed Sir David tensely. "He's late."

As he said that, a ladder swung over the wall and a hand waved at us. Sir David waved back. The zodiac bumped into the wall, and Sir David was off and climbing as we turned away. With outboard at full power, we headed upriver.

Elated but with mixed feelings, I slapped Tosh on the back. My heart was pounding even more.

"Lambeth Pier," shouted Tosh. "It's right next to the main road near Lambeth Palace. We'll grab a taxi to Waterloo Station."

I looked back at the wall and saw two figures waving at us. It was a great feeling to know we saved the Speaker of the House from assassination. My elation lasted a second as a loud pop, followed by hissing air from the zodiac, alerted us to something nasty.

"They bleedin' got us, guv. There's a shooter. It won't be long before we're swimming. We might make it, but be prepared to take your coat off just in case."

I threw my coat off.

"Hang on, guv. I'll zigzag to make us a hard target. If we don't get another hole, we have four or five minutes."

The zodiac swerved back and forth while I held on. The shot came from the Westminster bank, but we were further away, and Lambeth pier was getting closer. A police launch was closing fast from the Westminster pier, its siren wailing.

"Bleedin' blues and twos," shouted Tosh. "That's all we need."

The zodiac was lower in the water and had slowed. We were not far from the end of the pier as the police launch closed on us.

"Jump, guv! Don't worry about me!"

Tosh had the outboard at full throttle and was feet from the pier. As we closed within a yard, I jumped, coat under my arm. Tosh missed the top of the walkway but managed to grab the edge of the pier and haul himself up as the police launch arrived, the loud hailer ordering us to stop. Naturally, we ran.

"I'll get us a taxi, guv. There's plenty around here." Tosh ran ahead of me, stopped a black taxi, and we piled in. "Waterloo and hurry, mate." Tosh looked at his soaked feet.

"I know," I said, "A new pair of trainers on expenses." It was meant as an uplifting comment, but it had no effect on him.

Moments later, the cab dropped us off. "Subway. We need the subway in any direction, guv."

Tosh didn't stand on ceremony. I followed him, jumping over the ticket gates to the platforms. Shouts from staff echoed after

The Defector's Diary

us. One train was standing at the first platform we found. The illuminated board showed it going to Edgeware. We joined several commuters boarding and made our way to a couple of seats at one end of the carriage, hoping the doors would close before the staff caught up with us.

Moments later, the train moved off and I grinned at Tosh. His trainers were wet, and a small puddle had formed on the floor around his feet.

We were both enjoying the moment, but I knew we would not be finished until Cranthorp was pushed off the seat he was about to occupy. In the meantime, Cranthorp was not going to rest until he dealt with me and Tosh.

"So what's next?" asked Tosh. "I can't contact anyone now I'm out of work."

I realized that I would have a difficult time, too. Max, Dianne, Sir David's ex-wife and Myer could be reached by phone, but I could not turn up at my home or Herald office.

"Bugger, guv, how are we gonna' get to Myer and the ladies. They'll be at the opera tonight and the Savoy after the performance. We should warn Myer and the women to stay at Dianne's hotel for the time being. There's gonna' be a real media frenzy when Sir David makes his speech in parliament. The BBC will televise the proceedings."

With all the excitement of the last few hours, I had not given thought to what effect Sir David's speech would have on the public or the security authorities. Cranthorp, for the time being, would be able to manipulate the police and SIS until I could get Max to use his persuasive powers with Downing Street.

"I have no idea at the moment, Tosh, but you are right. You call Myer and I'll get a hold of Dianne."

Dianne answered at once and was quite upbeat. "You did it. Well done. I was just talking to Myer and he is really pleased and looking forward to tonight."

I interrupted her. "Darling, I am sorry to spoil your day, but

Tosh and I are in no-man's land. Cranthorp is going to try even harder now to deal with us. His agents, not to mention the police, are going to be everywhere. We are on the underground at the moment but the moment we get off we are going to be sitting ducks. We are-"

Dianne interrupted. "Then I'll go and see Max and work something out."

"No", I replied. "That's what Cranthorp is hoping you will do. The best course of action is for you to call Max and stay at your hotel. I am also getting Myer and Sir David's ex to get to you so that you are both safe. Cranthorp will not try anything while you are in the hotel. When Tosh and I-"

Dianne cut in again. "Okay, I see the sense in that but what are you going to do? Can you get to the hotel or, I hate to say this, what about one of Tosh's hideaways?"

I smiled. A great solution but a surprise that Dianne could suggest it.

"Good idea. Let's make a call later when Tosh and I have settled. We need to work out what to do about Cranthorp and the other conspirators, especially Labrum. They have to be named and dealt with."

The call ended and I looked at Tosh who was shaking his head.

"I got through to Myer. He's already picked up Sir David's ex-wife and is at her place. I told him to get to Dianne's hotel as soon as possible and take Mrs ..... with him. So he's gonna' be on his way shortly."

"Okay, so that leaves us. We need somewhere to hide and make our move to topple Cranthorp and expose the others involved. Dianne had a great idea. She has suggested we use one of your hideouts in London. Perhaps one of your seedy joints you love so much."

"I know just the place, guv." Tosh rolled his eyes. "Your missus suggested that? Blimey! As it happens I know the ideal place

The Defector's Diary

in Soho."

I wasn't surprised he knew a club we could use and Soho would be ideal. It would not be far from the hotel Dianne and the others were staying at.

"We need to sort our route out," said Tosh. "If we can get a taxi as soon as we get out of here then we should be okay. That's if Cranthorp hasn't had time to cover the stops along this line. He'll know by now we are on this train."

That was a sobering thought. I looked up at the underground map of our line on the wall above us. We were on the Northern Line.

"We get off at Tottenham Court Road," said Tosh, reading my mind. "From there it's a short taxi ride to Soho. With a bit of luck, Cranthorp will have his people watching Covent Garden. That's the closest station to The Savoy Hotel. It's on the Piccadilly Line and some distance from where we get off. We have one escalator to get up to street level and there should be plenty of taxi's about this time of day."

We had a plan. I was already thinking ahead to my conversation with Max. I had to have my story in the paper the following day. SIS, through the Prime Minister's office, might have gagged the paper. Writing my column would take too long. I needed Max to arrange for me to dictate my work over the phone. I looked at my watch. It was nearly nine-thirty, and Sir David would be making his speech. A few minutes later, we reached our stop.

Tosh tugged my arm as we stood. "Whatever happens, guv, just focus on getting into a taxi. If I'm not with you don't worry. I'll get my own and follow."

The doors slid back and we both made for the escalators, with ourselves part hidden within a crowd of commuters. In the main entrance there were people standing about, some by the exit including two police officers. I looked at the ground and walked past them with a small group of girls.

"Guv!"

I looked up, relieved that Tosh had already found us a taxi.

"The Pink Toothbrush, mate," ordered Tosh. "The one in Soho."

* * *

"Well, it's been some time since you showed up, you naughty little boy. Where have you been?"

Fiona to my mind, did not look like a Fiona. Dressed in a light blue trouser suit and wearing shiny black high heels, she was taller than both of us. Her blonde hair, a mass of curls down to her shoulders, looked as though it were a wig. Stiff with hair lacquer that stunk the room out, I was fascinated by her facial looks. Thick powder covered a face that looked like a drunk make-up artist had gone to town on it. Her pronounced lips, overgrown with botex treatment, shone bright glossy red and her eyes were almost hidden behind long false eyelashes. Tosh had explained that Fiona was once a film star who made money from sex education films but had retired due to a partner's heart attack during filming. He couldn't stop laughing as he told me. It was a good laugh and one we needed.

"Okay, darlings, you can share a room I have upstairs and use the bathroom next door. I take it I don't know you are here?"

Tosh nodded.

After settling in, Tosh had arranged to have his clothes and shoes dried out. Borrowing some jeans and a sweater from Fiona, he joined me. While he called Myer to see if Myer and the women had reached the hotel safely, I called Max and arranged a secretary to write my column as I dictated it.

"I will be getting instructions soon to stop your column," said Max. "I'm going to run it anyway. Cranthorp does not run this country. We have a government that deals with this sort of thing - when they know about it. Sir David finished his speech about five minutes ago. There was silence in the House for a minute

The Defector's Diary

and then all hell erupted. MP's on both sides of the House applauded Sir David. He tore holes in SIS and the Bilderberg Club. Myer will probably be very upset that Sir David didn't remark about the honest integrity of the club's intentions. I think Sir David did a great job in making sure the club is seen as unimportant in the public's eyes. Myer did get a thank you in the speech for whistle-blowing the affair so that keeps him out of jail. Of course, you and Tosh are a different matter."

I was a little concerned but pleased that the Bilderberg Club's intentions had been revealed. Cranthorp was still after silencing us. Sir David had not mentioned the role that SIS had played in the situation. The public would not know the involvement of senior SIS executives but they would be dealt with. According to Max Downing Street were issuing orders to the Police Commissioner for the arrest of Sir John Carlton and his assistant, Driscol. Lord Gresham was already under arrest with some of his people too.

"Max, Cranthorp should be arrested right away. He will know where all the conspirators are. There must be dozens of them, and it's not just here but abroad as well."

"Lord Gresham and Sir Carlton will not want to do time, Pete. They'll sing," answered Max. "They will know who the top man is. We know he was part of the Bilderberg Club committee."

"Well you have my story, Max. Cranthorp is now in charge of SIS until Whitehall do something about him. You'll see, they will spend months investigating and then brush things under the carpet. What do me and Tosh do in the meantime? Go on holiday?" I was getting angry. "Max, Dianne, Sir David and Myer are in danger as well. Cranthorp has to be stopped."

"There's only one way he can be put out of action, Pete. It's a big gamble, but it would certainly get Whitehall's attention. I could insert his name where you have written about a 'senior SIS officer was part of this dangerous conspiracy.'

He would deny any wrong-doing and my neck and yours will

be on the block. What you need is something that proves he was involved. It could be something very small but the only way you'll get that is by talking to him and record your conversation. Problem is, he wants to get rid of you and Tosh."

Max had given me an idea. "Okay, thanks Max. If you can do anything with the new press officer at number 10 it might prove helpful."

There was a click on the line and silence. Tosh had been listening.

"This conspiracy got no further than a few demonstrations thanks to Sir David's speech this morning. Now all we have to do is find a way to deal with Cranthorp. By the way, did you get a hold of Myer?"

Tosh nodded. "Yes, him and the ladies are safe in the hotel and I told him they must stay put."

Tosh gave me a sly look. "Apart from a bullet through his head, I have a suggestion about Cranthorp, guv."

I leaned against the wall in our dingy little room. It had white paint peeling from the ceiling and small areas of mold above the skirting board in one corner. The floor was partly covered by some worn linoleum, once covered in a floral design. The bed was something Tosh would be at home on. I had a small red sofa to sleep on. I wouldn't say I liked the thought that I might be in the room for a while, sharing with Tosh.

"What's your suggestion?" I asked.

"You'll think this is a bit up the wall, but it might work if we can fool Cranthorp into seeing us."

I grinned at him. "Cranthorp is a clever man. He would never agree to seeing us without bringing along a few of his agents. What we need is impossible, Tosh. We need an admission of guilt, even if it is about something small that puts him in Adam's flat or the Dutch boys flat."

"Supposing, guv, someone lets Cranthorp know that Sir David will be at the ruins of his cottage to pick up any bits and pieces

The Defector's Diary

worth saving. If Sir David is willing to act as the bait, we could arrange to be in place before Sir David arrives. Cranthorp is hardly likely to have anyone with him who could witness him killing Sir David."

I was aware that Sir David was also in the firing line.

"Look," continued Tosh, you've got a digital recorder. You could switch that on after I corner Cranthorp. The rest is up to you. Keep him talking and try to trick him into any information that proves he was involved in any way."

I was beginning to warm to the idea. "Slight change," I said. "Someone lets it slip that Sir David is going to the bungalow to sift the wreckage on a certain day. Cranthorp will get there hours before that time, but Sir David will not arrive. We will be there even earlier and wait for Cranthorp. You then corner him, and I join you. What do you think?"

We felt good. We had a plan that might work. At least there was a plan, and I decided to call Myer. Sir David had to be safe as well, and the hotel Myer was at was an ideal place for them all. I called Myer and put our idea to him.

"Great idea, Pete, but a risky one. I can put it about with some colleagues in Whitehall. One of Cranthorp's goons will hear and warn him. I'm sure your plan will work but will Cranthorp turn up alone?"

Chapter Forty-One

I LOOKED AT MY WATCH. Five-thirty on a cold October morning had both Tosh and I shivering despite warm coats and gloves. The first part of our plan was something Tosh was the expert at. He had decided that from a certain spot in the woods opposite Sir David's ruined bungalow, we would be able to see a car approaching from the end of the road. We had parked a mile away to hide our presence as much as possible. We walked through the wooded area and were pretty sure Cranthorp had not turned up.

"Guv, you hide behind what's left of the chimney stack. If he's gonna' come he'll be here shortly. He won't leave it any later. It's still a bit dark, ideal conditions for Cranthorp. He'll probably have a rifle and pistol backup."

Tosh's matter-of-fact manner did little to put me at ease. I left him standing behind a tree and moved off toward the ruined bungalow.

"Move!"

I heard Tosh shout a warning before I heard the sound of an engine. Bricks and debris were scattered over the ground, and I hopped over them carefully. Heavy breathing caused clouds of vapour. I covered my mouth with a hand and peered around the chimney stack. I couldn't see the car nor hear the engine. If it was Cranthorp, I imagined he was making his way through the trees to take up a position opposite the bungalow. I stood, moving each foot up and down. My toes were frozen. I looked across the road and turned to both sides, hoping not to see Cranthorp about to pounce.

The Defector's Diary

When I looked across to the woods again, I was surprised to see Cranthorp advancing toward me. Behind him, Tosh followed, carrying a rifle in one hand and a pistol in the other. I fumbled for a moment with the recorder in my pocket and pressed the record tab. A small microphone attached under my coat collar to the recorder by wire would, I hoped give me a clear recording of Cranthorp's conversation with me. My phone was in my top pocket. I pulled it out and pressed the 'recall last number button, hoping Max would answer and hear what was going on.

Without a word, Cranthorp came across the debris and stood in front of me with a smirk spread across his face.

"Well, hello old boy. He got me this time." He thumbed over his shoulder at Tosh. "I really think you should have thought this through. For your information, my people know where I am."

"You mean your fellow thugs from the Club," I said. "I don't think so. Your fellow thugs are pooping themselves at the moment, looking to save their jobs. You may be fooling everyone at the moment but after Sir David's speech yesterday and my story in the paper today, you are going to be quietly replaced by Number 10. I am also going to report your part in the deaths of Adam Denton and the young Dutch student, not forgetting a Czech spy, Valarie Forst."

"All part of an ongoing intelligence report and investigation that will never be disclosed in public, Pete. You know that."

"Of course," I replied, "but your attempt to kill Sir David and both Tosh and myself cannot be part of your investigation. In fact, with Sir David's testimony alone, you will face justice."

Cranthorp laughed. "Pete, you really have to face reality. I had nothing to do with any of this. When I heard you, or should I say Sir David would be here today I came to talk about being generous in offering you and Tosh a peaceful end to this whole dirty business. You have been an integral part of my official investigation since Adam disappeared. Of course, I couldn't tell you about this. I should have sent you home as soon as you reached Prague.

Adam was already dead, but something told me you might come in useful. We had a Czech agent to find who had stolen a diary from Commissioner Novotney. Adam had been seduced by her, but we played along when she offered information, but she fooled us."

Tosh, who had been guarding Cranthorp with the pistol, interrupted our conversation.

"Cranthorp, you are talking to the two of us who you tried to kill. Verbal diarrhoea is flowing out of your mouth."

I guessed Cranthorp had been his usual smart self. "I'm assuming you think we're recording your conversation otherwise you wouldn't tell stupid lies. You also know we can't arrest the head of SIS. The thing is, Cranthorp, you don't just have us to worry about. Lord Gresham and Sir John Carlton will never see the inside of a cell after they name names including yours. Tell me just one thing for the peace of my mind, when did you first meet Adam? Last year or the year before?"

Cranthorp smiled. "Excuse me, dear boy but I only met Adam once, early this year, when he saw me about Valarie being of use to us. I never saw him again until he was pulled out of the river." He stamped his feet. "Further to that I have to remind you I cannot comment on anything regarding National Security. If you have finished, Pete, I would love to get back to my office. I have a meeting with the PM this evening about dealing with unnecessary media rubbish being published about the SIS and ways of dealing with those papers involved."

I knew he was lying; I remembered the photo in Adam's flat. The date on the back proved the lie. A small point but nonetheless, a lie.

Tosh pushed him forward.

"We'll keep your weapons, Cranthorp. I'm glad we had a little chat. At least the Bilderberg Clubs conspiracy failed."

Cranthorp dug his hands in his pockets. "Never fear, we'll try ag..."

The Defector's Diary

His face contorted in anger as he realized his mistake. He swung around, snatching the pistol from Tosh's hand and pushing him to the ground, took aim. There was a click. The safety catch was still on.

"Run Pete!"

I tripped backwards and managed to fall behind the fireplace and chimney stack.

Tosh raised the rifle, but Cranthorp, unable to open the catch and re-aim the pistol, ran toward the woods. Taking a wild shot, Tosh fired in the direction of Cranthorp. The bullet pinged off the road near his feet as he reached the grass verge. Seconds later, all hell let loose as more shots from a second weapon rained across the open ground at the ruins. Tosh had joined me behind the chimney stack.

"Guv, it has to be that bastard, Labrum. Cranthorp wouldn't trust anyone else."

Tosh examined the rifle and pistol taken from Cranthorp.

"I told you Cranthorp was the best in our trade, didn't I? He only loaded two bullets in each firearm. He wouldn't need more than that to kill someone and if the gun gets captured, he'll try to get his target to fire those rounds off. Then he'll come for you."

Tosh was right. Cranthorp was someone very dangerous. We were in a precarious position. In the quiet that followed the shot from the woods, I thought I heard someone shouting at me.

"Someone trying to get your attention, guv? Sounds like your phone."

With all that had happened in the short time since Cranthorp appeared, I forgot I had called Max or called his number just as Cranthorp appeared. I pulled the phone from my top pocket and answered.

"Pete, it's Max."

I put the phone speaker on for Tosh to hear.

"I guess you called me to record what was going on in case your recorder had failed to work properly. Listen carefully. I have had Number 10 listening in live. They now know Cranthorp's involvement in Bilderberg. I'll explain later. For now, you must do your best until help arrives. The PM has authorized an army team to get you out. If you have power left in your battery, keep the phone live. Don't bloody die on me. You have a big story to write. Be safe, Pete."

Tosh nodded, a grim look on his face. "As long as we don't fire at them, they will be wary about approaching us. We need to be aware if they try to cross the road to our left or right to come around behind us."

We both ducked as a bullet smashed into the bricks just above our heads. Chips of brick and a cloud of dust came down on top of us. I looked back across the field behind the cottage where we had escaped the blast a couple of days earlier.

"Good idea, guv," said Tosh. "Better to hide in the tall grass than stand here behind a bleedin' chimney stack."

With the stack directly behind us, we both stooped low and ran as fast as we could over the rubble and into the field. A small copse of blackberry and hawthorn bushes tangled with the grass to our left and we dived for cover behind them as another shot rang out.

"They're coming, guv. Time for us to split up. I'll try to draw them to me. You just get your arse out of here in a straight line behind us." He pulled a pistol from his coat pocket. "This is mine and it's fully loaded. Remember, if you fear for your life, don't hesitate. Shoot first and spew up after."

We both froze as the hawthorn bushes moved. Through the undergrowth and mass of hawthorn, Labrum's legs slowly crept toward us. Tosh raised the pistol before springing up himself next to me. From where I crouched, Tosh's shot deafened me. Labrum fell to the ground and lay moaning for what seemed a long time. His eyes were looking directly at me beneath the bushes but were unseeing. They closed as the moaning stopped.

"Well done, Tosh! You still have what it takes despite your

The Defector's Diary

old age."

Cranthorp was nearby but in the tall grass it was hard to know where he was. Tosh left me, indicating I should stay put. Beside me, he had left his own pistol. He worked his way to the end of the bushes and disappeared. Instantly, there were two shots. Desperate, I panicked and picked up the pistol. Without thinking, I moved back from the bushes. Two shots rang out as I rolled over and looked for the safety catch on Tosh's gun. With trembling fingers I pushed the catch forward. My mind was spinning out of control as I fumbled. Two more simultaneous shots rang out and smoke drifted through the bushes as I tried to make myself as small as possible. A sudden calm and the sound of long grass being gently blown by a stiff breeze surrounded me.

"Sorry, old boy, poor old Tosh has fired his last shot. Now it's your turn, Pete. What a shame poor Dianne will not see you again - well, not alive anyway."

His sarcasm and disregard for life blew away any fear of dying out of my head. So full of anger and thoughts of revenge, I ran forward and caught a glimpse of him a few yards away. I raised the pistol and kept firing in his direction. I felt a sharp pain in my shoulder seconds later and dropped the gun as I fell. The roar of a helicopter engine and the sound of automatic fire confused me as I lay quite still. Cranthorp did not appear. The uniform of a soldier did a few moments later.

"Compliments of the army, sir. I am Captain Carr. I'll have your arm bandaged up in a second. You've got a bullet in your arm."

"My friend," I managed to say. "He's over there." I tried to point, but I was feeling weak.

"Don't worry, sir. We'll sort him out too."

"The other man?" I asked.

The captain smiled. "He's lucky to be alive, sir. You emptied your entire cartridge at him. He was doing a dance avoiding your shots when we caught him.

Chapter Forty-Two

THREE MONTHS LATER...
Dianne flicked the TV on for the lunchtime news. "It doesn't seem that long ago that I was worried this would never happen."

I gently put a hand on her stomach. "It isn't that long ago that I thought I wouldn't see you again."

We hugged, then sat on the couch just as the doorbell rang.

"Oh, for goodness sake. Are you expecting someone, Pete?"

"No," I replied. "I'll go and find out."

For a moment, I felt a knot in my stomach. I kept thinking of Cranthorp every time I walked around a corner or drove to work. Along with all the top conspirators, Cranthorp was awaiting trial, and I was waiting to give evidence. Something else, more important, had overshadowed any worries I had about making sure justice was done. As I opened the door, a grinning face greeted me.

"Hello, guv. Lovely day, ain't it?" Tosh stood in the doorway dressed in a navy suit and highly polished shoes. A fresh white shirt was adorned with what I guessed a regimental tie.

"Well, you're like a jack-in-the-box. You have a habit of appearing and disappearing," I said and smiled. I was pleased to see him again before he retired to wherever he was going. He had been released from hospital a month earlier, and we had all celebrated with Myer and Sir David.

"Who are you talking to, Pete?" Dianne's voice came from the lounge.

Tosh and I cringed. We walked into the lounge, and Dianne's

The Defector's Diary

face was a picture. Her expression turned from amazement to a frown.

"What, may I ask, are you doing here, and why are you dressed in unusual attire?"

We all burst into laughter.

"Morning, Mrs W. I came to say goodbye. I got myself a flat over this terrific club in Marseille. Anyways, I came to apologize for all the trouble we very nicely got out of, thanks to the guv 'nor here."

I put an arm around his shoulders. "I'm glad the dynamic duo got Sir David safely back to Westminster."

Tosh noticed the baby swing I had fixed by the back door.

"Blimey, that's a nice surprise, Mrs W. Congrats to you. A great New Year present for you both."

A news flash appeared on the TV lunchtime news from outside St Thomas Hospital in London.

"The Public Health Authority announced today that there were several suspicious cases involving nausea, loss of vision, and respiratory problems reported by hospitals in and around London during the last twenty-four hours. There are no deaths reported, but the authorities urge the public to report any similar symptoms at once. Scientists from Porton Down, the government's watchdog on biochemical warfare have been asked to investigate. Although no official statement has been made, a Whitehall spokesperson confirmed that nothing, including a bioterrorist nerve gas attack, could be ruled out. A statement by the Minister for Health will be made later today."

Dianne stamped her foot. "NG - damn Nerve Gas!"

"We missed it," said Tosh softly.

The phone rang, and I knew who it was.

"Pete," snarled Max, "get here as quick as you can. Go and find Tosh and bring the bloody man with you—and apologize to Dianne for me.

About the Author

Ray C Doyle writes hard-hitting political stories that resonate with the truth that lies beneath daily headlines. Political corruption and industrial espionage are rife today. Ray's exceptional talent with words takes these headlines and upgrades them into a fiction of the highest quality.

Ray's main character, Pete West lies somewhere between the noir world of Chandler's Philip Marlowe and the enforced moral principles in a corrupt political world found in LeeChild's Jack Reacher series.

These classic tropes come together to produce a new and exciting character-driven trilogy of hard-boiled, noir novels in the world of Pete West.

To learn more about Ray C Doyle visit:
Facebook: www.facebook.com/AuthorRaymondStone

More Books by Ray C Doyle

Lara's Secret
Book 1: Pete West mystery series

The Blind Pigeon
Book 2: Pete West mystery series

Printed in Great Britain
by Amazon